Will a k D0683312

A Ring
for Christmas

Three exhilarating Christmas romances from
three beloved Mills & Boon authors!

A Ring
for Christmas

JOAN ELLIOTT PICKART

CATHY GILLEN THACKER

MARGARET ALLISON

MILLS &
BOON

First published in Great Britain 2010
Harlequin Mills & Boon Limited,
Eton House, 18-24 Paradise Road, Richmond, Surrey TW9 1SR

A RING FOR CHRISTMAS © by Harlequin Enterprises II B.V./S.à.r.l 2010

A Bride by Christmas, Christmas Lullaby and *Mistletoe Manoeuvres* were first published in Great Britain by Harlequin Mills & Boon Limited in separate, single volumes.

A Bride by Christmas © Joan Elliott Pickart 2005
Christmas Lullaby © Cathy Gillen Thacker 2005
Mistletoe Manoeuvres © Margaret Allison 2005

ISBN: 978 0 263 88050 2

05-1210

Printed and bound in Spain
by Litografía Rosés S.A., Barcelona

A BRIDE
BY CHRISTMAS

BY
JOAN ELLIOTT PICKART

Joan Elliott Pickart is the author of over eighty novels. When she isn't writing, she enjoys watching football, knitting, reading, gardening and attending craft shows on the town square. Joan has three all-grown-up daughters and a fantastic little grandson.

In September of 1995 Joan travelled to China to adopt her fourth daughter, Autumn. Joan and Autumn have settled into their cosy cottage in a charming small town in the high pine country of Arizona.

For all the lovely ladies at Willow Wind

One

Luke St. John walked slowly up the wide steps leading to the porch, and the carved wooden doors of the large Episcopal church. He stopped at the doors, marveling at their intricate craftsmanship.

It really was a majestic structure, he thought, and he could understand why his brother and Ginger had chosen to be married here tomorrow. The event had been many months in the planning, and Robert had confided that Ginger had changed her mind about colors and endless other details so many times the wedding coordinator must be ready to strangle his bride-to-be.

Luke smiled as he opened one of the doors and entered the vestibule.

Ginger Barrington, he mused, was an endearing yet

rather ditzy young woman who had been given a blank check by her father to have the wedding of her dreams. The last he'd heard, Ginger had chosen seven bridesmaids for the don't-worry-about-the-cost event.

Whatever. The people in the Barrington-St. John social circle were accustomed to these kinds of extravaganzas. What was important was that Ginger and Robert were deeply in love—and they were, they really were.

Strange, Luke thought. He'd actually felt a twinge of envy on more than one occasion as he'd watched the relationship between Robert and Ginger develop. He'd been startled each time he'd registered that green-around-the-edges feeling. He dated independent career women and that suited him just fine. But then again…

Luke shook his head to halt his jumbled thoughts and glanced at his watch.

He was early for the rehearsal, he knew, but a business meeting on this side of town had ended sooner than expected. There wasn't time to go home, nor any point in returning to the office, so he'd come here with the idea of sitting in the quiet church and relaxing until the others arrived.

Luke crossed the vestibule, entered the large sanctuary, then walked down the aisle past about a dozen pews to finally settle onto one. He swept his gaze over the high ceiling and exquisite stained-glass windows, nodding again in approval.

His attention was caught by a side door opening close to the altar. A woman entered carrying a cardboard box. His gaze was riveted on her as she crossed to the center aisle and placed the box on the first pew, immediately removing a large yellow satin bow.

Luke felt a sudden pain in his chest and drew a sharp breath as he realized he hadn't breathed since the woman had appeared. He leaned forward, resting his arms on the rail in front of him, and drank in the sight of her, missing no detail.

She was so beautiful, Luke thought rather hazily. No, that wasn't the word he wanted. Beautiful was what the career women he dated strove for, which resulted in cookie-cutter perfection in clothes, hair and makeup that varied little from one to the next.

No, this woman, who was now attaching the satin bow to the side of the first pew was…pretty. Yes, that was the word. Pretty in a wholesome, breath-of-fresh-air way that was knocking him for a loop. She was sunshine on a cloudy day, real, what-you-see-is-what-you-get real, and he'd bet ten bucks she wasn't wearing any makeup at all.

Her strawberry-blond hair tumbled to her shoulders in what he was convinced were natural curls, and even from this distance he could see that her eyes were big and brown. Fawn eyes. Pretty, pretty eyes. She was wearing a simple pale pink sundress that suited her to perfection.

Whew, Luke thought. He'd felt it, a funny little hitch in the much-needed breath he'd taken and the increased tempo of his heart. Nothing like this had ever happened to him before. Nothing. This woman had definitely made a strange and totally unfamiliar impact on him.

Luke continued to watch as the woman attached a mint-green bow to the second pew, then matching ones on the other side of the aisle, making it subtly clear that those four rows were reserved for the families of the bride and groom.

She might, he guessed, be the wedding coordinator whom Ginger had driven to the brink of insanity. She appeared very young for such a lofty title, was maybe twenty-four or twenty-five. So, okay, at thirty-two he wasn't too old for her. Good. That was good.

But…a wedding coordinator? Why did a person decide to become one of those? Because their own wedding had been so wonderful they wanted to share the bliss of an error-free event with others? No. No way. She was not married. That was not acceptable. She was a wedding coordinator because she was a romantic, old-fashioned woman who adored weddings and was very good at taking care of a zillion details at the same time. Yes. That was much better.

He had to meet this woman, Luke thought with a sense of urgency. He had to hear her voice, look deep into those incredible brown eyes of hers. He had to connect with her before she disappeared from his life as quickly as she'd appeared. He had to… Man, he had to get a grip. He didn't know what was happening to him, but it was a tad scary, that was for sure.

The sound of voices on the porch reached Luke and he got to his feet and stepped into the aisle just as the woman turned toward him. She gasped in shock that he was standing there and took a step backward.

"I'm sorry," he said, walking forward. "I didn't mean to startle you. I arrived early and I was just sitting here quietly and…" He stopped in front of her, gazed into her eyes and totally forgot what he was going to say.

"I…" the woman said, still looking directly into his eyes. "I'm…" Whoever I am. Heavens, those eyes, those eyes were dark, fathomless pools that a woman could just drown in and not even struggle to escape. And that voice. So masculine and rumbly and yet…it seemed to stroke her like soft, sensuous velvet, causing her skin to tingle and…

He was tall, had wide shoulders, long legs, rough-hewn features and thick, glorious black hair. He looked like someone straight out of central casting.

"You're…who?" Luke said, leaning slightly toward her.

"Who what?" she said, then blinked. "Oh! Yes, of course. I'm Maggie Jenkins, the wedding coordinator. I own Roses and Wishes, which is gaining a fine reputation for coordinating weddings, because that's what I do. I…coordinate…weddings. I'm also babbling, so forget all that. I'm a tad exhausted at the moment, you see. And you are?"

Enchanted, Luke thought, smiling. Maggie Jenkins. Maggie. He liked her name. It suited her, it really did. Oh, yes, hello, Maggie Jenkins, who was not wearing a wedding ring, thank goodness.

"Luke St. John," he said. "The brother of the nervous groom and the best man for this gala event."

"Pleased to meet you," Maggie said, tearing her gaze

from Luke's. "I believe the others have arrived. I'd better go greet everyone and get this rehearsal going so we stay on schedule, because dinner's booked at the restaurant afterward. Excuse me."

Luke turned to watch her hurry down the aisle as the large group of people appeared. He didn't move to join the others. Not yet. He just stood there drinking in the sight of Maggie.

Maggie stifled a yawn of fatigue as she plastered a plastic smile on her tired face and stopped in front of the chattering wedding party.

Was that heat she felt on her back? she thought suddenly. Was Luke St. John staring at her with those…those eyes? Maggie, stop it. She had made a complete idiot of herself with Luke, had overreacted to his masculine magnetism only because she was so tired she couldn't think straight. Once rested, she would view Luke St. John as a very handsome man but big macho deal.

"Hello, everyone," Maggie said brightly.

"Oh, Maggie," Ginger said, beaming, "isn't this exciting? Tomorrow is the big day. I can hardly believe it's finally here."

You're not the only one, Maggie thought, smiling and nodding at the petite blonde who boasted a golden tan and was wearing a royal-blue raw silk jumpsuit.

"Did I check with you to see if you'd found someone to supply only pale yellow and mint-green yogurt-covered almonds for the nut cups at the reception?" Ginger said, frowning.

"Yes, you did," Maggie said. "And, yes, I did. Well,

sort of. I had to order extra nuts, then pick out the two colors we needed." Which took until after two o'clock this morning. "I was going to ask you what you wanted me to do with the almonds we didn't use."

"Whatever," Ginger said, waving one hand in the air. "Where's my sweetie? Oh, Robert, there you are, honey. Do you realize we'll soon be winging our way to Greece? We'll have a whole month to—What's wrong? You don't look like a happy groom."

The handsome young man in his midtwenties, who was wearing slacks and a dress shirt open at the neck, slid one arm across Ginger's shoulders.

"My brother isn't here yet," he said. "We can't have a rehearsal without the best man."

"I'm right here," Luke said, striding toward the group.

"I'm going to go tell Reverend Mason we're ready to begin the rehearsal," Maggie said quickly. "He's in his office and told me to come get him when we were all set."

"Maggie, hon, wait a sec," an attractive young woman said. "I've lost two pounds since the final fitting of my bridesmaid dress. Do you think it could be nipped in a bit before the ceremony tomorrow night?"

Over my dead body, Maggie thought. Don't even think about it...*hon.*

"That won't be necessary...Tiffy, isn't it?" Maggie said, her voice dripping with sweetness. "That's the beauty of that style of gown. There's room for a fluctuation of a few pounds here and there. I promise that you have nothing to worry about."

Nicely done, Luke thought, swallowing a burst of laughter. Maggie had handled the spoiled and pampered Tiffy like a pro. She was really something, this Maggie Jenkins.

"Look on the bright side, Tiffy," one of the other bridesmaids said. "You can eat your little heart out at the wedding reception—and at the rehearsal dinner tonight, for that matter. You know Ginger and Mrs. Barrington picked goodies to die for. Eat and enjoy."

"Well, there is that, Melissa Ann," Tiffy said thoughtfully, then wandered away.

Bless you, Melissa Ann, Maggie thought wearily.

"And don't forget all those delicious green and yellow yogurt-covered almonds," Luke said, finally indulging in a chuckle. He paused. "Maggie, did you really have to sort through tons of those things to get the two colors?"

"No detail is too small for Roses and Wishes," Maggie said, not looking in Luke's direction.

As Maggie rushed away to get the priest, Luke turned to watch her go, a smile tugging at the corners of his mouth.

"Luke?" Robert said.

"Hmm?" he said, still staring after Maggie.

"What's the matter with you?" Robert said. "You're standing here with your back to everyone. Could you be a little more sociable, for Pete's sake?"

Luke snapped his head around to look at his brother. "Yes, certainly. Sorry." He paused. "I must say, Robert, that I'm impressed with the job Maggie Jenkins has done for you and Ginger. Maggie is quite young to have her own business. It's interesting, too, that she's a wedding coordinator who isn't married." Didn't hurt to double-check on that. "Don't you think? You know, someone who didn't have a fabulous wedding of their own?"

Robert shrugged.

"I asked Maggie about that," Ginger said, joining the brothers and slipping her arm through Robert's. "She pointed out that not all pediatricians have children. Maggie loves the challenge of planning a perfect wedding down to the smallest detail. She just doesn't want one of her own. She told me that. She never intends to get married."

Luke frowned. "Why not?"

"Well, gracious, Luke," Ginger said, wrinkling her nose, "it wouldn't have been polite to ask that. I swear, men should be required to take the same social-graces classes that all of us women do." She shifted her attention to Robert. "Sweetie, what if people don't like yogurt-covered almonds? Do you think I should ask Maggie to change what's in the nut cups before tomorrow night?"

"No," Luke said quickly. "Did you notice the shadows under Maggie's eyes, Ginger? She's obviously exhausted, and I'm sure you learned in your social-graces classes that you should be aware of the needs of those around you.

"Besides, I've attended more gala events than you due to the simple fact that I'm older than you are. I assure you that my vast experience has shown me that most people are very fond of yogurt-covered almonds."

"Really?" Ginger said, beaming.

"Guaranteed," Luke said. "So don't even entertain the idea of asking Maggie to stay up all night redoing the nut cups."

"Well, if you say so, Luke," Ginger said. "I won't… Oh, there's Maggie with Reverend Mason. I'd best go say hi."

Ginger hustled up the aisle and Robert stared at his older brother.

"You're suddenly an expert on the popularity of almonds?" Robert said incredulously. "Where did that come from? And you're aware that Maggie is exhausted? What did she do? Say, 'Hi, I'm Maggie and I'm wiped out'?"

"I'm an attorney, Robert," Luke said. "A good lawyer learns to observe people for subtle little nuances that can be extremely important in the outcome of a given case."

"That is such a bunch of crock," Robert said with a hoot of laughter.

"Yeah, well…" Luke frowned. "Forget it."

"You sure sound—what word do I want?—protective. Yes, that's it, protective of Ms. Maggie, big brother. What gives?"

"Nothing 'gives.' Look, just concentrate on marrying Ginger." Luke paused. "You know, Robert, I'm rather…envious of what you and Ginger have together. I've watched you two over the past months, seen you fall deeply in love, make plans for a future together. It's good and I'm really happy for you both. Yep, I admit I'm a little bit jealous."

"You? Envious of me?" Robert said, splaying one hand on his chest. "I find that a tad hard to believe. You have women beating down your door. You've always gone for the type who just wants to have fun but not settle down. There are seven bridesmaids over there who fit that bill. Just take your pick."

Luke watched Maggie approach with the priest and Ginger.

"Things change," he said quietly.

Reverend Mason greeted everyone and explained that they would walk through the basics of the wedding ceremony so everything would go smoothly the next evening.

"Right," he said finally. "Ginger, if you'll stand at the back of the church with your father and be ready to come down the aisle after your bridesmaids and…"

"Oh, no," Ginger said, shaking her head. "No, no, no, I can't do that."

"Why not?" Robert said frantically. "You're not changing your mind about marrying me, are you?"

"Don't be silly, sweetie," Ginger said, kissing him on the cheek. "But you know how it's bad luck for the groom to see the bride on their wedding day before the ceremony? Well, it's also bad luck for the bride and groom to act out those roles at the rehearsal. Didn't you know that?"

"Can't say that I did," Robert said, drawing a deep breath of relief. "So now what?"

"You and I will sit and watch very carefully," Ginger continued, "so we'll know what we're to do tomorrow night."

"Watch who?" Robert said. "We're the bride and groom, remember?"

"We use stand-ins for the rehearsal, silly," Ginger said. "Let's see. Okay. Your father will be the best man and pretend he has the ring, and Luke will be the groom. And…" She glanced around. "Yes, of course. Maggie, you'll be the bride."

"Got it," Luke said.

"I don't think that's a great idea," Maggie said, feeling the color drain from her face. "No. Bad plan. Bad, bad. I need to… Yes, I need to stay at the back of the church and control the spacing of the bridesmaids starting down the aisle."

"What is the spacing?" Luke said pleasantly.

"Three pews apart, but…"

"Have you got that, ladies?" Luke said, looking at Ginger's girlfriends.

Seven heads bobbed up and down.

"Done," Luke said. "That leaves you free to be way behind them with Ginger's dad ready to be…the bride, Maggie. And I'll be the groom."

"Excellent," Reverend Mason said. "Let's take our places, please. The groomsmen need to be up front with our stand-in best man and groom. Mothers, take your places, please. Ginger and Robert, sit where you can observe and hear me clearly."

"But—" Maggie pointed one finger in the air.

"See you soon, future wife," Luke said, smiling at Maggie.

"But—"

"Come along…Ginger," Mr. Barrington said, chuckling as he tucked Maggie's hand in the crook of his arm. "This reminds me of a baseball game. Instead of a designated hitter, you're the designated bride."

She didn't want to be a bride, Maggie thought miserably as Ginger's father led her to the back of the church. Well, she did, but it would never happen. She wouldn't allow it to happen because… No, she was not a bride. Not a real one or a pretend one or a designated one. Not a bride. Not now, not ever.

And to make matters even worse, the stand-in groom was Luke St. John, a man who had made her forget her own name. Good grief, she wanted to go home. Right now.

Everyone except Maggie was chattering and laughing as they took their places, then silence fell as Reverend Mason raised one hand for quiet. He stood at the front of the church with Luke next to him, then the other men in a straight row alongside.

"The organ music you picked for the procession has now begun," the priest said, smiling. "Pretend you hear it. We're ready for the bridesmaids to come forward. What was it? Oh, yes, three pews apart, my dears."

As Tiffy started off, Ginger's father bent down to whisper to Maggie.

"I hope Ginger looks happier tomorrow night than you do at the moment," he said. "I think this is rather fun, don't you, Maggie?"

"That's not quite the word I would pick, sir," she said, attempting and failing to produce a smile.

"But your groom is Luke St. John," Mr. Barrington

said. "He's considered quite a catch in this town. You have to get into your role and realize you're the envy of a multitude of women in Phoenix. Will that thought make you smile?"

"Not really," Maggie said gloomily.

"Well, fake it. My daughter is so superstitious about all this nonsense that she'll probably pitch a fit if you look like you're about to have a root canal. You can be Ginger marrying Robert or Maggie marrying Luke. Take your pick, but remember this is a wedding, not a funeral. *Smile.*"

Maggie nodded jerkily and plastered such a wide smile on her face that her cheeks hurt.

"Now you look like someone just stepped on your foot," Mr. Barrington said.

"Don't get picky," Maggie said, glaring at him while keeping her plastic smile in place. "This is the best I can do."

"For a wedding coordinator," Mr. Barrington said, "you have a strange attitude about being a bride. Fascinating."

No, try terrifying, Maggie thought. Try never going to happen. Try…*she wanted to go home.*

"Now the actual wedding march begins," Reverend Mason said in the distance. "Give the congregation time to rise and turn in your direction and…now…here comes the lovely bride."

TWO

He could hear the wedding march, Luke thought. *He could.* A part of him knew that was impossible, yet it was there quite clearly, the wondrous music filling the church to overflowing.

And in the distance, walking in measured steps on the arm of Ginger's father, was Maggie, his bride. *His.* She was lovely, just exquisite. His heart was thundering at the mere sight of her as she came closer and closer and…

Maggie and Mr. Barrington stopped in front of the priest.

"I will ask at this point," Reverend Mason said, "who gives this woman in marriage. And you, Mr. Barrington, will reply 'Her mother and I,' then you'll take your daughter's hand and place it in Robert's."

"Her mother and I," Mr. Barrington boomed, then grasped Maggie's hand.

Without realizing he had moved, Luke stepped forward and extended his hand to receive Maggie's. As Mr. Barrington placed Maggie's hand in Luke's, their eyes met and time stopped.

Dear heaven, Maggie thought, unable to tear her gaze from the mesmerizing depths of Luke's eyes. Luke's hand was so strong yet so gentle as it wrapped around hers. And the heat. Good grief, the heat from his hand was traveling up her arm, across her breasts, then swirling and churning throughout her, causing a flush she could feel staining her cheeks.

She had to get her hand back. And she would. In a minute.

And she had to quit, just stop, looking into Luke's eyes. And she would. In a minute.

"We are gathered here," Reverend Mason said, "to unite this man and this woman in holy matrimony."

Yes, Luke thought, that was exactly why they were there. This man, him, and this woman, Maggie, were about to be united in holy matrimony, become husband and wife until death parted them.

He had never in his entire life felt like this. He was consumed with a soothing warmth of peace that was somehow combined with the coiling heat of desire. The chill within him that he now knew had been loneliness was gone, pushed into oblivion, never to return because Maggie was here. He'd waited an eternity for this, for her, to find his soul mate, and she was here at long last. Maggie.

Oh, man, this was nuts, he thought, unable to stop a smile from forming on his lips. He was an attorney who dealt in facts, absolutes, things being either black or white, proven data, and... Yet he had suddenly been flung—there was no other word for it—flung helter-skelter into a strange new world that embraced the romantic notion of love at first sight.

Oh, yeah, this was crazy. And wonderful. And hard to believe, but he did believe it with his entire being—heart, mind, body and soul.

Maggie Jenkins had come, she had seen, she had conquered. By doing nothing more than being, she had stolen his heart for all time, and he didn't want it back. Not ever. He loved her. It was as simple and as complicated as that. It was exciting and terrifying at the same time. It couldn't, shouldn't, be true, but yet it was.

He was in forever love with Maggie.

"After you have lit the single candle from the ones that will be burning next to it," Reverend Mason was saying, "blow out the others and place them back in the holders. The single burning candle will represent your union, becoming one entity."

Yes, Luke thought firmly.

Yes, Maggie thought dreamily. Wasn't that just the sweetest thing?

Reverend Mason's word became a buzz, like a multitude of bees in the background, as Maggie and Luke continued to look directly into each other's eyes. Then suddenly what the priest said was loud and clear.

"You may kiss the bride."

Luke framed Maggie's face in his hands, looked at her intently for a long, heart-stopping moment, then slowly, so slowly, lowered his head and captured her lips in a kiss that was so tender, so reverent, so…theirs, that tears filled Maggie's eyes. She savored the taste, the feel, the very essence of Luke, yearning for the kiss to never end.

Reverend Mason cleared his throat. "Yes, well, that's fine. Thank you, Luke, Maggie, for playing out your roles so convincingly."

Luke raised his head and both he and Maggie stared at the priest as though they had never seen him before in their lives.

"I, um…" Reverend Mason continued, "I will then introduce Mr. and Mrs. Robert St. John to the congregation, the organ music will burst forth and the recessional will take place. Any questions?"

Ginger jumped to her feet. "No, no questions. It's going to be so beautiful. I can hardly wait until tomorrow night. Thank you so much, Reverend Mason. We're off to the restaurant now for the rehearsal dinner. I do hope you and your wife will join us as planned."

"We'd be delighted," he said, sliding one more glance at Luke and Maggie, who were still staring at him with rather stunned expressions on their faces.

Maggie shook her head slightly to escape from the eerie spell that seemed to have transported her to a faraway place. She stepped back from Luke, averting her eyes, then spun around and forced another big smile onto her lips. Lips that still held the taste of Luke, the feel of Luke, tingled from the kiss shared with Luke.

"Ginger," Maggie said, "I'll come to the restaurant to make certain that everything is as it should be, then I'm going to scoot on home."

"But you're supposed to have dinner with us, Maggie," Ginger said, pouting prettily.

"I had a late lunch," Maggie said. "I couldn't eat a bite. Really."

"Don't be silly, my dear," Mr. Barrington said. "We all know how hard you've worked all these months to make this event perfect for our Ginger. I insist that you join us for dinner, even if you don't eat much. Good. That's settled. Me? I'm starving. Let's get going."

"But—" Maggie said.

"Come along, Mrs. St. John," Luke said, encircling her shoulders with his arm.

"What?" Maggie said, staring up at him with wide eyes. "Who?"

"Oh, sorry," Luke said, smiling. "I'm still in my role, I guess. You and I did get married a few minutes ago, you know. Maggie St. John. It has a nice ring to it, don't you think?"

"*Ginger* St. John has a nice ring to it," she said. "That's who I was pretending to be, remember? I'm Maggie *Jenkins* and that's who I intend to remain."

"Ah," Luke said, nodding.

"And what does 'ah' mean?" she said.

"Only that none of us have crystal balls to see into the future, Maggie *Jenkins*," he said. "Who knows what might happen? Shall we go?"

Without speaking further, Maggie grabbed the box

that had held the satin bows, then marched down the aisle, snatching her purse from the last pew as she went.

Outside the summer sky was a black velvet canopy sprinkled with twinkling diamondlike stars and a silvery moon, all of which went unnoticed by Maggie as she stomped to her ten-year-old van and slid behind the wheel.

As she took her place in the line of vehicles headed to the restaurant she drew a deep, shuddering breath.

Don't think, she ordered herself. Don't dwell on what took place in that church. Don't relive that kiss, or see again the smoldering passion in Luke's eyes or feel the tenderness of his hands on her flushed face or acknowledge the desire that had swept through her. Do not do that, Maggie Jenkins. Okay. Fine. She wouldn't. *She would not.*

But, darn it, what had happened back there? She had never in her life experienced anything so…so…whatever that had been. It was as though everyone had disappeared, leaving only her and Luke in a wondrous place that was theirs alone. The bride. The groom. The kiss. The undefinable something that in its intensity took desire beyond description. Luke.

Maggie sighed. It was a dreamy, wistful, womanly sigh that caused a soft smile to form on her lips. In the next instant she smacked the steering wheel with the palm of her hand.

"Cut it out, Maggie Jenkins," she yelled. "Just stop it right now. You are acting so ridiculous, it's a crime."

It was amazing, she mentally rushed on, how asinine a person could behave, think, feel, when they were totally exhausted. That, of course, was the explanation for what had happened. Overreaction due to overfatigue. It was all so simple now that she calmed down and thought about it like a rational human being.

At least no one had been aware of how silly she'd behaved while performing in her role of the bride. Well, Reverend Mason had given her and Luke a rather inquisitive look, but everyone else had been oblivious to the nonsense between them.

Well, that was probably not even accurate. Luke had been doing a stand-in thing for his brother, nothing more. She was the one who had gotten all wiggy and weird, not him. Luke had just been pretending to be Robert and seeing her as Ginger. End of story.

Maggie flicked on her blinker and followed the cars into the parking lot of the restaurant.

She'd nibble a bit of dinner, she thought, then be on her way home to bed as quickly as was socially acceptable. Everything was fine. Just fine. She was erasing what had happened from her beleaguered mind. So there.

As the chattering group entered the restaurant, Robert pulled Luke to one side and spoke to his older brother in a quiet voice.

"Luke, my man," Robert said, "care to explain what was going on between you and Maggie during that rehearsal?"

"What do you mean?" Luke said. "We were just playing out the roles Ginger assigned us, that's all."

"Yeah, right," Robert said with a snort. "From where I was sitting, it didn't look like 'let's pretend.' No way.

You've been acting very strange ever since you met Maggie, Luke."

"Robert, Robert, Robert," Luke said, shaking his head. "You've got a typical case of prewedding jitters, not thinking clearly, seeing things that aren't there, the whole nine yards. You'd better get it together or you're liable to pass out at the altar tomorrow night. Trust me. I've been in a great many wedding parties over the years and I've seen your symptoms time and again."

"Really?" Robert said, pressing a fingertip on his chest. "Now that you mention it, my heart is beating really fast."

"That's one of the signs," Luke said, nodding. "I'm telling you, little brother, you've got to calm down. Ginger will never forgive you if you spoil this shindig by falling flat on your face before you can say 'I do.'"

"You're right," Robert said. "Okay. Deep breath. In. Out. I'm cool. I'm fine."

"Robert," Ginger said, coming back to where the brothers were standing. "They're waiting to seat us. Is something wrong?"

"Robert was just very emotionally moved by the rehearsal at the church," Luke said. "But all is well now. You're marrying a very romantic man here, Ginger."

"Ohhh, you are so sweet," Ginger said, giving Robert a quick kiss on the lips. "I love you so much."

"I love you, too, sugar," Robert said.

And unbelievable as it was, Luke thought, he loved Maggie Jenkins. This was definitely a fantastic life-changing night.

The restaurant where the dinner was being held was a five-star establishment, and Maggie had reserved a private dining room for the wedding party.

"Oh," she said softly when she entered the room.

Everything looked wonderful. The staff had really gone all out, per her instructions. The chandeliers were dimmed to create a rosy hue over the room. The crystal glasses gleamed and the sterling silverware sparkled. Wafer-thin china finger bowls sat by each place setting, and yellow rose petals were scattered whimsically down the center of the table that was covered in a pristine white cloth with lace edging.

Nodding in approval at the lovely and oh-so-romantic atmosphere, Maggie hung back with the intention of claiming a seat close to the door so she could make her early exit without creating a fuss. Just as she was about to sit down, Luke took her arm.

"Whoa," he said. "The pretend bride and groom are supposed to sit close to the real bride and groom at this dinner. It's part of the superstition."

"It is not," Maggie said, frowning.

"It certainly is," Luke said indignantly. "You wouldn't want to upset Ginger, would you? I mean, hey, anyone who spends hours sorting through yogurt-covered almonds to get the proper colors for the nut cups certainly wouldn't do anything to blow it in the home stretch."

"Well, Roses and Wishes does aim to please."

"My point exactly," Luke said, propelling Maggie toward the middle of the table. "Which is why you and I are going to sit close to the bride and groom before Ginger flips out."

"But I don't intend to stay long and I—"

"Here we are," Luke said, pulling out a chair. "Right across from the happy couple."

"Mmm," Maggie said, shooting a glare in Luke's direction, then plunking down in the chair.

Waitresses appeared, wineglasses were filled. Soups, then salads came and went. Then huge plates of roast beef, baked potatoes and artfully arranged asparagus were set in front of the diners.

Maggie stifled yet another yawn and stared down at the meal.

"Eat," Luke whispered in her ear.

"I'm too tired to eat."

"If you don't eat, Ginger will think something has gone wrong with the wedding plans and you're upset," Luke said, "which will cause her to—" he shuddered "—I don't even want to think about it."

Maggie sighed and picked up her fork.

The conversations around the table were lively with laughter erupting from one end of the table, then later the other. Everyone was having a wonderful time.

And Maggie was falling asleep.

The four sips of wine she'd consumed were her final undoing, and she was suddenly unable to keep her eyes open. Just as she began to slide off the front of her chair, Luke flung his arm around her and hauled her back up. Maggie blinked and shook her head slightly.

"That was a great story, Maggie," Luke said, his arm

still holding her upright. "Really funny. Ah, here comes the waitress with some coffee. Would you care for some? Yes, you would."

"Yes, I would," Maggie mumbled.

"I want to hear the funny story," Ginger said. "Share with us, Maggie."

"Um…" Maggie said, a blank expression on her face.

"Right," Luke said. "Well, you see, Maggie coordinated a wedding where the bride and groom wanted to be married on horseback. That included the minister sitting on a huge stallion, you understand. The stallion was a horny beast, and just as the minister was to pronounce the couple officially wed, the stallion caught the scent of a mare in an adjoining pasture and took off—bam!— just whisked that minister away in a trail of dust."

Everyone erupted in appropriate laughter, then continued on with their own conversations.

"That was the dumbest thing I've ever heard," Maggie said to Luke under her breath.

"I thought it was pretty good considering I was winging it," Luke said, smiling at her.

"Would you please remove your arm from my person before someone wonders why it is there?"

"Just as soon as you get a few jolts of caffeine in you, my bride," Luke said.

"I am not your bride," Maggie said through clenched teeth. "Your arm is disturbing me."

"Oh?"

"What I mean is," she said, "it's heavy. Your arm. And warm. Much too warm. The air-conditioning is on, but there are a great many people in this room and…much too warm. Hot."

"You're hot?" Luke said, an expression of pure innocence on his face. "Because I have my arm around you? Because I'm very close to you and you're very close to me? Isn't that interesting?"

The waitress filled Maggie's coffee cup, then Luke's, then moved on down the table. Maggie leaned forward to grasp her cup, aware that Luke's arm seemed to be permanently attached to her body. She took a sip of coffee, blew on the remainder to cool it, then drained the cup.

"All better," she said. "I'm wide awake, ready to rock and roll. You may have your arm back now, Luke." That strong, masculine and oh-so-hot arm. "Thank you for your assistance."

"Glad to help," Luke said slowly, very slowly removing his arm. He paused. "So tell me, Maggie, why is it that someone whose focus is on producing picture-perfect weddings doesn't want a wedding of her own? Someone mentioned that you don't intend to marry. I'm curious as to why."

"It's a long story," Maggie said, running one fingertip around the rim of her coffee cup.

"I'm listening."

"I'd rather not discuss it." Maggie pushed her chair back and got to her feet. "Thank you for a lovely dinner," she said to Ginger and Robert. "I'll see everyone at the church tomorrow night. 'Bye for now."

"Hey, wait a minute," Luke said, getting quickly to

his feet. "I think it would be best if I drove you home. You might fall asleep at the wheel."

"Oh, no, I'm perfectly fine now that I've had that coffee. Ta ta."

As Maggie hurried from the room with a chorus of goodbyes following her out the door, Luke slouched back in his chair, a frown knitting his brows.

"Damn coffee," he said, looking at Maggie's empty cup.

"What's wrong with the coffee?" Ginger said, peering into her own cup.

"It's fine, honey," Robert said, then slid a grin at Luke. "It perks up sleepy people that other people wish hadn't gotten perked."

"Pardon me?" Ginger said.

"Nothing," Robert said, chuckling. "It's a guy thing between me and Luke. You know Luke, Ginger. He was the groom tonight and Maggie was the bride. Don't you think they made a smashing couple?"

"We're going to discuss smashing in regard to your nose if you don't shut up," Luke said.

Robert burst into laughter. Ginger looked totally confused. Mrs. St. John told her sons to behave themselves, and Luke got to his feet and said he was leaving.

"Great meal," he said. "In fact, the entire evening was very special. Definitely memorable."

"Do tell," Robert said, still beaming.

Luke made an imaginary gun out of his thumb and forefinger and shot his brother, who laughed so hard he got the hiccups.

* * *

Roses and Wishes took up the first floor of an older Victorian house that Maggie rented in an area of Phoenix that had been rezoned for businesses. Maggie lived upstairs, having furnished one of the bedrooms as a small living room.

The kitchen was on the main floor, as well as a powder room. The original living room was the reception area where albums with pictures of weddings were displayed and comfortable chairs grouped for discussing forthcoming ceremonies. The dining room was Maggie's office.

Maggie's favorite feature of the entire place was the enormous old-fashioned claw-foot bathtub in the upstairs bathroom that allowed her to indulge in long, leisurely soaks with soothing warm water up to her chin.

An hour after leaving the restaurant, having battled the traffic to get home, Maggie sank gratefully into the beckoning bubbles in the tub, rested her head on a spongy pillow on the rim and closed her eyes.

Good grief, she thought, what a night this had been. It had been awful, just awful. Luke St. John was a menace. Yes, that was a great word. A menace. A very dangerous, sensuous member of the male species who was a…a menace to her state of mind and did funny little weird things to her body. Her libido or some such thing. Her womanliness in general. He had nudged awake desire within her that she had worked very hard to put to sleep, to tuck away and ignore. Definitely a menace.

No wonder he had women crawling out of the woodwork trying to get his attention. He had an unexplainable something that pushed sexual buttons in women that they didn't even know they possessed.

Well, she was wise to him now. Granted, part of her overreaction to Luke St. John was due to her exhaustion, but she had a sneaky feeling that even well-rested she might be susceptible to his whatever-it-was.

So. Tomorrow night at the wedding and the reception following she was going to make very certain that she kept her distance from Mr. St. John.

There would be no more gazing into his incredible eyes. No more strong, *hot* arms encircling her. And heaven forbid, no more kisses shared that caused her to have naughty images of tearing his clothes off and ravishing his body right there in front of Reverend Mason.

There. It was settled. She had her plan. She'd stay away from Luke tomorrow night, the wedding would take place without a hitch and she'd never see him again.

Maggie opened her eyes and frowned.

Never see Luke again? Never? Ever? No, of course she wouldn't. He was a member of the jet-set money crowd, and she was among those who hoped they could make next month's rent. There was simply no way that their paths would cross again.

Why was that depressing?

"Oh, stop it," she said aloud, then closed her eyes again.

That was a thought from the tired part of her brain that the coffee hadn't reached. She was now blanking her mind, relaxing in her wonderful bathtub, preparing to sleep away the hours of the night and awake rejuvenated and back to normal with no lingering images or wanton thoughts of Luke St. John.

"Mmm," Maggie said, feeling the misty fog of sleep begin to dim her senses. "Mmm."

Maggie began to slide slowly lower in the tub. Then lower and lower…until she disappeared beneath the frothy bubbles.

She shot upward, sputtering as she swallowed a mouthful of suds, the wild motions causing water to splash out of the tub and onto the floor.

Her hair was covered in bubbles, which made her look like a frosted cake and, she knew, would result in a sticky mess that would have to be properly shampooed. The floor would have to be mopped, her towel that she'd placed next to the tub was soaked and…

And Maggie burst into tears.

She cried because she'd scared herself to death by sinking under the water and because the bubbles tasted terrible and now her stomach was upset. She cried because she was too tired to shampoo her hair and mop the floor and deal with a soggy towel and…

She cried because no matter how hard she tried she couldn't forget what it had been like to be kissed by Luke St. John and she didn't know how to deal with all the new and foreign feelings she'd experienced.

She cried because after tomorrow night she'd never see Luke again, which *she knew,* she knew, was for the best, but sometimes the best was really stinky and just so sad.

She cried because…because, darn it anyway, she felt like it.

So Maggie cried until she had no more tears to shed and the water in the tub was cold and her hair had dried and was a gummy disaster sticking up in weird spiky things and her sinuses were clogged, causing a roaring headache.

Maggie sniffled as she got out of the tub, picked up the soggy towel and threw it in the water. She marched into her bedroom and crawled beneath the sheets.

And during the night spent on damp linens and a gooey pillow, she dreamed of Luke St. John.

Three

Unable to sleep after the events of the unsettling evening, Luke gave up and left his bed, pulling on a lightweight robe. He wandered through his penthouse apartment, finally stopping by a wall of windows to look out over the city lights that shone into infinity.

Thoughts tumbled through his mind one after another, and he pressed the heels of his hands to his throbbing temples for a moment in a futile attempt to halt the onslaught.

Maggie, he thought, crossing his arms over his chest. She was all and everything he had ever hoped to find in a woman. He had only known her for a handful of hours, yet he knew she was the one, his life's partner.

Half of him wanted to shout the fantastic news from

the rooftops, tell the world that he was in love, had found the woman of his heart.

Another section of his being was terrified that Maggie would never come to feel the same way about him, that she would slip away from him like sand falling from the palm of his hand.

Maggie, for reasons she refused to share so far, never intended to marry. That was not good, not good at all. The mystifying question was why. Had she been terribly hurt by a man in the past? Oh, he'd take the guy apart. He'd…Whoa, he would just waste mental energy going off in that direction.

Maybe Maggie was so focused on her career she saw no room for a man in her life. No, that didn't work for him. He'd dated a multitude of women with that mindset and they were all popped out of the same mold. Maggie wasn't like them, not even close. She didn't have the brittle edginess, that step-over-the-bodies-to-get-to-the-top mentality he was so tired of dealing with.

Maggie was so down to earth, so…real. She'd started a business that made dreams come true for brides, made their weddings a special, memory-making event in their lives.

Ginger and Robert's day was going to be perfect because Maggie had seen to every detail, including sorting through a mountain of yogurt-covered almonds to select Ginger's choice of colors.

Yes, Maggie knew how to make dreams come true, yet she didn't want any of those spectacular weddings to be hers, didn't want to be the bride who would see her groom waiting eagerly for her at the altar as she made her way down the aisle.

Why?

It was as though Maggie had built tall, strong walls around her heart, and his greatest fear was that he wouldn't be able to break through them, get a chance to capture her heart as she had his.

The flicker of hope he had, Luke mused as he continued to stare out the window, was that he'd felt Maggie respond to his kiss during the rehearsal, had seen the desire in her big brown eyes directed toward him. *Him.*

That kiss had been the beginning of the chipping away of that barrier surrounding Maggie. It was a start, a positive one, but he had a long, long way to go.

His first impulse was to ask Maggie out, wine and dine and court her, but a cold knot in his gut told him she'd turn him down flat if he invited her to join him for a night on the town. She'd been upset, really flustered by her reaction to the kiss they'd shared and had beat a hasty retreat from the rehearsal dinner as quickly as she could.

No, the traditional program of flowers, candy and romantic dinners wasn't going to work because he just somehow knew he wasn't going to get a chance to put those things in motion.

He needed a new and innovative plan, Luke thought, narrowing his eyes. And he'd better come up with it very quickly. He'd see Maggie at the wedding and reception, but beyond that he envisioned her being set on automatic "no" if he attempted to get her to go out with him.

Ah, Maggie, why? he thought dismally. What secret

something held her in an iron fist that made her determined to never fall in love, never marry, never be the bride in one of her meticulously planned weddings?

He didn't know the answer to that tormenting question. Nor did he know the answer to how he was going to see Maggie again after Robert and Ginger's wedding. And he didn't know the answer to how he would face a cold and empty future without her.

Well, the first order of business, he thought, heading back toward his bedroom, was to get some sleep. He was about to begin the greatest battle of his life and he intended to win. Somehow. He would be the victor. Somehow. He would crumble Maggie's walls into dust and share her sunshine world with her for all time. Somehow.

Late the next morning Maggie entered the small house where her mother lived and presented her with a lumpy plastic bag.

"What's this, sweetheart?" Martha Jenkins said, holding the bag at eye level.

"Almonds," Maggie said, sitting down at the kitchen table. "Yogurt-covered almonds in every shade of the rainbow except yellow and mint-green."

Martha laughed as she sat opposite Maggie and opened the bag. Martha was a rather attractive woman, although not one that would turn heads when she walked into a room. Her brown hair was streaked with gray, which she felt no need to hide, and she had given up long ago trying to lose the twenty pounds that had crept up on her over the years.

"Just what my pudgy person doesn't need," she said. "But, what the heck, I'll eat every one of them. Are these left over from something you did for the big wedding tonight?" She popped two of the nuts into her mouth.

Maggie nodded. "Nut cups. Nut cups, you understand, that only boast yellow and mint-green yogurt-covered almonds, to please my picky bride." She paused. "No, that's not fair. Ginger is very sweet. She just had trouble making up her mind about things for a stretch of time there. But when you think about it, she has every right to have things perfect for her special event."

"That's true," Martha said, then sighed. "But that doesn't guarantee a happy marriage, does it? The bubble bursts and that's that, as evidenced by the fact that I divorced your father when you were ten. Off he went, never to be seen or heard from again." She ate four more almonds. "These are yummy."

"I think Ginger and Robert are going to be a forever couple, Mom," Maggie said. "If you could see them together... Oh, never mind."

"Maggie, honey, I worry so about you," Martha said. "Why on earth did you become a wedding coordinator when there are so many other things you could have done? Why torture yourself creating those beautiful events for other people when—"

"When I know I can never get married myself?" Maggie finished for her.

"Yes," Martha said, patting her daughter's hand. "Exactly."

A sudden and vivid image of Luke flashed through Maggie's mind and a shiver coursed through her.

"Maybe you're right," she said quietly. "Maybe launching Roses and Wishes was a terrible mistake. I've been fine for the past year with all the preparations being for other people, but…" She stopped and shook her head.

"Is there something different about this wedding that's upsetting you?" Martha said, frowning.

"No, not really," Maggie said quickly, forcing a smile to appear on her lips. "It's just the largest wedding I've done, and after so many months I think I'm just registering a sense of loss, sort of hating to say goodbye to all those people.

"I'm hoping, of course, that my reputation will soar because of Ginger and Robert's event and I'll get to do some ritzier weddings. I guess that's what I want. Oh, ignore me. I'm in a strange mood. Eat another almond, Mom. Yogurt is good for a person."

"Nuts are fattening," Martha said, laughing.

"How are things at the store?"

"Same old, same old," Martha said with a shrug. "I manage the children's clothing department by rote now, I've been doing it for so long. I don't love it, I don't hate it, I just do it. Keeps this roof over my head. I really can't complain, sweetheart. I made my way up the ladder from a salesclerk to the manager and I'm proud of that."

"You should be," Maggie said, nodding. "I'm proud of you, too."

"I'll just keep plugging along until I retire. Since I

just turned fifty, I have a ways to go, though." Martha paused. "Do you feel that type of settled in with Roses and Wishes? Do you see yourself running your business for many years to come?"

"I'm not sure," Maggie said, then popped an almond in her mouth. "As I said, I'm having sort of a letdown after working on this big wedding so long. I'll have a better idea how I really feel after tonight and I get some more sleep, sleep, sleep. I'm exhausted and now isn't the time to analyze how I feel about Roses and Wishes."

"True." Martha nodded, then sighed. "Oh, Maggie, I wish things were different. I'd like to think you'd be planning one of those beautiful weddings for yourself someday, but... Hardly seems fair, does it? I know, I know, no one said that life is fair."

"No," Maggie said quietly, "no one said that."

Mother and daughter chatted for a while longer, Martha bringing Maggie up to date on the gossip in the neighborhood, including the news that another of Maggie's childhood friends was getting married, which did nothing to improve Maggie's rather gloomy mood.

Another bride, she thought as she hugged her mother, then left the house. Another bride that wasn't her. Her mom had said she'd reminded the bride-to-be about Roses and Wishes but, due to a very limited budget, the newly engaged couple planned to exchange vows at the courthouse.

No, she thought as she drove away, she wasn't getting more depressed by the minute because her friend hadn't chosen Roses and Wishes to plan her wedding. It was because her friend was *having* a wedding, had found her special someone and would live happily ever after.

Happily ever after, Maggie mused, then sighed. Every bride and groom believed that was their destiny, that they would be together until death parted them, and for some that was gloriously true. But for others?

"Don't go there, Maggie," she ordered herself aloud. "Go home and eat a ton of yogurt-covered almonds and quit thinking." She drew a wobbly breath. "And whatever you do, do *not* dwell on Luke St. John."

Months ago Maggie had splurged on what she referred to in her mind as The Dress. It was sea-green chiffon with a camisole top and a skirt that swirled in changing hues of color just below her knees. Her shoes were strappy evening sandals with three-inch heels. If the event was during the Phoenix winter, she added a lacy off-white shawl that had belonged to her grandmother.

The fact that she wore the same dress to each wedding was immaterial, she knew, because she went unnoticed, was just a busy figure in the background who bustled around making certain everything went as planned.

Wearing The Dress, Maggie arrived at the church an hour before the ceremony was to begin and checked to see that the flowers were delivered and in place. Two of the candles in front of the altar were yellow, and the single one that represented Ginger and Robert united was mint-green.

Maggie stood in the silent church in front of the candles, remembering how Reverend Mason had explained their meaning while she and Luke were playing out the roles of bride and groom.

Knowing she was acting ridiculous, Maggie slid one of the yellow tapers free, then glanced to the right, envisioning Luke holding the other one. In her mind's eye she saw them moving at the same time, igniting the one larger candle in the center. She blew out the imaginary flame that declared her to be a single entity and saw— oh, yes, she really saw—the dancing light from the larger candle in the middle.

Maggie, stop it, she ordered herself as she replaced the yellow taper. Enough of this foolishness.

She turned and her breath caught as she saw Luke standing at the back of the church, watching her as he held a garment bag over his shoulder with one finger.

Squaring her shoulders and lifting her chin, she walked up the aisle to where Luke stood.

"Hello, Luke," she said, looking at an empty space just above his head. "I was just making certain the candles weren't stuck in the holders or anything. Details, details, details. You just wouldn't believe how many little things there are to keep track of for an event like this. And that's my job, by golly, checking all those details and…"

"You look beautiful." Luke's voice was rich, deep and so very male and sensuous that a shiver coursed through Maggie. "Pretty as a bride."

"Oh, well, thank you," Maggie said, still not meeting his gaze. "This is The Dress. What I mean is— Never mind. It's not important. I assume that's your tux you're holding. Ginger changed her mind three times on the color of the tuxedos before settling on pale gray. I hope you don't mind wearing a ruffled shirt, because she didn't budge on ruffled shirts. So. Well. I'd best go into the bride's dressing room and…"

"Maggie, look at me," Luke said quietly.

"Gosh, I just don't have time to do that, Luke."

"Look…at…me."

Maggie slowly shifted her eyes to Luke's and immediately felt light-headed, as though she might float off into oblivion.

"Yes?" she said softly.

"Will you save me a dance at the reception?"

"No, I can't because I don't actually take part, per se, in the reception activities. I hover around in the background checking those pesky little details I told you about. So, nope, no dance. Sorry 'bout that. Gotta go. 'Bye."

"Maggie, do I make you nervous?" Luke said, frowning.

"Nervous? Me?" she said, waving one hand in the air. "Don't be silly. It's not you, it's the whole evening ahead. The reputation of Roses and Wishes is at stake here. Everything has to be perfect."

"Ah," he said, nodding. "That includes keeping all members of the wedding party happy. Right?"

"Well, yes, I suppose so."

"Then promise you'll dance with me. Just one dance, Maggie. That's not too much to ask, is it? You wouldn't want to make the best man grumpy, would you? Heaven forbid."

Maggie narrowed her eyes. "Do you always get what you want, Luke?"

"When it's very important to me, I do," he said, still looking directly into her eyes. "Is it a deal? One dance?"

"Jeez Louise, all right," Maggie said. "But if some detail goes wrong while I'm dancing that dance, it will be your fault, Luke St. John."

"Fair enough," he said, smiling. "I'll see you later then."

"Fine," she said, then scooted around him and hurried away.

Luke stood statue-still for a long moment, staring at the candles that symbolized two becoming one. He nodded, then turned and walked slowly toward the room where the men in the wedding party were to change into their pale gray tuxedos.

Maggie had prepared herself to deal with a totally jangled and nervous-to-the max prewedding Ginger. To Maggie's amazement and heartfelt delight, Ginger had a quiet serenity about her when she arrived in the dressing room at the church.

"Are you really okay?" Maggie said, peering at the bride.

"I'm about to marry the man I love with my whole heart, Maggie," Ginger said softly. "That's all I can think about, focus on. It's strange, isn't it? I made such a fuss about having the right colored almonds in the nut cups, and suddenly none of that is important."

"I think that's wonderful," Maggie said, smiling.

"And you're absolutely beautiful in your dress, Ginger. I hope you and Robert will be very, very happy together."

"Oh, we will be," Ginger said, nodding. "We will be."

Forever? Maggie thought. Until death parted them and even beyond? What were the chances of that?

"Mother," Ginger said, bringing Maggie back to the moment at hand, "you've got to stop crying or you'll be all blotchy in the photographs."

"I know, I know," Mrs. Barrington said, dabbing at her nose with yet another tissue. "But you're my baby girl and... Ohhh, I'm a wreck."

"It's time," Maggie said, looking at her watch. "Mothers, please go and have the ushers seat you now. Bridesmaids, head for the vestibule. You're all simply gorgeous."

"I look like one of those yogurt-covered almonds," Tiffy said, frowning at her reflection in the mirror. "I don't want to do this."

Maggie stepped in front of Tiffy to block her view of herself in the mirror.

"If you want to live to see another day," Maggie said so only Tiffy could hear, "you'll go get in line, Tiffy."

"You can't talk to me like that."

"I just did," Maggie said.

"Oh. Right. Okay. I'm going," Tiffy said, giving Maggie a wary look, then hurrying from the room.

Maggie threw up her hands. "Well, if Tiffy ever gets married, Roses and Wishes sure isn't going to get the chance to coordinate *her* wedding."

* * *

Over three hundred guests witnessed the wedding of Ginger Barrington and Robert St. John. From her usual place in the last pew in the church, Maggie Jenkins indulged herself by watching Luke St. John during the entire picture-perfect ceremony.

What Luke did for a pale gray tuxedo, she thought dreamily, was sinful. The color accentuated his dark hair and tanned skin. The custom-tailored tux made his shoulders look a block wide. And those strong but gentle hands produced the ring right on cue.

The smile that broke across Luke's face when Robert kissed his wife sent shivers coursing down Maggie's spine.

Reverend Mason introduced Mr. and Mrs. Robert St. John to the congregation, then the organ music swelled and the recessional took place, the smiling bride and groom leading the way back down the aisle. When Luke and the maid of honor went by where Maggie stood, he met her gaze for a brief moment and a frisson of heat swirled throughout her.

How on earth, Maggie thought, very aware of her racing heart, was she going to survive her dance with Luke? A promise was a promise, but… If she was just so busy tending to those details, details, details and managed to keep some distance between her and Luke, the dance might never take place. It would take some fancy footwork on her part and she'd have to stay on red alert as to where Luke was at all times, but she could pull this off.

"Good plan," she said under her breath. "Maggie, you're brilliant."

* * *

The reception was being held at one of the exclusive country clubs in Phoenix. A dinner buffet greeted the guests and the huge ballroom was filled with a multitude of round tables each topped with a mint-green or yellow tablecloth and contrasting color candle burning in a glass cylinder in the center. A ten-piece band would play quietly during the meal, then change to Ginger's choice of dance music after the champagne toasts had been made and the four-tier cake had been cut and served by the army of waiters.

As everything continued to go like clockwork, Maggie began to relax and a wave of utter fatigue swept over her. She sat on a folding chair in a dim corner of the room, nibbling on a small plate of food, and nodded in approval at the final outcome of her months of labor.

She'd done it, she thought. Roses and Wishes had hopefully now wiggled its way into the high-society scene of Phoenix. She'd seen the business cards she'd propped next to the candleholder on each table being slipped into purses and given to men to place in their pockets. Fantastic.

Maggie frowned as she recalled the conversation with her mother regarding whether Maggie truly wanted to continue to plan weddings for bride after bride while knowing she herself would never have that title. Well, she wasn't going to dwell on that now, for heaven's sake. She intended to bask in her glory tonight of a job well done for Ginger and Robert St. John.

Maggie placed her plate on the tray of a passing

waiter, then smiled as Ginger and Robert took the floor for the first dance.

How lovely, she thought. They looked so happy, had eyes only for each other as they moved around the gleaming expanse. They danced so well together and—

Maggie suddenly sat bolt upright in her chair.

Dancing, she thought frantically. Other couples were now joining the bride and groom to enjoy the terrific music and so many people were dancing, for heaven's sake. Where was Luke? She had to keep careful track of Luke.

There he was dancing with Ginger. Now he'd shifted to his mother. Fine. My, my, he was poetry in motion, so graceful for a man of his size. Oops. He'd bowed slightly and given his mother's hand to his father and— no, no, no—he was headed toward her secret little corner, was working his way through the crowd on the dance floor. She was out of there.

Maggie jumped to her feet and hurried to the head table, where she gave instructions for the top layer of the cake to be boxed up so it could be frozen and brought out again on Ginger and Robert's first anniversary celebration.

"Give it to the mother of the bride," Maggie told a waiter. "She agreed to take care of it tonight."

"You told us that at the meeting we had last week," the waiter said, frowning. "I've got it covered, Maggie."

"Of course you do," Maggie said, patting him on the arm. "I'm sorry for nagging." She looked quickly into the distance and saw Luke advancing. "How's the supply of champagne holding up?"

"Fine," the waiter said, rolling his eyes. "Trust me. Everything is going great. Isn't there something else you should be doing?"

"Right." Maggie pointed one finger in the air. "I do believe I'll visit the powder room."

"Good idea," the man said drily. "Don't feel you have to check back here."

"Keep up the great work," Maggie said, then rushed away.

When Maggie entered the powder room, she absently registered the fact that it was bigger than her entire living space at home. There was a huge sitting area with love seats, easy chairs and coffee tables holding attractive baskets of artificial flowers.

Beyond all of that were the stalls, a long mirror surrounded by makeup bulbs and a vanity with eight or ten sinks. The noise level was high as women stood two deep in front of the mirror, touching up their postdinner lipstick, one row peering over the shoulders of the other as they chatted and laughed, a good time obviously being had by all.

There was no point in staying in here with this crowd, Maggie thought, shaking her head. The noise was enough to give her a headache and, besides, her purse was locked in a cabinet in the kitchen, so she had nothing to repair her lipstick with.

Well, there was no problem really about leaving the powder room, because even if Luke had figured out where she had been headed, he wouldn't do anything as crass as to plant himself outside the door of the women's restroom. People with money were very big on proper social decorum, and that maneuver definitely wouldn't go down well here.

Nodding in satisfaction that she was so far doing a dandy job of keeping a safe distance between herself and Luke, Maggie opened the door and walked out into the hallway beyond.

And walked smack-dab into the solid, unmoving body of Luke St. John.

Four

Maggie gasped and staggered slightly, causing Luke to grip her upper arms to steady her.

"Well," he said, not releasing his hold on her, "fancy meeting you here, Maggie."

"Luke," she said, looking quickly to each side, "you can't hang around outside the women's restroom. It's not…couth, not nice at all. Your mother would be mortified."

"My mother isn't here," he said, frowning. "You are. Ever since the music began you've been bouncing around the room out there like a Ping-Pong ball. I have the distinct impression that you don't intend to keep your promise to dance with me. Talk about mortifying a mother. How would yours feel if she knew her daughter hadn't kept her word?"

Maggie opened her mouth to say something in her defense, only to realize she was guilty as charged.

"How about," she said, narrowing her eyes in concentration, "I had details, details, details to check on?"

"Nope," Luke said. "Everything is going like a fine-tuned machine. I'm betting that there's nothing left to check on."

"Oh." Maggie paused. "Well, then, try this. I needed to freshen my lipstick, like all the others in the powder room are doing."

"I might buy that," Luke said, nodding, "except where is your tube of lipstick? No purse, no lipstick."

"Oh."

"Maggie," Luke said, his voice gentling, "don't you want to dance with me?"

"Yes, I do. It's just that I—"

"Good. That's settled then." Luke released her arms and grasped one of her hands with one of his. "Let's go."

"But…"

The door to the powder room opened and three young women emerged, stopping before they bumped into Luke and Maggie.

"Well, Luke St. John," one of the women said, smiling coyly, "what on earth are you doing skulking around outside our private little place? Are you lost, gorgeous man?"

"Not at all," Luke said, tightening his hold on Maggie's hand as she tried to pull free. "I just came to collect my partner for the next waltz. I thought it would be extremely polite on my part to escort her to the dance floor."

"Well, isn't that just the sweetest thing?" one of the other women said.

"That's the way I see it," Luke said. "Come along, Maggie."

"You're a lucky girl, Maggie," the third woman said with a wistful sigh. "I've been trying to get Luke to *collect* me for all kinds of things for years and nothing has worked. What do you know that I don't?"

"I have no idea," Maggie said wearily.

"Enjoy your evening, ladies," Luke said, starting down the hallway with Maggie in tow.

Just as Maggie and Luke reentered the main room, a song ended and the band paused, then began to play a slow, dreamy waltz.

"Perfect," Luke said, smiling as he led Maggie onto the crowded, gleaming floor.

And then Maggie was in Luke's embrace, swaying to the music as though they had spent a lifetime dancing together. He nestled her close to his body and she totally ignored the naggy little voice in her mind that was telling her she was in a danger zone, should move backward, keep space between them.

"Mmm," Luke said, "you smell so nice. What kind of perfume is that?"

"Soap," Maggie said.

Luke chuckled and the sexy sound caused Maggie to shiver.

"Are you cold?" Luke said, pulling her even closer.

Maggie's breasts were crushed to the hard wall of Luke's chest in a sweet pain that made her acutely aware of her femininity in contrast to his blatant maleness. Heat swirled within her, finally pulsing low in her body.

"No. I'm...I'm definitely not cold."

"You feel so good in my arms, Maggie. Perfect, absolutely perfect."

"Well..." Maggie started, then for the life of her couldn't think of one intelligent thing to say.

And the music played on.

The crowd surrounding them disappeared, along with the buzz of conversation from those on the sidelines who weren't dancing. The room itself no longer existed. It was just the two of them and the music, encased in a sensual mist.

Ah, Maggie, Luke thought. He wanted this dance to last forever. Holding Maggie in his arms was heaven in its purest form. She fit against him as though she'd been custom-made. Well, that was actually true. Yes, custommade just for him because she was his other half, and he loved her with an intensity that was beyond description.

They were dancing like Cinderella and the prince at the ball, Luke mentally rambled on. But in that fairy tale it all fell apart at the stroke of midnight. That poor slob of a prince was left with empty arms and an aching heart, wondering if he'd ever see his newfound love again.

Well, that wasn't going to happen to Luke St. John, damn it. No way. Because he was going to come up with a rock-solid plan that would enable him to see Maggie on a regular basis without running the risk of her turning him down.

But how in hell was he going to do that?

Where was this genius-level plan going to come from? He'd searched his brain for it until he was exhausted, and it wasn't there, he'd come up empty.

Think, St. John. His entire future happiness depended on that unknown plan.

The song ended.

No, Luke thought frantically. Not yet.

"Luke?" Maggie looked up at him as they stopped moving, realizing that he had not relinquished his hold on her one iota.

"Yes?"

"Could we dance to just one more song?"

"Yes," he said. They would dance to a lifetime of songs played just for them. "It will be my pleasure."

Another waltz began and they swayed to the lilting music.

What on earth had possessed her to ask Luke to dance with her again? Maggie thought, feeling a flush of embarrassment warm her cheeks. How brazen was that, for Pete's sake? Not only brazen but dumb, really dumb. She was supposed to be putting distance between them, not practically begging to be kept nestled close, so enticingly close, to his body.

But he felt so good and smelled so good and he danced so smoothly she was transformed into Ginger Rogers. Oh, what harm could one more dance do? She'd never see Luke again after tonight, so why not have the memory of two fantasy-filled dances instead of just one? Sure, why not?

It was sort of like the story of Cinderella, only this handsome prince wasn't going to run all over the kingdom of Phoenix trying on a shoe to find her. No this was it, all there would be, and the very thought of that was so depressing it was enough to make her weep buckets.

Soon—much, much too soon—the song ended. Maggie drew a steadying breath, then stepped back out of Luke's arms.

"Thank you," she said, smiling slightly. "That was lovely. I… Well, I have things to check on regarding the cleanup crew and what have you so… It was nice meeting you, Luke. Goodbye."

"Good night, Maggie," he said quietly.

Maggie made her way through the crowd on the dance floor, and Luke watched her go before weaving through the guests to return to the head table. He sat down next to his father, a distinguished-looking man with a trim build and salt-and-pepper hair.

"Everything went very well this evening, don't you think?" Mason St. John said. "Your brother and Ginger must be pleased."

"Mmm." Luke rocked his chair back on two legs and folded his arms over his chest.

"Your mother is still out there dancing," his father continued. "She's having a marvelous time."

"Mmm."

"The wedding cake was the best I've ever tasted,"

Mason said. "Some I've had over the years have been like sawdust with a plastic bride and groom on top."

"Mmm."

"I do believe you've met your match in Maggie Jenkins, son," Mason said. "You have all the signs of a man who has had the pins knocked out from under him."

"Mmm," Luke said, then blinked and thudded the chair back onto four legs. "What?"

Mason chuckled. "I thought that might get your attention. I've been watching you, Luke. You're a goner. I was beginning to believe there wasn't a woman in Phoenix who could stake a claim on you, but Maggie Jenkins obviously has. What I don't understand is why you look so gloomy."

"It's very simple, Dad," Luke said. "Maggie may plan fantastic weddings but she doesn't want one for herself. She has no intention of marrying. I don't know if you believe in love at first sight, but it has happened to me big-time. I am irrevocably in love with a woman who wants no part of 'until death do us part.'"

"Well, for the record," Mason said, "I certainly do believe in love at first sight. I fell in love with your mother when we were in the seventh grade and one of the rubber bands from her braces flew off and smacked me right in the eye. As for your Maggie? It doesn't take a genius to figure out that you need a plan."

"Oh, man," Luke said, squeezing the bridge of his nose, "don't say that word. I've worn out my brain already trying to come up with exactly that—a plan. And I'm running on empty.

"Maggie isn't going to go for the wine-and-dine routine. No way. She'd head for the hills before she got tangled up in anything that even hinted of courtship, a serious relationship. I can literally see, feel, the walls she's built around herself."

"So chip away at them. That's where the plan comes in," Mason said. "Come on, Luke. You're a St. John. We go for the gusto, we're winners, we don't even entertain the word *defeat*."

"In the courtroom," Luke said. "Dealing with women is a whole different arena, Dad. It calls for understanding the female mind, and I'm not sure there's a man on this planet who can do that."

"Good point. I certainly don't know what makes those wonderful creatures tick, even after all these years," Mason said, stroking his chin. "Well, now, this is going to be quite a challenge for you, isn't it?"

"The most important fight of my life," Luke said. "I really, *really* need an idea."

"Yep," Mason said, nodding. "Keep me posted on this, son."

"Yeah, okay. In the meantime, pass that champagne bottle down here, will you? Maybe there's a magic answer waiting for me in the bubbly."

Mason laughed as he handed his son the bottle. "All that is in there is a hangover waiting to happen."

"Whatever," Luke said, then filled his glass to the brim.

Late the next morning Luke rolled onto his back in bed, opened his eyes and groaned. He closed his eyes again, pressed his hand to his throbbing forehead, then dropped his arms to the bed with a thud.

He was a dying man, he thought, eyes still tightly closed. Some idiot was playing a bongo drum in this brain, every tooth in his mouth ached and even his hair hurt. To even hope to survive he'd have to cut off his head and grow a new one.

"Ohhh, I hate champagne," he said aloud, with another groan thrown in for good measure. "I'm never drinking that junk again. This is somehow all Maggie Jenkins's fault, damn it."

Luke opened his eyes slowly, then eased upward and moved his feet cautiously to the floor. He propped his elbows on his knees and cradled his throbbing head in his hands.

He couldn't believe he'd done this, he thought miserably. He hadn't gotten smashed since his freshman year in college many years ago. But there he'd sat, filling his glass with expensive champagne, chugging it down, filling it again and again and again.

He vaguely remembered his father watching him and chuckling with maddening regularity, then finally extending his hand and asking for Luke's car keys.

So how had he gotten home? Oh, yeah, his dad had driven him with his mother following in their vehicle. Well, at least his SUV must be parked in the garage beneath the building. His mother had seemed to get a kick out of her oldest son's condition, too, now that he thought about it. What rotten parents.

At least Robert didn't know what his big brother had

done. Robert and Ginger had changed into their traveling clothes and with all the proper fuss had left the reception to catch the plane to their honeymoon in Greece.

Their honeymoon. Because they had just gotten married. Mr. and Mrs. Robert St. John. Robert and Ginger were so happy it was nauseating. No, that wasn't fair. He was sincerely pleased that Robert had found his happiness in ditzy Ginger. By this time next year they would no doubt have produced the first St. John grandchild. How crummy was that?

"Knock it off," Luke said, the sound of his own voice increasing the pain in his head.

He was so jealous of Robert and Ginger, it was a crime. And envious of his parents and every other dewy-eyed in-love couple on the face of the earth.

Well, watch out world, because Luke St. John was in love, too, and…and had gotten as drunk as a skunk because the woman of his heart wasn't remotely close to being in love with him. What a bummer.

Luke staggered to his feet, steadied, then shuffled into the bathroom, where he stood under a very hot shower for a very long time. He dressed in jeans and a T-shirt, consumed four cups of coffee with four matching aspirins and decided he might, just might, live.

He wandered into the living room and slouched onto the large sofa, resting his head on the top and staring at the ceiling.

How many people, he wondered, would decide to take the big step and get married after witnessing the faultless Barrington-St. John wedding Maggie had produced the night before? Would her phone be ringing off the hook Monday morning with newly engaged brides-to-be? That was sure what *he* would like to be doing come the first of the week—helping to plan the wedding of all weddings and…

Luke sat bolt upward, then smacked one hand against his forehead as the sudden motion caused a lightning bolt to shoot through his head.

There it is, he thought, his hear racing. Even through the last lingering fog of his hangover it was taking shape, coming together, clicking into place.

The Plan.

"Yes," he said, punching one fist high in the air.

Maggie spent Sunday catching up on Roses and Wishes paperwork, tackling a mound of laundry and cleaning her neglected apartment on the upper floor of the old house.

That done, she shopped for groceries for her Mother Hubbard cupboards. She prepared a nice dinner for herself of baked chicken, mashed potatoes and gravy and a fruit salad, with the smug knowledge that the effort would provide enough leftovers for several days.

What she did *not* do was think.

Upon waking that morning she'd made a firm vow that she would not dwell on the subject of Luke St. John. Not relive the kiss at the altar during the rehearsal or the dances they'd shared.

No remembrances would be allowed of the heated sensations that had consumed her when Luke's lips had captured hers and while she had been held so tightly in his arms during the dreamy waltzes.

She'd shoo away any images that threatened to creep into her mental vision of Luke's deep brown eyes, his thick beckoning-to-her-fingers hair, his wide shoulders and those incredible strong but gentle hands of his.

Through the entire day she concentrated on her chores and kept busy, busy, busy, becoming extremely proud of herself for her restraint and self-control.

Luke and the success of the Barrington-St. John wedding were now old news, done, finished, kaput, and her thoughts were directed toward the start of the fresh week at Roses and Wishes. She focused on the hope that new business from all those cards she'd seen tucked away at the reception would cause the phone to ring off the hook.

She mentally patted herself on the back for doing such a stellar job of keeping her vow. The day had gone exactly as she'd planned.

But then she ran out of things to do.

She had spit-shined the kitchen after dinner, taken a leisurely bubble bath in her super-duper tub, then settled onto the sofa in an old-fashioned, pale pink, soft cotton granny nightgown that was perfect for the warm summer night.

Glancing at the little clock on the end table, she frowned when she saw that it was only a few minutes after eight o'clock. She was tired from her nonstop day but not sleepy enough to go to bed.

"Television," she said, snatching up the remote.

She channel surfed three times, sighed, then turned off the TV realizing there was just nothing on that she wanted to watch.

"Read a book," she said, grabbing a paperback novel on the coffee table.

After reading the same page four times and having no idea what it said, she plunked the book back onto the table and glared at it.

She wiggled into a more comfortable position on the rather lumpy sofa, crossed her arms over her breasts and stared into space.

And thought of Luke St. John.

"This is dumb, dumb, dumb," she said with a cluck of self-disgust.

Well, she thought, maybe not. Perhaps she was approaching this all wrong. Granted, she'd kept Luke at bay during the hours of the day, but she couldn't continue such a frenzied schedule or she'd collapse into an exhausted heap on the floor.

So. New idea. She *would* indulge in dwelling on all that had transpired between her and Luke, *would* allow images of his masculine magnificence to consume her mind, *would* invite the womanly sensual sensations to once again swirl and churn and burn within her. Then she'd wrap all those things up like a precious treasure and tuck them away in a secret chamber of her heart and be done with them for all time. The end.

"Very good," she said with a decisive nod. "Go for it, Maggie."

And she did.

And spent a long night tossing and turning in her bed, alternating between hot waves of overpowering desire and the chill of loneliness.

Late the next morning Maggie sat in the office of Roses and Wishes and stared gloomily at the telephone, which had not rung once since she'd come downstairs.

Well, that was fine, she rationalized. It didn't mean she wasn't going to garner any new business from the success of the Barrington-St. John wedding. She was being much too impatient, that's all. Brides-to-be had to come back to earth from cloud nine and start thinking about what kind of wedding they wished to have. They'd mentally sift and sort, mull it over, then eventually call Roses and Wishes to set things in motion. Sure.

Maggie left the office and went into the reception area, where she straightened albums that didn't need straightening, dusted what wasn't dusty. She switched two easy chairs to opposite sides of the love seat, then put them back where they'd been.

With a sigh she trudged back into the office, sank onto the chair behind the desk and, for lack of anything better to do, doodled on a legal pad and munched on yogurt-covered almonds.

She was tired, she mused, and that was Luke St. John's fault. She'd given him several hours of her evening last night, but she'd certainly not invited him into her bed and the dreams she'd had when she'd finally managed to doze off. Pushy, rude man. He'd refused to stay beyond her bedroom door as ordered, darn it.

The bell over the front door jingled, indicating someone had entered the house, and Maggie jumped to her feet, nearly tipping over the chair in the process.

She told herself to get a professional grip, for heaven's sake, took a steadying breath as she smoothed her pale blue top over the waistband of her white slacks and actually managed to walk to the main area in a fairly slow, ladylike manner.

Then stopped dead and forgot to breathe.

"Hello, Maggie," Luke St. John said from where he stood just inside the door.

This was absurd, Maggie thought, taking a gulp of much-needed air. Luke wasn't really standing there looking incredibly gorgeous in jeans and an open-necked gray dress shirt. She'd conjured up his image from the wanton section of her brain that insisted on reliving all the sensationally sensuous... This was ridiculous.

"Maggie?" Luke closed the distance between them and frowned. "Hello?"

"You're not here," she said, flapping one hand in the air. "Poof. You're gone." She paused, waited, then tentatively pressed one fingertip to Luke's imaginary chest, which was definitely hard as a rock. Her eyes widened as she stared up at him. "Oh, my gosh, you really are here. Why are you here?"

Luke folded his arms across his chest and stared down at the floor, his shoulders shaking with muffled laughter.

Oh, man, he thought, how he loved this woman. She was obviously jangled by his unexpected arrival at

Roses and Wishes, and that was good news. Great news. If he hadn't had an impact on Maggie, she wouldn't give a damn if he suddenly popped into her place of business.

She was flustered and didn't know how to hide it, and that was so endearing. Maggie was genuine and honest. He wanted to take her into his arms and…

"Mr. St. John?" Maggie said, planting her hands on her hips. "May I help you?"

"I'm beyond help," he said, meeting her gaze with merriment dancing in his brown eyes.

"Pardon me?"

"Never mind." Luke forced a serious expression onto his face. "Yes, you may assist me, Ms. Jenkins. I am in desperate need of your expertise."

This was it, he thought, feeling a sudden trickle of sweat run down his chest. He was putting The Plan into motion. And it would work. It *had* to work.

"My expertise?" Maggie said, cocking her head slightly to one side. "About what?"

"Weddings. I am responsible for planning a wedding, every detail, beginning to end. No expense spared."

Dear heaven, no, Maggie thought, feeling the color drain from her face. Luke St. John was getting married. How could he do such a thing? He hadn't even brought a date to his brother's wedding, for crying out loud. And crying out loud was what she was about to do, because she could feel the tears stinging at the back of her eyes and…

"Are you all right?" Luke said, frowning. "You're very pale all of a sudden. Why don't we sit down on this nice love seat you have?"

"*I'll* sit on the love seat," she said, shooting him a dark look, "and *you* sit on that easy chair."

Luke raised both hands palms out. "No problem. Whatever makes you comfortable."

Once seated, Maggie directed her attention to an invisible piece of lint on one of her knees.

"I must say, Luke," she said, wishing her voice sounded steadier than the quivering little noise she was hearing, "that I'm surprised by your announcement. I mean, you didn't have a…a companion with you at Ginger and Robert's wedding or…

"What did you do? Put all your women's names in a hat, pull one out and decide to marry her because your brother is obviously so happy, so what the heck, why not?" She paused. "Sorry. That was rude. Very rude." She cleared her throat. "So. You wish to hire me—Roses and Wishes—to coordinate your wedding. I appreciate your confidence. It is a bit unusual that you're tending to this and not your bride-to-be, as it's traditional that the woman… Forget that. To each his own. How many people are you going to invite?"

Luke propped one ankle on his other knee and smiled pleasantly. "A lot."

"Could you be a tad more specific?"

"Not at the moment. Just go with a lot for now."

"And when do you plan to have this life-changing event?" Maggie said, looking over at him.

"The sooner the better," he said. "But I'm not exactly sure at this point in time."

"I see." Maggie frowned. "No, I don't. Call me stupid, but this isn't making one bit of sense. You want me to coordinate a wedding for a lot, number unknown, of guests, and it's to be held the sooner the better, but you don't have a clue as to when."

Luke nodded. "That's it in a nutshell."

A rather hysterical giggle escaped from Maggie's lips. "Do you know anything for certain? Like, for example, who the bride is?"

"Oh, yes, ma'am," he said. "That is etched in stone."

"How nice," she said miserably. "What I mean is… I'm not sure what I mean. This is very confusing."

"It is?" Luke said, an expression of pure innocence on his face. "I need a wedding planned, you're a wedding planner—coordinator, whatever." He shrugged. "Seems to me I've come to the right place, especially after seeing what a dynamite job you did for Ginger and Robert."

"But Ginger knew what she wanted and when she wanted it," Maggie said, throwing up her hands. "Well, sort of. She did change her mind about a ton of things, but generally speaking, she knew. You know—three hundred, give or take, guests, a summer wedding, seven bridesmaids, yogurt-covered almonds in the nut cups, details like that."

"Oh," Luke said, nodding. "Well, I don't know any of that stuff. Except forget the almonds. I don't like almonds, yogurt-covered or otherwise."

"Oh, well, with that data I'm ready to roll," Maggie said, throwing up her hands again. "No almonds in the nut cups." She shook her head. "This is insane."

"Tell me this, Maggie," Luke said, leaning toward her. "How long does it take to put on a production like Ginger and Robert's shindig?"

"At least six months," she said, "and that's going full speed ahead."

"Really? That long? Grim, very grim. Well, if that's the best you can do… Okay, let's aim for a Christmas wedding. How's that?"

Sure, Maggie thought, feeling the threat of tears again. Merry Christmas to Maggie Jenkins. She could watch Luke St. John get married. Hooray.

Darn it, what difference did it make? Why was she falling apart because Luke suddenly realized he was in love with one of the high-society women he dated and wanted to get married and live happily ever after? It had nothing to do with her beyond being a real coup for Roses and Wishes.

So why did she feel so sad?

Why did she want to crawl into bed and cry for a week?

Forget it, just forget it. She wasn't talking to herself about this anymore because she was being absolutely, positively ridiculous.

"Maggie?" Luke said. "Does that work for you? A Christmas wedding?"

"Yes," she said softly as she looked at a spot in space a couple of inches above Luke's head. "A Christmas wedding will be just fine, very beautiful and…special. Definitely a Christmas to remember forever."

Five

Luke nodded and rubbed his hands together. "Actually this schedule will work out perfectly. A holiday wedding. That's really romantic, don't you think?"

"What? Uh, yes, very romantic," Maggie said with a rather wistful sigh as she shifted her gaze to the opposite wall. "It's a magical time of year as it is. And to be getting married then, too? Goodness, that's over the top or however you want to put it."

"Yep." Luke paused and looked at Maggie intently. "I'll tell…*them*…the good news."

Maggie snapped her head around to stare at Luke. "Them? Them who?" She paused. "You mean the families?"

"Nooo," Luke said slowly. "I was referring to the bride and groom."

"Pardon me?" she said, obviously confused.

"Oh," Luke said, snapping his fingers, "I didn't make myself clear on this at all, did I? I do apologize, Maggie. The wedding we're discussing is for my cousin and his fiancée."

"What?" Maggie blinked. "You mean *you're* not… What?"

"Let me start at the top," Luke said, lacing his fingers on his chest. "My cousin…Clyde…"

Jeez, what a name, he thought, inwardly groaning. He should have given thought to the identity of these people before he got here. The bride, the bride. What was the bride's name?

He looked frantically around the room, his gaze falling on the cover of a thick photograph album imprinted with the words *Precious Memories* in gold.

"…and the love of his life…Precious," he went on, "are in London working for the State Department."

"Clyde and Precious?" Maggie said, raising her eyebrows.

"Yep, good ol' cousin Clyde. Anyway, they decided they'd best get married here in Phoenix to keep the families from murdering them. However, they agreed to stay on in their positions as long as possible to train their replacements before returning to the States.

"They did stipulate to their boss, though, that they definitely wanted to be back home for the holidays. So, you see, a wedding at that time of year keeps everybody happy. Are you happy, Maggie?"

"I'm ecstatic," she said, smiling. Because Luke wasn't getting married. He wasn't. Thank goodness, because... Because why? She didn't know, but there was no denying that the dark cloud that had settled over her was gone, poof, just disappeared, because Luke wasn't talking about *his* wedding. "Ecstatic because... Yes, because this is wonderful news for...for Roses and Wishes."

"Of course," Luke said, nodding. "Now let me make something very clear. Precious is a rather unusual young woman. She'd much prefer to just go to City Hall in her jeans and marry her beloved Clyde, but the mothers would freak and Clyde and Precious would never hear the end of it.

"So when I spoke with them on the phone yesterday I suggested that they hire you to arrange the whole she-bang and all they have to do is show up. They're thrilled. Precious said she'd go along with any decisions you make. Clyde? Hey, guys don't care about this kind of stuff. It's a woman thing."

"You mean I get to plan the whole wedding, make it the way I want it to be and... What about the mothers? The mothers will never let me do that. They'll want to step in and put this production together."

"No way," Luke said. "They're as different as day and night, those mothers. My aunt and Precious's mom together are a war waiting to happen. They're not going to know a thing about it.

"They'll get an invitation in the mail, just like everyone else who is invited. They'll pout for a while, I suppose, but then they'll jump right into fast-forward and start thinking about becoming grandmothers, and all will be well."

"This is crazy," Maggie said, shaking her head.

"No, this is exactly the way it should be done." Luke leaned forward, only inches from Maggie as he looked directly into her eyes. "You pretend this is *your* dream wedding, Maggie. Make the decisions based on what *you* would want if *you* were getting married."

"Oh…my…gracious," Maggie whispered.

"The thing is, Clyde and Precious feel they'd better be kept up to date on what's what, you know what I mean? Just in case the moms quiz them later on why they decided on something. For example, if you have them get married in a hot-air balloon, they want to be prepared with a solid story about how they have this thing for hot-air balloons. Get it?"

"I…"

"Therefore, I'll be sticking pretty close to you through this whole endeavor so I have all the details straight to pass along to them as we go. My father will take up the slack for me at the office to free up some of my time because Clyde is his favorite nephew. My dad is semiretired, but for this occasion he's willing to put in extra hours.

"So I'd say that about covers it. Remember, no expense spared. Oh, and Precious is about your size, so there shouldn't be any problem about your picking out her wedding dress—if you want a traditional wedding dress. That's up to you. Any questions?"

"I-I'm stunned," Maggie said, shaking her head. "I'm having difficulty comprehending all this because it's so… I can't even think of a word to describe it."

Try *brilliant*, Luke thought smugly. The Plan was nothing short of brilliant. Maggie would produce the wedding of *her* dreams. He had set it up perfectly to be able to stick close to her through the whole thing and he'd be chipping away at those walls of hers little by little, brick by emotional brick.

She would come to love him, just as he loved her. God, she just had to fall in love with him, want to marry him and spend the rest of her life by his side. *Ah, please, Maggie.*

"Will you do it?" Luke said. "I mean, take on this project?"

"Well, yes, of course I will. Yes."

"Great. That's even more than great. Thank you, Maggie, from the bottom of my heart. I'm really grateful. That is, Clyde and Precious will be very grateful to you for doing this." Luke paused. "I realize that you don't wish to ever marry, but that doesn't mean you haven't thought about the kind of wedding you'd like to have if you intended to marry, even though you don't…intend to marry. Right? Did that make sense?"

"I think so," Maggie said, frowning slightly. "Yes, I understand what you said. And I suppose I do wonder about how I would do things each time I coordinate a wedding. It's human nature, you know what I mean?

"For example, when Ginger finally settled on pale yellow as one of her colors, I couldn't help feeling that with so many blond bridesmaids a deeper shade would have been more striking. Of course, I didn't say that to Ginger, but I *was* thinking it."

"There you go," Luke said, nodding. "That's exactly what I was referring to. Have you ever put together a holiday wedding before?"

"No."

"Then you won't be influenced by a previous bride's choices. The decisions will be exclusively yours." Luke beamed. "Won't that be fun?"

"I…"

"You're not scheduled to do another wedding right away, are you?" Luke said. "You're free to concentrate totally on Clyde and Precious's do?"

"Their wedding will have Roses and Wishes' undivided attention," Maggie said, smiling.

"Great." Luke frowned. "Mmm. The church. Which one would you pick?"

"Me? Well, I happen to be Episcopalian, but—"

"Terrific. You can book the same church that Ginger and Robert had. That will suit Clyde and Precious just fine."

"Well, sure. Okay. Goodness, my head is spinning. This is rather overwhelming because it's so…strange. What about bridesmaids? The dresses have to be custom-fitted, you know."

Oops, Luke thought. Quick, St. John, come up with a solution to that.

"Well," he said slowly. "Who would you choose as your attendants?"

"Me? My sister and my best friend."

"That's all? Just two?"

Maggie laughed. "Not everyone has seven bridesmaids like Ginger, Luke."

"True," he said. "Two. I'll pass that on to Precious. Why don't you find out what size dresses your two choices wear, and the seamstress or whatever you call her can adjust to the size of Precious's bridesmaids."

"Well, it's not perfect, but it might work if there's time enough to nip and tuck before the actual wedding—provided, of course, that everyone is at least close to matching in size. My sister Janet wears a twelve. My best friend Patty is a ten."

"And you?"

"Me? I wear a size eight."

"Got it. I'll double-check all three of those numbers with Precious." Luke paused. "There. Problem solved. We're a good team, Maggie Jenkins." Luke looked directly into Maggie's big brown eyes. "A very good team. You. Me. Together."

"Together," Maggie whispered as she stared into Luke's mesmerizing eyes.

She was about to start planning her fantasy wedding, Maggie mused dreamily. The one she would never have but had thought about so very much. And Luke St. John would be beside her every step of the way, as though he was the groom and she was the bride and… This was totally bizarre.

And very, very dangerous.

She had to keep herself grounded in reality through the months ahead, not get emotionally caught up in what she and Luke were doing. It was an unusual project assigned to Roses and Wishes, that's all.

The bride was Precious, the groom was Clyde. She must remember that at all times. And keeping her head and heart straight would be a lot easier if she quit gazing into those compelling eyes of Luke's.

"Well," Maggie said much too loudly and causing Luke to jerk at her sudden outburst, "this has certainly been an interesting meeting." She got to her feet. "As the owner of Roses and Wishes, I'd like to sincerely thank you for your confidence in me to coordinate the perfect wedding for Precious and Clyde."

"You're welcome," Luke said, rising. "Just out of curiosity, what will you do first?"

"Select the colors. There are so many things—details, details, details—that have to tie into them that it's important they are chosen early on." Maggie laughed. "The way Ginger kept changing her mind about her colors was nerve-racking, to say the least."

"You won't have to worry about that type of thing this time, will you?" Luke said, smiling. "You're planning *your* wedding—so to speak."

"Well, yes, so to speak. But not really. Well, sort of, because whatever I decide is how it will be. But then again… Never mind. It's going to take a while to adjust to such a once-in-a-lifetime endeavor."

"That's what weddings should be, don't you think?"

Luke said quietly. "A once-in-a-lifetime, forever-and-ever event for the bride and groom?"

"Of course." Maggie sighed. "But in today's society the forever-and-ever part doesn't mean much to some couples."

"There hasn't been a divorce in our family," Luke said, "for as far back as anyone can remember."

Maggie's eyes widened. "You're kidding. That's amazing."

"Not really," Luke said, shaking his head. "I believe that St. Johns are just very good at listening to their hearts, knowing what is right and real and falling in love with someone who is on the same wavelength. My dad fell in love with my mother when they were in the seventh grade. I kid you not, it's true."

"Awesome," Maggie said. "That's a rather dopey word to use, but it fits. Seventh grade? And there hasn't been even one divorce in your family history? Totally awesome. Almost unbelievable. You don't suppose some of those couples stayed together even though they were miserable because they didn't want to be the first to break that magical spell, do you?"

"Nope," Luke said. "No way. A stranger seeing any of my family with their partners would be able to tell that they're deeply in love. Ginger and Robert will grow old together and be just as happy as they were at their wedding. So will…Precious and Clyde. Yeah, so will Precious and Clyde."

"That's so beautiful," Maggie said wistfully.

"What about *your* family, Maggie?"

She frowned. "We're…" She mumbled something that wasn't quite clear.

"Pardon me?" Luke said, frowning.

"Never mind," she said quickly. "Well, I have my work cut out for me, don't I? And the first order of business is choosing colors for a Christmas wedding."

"I'll leave you to get started on the plans," Luke said, "but I'll be in touch very soon. Goodbye for now, Maggie, and thank you."

"Oh, I thank you, Luke. Goodbye."

As Luke closed the door behind him, Maggie sank onto the love seat and drew a steadying breath as she continued to digest all that had just happened. Then she shifted her gaze to the center of the table that held the albums.

It had been her plan when she'd opened Roses and Wishes, she thought, to always have a vase of roses, her very favorite flower, right there in that spot. She soon realized, however, that the budget would not allow for such an extravagance.

Roses. She would carry… No, no, *Precious* would carry a bouquet of red roses with baby's breath and Christmas greenery all tied together with one red and one white satin ribbon.

She'd named her fledgling business Roses and Wishes because it held a secret meaning for her. Her wishes were simple but not hers to have. A husband, children, a home. Life with a man who loved her as much as she loved him.

Roses. She'd be a bride who carried roses down the

aisle and later grew them in the garden behind the home she shared with her family.

Roses and Wishes. She'd wanted that name where she could see it, her attempt to find fulfillment in helping brides make their wishes come true. Well, this time she got to go one step further. She had chosen roses for the bridal bouquet. Gorgeous, fragrant red roses.

Maggie smiled and leaned her head back on the back of the love seat.

The colors must be chosen for this Christmas wedding, she mused. Well, it really wasn't that difficult. Red roses. And the attendants would wear rich forest-green satin dresses with shoes to match. They would carry bouquets of red and white baby carnations.

The taper candles that would be used to light the one signifying a single entity would be white and the center candle would be red.

And her dress? It would be white as freshly fallen snow, simple but elegant, with a train and a frothy veil— a veil that Luke would lift at the proper moment to kiss his bride and...

"No," Maggie said, jumping to her feet. "Stop it right now. Back up and get it right, Maggie Jenkins."

Precious's dress. Precious's veil. Clyde's kiss for his new wife. This was Precious and Clyde's wedding she was coordinating.

"Thank you," she said, dropping back down on the love seat. "That's better. Don't make that mistake again, Ms. Jenkins. Not once in the months ahead while you tend to the details, details, details."

* * *

As Luke maneuvered his SUV through the heavy Phoenix traffic, he made no attempt to curb the wide smile on his face.

He'd done it, he thought, tapping his fingertip on the steering wheel. He'd set his brilliant plan in motion and it had worked, it had actually worked. Maggie was now committed to coordinating a fantastic wedding for his imaginary cousin Clyde and the ever-famous Precious. Man, he really should have given thought to names for the bride and groom before he'd gone to Roses and Wishes. Oh, well.

Back to The Plan. Maggie would create the wedding of her dreams. *Her* dreams. And if everything went as he hoped and prayed, that wedding would actually take place. Maggie Jenkins would marry Luke St. John at some point during the Christmas holidays.

Of course, there was a long way to go before that ceremony happened. Maggie had to fall in love with him, just as he had with her. She was attracted to him, unsettled by him, was feeling something for him already, he was sure of that.

She had to fall in love with him and trust him enough to be willing to allow him to crumble into dust those protective walls she'd constructed around herself, so he could reach out and take her into his arms…forever.

Yeah, he had his tasks cut out for him, but Maggie was worth fighting for and he intended to win. He *had* to win.

Luke frowned as he suddenly recalled Maggie's

strange response when the conversation had centered on all the happy marriages in his family. He'd asked about her family and—what had she said? She'd sort of mumbled a word and he just wasn't sure what it had been. When he'd pressed, she'd quickly changed the subject.

"Damn," Luke said, smacking the steering wheel with the heel of one hand.

Maybe it was an important clue about Maggie's aversion to getting married, to being determined to plan weddings for other people but never for herself.

He'd said…then she'd said… Oh, hell, what had Maggie said?

Six

That evening Maggie and her best friend Patty sat on the floor in Maggie's minuscule living room eating take-out pizza, sipping sodas and going through a tower of bride magazines page by page.

The two had been friends since elementary school and now, at twenty-five years old, neither could imagine dealing with the ups and downs of life without the other's support.

Patty taught first grade at the same school she and Maggie had attended. Patty's parents had been killed in an automobile accident five years before, so now every spare cent she had went toward putting her younger brother through college.

"Look at this," Patty said, tapping one fingertip on a

page of the magazine in front of her. "Tiny Christmas balls nestled in the bridesmaids' bouquets. Do you like that idea?"

Maggie wrinkled her nose. "It's a bit much, I think. I don't want to overdo the Christmas theme." She laughed. "After all, this is a wedding, hon, not an office party."

"True," Patty said, turning the page. "Forget the icky ornaments." She took another bite of pizza and looked at Maggie. "It's so strange to be sitting here doing this, Maggie. I get so caught up in it, I have to keep reminding myself that we're not really planning *your* wedding."

"I know," Maggie said, sighing, "but this is the closest we'll ever get to actually doing that, so enjoy."

"Don't get me started on that subject," Patty said, shaking her head. "The fact that you won't even consider the possibility of falling in love and getting married because—"

"Patty."

"Okay, okay, I'll shut up." Patty paused. "This whole project is weird. Who ever heard of a bride who didn't give a damn about the plans for her own wedding? Are you sure this Precious person is playing with a full deck?"

Maggie shrugged. "Luke said Precious would just as soon get married wearing jeans at a courthouse. This production is to satisfy the mothers. Mothers I don't have to deal with, which is a blessing. This will be the wedding of…well, *my* dreams. Roses and wishes and…

Anyway, I intend to thoroughly go for it because nothing like this will ever happen again. The only person I have to report to is Luke."

"Luke St. John," Patty said wistfully. "I've seen his picture in the newspaper. He is so gorgeous, he's hot! To think that you actually danced with him at his brother's wedding reception." She stared into space. "To be held in the arms of Luke St. John must have been heaven on earth."

"Close, very close," Maggie said, nodding. "He's a marvelous dancer, made me feel like I was floating on a cloud and…" Sudden heat stained her cheeks a pretty pink. "Forget that. Do you think having the bridesmaids wearing green is corny? Maybe I should start over in my mind and not address the Christmas thing at all."

"Oh, no, don't do that," Patty said. "People will expect a festive touch. Besides, it's what you want. Right?"

"Well, yes."

"Then it's settled. Stay with the Christmas theme, but don't go over the top. What did your sister say about all this?"

"Janet said it was nuts," Maggie said, smiling, "but that she'd be delighted to be fitted for a beautiful dress even if she doesn't get to actually wear it anywhere. As a single mom with three kids, she said they don't provide fittings—la-di-da—in the thrift shops where she buys her clothes."

"How funny." Patty laughed, then frowned. "What

was your mom's reaction? She must think Precious has a screw loose."

"She didn't dwell on Precious's mind-set," Maggie said. "Eat that last piece of pizza. I'm stuffed."

"No problem," she said, reaching for the slice. "So what *did* your mom focus on about this crazy situation?"

"She's worried about me, Patty," Maggie said quietly. "She's afraid that I'll spend all these weeks planning my dream wedding and then fall apart when I have to face the reality of it being for someone else."

She sighed. "In fact, she's concerned about me being a wedding coordinator in the first place. She thinks it was a stupid business for me to start considering I'll never have a wedding of my own. She's afraid I'll spend my life being so sad because I'll be constantly reminded that... Oh, you know."

"What I know," Patty said, shaking her head, "is you won't budge on the subject of your not getting married, and your mom and Janet—and even your brother, for all I know—are on the same wavelength about it. I'm totally outnumbered when it comes to convincing you otherwise."

"So don't try. Heavens, look at this picture in this magazine. The bridal bouquet has green and red candles in it and they're lit, for heaven's sake."

"It boggles the mind," Patty said, laughing. "Talk about being hot. Which brings me back to the subject of Luke St. John. You said he's really nice, not snooty even though he's as rich as Midas?"

"Yes." Maggie nodded. "He's very, very nice."

"And he has a sense of humor and a good relationship with his family and dances like a dream and looks as good in jeans as he does in a tux and... Maggie, you'd better be very careful during the weeks ahead. You're going to be seeing a lot of Luke because of this wedding. Luke sounds like he's capable of smashing hearts to smithereens. I don't want one of those hearts to be yours."

"Believe me, I don't either," Maggie said. "I'm very aware of Luke's...attributes, shall we say. But fear not, because I'm on red alert, the walls are up, the door is barred. There's not a chance on earth that I'll fall head over heels in love with Mr. Luke St. John. Nope. That isn't going to happen."

"And now," Luke said, "I have to make certain that Maggie falls head over heels in love with me."

Mason St. John chuckled. "That's definitely top of the list considering you want to marry Maggie Jenkins, have a slew of little St. Johns, then grow old and creaky together."

"Right," Luke said, then cut a chunk out of the enormous steak on the plate in front of him.

Father and son were dining at Mason's club, which he had yet to convince Luke to join. Luke had made it clear several years before that he'd consider a membership once the private establishment got with the program and allowed women to join.

"I must say, Luke," Mason said after consuming several forkfuls of succulent roast beef, "that I'm impressed with this plan you've come up with. It's brilliant. And I'm more than happy to cover things for you at the office as this scheme unfolds."

"I appreciate that, Dad. Remember, not a word of this to Mom. She couldn't keep a secret if her life depended on it, plus she'd be calling me constantly with advice about how to win Maggie's heart."

"That she would, bless her," Mason said, smiling. "I just wish you'd... Oh, Lord." His shoulders started shaking with laughter as he pressed his napkin to his lips.

Luke frowned. "Don't go there. I thought you were going to get us kicked out of here earlier because you were laughing so loud. Just don't think about it."

"I'm trying not to, but...Clyde and Precious?"

"I forgot to think of names for my fictitious bride and groom before I went to see Maggie. I was under pressure. I realize they're grim but..." Luke shrugged.

"What's Clyde's last name?" Mason said. "Is he a St. John? Clyde St. John." He started laughing again. "I can't handle that."

"Okay, okay. Knock it off. All right, let's see. Clyde's mother is your sister and she married... Who did she marry?"

"John Smith."

"That's really original," Luke said, rolling his eyes heavenward. "All right. Whatever. Clyde Smith is going to marry Precious, um...Peterson."

"Precious Peterson?" Mason said with a hoot of merriment that drew several frowns from other diners. "Sorry. So this extravaganza is the Peterson-Smith wedding. Got it. Having it during the Christmas holidays is a nice touch. Very romantic." He took a sip of wine. "What happens next?"

"I wait for Maggie to make some decisions and contact me so I can pass on the data to Precious and Clyde. Well, Precious at least. Clyde will go along with things just like any other groom would. Your favorite nephew is a laid-back, go-with-the-flow guy."

"Ah," Mason said, nodding.

"I have to concentrate on Maggie, chip away at those barriers of hers, get her to allow herself to fall in love with me."

"Ah."

"There's a special…something…already happening between Maggie and me, Dad, I know there is. It's rare, important, real. You should have seen her face when she thought I wanted her to plan my wedding to some other woman. She tried to hide it, but she was upset, I know she was. When I finally told her that it was cousin Clyde's wedding, she just lit up. She feels something for me, she cares. I have to nurture that, make it grow, get her to trust me, come to love me as I love her, then agree to be my wife for all time."

"Ah."

Luke glared at his father. "Can't you say anything else besides 'ah'? A little advice would be helpful here, you know."

Mason set his fork and knife on the edge of his plate, folded his arms over his chest and looked at his son.

"Love is very complicated," Mason said quietly. "But

at the same time it's very simple." He shook his head. "It's hard to explain. You construct a sturdy foundation together and build on that as the years go by. One of the bricks in that foundation, Luke, is honesty. Your plan to win Maggie's heart is based on duplicity."

"But—"

"I know, I know," Mason said, raising one hand. "You're convinced that if you try to court Maggie, she'll refuse to see you, won't run the risk of finding herself in a serious relationship. I understand the need for this plan you've come up with. The thing is, will Maggie understand when she knows the truth? Women don't like to be duped. This whole thing could backfire on you."

"You're thoroughly depressing me," Luke said, leaning back in his chair.

"Well, in all fairness, I don't see where you have any choice but to do it this way," Mason continued. "The usual wine-and-dine scenario is not going to work with your young lady, so you've been forced to come up with an alternative approach. A very clever one, I might add."

He chuckled. "Except for the names! I want you to be happy, Luke. I hope your dream for a life with Maggie becomes your reality, I really do."

"Thanks, Dad. This plan will work. It has to. A future without Maggie is not something I'm willing to accept. I'm going to win the heart, the love, of Maggie Jenkins."

At one o'clock the next afternoon Maggie entered a popular downtown restaurant and immediately scooted into the ladies' room. She stood in front of the long mirror above the half dozen sinks and glared at her reflection.

She was nervous, she thought, and furious at herself because she was. Luke had called her early that morning and asked if it would be too much trouble for her to meet him for lunch.

He was waiting for a scheduled long-distance call regarding a case he was about to wrap up and couldn't leave the office to come to Roses and Wishes. The afternoon was jam-packed with bringing his father up to date on Luke's ongoing cases.

He'd spoken with Clyde and Precious, Luke had told her, and wanted to pass on the information he had and blah, blah, blah.

"Oh, sure," Maggie said, still glowering at her image. "Lunch? *Do* lunch? No problem."

Right, she thought dismally. No problem, except for the fact that she was a nervous wreck. That was so dumb. Dumber than dumb. Luke was a client of hers, of Roses and Wishes, nothing more. They were working together to coordinate the wedding of his cousin Clyde and the bride-to-be Precious. The end.

The really humiliating part was that she knew why she was shaky about seeing Luke. Last night she'd had the most sensuous dream imaginable about the two of them. Goodness. She'd wakened in the night all…all hot and bothered, and try as she may she couldn't erase the pictures in her mind of a naked Luke reaching for a naked her, taking her into his naked arms and…

"Stop it." Maggie spun around and stomped out of the ladies' room. "You are just so ridiculous."

She gave her name to the hostess and was immediately shown to a table at the far end of the large room. Luke stood as he saw her coming.

Thank the Lord, Maggie thought giddily, he has his clothes on. Nice suit. Very lawyer-looking suit. Did she look frumpy in white slacks and a flowered blouse? She should have worn a skirt or dress but hadn't wanted to arrive there with naked legs and… Oh, God, she was totally losing it.

"Hello, Maggie," Luke said, smiling, when she reached the table. "It's nice to see you."

Maggie's eyes widened. "See me?" She shook her head slightly and slid onto her chair. "Yes, of course, nice to see me. It's nice to…see you, too, Luke. I really like that suit you're wearing. Excellent suit. I'm *so* glad you're wearing that suit."

Luke frowned. "Are you all right?"

"What? Oh, yes, of course, I am." Maggie busied herself spreading the linen napkin on her lap. "I just didn't sleep very well last night and—" she looked at Luke again "—I'm hungry."

"Well, we can fix that easily enough." Luke signaled to the waitress. "Order whatever you'd like."

The waitress appeared at the table. Maggie ordered the first thing she saw on the menu and told herself to get a grip. Luke asked for a steak sandwich and home fries.

"I really appreciate your coming all the way downtown," Luke said as the waitress hurried off.

"Not a problem," Maggie said. "Did you receive the call you were waiting for?"

"Call? Oh. Yes. Right on schedule." Luke took a sip of water.

Man, I'm crummy at this cloak-and-dagger stuff, he thought. He'd nearly forgotten about his imaginary "appointment" with the telephone. He'd decided to push his luck and attempt to meet with Maggie somewhere other than at Roses and Wishes. The long-distance call had been a great idea, but he'd blow it big-time if he didn't remember what he'd told her.

"What was it you wanted to discuss with me about your conversation with Precious and Clyde?" Maggie said.

"Why don't we enjoy our lunch first, then get into all that after we eat," he said, smiling.

"But you said you have a very busy afternoon," Maggie said.

"Yes, so I do," Luke said, frowning. *Really* crummy at this. "All right. Precious and Clyde will be arriving in Phoenix in the middle of December, so the holiday wedding is great. Right on the money."

Maggie smiled. "Good. I've chosen the flowers and the color of the bridesmaids' dresses with a Christmas theme in mind. Did you ask Precious about her dress size and those of her friends?"

"They're exactly the same as yours, your sister's and your best friend's."

"Isn't that something?" Maggie said. "Then it will just be a matter of nip and tuck."

"Indeed."

Their lunch arrived and Maggie was amazed to find that she'd ordered grilled salmon and steamed vegetables, which weren't exactly her favorite foods but would do in a pinch.

"Now then," Luke said after they'd taken the edge off their appetites. "Clyde and Precious said that they will have just made that long flight from London a couple of weeks before the wedding. They'd prefer to not have to pack their suitcases again and go winging off on a honeymoon right away, which makes sense."

Maggie cocked her head slightly to one side. "They don't want a honeymoon?"

Get this right, fumble-brain, Luke ordered himself. He wanted to plan that oh-so-important honeymoon trip with Maggie when she was engaged to marry him. It was something that they should do together for real, not as part of this charade.

"They'll have a trip later on," he said, narrowing his eyes in concentration. "So what they want is a honeymoon suite here in Phoenix for a few days following the wedding."

Maggie nodded slowly. "I understand. Well, I really don't know what's available because my couples have always left town after the reception. I'll visit some honeymoon suites in the posh hotels and report back to you."

"I thought I'd do that investigating with you," Luke said. "I'll have the time once I bring my father up to speed on my cases at the office, and as the old saying goes, two heads are better than one. You don't mind if I tag along, do you?"

A teenage boy appeared at the table at that moment to refill their water glasses, and Maggie fought the urge to jump up and hug him for giving her a moment to gather her racing thoughts before answering Luke's question.

Visit honeymoon suites with Luke St. John? she mentally repeated. *Honeymoon* suites, where people did what she and Luke had been about to do in her wanton dream? That was not a good idea at all. No, it was a bad plan. Bad, bad. And dumb and dangerous and—

"Maggie?"

But what reasonable excuse could she dish out to Luke as to why he shouldn't come along on the honeymoon-suite tour? she asked herself frantically. Sorry, Mr. You Melt My Bones, but there's a very good chance I might tear your clothes off in one of those romantic suites and get you naked as a jaybird, just like in my dream? Yeah, right, she'd just lay that on him. Not.

"Maggie, are you with me here?" Luke said, leaning slightly toward her.

"What?" she said. "Oh, yes, sure thing, Luke. You can come along to look at the accommodations if you like. But doesn't that sound just a tad boring to you?"

"Nooo," Luke said slowly, then smiled. "Not at all. Not even close."

Maggie narrowed her eyes. "Why not?"

Because he'd be envisioning the two of them in each of those suites, newly married, husband and wife, about to begin their honeymoon here in Phoenix before leaving on their dream trip. No, that didn't sound the least bit boring.

"Why not?" he said. Quick, St. John. Come up with something reasonable. "Because, like you, I've never seen a honeymoon suite in any of the ritzy hotels in town. It will be informative, interesting. Anytime a person has an opportunity to experience something new they should jump at the chance. It's good for the gray matter." He tapped his temple with a fingertip. "Know what I mean?"

"Not really," Maggie said, frowning, "but I'll take your word for it." She paused. "I think it would be best if I made actual appointments for our inspections. I'll get back to you on that."

"Fine. And you said you'd decided on the flowers for the wedding. What did you choose? No, wait, let me guess." Luke drummed the fingers of one hand on the table. "Hmm. You named your business Roses and Wishes. I'm betting that the bridal bouquet is roses, red for the holiday theme with some kind of Christmassy greens and those fluffy things that look sort of like snow."

"Baby's breath," Maggie said hardly above a whisper as she stared at Luke.

"Yeah, that's what it's called. How close did I come to being right?"

"That's exactly what I chose, but…but how did you know?"

Luke reached across the table and covered one of Maggie's hands with one of his. He gazed directly into her big brown eyes and when he spoke again his voice was slightly raspy and very, very…male. Maggie shivered.

"I knew because you're Maggie," he said. My Maggie. Forever.

"Oh," she said. Get your hand back, Maggie Jenkins. The heat—the heat from Luke's hand was traveling up her arm and across her breasts that were suddenly achy and... Get your dumb hand back. Sometime within the next hour. "Huh? You knew what flowers I'd pick right down to the baby's breath because I'm Maggie? I don't think that makes sense."

"It does to me," he said, tightening his grip slightly on her hand. "Yes, ma'am, it certainly does."

"Would you care for some dessert today?"

Maggie snatched her hand from beneath Luke's and looked up at the waitress.

"Dessert," she said, hearing the thread of breathlessness in her voice. "Dessert is a good thing. Yes, it certainly is, but I'm much too full to eat another bite of anything so...no, thank you."

Bingo, Luke thought. Maggie was flustered and that was dynamite. The heat that had rocketed throughout his body as he'd held her hand had traveled through her, too, he was certain of it. Her cheeks were flushed a delicate pink and her voice was trembling slightly. Fantastic.

"And you, sir?" the waitress said. "We have a scrumptious Black Forest cake today."

"A man certainly can't pass up Black Forest cake," Luke said. "Why don't you bring me a slice. With two forks, just in case the lady changes her mind and decides to share it with me."

"You bet," the waitress said. "I'll be right back."

A busboy cleared their dishes, and moments later the

waitress set an enormous slice of cake in the center of the table and placed a fork in front of Maggie, then Luke.

"Enjoy," the woman said, then zoomed away.

"Help yourself, Maggie," Luke said. "Look at that creation. Chocolate cake with whipped cream between the layers and all those cherries in sauce dribbling down the sides like a delicious waterfall. How can you resist a treat like this?"

What she wanted to know, Maggie thought miserably, was how could Luke make the description of a slab of cake sound like the most seductive thing she had ever heard in her entire life? The man just didn't quit.

"Well, maybe just one bite," she said, picking up the fork. She filled her fork, making sure it included one of the fat, gooey cherries. "Mmm."

"Oops," Luke said, reaching for a napkin. "You've got a dab of cherry sauce. I'll get it for you."

He leaned across the table and gently, so gently, dabbed at the spot of sauce, then shifted his eyes to look directly into Maggie's.

Her bones were dissolving, Maggie thought, unable to tear her gaze from Luke's. There was nothing sensuous about having her sloppy eating mopped up like a toddler in a high chair, darn it, but… Oh, yes, there was.

There was something so intimate about Luke tenderly stroking that napkin by her lips as though it was the most important thing he had ever done. She was going to slide off that chair and turn into a puddle on the floor.

"All better," he said, his voice husky. "Good cake?"

"Mmm," Maggie said dreamily. "The best cake I've ever…really yummy."

"Well, it's sure calling my name."

Maggie watched with rapt attention as Luke leveled a serving onto his fork, lifted it to his mouth, then closed his lips—those, oh-so-kissable lips—over the treat, then slowly pulled the fork free.

"Mmm," he said, closing his eyes as he savored the taste.

She couldn't handle this, Maggie thought frantically. She was going up in flames, burning inside with a heat like nothing she had ever experienced before.

Luke set the fork on the table and reached over to take both of Maggie's hands in his.

"Ah, Maggie," he said, "what are you doing to me? What is this thing that spins out of control between us?" It's love, Maggie Jenkins. True and forever love. "You feel it, I know you do."

"No, I don't," she said, trying to pull her hands free. Luke tightened his hold. "Well, yes, I do, but it's just physical attraction between two people who are…physically attracted to each other. I would call it lust, but that's kind of a tacky word. It's certainly nothing to be pursued or acted upon or… May I have my hands back now, please, Luke?"

"In a minute. So you admit that you're physically attracted to me?"

"Well…yes."

"You desire me? Do you, Maggie? Lust is a tacky word. Desire is something else entirely."

"Semantics."

"No, Maggie, emotions. Emotions are intertwined with desire. I truly believe that. The tricky part is to know what those emotions are, what they mean, unwrap them layer by layer like a wondrous gift."

"That's very poetic," Maggie said softly.

"I'm not attempting to be poetic. I'm just expressing how I feel. I want to know what that gift holds for us. Don't you?"

Maggie pulled her hands free and shook her head. "No, I can't."

"Why not?"

"Luke, you just don't understand."

"Then explain it to me. Please, Maggie. What are you afraid of? Why are you so determined to never marry, to plan weddings for so many brides but never one for yourself? Why have you built those tall, strong walls around your heart? There's something happening between us that could be very important, but whenever I bring it up you act like you're about to bolt. Talk to me. Please."

Maggie clutched her hands tightly in her lap and stared at them for a long, mind-searching moment. She nodded slowly, then met Luke's gaze again.

"All right," she said, her voice trembling slightly. "Perhaps I *should* tell you the truth about me, why none of the weddings I coordinate will ever be mine, why I'll never be a bride."

Luke's heart thudded so wildly he could hear the echo of it in his ears.

"It goes back as many generations as my family has been able to track, without skipping even one," Maggie continued. "There's no escaping it, no reason to believe it won't continue on and on into infinity." She sighed. "Oh, people try to beat the odds—my mother, sister, my brother—but it's foolish to do that because it's hopeless."

"My God, Maggie," Luke said, feeling the color drain from his face. "Is it a disease that can't be cured?"

"Well, I don't know if I'd call it a disease exactly, but there is definitely no cure for it. It happens over and over and over again. It's harsh and heartbreaking and I don't intend to allow it to happen to me. I will never, ever get married."

"What—" Luke cleared his throat "—what is it? Does it have an official name?"

"Yes, it definitely has a name," she said. "We're all doomed. It would be so foolish to believe I would be spared, because it wouldn't happen, Luke. My mother, sister, brother all thought they could escape from it, but…" She shook her head.

"What is it?" he said, leaning toward her. "You're ripping me up here, Maggie. *What is it?*"

Maggie took a shuddering breath, then blinked against sudden and unwelcome tears.

"It's…" she said, a sob catching in her throat. "It's the Jenkins Jinx."

Seven

It took several mental beats for Luke to really compute what Maggie had just said. He opened his mouth to reply, then shut it again as he replayed the words once more in his head.

The Jenkins Jinx? he thought incredulously. Did he have a clue as to what Maggie was talking about? No, he did not. A jinx of some kind that had a bearing on Maggie's negative attitude to marriage? Did people really believe in jinxes these days? A jinx that did what? Oh, man, this was nuts.

It would certainly clear things up if Maggie would suddenly laugh and tell him she was just kidding, that what she had said was a silly joke, then tell him the real reason she didn't intend to ever be the bride in one of her beautifully coordinated weddings.

But the fact that at the moment Maggie was a study in misery and that tears were shimmering in her big brown eyes told him that she was dead serious about the Jenkins Jinx.

"Maggie," Luke said finally, "we need to talk about this…this Jenkins Jinx thing, but you're obviously upset, so let's get out of here." He signaled to the waitress for the check. "I'll take you home, back to Roses and Wishes, and we'll discuss this there. Okay?"

"You said you had a very busy afternoon at work," Maggie said, then sniffled and dabbed her nose with the napkin.

"That's what cell phones are for," he said. "So bosses can call efficient secretaries and have them reschedule whatever is on the calendar. My father won't mind getting the word that he's free to go golfing."

"But I drove my van here so you can't take me home."

"I'll bring you back later for your van or you can drive yourself if you feel you're up to it," he said. "We're not postponing this discussion, Maggie."

Maggie sighed in defeat. "I had a feeling you'd say that. I'll drive myself. Meet me at Roses and Wishes." She got to her feet and hurried away.

Luke rose, dropped several bills onto the table, then accepted the check from the waitress.

"Is everything all right, sir?" the woman said.

"Ask me later," Luke said absently, "because right now I really don't know."

* * *

Maggie drove blindly to Roses and Wishes, wishing she could turn back the clock to before her momentous announcement about the Jenkins Jinx.

No, she thought with yet another sad-sounding sigh, there was no point in pretending the Jenkins Jinx didn't exist. Luke was pressing her to explore, actually embrace, the strange whatever-it-was that was happening between them, and it wasn't fair to keep the jinx a secret.

She dashed an errant tear from her cheek.

It just would have been nice, she mused wistfully, to have had more time with Luke, enjoy his company, allow herself to feel so feminine and desirable, before revealing the god-awful truth.

Once she explained it all to Luke, it would hover between them like a palpable entity, a living thing that would make him uncomfortable because she was a weird person from a very weird family.

"I'm so sad," Maggie said as she parked in front of Roses and Wishes. "So very, very sad."

She waited in the van until Luke arrived, then they entered the house together. Maggie left the Closed sign on the door.

"Let's go upstairs to the living room," she said, sounding extremely weary.

"Whatever you say," he said quietly.

In the tiny living room Maggie sank onto a rocking chair and Luke settled on the sofa, spreading his arms across the top as he looked at Maggie intently. She rocked back and forth for several minutes, staring into space.

"Maggie," Luke said, "you can't pretend I'm not sitting here waiting for you to talk to me."

She shifted her gaze to meet his.

"I know," she said. "It's just that I hate to... Never mind. You have the right to know what I meant by the Jenkins Jinx." She drew a steadying breath. "I told you that it goes back many generations in our family."

Luke nodded, aware that the lunch he'd consumed now felt like a rock in the pit of his stomach.

"We all have had to face the devastating fact," Maggie continued, "that for unknown reasons it is impossible for any of us to live happily ever after with our chosen mate. It just isn't going to happen, no matter what. And that, Luke, is the Jenkins Jinx."

Luke moved his arms forward to rest his elbows on his knees and make a steeple of his fingers.

"I beg your pardon?" he said, frowning.

"You heard me."

"Okay, I heard you, but I can't fathom that you actually believe that a jinx, a spell, whatever, has been cast over your entire family."

"Like a gloomy dark cloud," Maggie said, nodding.

"Maggie, come on, give me a break. Things like that don't really happen. So, yes, some of the couples in your clan got divorced, but—"

"Everyone got divorced."

"Everyone?" Luke said, raising his eyebrows.

"Everyone. We researched our family tree as far back as we could and, yes, everyone."

"That's rather…strange." Luke sank back against the cushions. "Whew."

"That's the Jenkins Jinx," Maggie said. "No one understands why we're plagued by it, what we did to draw this lousy card, but there's no denying the truth of it. Oh, there are those who feel they'll be the one to break the spell, end it for all time, because they're so in love, so sure when they marry that it's forever. Then—bam!— it all falls apart and yet another gleeful divorce attorney has a bill to send.

"My mother was a starry-eyed bride," she said. "My father left us when I was ten. Poof. Gone. My sister has been divorced twice, my brother once. My grandparents, great-grandparents… Oh, I can go even further back than that, I guarantee you. We all agree we're doomed."

"But—"

"Therefore, Luke, I never intend to fall in love and marry. I'm not going to have my dreams shattered and my heart broken. I'm not. So I create fairy-tale-perfect weddings for others to…to satisfy my romantic soul. But I'm beginning to wonder if Roses and Wishes is a dumb thing to be doing because it just emphasizes over and over what I'll never have."

"But you're planning the wedding of *your* dreams for Precious and Clyde," Luke said.

"Yes, and it's probably foolish, but I'm giving it to myself like a gift to cherish before I make a decision about whether I want to continue as a wedding coordinator."

Luke got to his feet and began to pace—as well as

he could in the limited space. He dragged a restless hand through his hair and narrowed his eyes in deep concentration. He finally stopped in front of Maggie's rocking chair, planted his hands on the arms and leaned down, speaking close to her lips as she stared at him in wide-eyed surprise.

"No," he said.

"No…what?" she said, aware, so very aware, that his lips were mere inches from hers.

"No, I won't accept this," he said. "So, okay, your family seems to have had more than your share of divorces, but there is no such thing as an honest-to-goodness jinx, Maggie."

"That's what my sister's second husband said—at first."

"Maggie, you're an intelligent woman," Luke said, his voice rising. "How can you buy into this malarkey?"

"Facts are facts," she said, matching his volume. "We checked as far back as we possibly could, hoping, praying, we'd find even one couple that stayed together on our family tree. There wasn't one. Not one, Luke. The jinx is real and I won't allow myself to think I could be the one to break it, make it disappear, because it's here to stay. That's the way it is and there's nothing I can do about it."

"It's impossible," he said none too quietly. "A jinx is a superstition, a…a… Damn it, this is the most frustrating conversation I've ever had in my entire life."

"Well, excuse me all the way to Sunday," Maggie yelled, "but the truth is the truth."

'Oh? Well, try this truth on for size, lady," Luke hollered.

He released his white-knuckle hold on the arms of the rocking chair, gripped Maggie's shoulders, hauled her to her feet…and kissed her.

Maggie stiffened in shock, but as Luke's kiss gentled and he dropped his hands from her shoulders to wrap his arms around her and bring her close to his body, she nestled against him. Her arms floated upward to encircle his neck, her fingertips inching into his thick ebony hair.

The kiss was hot. It was desire, not lust, with unnamed emotions intertwining with the want and need. The kiss was powerful enough to push aside for that tick of time the existence of the Jenkins Jinx and allow them to savor the taste, the feel, the very essence of each other. The kiss was theirs.

Luke broke away first to draw a much-needed breath but didn't release his hold on Maggie. She gazed up at him, a dreamy expression on her face, her lips moist and slightly parted, beckoning.

"Ah, Maggie," Luke said, his voice gritty with passion. "I want to make love with you so damn much. From the moment I first saw you I… Do you want me, Maggie? Do you want to make love with me?"

"Yes, I do," she whispered. "But—"

"Forget the jinx thing for now. We'll tackle that later…later…yes. All I can concentrate on now is you, me, what we'll share. But, Maggie, I would never take advantage of you, pressure you, attempt to seduce you into doing something you'll regret." He paused. "I guess what I'm saying is, it's your decision."

Oh, Maggie thought foggily. How could she decide when she couldn't even think clearly? Okay, okay, she was getting a grip now, ignoring the fact that she was still being held in Luke's strong arms, still molded to his aroused body, still…thinking. Yes, she was thinking.

And she wanted him.

She wanted to make love with him because she cared for him so very much and he cared for her, she knew he did.

And because when he realized that the Jenkins Jinx was true, he would chalk her up as being a very weird, creepy woman and keep her at a safe distance from him.

And because she intended to give herself this intimate joining with Luke St. John so she'd have a precious memory to make up for all she would never have because of the Jenkins Jinx.

"Maggie?"

"Make love with me, Luke," she said softly, looking directly into his dark eyes. "I won't be sorry. I'll have no regrets, I promise. We have no future together. None. The jinx is real and I've accepted that. Nothing you can say or do will change my mind about it. But now? Right now? I want—I desire you. So, please, make love with me."

With a groan that rumbled from deep in his chest, Luke captured Maggie's mouth once again in a searing kiss. She returned the kiss in total abandon, holding nothing back, giving as much as she was receiving.

Luke lifted his head, then swung Maggie up into his

arms. She pointed in the direction of her bedroom and he carried her there with long, purposeful strides.

He set her on her feet next to the double bed, absently registering that the room was femininity personified, just like Maggie, with a bedspread patterned with pale pink roses and a matching skirt on a small round table that held a clock and a telephone. The curtains were pink and the dresser was white wicker.

Maggie swept back the spread and blankets to reveal sheets with tiny pink rosebuds, then turned to face Luke again.

"I'm very nervous," she said. "I really don't have the kind of experience that I'm certain you're accustomed to and I—"

"Shh," he said, placing one fingertip gently on her lips. "We're going to be wonderful together, Maggie."

And they were.

With sudden confidence that came from a place she couldn't fathom, Maggie nodded, and as Luke shed his clothes, she removed her own. They stood naked before each other, rejoicing in what they saw, what would be theirs, given willingly.

He lifted her into his arms again, settled her in the center of the bed, then followed her down, his mouth melting over hers.

It was ecstasy. They kissed, caressed, discovered each other's mysteries with awe and wonder. Where hands traveled, lips followed, igniting the heat of their desire into leaping flames that threatened to consume them both.

Luke left her only long enough to roll on protection, then returned to her outstretched arms. When they could bear no more, he moved over her and into her with a thrust that filled her and brought a gasp of pure pleasure from her lips.

The rocking rhythm began, then increased in tempo until it was wild and earthy, wondrous, synchronized to perfection as though they had been lovers forever.

They soared. Higher. Closer. Calling to the other, clinging fast, then bursting upon the place they sought only seconds apart.

"Luke!"

"Oh, Maggie. My Maggie."

They drifted slowly back, then Luke mustered his last ounce of energy to move off her and tuck her close to his side, his lips resting lightly on her moist forehead. She rested one hand on the dark curls on his broad chest, feeling his heart settle into a quieter, steady beat.

"Thank you," Luke said quietly.

"And I thank *you*," Maggie whispered, "for the beautiful memories to keep."

Maggie's lashes drifted down and she slept, content, sated, a soft smile on her lips. Luke held her, sifting his fingers through her silky strawberry-blond curls.

God, how he loved this woman, he thought, feeling a foreign ache tighten his throat. She had given of herself so freely, so honestly, to him. *Him.* She cared deeply for him, he knew that, might even be falling in love with him just as he was already deeply in love with her.

He couldn't lose her. No, the mere thought of it was

more than he could bear. He knew the name of the enemy now—the Jenkins Jinx. That he believed it to be crazy, borderline nuts, meant nothing because Maggie was convinced it was true and planned to never marry to protect her heart from being shattered.

The battle lines were drawn. He was literally fighting for his life, his future happiness, his forever. And he would be the victor, for himself, for Maggie, for what they would have together until death parted them and beyond.

He would win. Somehow. He had to.

"I love you, Maggie Jenkins," he whispered, tightening his hold on her. "You are my life. My wife. Mine."

A little over an hour later Maggie stirred and opened her eyes, only to blink against the bright sunlight streaming through the window.

Luke, she thought, as the mist of sleep lifted.

She turned her head on the pillow to see the empty expanse of bed next to her, then heard the sound of the shower running. She stretched leisurely, then pulled the sheet to beneath her chin, clutching it with both hands.

She'd made love with Luke, she thought, and it had been glorious, beyond her wildest fantasies. Did she regret what she had done? Was she sorry? No. Never.

Her life was not like other women's, with dreams of a husband, babies, hearth and home. To have experienced something as wondrous as she just had with a magnificent man like Luke St. John was more than she'd ever expected to receive, to possess as hers, to tuck away in the treasure chest in her heart.

Was this dangerous? she asked herself. Well, no, not if she stayed alert, kept a tight control over her emotions and the truth of her reality front and center. She could handle this. She would have this time with Luke. And when Precious and Clyde were married, that would be the end of Maggie Jenkins and Luke St. John. She knew that, understood that. Yes, she could handle this.

Luke came into the bedroom fully dressed, his hair damp from the shower. He sat on the edge of the bed and smiled at Maggie.

"Have a nice nap?"

"Lovely, thank you," she said, matching his smile.

"You're very pretty when you're sleeping, very peaceful." He paused. "I'd better get going. You'll let me know when you have some appointments to see honeymoon suites at various hotels?"

"Yes, of course. I'll call you."

"Good." He nodded. "Maggie, you don't have any regrets about what happened here, do you?"

"No, no, Luke, not at all. It was wonderful and I... No regrets. We both understand that this is temporary, what we're sharing, because my life is what it is— jinxed. I know you're not quite believing that yet, but it's true, trust me, and I'll never allow myself to think otherwise. That would be so foolish on my part and it isn't going to happen."

"Mmm." Luke frowned. "And no one in the entire history of your family has figured out a way to break the spell, the jinx?"

"No."

"Mmm." Luke stroked his chin thoughtfully. "Would you categorize the jinx as a superstition of sorts?"

"I… Well, not exactly, because it's true."

"But if you had to group it with something," he said, "a jinx would fall into the arena of superstitions for a lack of a better place to put it. Right?"

"I suppose so. I never thought about it like that." Maggie looked at him questioningly. "Why?"

"I'm just trying to be certain that I fully understand the Jenkins Jinx, what it is."

"It's my reality," Maggie said firmly. "Ask any member of my family and they'll verify what I'm saying. It's sad but true."

"Yeah." Luke leaned over and dropped a quick kiss on Maggie's lips. "I'll be waiting to hear from you about viewing the suites. Eager to hear from you. You'll contact me soon?"

"Yes, sir," she said, smiling at him warmly.

Luke drew one thumb lightly over her lips, which she felt to the very tip of her toes, then he got to his feet and left the room.

"'Bye," Maggie whispered, then sighed in delicious contentment.

After a frustrating stop-and-start drive across town in the surging Phoenix traffic Luke entered the plush offices of St. John and St. John, Attorneys at Law.

"Good afternoon, Mr. St. John," the receptionist said.

"Mmm," Luke said absently as he strode down the hall. The attractive young woman turned in her chair and watched him go, deciding he was definitely a man with something heavy on his mind.

Luke stopped at the desk of his secretary, a plump woman in her fifties, who looked up at him with a rather confused expression.

"I thought you said when you called that you weren't coming in this afternoon," she said.

"I need some data, Betty," he said. "Extensive research."

Betty picked up a pen and slid a steno pad in front of her.

"Okay," she said. "What can I do for you, Luke? What am I researching?"

"Superstitions."

"I beg your pardon? Superstitions? About what? Is this pertaining to a case you have on the docket?"

"Not exactly," he said, shoving his hands into his pockets. "Let's just say it's the most important project I've ever undertaken and let it go at that, shall we? Start with superstitions regarding brides, weddings, things like that, then go further into superstitions in general."

"Brides? You mean, like it's bad luck for the groom to see the bride in her wedding dress before she walks down the aisle?"

"Exactly." He shook his head. "Who comes up with this junk?"

Betty shrugged. "I have no idea, but that business about the dress has been around for as long as I can remember, and I'm borderline ancient." She tapped the pen against the pad of paper. "Okay. I get the drift of what you want about brides and what have you. Then I go to other things like not walking under a ladder or letting a black cat cross your path?"

"Right."

"When do you need this interesting info?"

"Yesterday," he said, then went on into his office.

Late that night Luke was stretched out on the sofa in his living room reading yet again the thick stack of papers that Betty had given him on superstitions.

He frowned in disbelief at some of them and couldn't help but laugh aloud at others. But for the most part he was digesting everything he read with serious intent.

He'd memorize as many of these wacky things as he could, he'd decided, then keep the papers close at hand for ready reference on others.

Luke reached over and set the papers on the coffee table fronting the sofa, then laced his fingers beneath his head where it rested on a puffy throw pillow.

The Plan was in effect, he mused, insofar as Maggie believed she was coordinating a wedding for cousin Clyde and his Precious.

However, now he knew Maggie's secret about the Jenkins Jinx, further genius-level action was definitely called for, an extension of The Plan. Through brilliant lawyer-type persuasion he'd gotten Maggie to agree that the jinx was a superstition. She'd done so rather reluctantly, but he'd take what he could get.

His mission, then, was to cleverly and carefully expose Maggie to superstition after superstition, casually pointing out that, son of a gun, nothing horrible had happened because they'd—they'd what?—walked under a ladder, for example. He'd stack up the evidence piece by piece, inching closer and closer to the Jenkins Jinx and the miraculous fact that Maggie was obviously the one who was going to break its hold on the family because she was immune to the consequences of superstitions.

Man, he was so sharp sometimes, it just blew his mind. This was shining-star thinking, damn it. It wouldn't be easy, that was for sure, would take planning and coordination and… He needed help. It was too big, too important to tackle alone.

Luke sat up and swung his feet to the floor.

His father, he thought. Mason St. John knew about The Plan and understood the need for it, although he did have some reservations about the consequences of duping Maggie. His dad was the perfect person to help with this new addition to the program.

Luke glanced at his watch and swore under his breath as he saw it was too late to call his father.

But first thing in the morning, he thought, he'd corner his dad and they'd map things out. Ah, yeah, this was good, very good. It was the next step in the battle that would eventually win the war.

Luke settled back on the sofa and smiled up at the ceiling.

Yes, there was going to be a Christmas wedding, all right. But Precious and Clyde—who were becoming strangely real to him—would have to make their own arrangements to tie the knot.

The wedding that was being put together at this very moment would unite Maggie Jenkins and Luke St. John in holy matrimony forever, declare them to be wife and husband, soul mates, partners in life and parents of the little miracles that would be the result of their exquisite lovemaking.

His Christmas bride, Luke thought. His Maggie.

Eight

Maggie spent the next two days tackling the stack of paperwork in her office at Roses and Wishes. It was her least favorite part of owning the business, and she often daydreamed about what it would be like to be successful enough to have a secretary.

Not only would the tedious paperwork be taken care of, but Roses and Wishes could remain open while Maggie was off and running to tend to the multitude of details, details, details needed to coordinate the perfect wedding.

But, she mused as she scrutinized another bill for Ginger and Robert's extravaganza, the budget didn't allow for such luxury as a secretary. And besides, she wasn't all that sure she intended to continue with this career choice she'd been so excited about at the onset.

Maggie sighed and read the bill once more, realizing that yet again she hadn't comprehended what was on the invoice. Why? Because her mind kept drifting off and settling on the exquisite lovemaking she'd enjoyed with Luke.

She should have had her desk cleared in one day but, no, not this time. Here it was late in the afternoon of the second day and she was still glued to her chair because her flighty brain wouldn't behave itself.

Maggie flipped the paper in the air, watched it settle on the pile she had yet to even look at, then plunked her elbow on the desktop and rested her chin in her palm.

All right, she thought decisively, this obviously wasn't working well. Sneaky and wonderful images of that afternoon with Luke kept creeping in and disrupting her concentration. So, therefore, she'd indulge in a trip down memory lane, relive every tantalizing, sensuous moment of what they'd shared and finally put it to rest. Then she'd be able to get her chores done like a proper little business owner should.

Maggie stared into space, making no attempt to erase the soft smile that formed on her lips as picture after picture slid into her mind and sensation after sensation swirled within her body.

Heat settled low within her, pulsing and hot, and she shifted slightly on the chair. Her breasts began to ache, yearning for the soothing feeling of Luke's hands, then mouth, on the sensitive flesh. Mercy. Her cheeks, she knew, were flushed and she could hear the increased tempo of her heart echoing in her ears.

Ecstasy in its purest form, she mused dreamily. That's what that joining had been. And at the peak of it, the climax? God, she had no idea it could be like that. It defied description, required words that hadn't even been invented yet.

Imagine what it would be like, she mentally rambled on, to be married to Luke, to be the recipient of all that magnificent masculinity night after night after… It boggled the mind.

Of course, there was more to marriage than just…well, than just that. She and Luke would laugh and talk, eat meals together, shop for groceries, discuss events from the six-o'clock news. They'd choose a house they both knew would be their home, then furnish it room by room, agreeing on choices, compromising where necessary.

And, of course, one of those rooms would be a nursery for the baby they'd create with their wondrous lovemaking. A baby boy? A girl? It wouldn't matter. Then a couple of years later another little miracle would arrive to join the first. Luke would be a fantastic father to all their children, whether they had two or four or…

But each night when tiny heads were nestled on pillows after stories had been read and prayers heard, it would be grown-up time, Maggie-and-Luke time, private time. And in their marriage bed they would reach eagerly for each other, the desire never waning, their heartfelt love growing deeper and stronger with each passing year. Their lips would meet and…

"Maggie?"

Maggie shifted her gaze to focus on the direction the voice had come from. Luke. He was standing right in front of her desk in all his masculine splendor.

He really wasn't there, she told herself, was a figment of her imagination due to the fantasy playing out in her head. No, he really wasn't there, so what the heck….

Maggie got to her feet, leaned forward to grip Luke's tie and pulled him toward her to plant a searing kiss on his lips.

But the very moment that their mouths met, a mortified Maggie realized that Luke really *was* there in living, breathing color. She released her hold on his tie and plunked back down in her chair, wishing she could disappear into thin air, never to be seen again.

"Well," Luke said, smoothing his tie and smiling at her, "that was quite a welcome. Hello to you, too, Maggie."

"'Lo," she mumbled, staring at the middle button on his shirt.

"You certainly make a man feel special, like you're glad to see him, I must say."

"I can explain that," Maggie said, finally meeting his gaze. She sighed and shook her head. "No, forget it. It's too ridiculous." She paused. "I guess you're here because you haven't heard from me regarding honeymoon suites, but I've been buried in paperwork and haven't had a chance to do any investigating yet."

"No, I'm here because I missed you," Luke said, settling onto one of the chairs opposite Maggie's desk. "That's it, pure and simple."

"Really?" A bright smile lit up Maggie's face, then

in the next instant she managed to erase it and adopt an expression of vague interest. "Oh?"

"Yep," Luke said, chuckling. "And since this tie I'm wearing may never be the same, I'd say you missed me, too."

"Well…" Maggie flipped one hand in the air. "Whatever."

"Mmm. My, my, Maggie, I'm surprised to see that you're wearing that shade of blue on a Thursday. You didn't go so far as to take a bath or shower this morning, did you?"

"Huh?" Maggie peered down at the string sweater she wore, then looked at Luke again, obviously confused. "What on earth are you talking about?"

Luke propped his elbows on the arms of the chair and tented his fingers.

"There are certain cultures," he said, "which believe the color blue represents the ocean, the sea. They also think that Thursday is the unluckiest day of the week. Therefore, to tempt fate by wearing that color on a Thursday, you're destined to have an accident in water, maybe even drown."

"That's the silliest thing I've ever heard," Maggie said, rolling her eyes heavenward.

"Not to the people who believe it."

"Which probably number about three. For heaven's sake, Luke, the wrong color on the wrong day and you're deader than a doornail? That's a nonsense-to-the-max superstition."

Luke shrugged with a rather nondescript expression on his face.

"Besides, I took a long bath in my wonderful tub this morning and lived to tell about it," she said, lifting her chin. "So there."

"No kidding? Well, maybe that superstition is garbage after all," he said thoughtfully. "It was so off-the-wall that I was leaning toward believing it. I mean, there must be enough evidence to substantiate it in the first place."

Maggie leaned toward him. "That tie of yours that I just wrinkled is blue, sort of sea-blue. Did you shower this morning?"

"Yes, I did."

"I rest my case. That superstition is nonsense."

Gotcha, Luke thought smugly. Score one for Luke St. John.

"So back to why you're here," Maggie said.

"Well, it's not because I'm bugging you about the honeymoon suites," Luke said. "One of my clients had a bit of an emergency and I had to put on my big-boy-lawyer clothes and meet with him for a long, boring lunch close to here. I just dropped in to say hello and to tell you that I missed you." He attempted once again to smooth his crumpled tie. "And to get my tie killed, I guess."

"I'd offer to replace it, but I don't think I could afford to do that on my budget. How much did it cost?"

"A hundred and fifty dollars."

"For a tie?" she said, nearly shrieking. "That's absurd."

"It's imported silk from Italy."

"Could I interest you in installment payments?"

Luke laughed. "Tell you what. You agree to have dinner with me tonight and we'll call it even."

"Well…"

"I'm in the mood for pizza, if that suits you, so dress very casually. But don't wear blue. Okay?"

"Pizza sounds great but, Luke, you've got to forget about that superstition because it really is nuts."

"I'll try," he said, rising with a dramatic sigh. "I'll pick you up at eight o'clock. I'll let you get back to work now. See you later."

"But…" Maggie said as Luke strode from the room. She smiled as she heard the front door of Roses and Wishes close behind him. "Eight o'clock will be just fine."

She picked up an invoice, then stared into space.

She'd really gotten carried away with her mental fantasy, she mused. Goodness, she'd gone all the way to being Luke's wife and having a slew of his babies. Well, that was all right…except, of course, for the embarrassing tie episode.

It didn't matter how much daydreaming she did because she knew, really knew, that all this was temporary. She could indulge in anything she wanted to with Luke St. John because once Precious and Clyde were married that would be that. No more Luke in her life. In the meantime? She was free to go for it because she had total command over her emotions. Everything was dandy.

That night Luke drove past several well-known pizza restaurants to the far side of Phoenix.

"You must really like the pizza here," Maggie said,

as they settled into a red vinyl booth. "You certainly were willing to drive a long way to reach this place."

"Best pizza in Phoenix," Luke said, glancing at his watch. "I'll go up and place our order. What would you like on yours?"

"Anything and everything except the little fishes," she said, smiling.

"Got it," he said, sliding out of the booth. "Soda?"

"Perfect."

A few minutes later Luke returned to sit across from Maggie and set a slip of paper on the table.

"I'm glad this is Thursday and not Friday," he said. "We have the number thirteen. Thirteen on a Friday is bad news, you know." He looked at his watch again.

"No worse than drowning in the bathtub because you wore the wrong color," Maggie said drily. "Luke, what is with this sudden preoccupation with superstitions?"

"It's not sudden," he said. Oh, man, his nose was going to grow. "I've always been superstitious, but don't talk about it much because people have a tendency to scoff."

"Scoff?"

"Yes, definitely scoff. But, you see, Maggie, I've been doing a great deal of thinking about what you told me about the Jenkins Jinx. My first reaction was to tell you that it was nonsense. I scoffed. And I apologize to you for doing that. Jinxes, superstitions, wives' tales all have merit. I want you to know that I respect your belief in the Jenkins Jinx."

"You do? I mean, you're not going to attempt to talk

me out of it? Tell me it's a bunch of baloney? Try to convince me that I could be a bride, get married, just like anyone else?"

"Nope."

"Oh."

Well, that was good, she thought. Wasn't it? Sure. Then why did she suddenly feel so sad, gloomy and depressed? Luke's acceptance of the Jenkins Jinx meant he was as fully prepared to walk away as she was after Precious and Clyde's wedding. No fuss, no muss. That was…great. But her stomach hurt. And her heart hurt. Her heart actually hurt. Damn it, what was the matter with her?

"Luke, my boy," a deep voice boomed, snapping Maggie back to attention.

"Well, Dad, my, my, what are you doing here?" Luke said, looking up at his father where he stood next to the table.

"Your mother got hungry for pizza so I called in an order and came to pick it up. This place has the best pizza in Phoenix, you know."

"Yes, I certainly know that and you're fortunate to live only a few blocks away," Luke said. "You remember Maggie."

"Certainly," Mason St. John said. "Delightful to see you again, my dear."

"My pleasure," Maggie said.

"Luke, I'm just beside myself," Mason said.

"Oh? Why is that, pray tell?" Luke said.

Pray tell? Maggie thought. For some dumb reason

Luke and his father sounded like they were reading words from a script and not doing a very good job of it. No, that was silly. So what, pray tell, was Mr. St. John beside himself about?

"I lost my acorn," Mason said.

Huh? Maggie thought, frowning slightly.

"Oh, no, anything but that, Father."

"I know, I know," Mason said, resting one hand on his heart. "I didn't tell your mother I was driving over here without my acorn. She'd be worried sick."

"For good reason," Luke said. "But fear not, because I always carry two." He leaned back so he could slide his hand into the front pocket of his jeans. "There you go, sir. One acorn."

Mason curled his fingers around the acorn Luke had placed in his hand, then slid the little nut into his pocket. He clamped one hand on Luke's shoulder.

"Bless you, son. Enjoy your pizza. Good night, Maggie. Farewell, Luke."

As Mason hurried away, the waitress appeared at the table and set a pitcher of soda in the center along with two glasses. Luke thanked the young girl, then filled the glasses. Maggie leaned forward, staring at Luke intently as she waited for an explanation about the bizarre interchange regarding the acorn. Luke glanced around.

"Sure is getting crowded in here, isn't it? That's understandable, though, when you consider that they serve—"

"The best pizza in Phoenix," Maggie finished for him. "Would you care to explain what just happened here?"

"The waitress delivered our soda," Luke said, smiling. "Hey, they just called number eleven. We're getting closer. Man, I'm starved."

"Luke," Maggie said, smacking the table with the palm of her hand. Luke cringed. "What was that whole weird thing with your father about the acorn?"

"Oh, *that*," Luke said. "Did they just call number twelve?"

"Luke," Maggie said, narrowing her eyes and drumming the fingers of one hand on the top of the table. "The acorn. Now."

"You bet," he said, nodding. "Well, it's very simple. It's good luck to carry an acorn on one's person. We St. Johns have toted acorns around for years. Years and years. Never go anywhere without our acorns, by golly. So you can see why my father was so upset about having lost his and not wishing my poor mother to know. But—" he grinned "—I saved his bacon because I always have two. Insurance, you know what I mean?"

Maggie leaned back in the booth and crossed her arms over her chest. "That's stupid," she said.

"It certainly is not," Luke said indignantly. "One could become jinxed, experience endless lousy luck if one didn't carry one's acorn, Maggie. Remind me to find an acorn for you." He paused. "Yo. They just called thirteen. That's us. I'll be back in a flash."

"But…" Maggie said, pointing one finger in the air, then realizing that Luke was long gone.

All the St. Johns were superstition freaks? she thought incredulously. They were intelligent, highly educated people, lawyers and what have you, for heaven's sake, but they flipped out if they lost their acorn? How weird was that?

Luke interrupted Maggie's racing thoughts by setting a huge, fragrant pizza in the center of the table, then sitting down again and rubbing his hands together.

"Now that looks delicious," he said, smiling. "Dig in and enjoy."

"I will, but…Luke, about this acorn thing. Your father didn't say he'd experienced any bad luck or mishaps or whatever while his acorn was missing. Correct?"

Luke nodded as he chewed a big bite of the hot pizza.

"So," Maggie continued, "doesn't that suggest that there is nothing to the superstition surrounding the acorn? That it is just that—a superstition, which is fun and cute but…isn't grounded in reality?"

Luke stared into space. "You've got a point there. When I was a kid I left my acorn in the pocket of my jeans and my mom washed them, turned the acorn into a mushy mess. It was quite a while before I could find another one because it was the wrong time of year. Nothing bad happened to me except that I flunked a spelling test, which was my fault because I didn't study for it."

Maggie picked up a slice of pizza and smiled, obviously pleased with herself. "See?" She took a bite of her dinner.

"I'll give this some serious thought," Luke said. Oh, this was going great, even better than he had hoped for. "Wait a minute here."

"Hmm?" Maggie said, her mouth full of pizza.

"I bet you didn't know that if you say goodbye to a friend on a bridge you'll never see each other again. Well, when I was fifteen I had this buddy. We did everything together, were really close. One summer we were riding our bikes and said goodbye at the end of the day on a bridge. I never saw him again. How do you like that?"

"Why didn't you ever see him again?" Maggie said.

"Because of the bridge thing, Maggie." Luke paused. "Well, not entirely, I guess. His dad was a creep, physically abused his mom and… She took off in the middle of the night with my buddy and disappeared.

"I figured it was because of the parting on the bridge, but now that I really think about it… Well, hell, so much for the bridge belief." He shook his head. "Amazing. All these years I was convinced…mmm."

Maggie smiled sweetly. "This pizza is delicious. Thank you for bringing me here."

"Sure, no problem," Luke said, frowning. "This is rather unsettling. The acorn. The bridge. I don't really have any concrete data to… Just goes to show ya, doesn't it? Things aren't always what they seem to be. Ready for some more soda?"

"No, I'm fine," Maggie said. "Don't be so hard on yourself, Luke. You got caught up in the theories about the acorn and the bridge, have believed them for so long you haven't questioned their validity in years. I think you're being very noble—there's a good word—to accept that the superstitions about them aren't real, aren't true."

"You're right," he said, "and I have you to thank for

showing me how ridiculous I was for buying into those tales." He deserved an Academy Award for this performance, he really did. "Let's just concentrate on the pizza now. This has been a pretty heavy topic for my weary brain. Enough for one night."

"Okay. Do you want to discuss Precious and Clyde's wedding?"

Luke smiled. "Maggie, I'd love to discuss the wedding. You have no idea how much it means to me."

"Well, the church is reserved for December twenty-third," Maggie said, her voice ringing with excitement. "And I got the ballroom at the Majestic Palms Hotel sewn up for the reception."

"The Majestic Palms," Luke said, nodding in approval. "Classy. Very nice."

"I have an appointment next week to meet with the chef to plan the buffet dinner at the reception. I still have oodles to do—you know, decide on the color of the tablecloths, the centerpieces, start shopping around for the exact shade of material I want for the brides-maids' dresses and, of course, there's the wedding dress itself."

"Yep."

"What about the invitations, Luke? Do you think Precious and Clyde would prefer traditional ones that say the name of the parents or a more modern version where the couple themselves are inviting everyone to share their special event?"

Uh-oh, Luke thought, then took a big bite of pizza to give himself time to consider his answer. The invitations couldn't be ordered with Precious and Clyde's names on them. They didn't even exist. Think, St. John.

"Um...why don't you hold off on the invitations for now," he said finally. "I should run that by Precious and Clyde just in case they have an idea as to what will make the mothers happy."

"Okay. Would you ask them how they feel about tiny holly berries edging the invitations? I thought that would be so festive for a Christmas wedding."

"I'm sure that part will be fine. There certainly are a lot of things to tend to for a picture-perfect wedding, aren't there?"

"It takes months," Maggie said, laughing, "and then—blink—the ceremony is over in about fifteen minutes." She frowned in the next instant. "And in our family the marriage lasts about that long, too."

Change the subject, Luke thought frantically. He didn't want Maggie centering on the Jenkins Jinx, not tonight. Her beautiful eyes sparkled when she talked about the plans for the wedding, and the expression on her face was pure joy.

Not only that, he needed more superstitions for her to dismiss, to attempt to talk him out of believing, if he was to build a solid foundation for his case.

No, the Jenkins Jinx was definitely off-limits this evening.

"You know," he said, "you've never seen my apartment. I was just thinking that I have some mint-chocolate-chip ice cream in my freezer. Would you like to go there for dessert?"

Maggie leaned toward him. "Mint-chocolate-chip?"

"That's the one."

"Two scoops?"

"Three scoops," he said, holding up that many fingers.

"I have no willpower when it comes to mint-chocolate-chip ice cream," Maggie said. "Oh, my, three scoops."

"I thought you might like that flavor," Luke said, appearing extremely pleased with himself. "See how well I'm getting to know you, Maggie? It boggles the mind."

It terrifies the mind, Maggie thought. They were becoming so connected, bonded, on the same wavelength and... Never mind. She wasn't going to get all in a dither about it.

She was about to have three scoops of mint-chocolate-chip ice cream. Ah, yes, life was good.

Nine

"**M**y goodness," Maggie said, taking in Luke's enormous living room. "This is incredible, just beautiful. I've never been in a penthouse apartment before. The view is fabulous. I'd probably lose track of time and just sit for hours gazing out those windows at the city lights. You must look forward to coming home each day after work, Luke."

Not anymore, Luke thought as he stared at the awed expression on Maggie's face. Now it was just a whole lot of empty space waiting for Maggie to fill it to overflowing with her sunshine, laughter and…well, by just being Maggie.

"Ready for that ice cream?" he said.

"Sure. Can I see the kitchen?"

Luke laughed. "Follow me. It's fun to experience this place through fresh eyes."

Maggie gushed on and on about the fantastic kitchen as Luke scooped out the ice cream. As he picked up the bowls to carry them to the table, he dropped one of the spoons.

"Darn," he said.

"I'll get it," Maggie said, retrieving the spoon from the floor and rinsing it under the faucet.

They settled onto chairs opposite each other at the round oak table and Maggie took several mouthfuls of the dessert before she realized that Luke was staring into space.

"What's wrong?" she said.

"I was just wondering what child was going to come visit me and I'm coming up blank."

"I beg your pardon?" Maggie said, obviously confused.

"When you drop a spoon it means a child will visit. A fork brings a woman to your door, and a knife indicates the visitor will be a man."

"Is that a fact," Maggie said drily.

"Yep."

"Mmm," Maggie said, frowning at him.

"It's true," Luke said, leaning toward her. "I dropped a knife last month and—bingo—Robert popped in for no reason other than he was in the neighborhood."

"Robert is your brother. It makes perfect sense that he'd like to see you. It has nothing to do with the knife you dropped, Luke."

"Oh, yeah? Well, another time it was a fork, and

you'd better believe I shoved all the dirty dishes in the dishwasher before the knock came at the door. And there she was, my mother, bringing me some brownies she'd baked." He paused. "I wonder what little kid… Are Girl Scouts selling cookies now or something?"

"Halt," Maggie said, raising one hand. "Has Robert ever come by unannounced before?"

"Well…yes."

"And is your mother in the habit of bringing you homemade baked goods?"

"Yes, but—"

"I rest my case. Your fumble-fingers with the silverware was just a coincidence, nothing more. Another one of those superstitions you should forget about."

"Think so?"

"Know so." Maggie took another spoonful of ice cream. "Mmm. This is delicious. You'd better start on yours before it melts."

"You're really punching holes in my superstitions, you know," Luke said, then started in on his dessert.

"They can control your life if you're not careful," Maggie said.

Luke laughed. "Not all of them. There's one just for women. If she goes out in public and her slip shows, it means her father loves her more than her mother does."

"No, Luke, it means that either her slip is too long or her dress is too short."

"What you're saying makes sense, I guess. Then again…hmm. I'll have to think about this." He paused.

"Enough about superstitions. I'm going to go put some music on. I'll be right back."

A few moments later Maggie stiffened in her chair as the sound of lilting music reached her.

Oh, God, she thought, that was one of the waltzes she and Luke had danced to at Ginger and Robert's wedding. The beautiful song evoked special memories she intended to keep for all time. Did Luke remember why that particular tune was so meaningful or was it just a coincidence that he had put it on? No, men didn't get caught up in things like that. Music was music.

Luke came back into the kitchen and stood next to Maggie's chair.

"Recognize that waltz?" he said quietly. "We danced to it at Robert and Ginger's wedding. I asked the band leader what it was and went out and bought it so I could play it when you came here."

"Really?" Maggie said, a warmth suffusing her and creating a flush on her cheeks. "You did that? Of course I remember it, Luke, but to think that you went to all this trouble to… I don't know what to say."

He extended one hand toward her. "Say you'll dance with me."

From a seemingly faraway dreamy place, Maggie watched her hand float up to grasp Luke's, then she was on her feet and in his embrace. He held her close, moving with the music as he glided them out of the kitchen and into the living room, which was filled with the melody from speakers mounted high on the wall in each corner of the large room.

Maggie nestled her head on Luke's shoulder as they danced, drinking in the feel of him, his aroma, the strength of his body. Around the room they went, so gracefully, so perfectly in step.

It was so romantic that tears burned at the back of Maggie's eyes and desire consumed her, making it impossible to think clearly. She could only feel and savor and wish for the music to never end.

But it did finish, and they stopped in front of the tall windows where the lights of the city spread out in all directions like a fairyland. Another song started, but they didn't move, just held fast to each other. Then Luke shifted enough so he could tilt Maggie's chin up with one gentle fingertip, lowered his head and kissed her.

The kiss was so soft and tender, so exactly right to mark the finish of the memory-filled waltz, that two tears spilled onto Maggie's cheeks. Luke deepened the kiss and she gave herself to him, swept away by the moment and the music and...Luke.

Then he slowly, so slowly, lowered her to the plush carpet. He stretched out next to her, bracing his weight on one forearm as he drew a thumb over her tears.

"You're so beautiful," he said, his voice husky. "I've actually daydreamed about this, about seeing you here in my home, right here in front of these windows with the world spread out before us as though it belongs only to us. Ah, Maggie, I..." *Love you with all that I am, all I will ever be, for eternity.* "I...want to make love to you so much, so very much."

"Yes," she whispered.

He kissed her, then they parted long enough to shed their clothes and reached for each other once again. An urgency engulfed them, a need so great it was indescribable.

With hands never still, they caressed.

With lips seeking more, they kissed.

With passion soaring to unbelievable heights, they waited until they could bear it no longer.

Then they joined, meshed into one entity that made it impossible to decipher where the body soft and feminine and the one so very masculine ended and began.

The music had stopped, but they could hear their special waltz as they rocked in gentle rhythm to the exquisite song that belonged to them alone. The tension built within them, tightening, spiraling, taking them higher, up and away, until they burst into the heavens with the lights of their world beyond the windows showing them the way.

It was ecstasy. It was nearly shattering in its splendor, an explosion of sensations like none before. They drifted, savoring, murmuring the name of the other, until they returned to rest on the lush carpet that cradled them.

Luke moved off Maggie, then shifted her so her back was to his front and they could gaze out at the lights. He buried his face in her fragrant hair for a long moment, then tucked her head beneath his chin.

Maggie drew a shuddering breath, then smothered a sob that threatened to escape from her throat.

Dear God, she thought, she loved him. She was in love with Luke St. John. There was no denying it, nowhere to hide from the truth of it, nowhere to run. She loved him. He was all, everything and more that she'd fantasized about finding in a man, the one who would steal her heart for all time if things were different. If she was a normal woman, not plagued by the Jenkins Jinx. She loved him, but she couldn't have him, and it was just so incredibly sad.

But for now? she thought, blinking back unwelcomed tears. He was hers. Until Precious and Clyde's wedding, Luke was hers. She would cherish every moment she had with him and ignore the ticking of the clock that would signal their goodbye.

"What we just shared was…" Luke said, then stopped speaking for a second. "No, I don't have the words."

"I don't either," Maggie said softly, "but I know that it was… I'll never forget this night, Luke."

"I won't either." He paused, then chuckled. "I think our ice cream has melted."

Maggie smiled. "I think my bones have melted."

Time lost meaning as they lay together in sated, comfortable silence, then Maggie finally sighed.

"I'm about to fall asleep," she said. "I'd better get home, Luke."

"Ah, Maggie, stay. Please," he said. "We'll sleep with our heads on the same pillow in my bed and have breakfast together in the morning."

"I don't think…"

"Please?"

Why not? Maggie thought. In for a penny, in for a pound, or however that saying went. She was hopelessly, irrevocably in love with this man. The damage was done, the heartbreak guaranteed when all of this ended. Why not share everything she could with Luke while it was possible?

"Yes," she said. "Yes, I'll stay."

"Thank you," Luke said, then shifted away from her, rolled to his feet and extended one hand to her. "Come on. I promise my bed is softer than this floor."

Maggie placed her hand in his and allowed him to draw her up into an embrace where his mouth melted over hers in a searing kiss. On legs that weren't quite steady she walked by his side to the large master bedroom that was decorated in gray and burgundy. Luke turned on a lamp on the nightstand, then flipped back the blankets to reveal burgundy sheets.

"Oh, wait," he said. "Make note of which side of the bed you get in on because you have to leave on the same side in the morning or you'll have bad luck."

"Here we go again," Maggie said, rolling her eyes. "Another St. John superstition."

"Well," he said, shrugging, "at least I have a variety to offer. You're zoned in on the Jenkins Jinx and that's it."

Maggie looked up at him and frowned. "Which has generations of proof that validates it."

"That may be true, but you've managed to punch holes in all the superstitions I've presented so far, shown me that there's room for doubt. The same may hold true for your jinx."

"No," Maggie said, taking a step backward. "I'm not going to even entertain the idea that the jinx can be broken. I've seen the heartache suffered by those who thought they could do exactly that. No."

"Okay," Luke said, raising both hands in a gesture of peace. "Forget I said that. I didn't mean to upset you on this incredibly perfect night." He swept one arm in the direction of the bed. "Madam?"

Maggie settled onto the bed with a sigh of pleasure.

"Oh, this is heavenly," she said.

"I'm going to go turn out the lights in the other rooms and dump the soupy ice cream," Luke said. "I'll be back in a few minutes."

"'Kay," she said, then yawned.

Luke chuckled, then strode from the room. When he returned, Maggie was sound asleep. He slipped carefully into the bed next to her, then propped up on one forearm to watch her sleep.

So lovely, he thought. Maggie was here with him, where she belonged. If only there was a golden ring on her finger symbolizing her being his wife, his partner in life.

He was winning little victories each time she made it clear that the newest superstition he'd declared was foolish, should be dismissed as nonsense. Each of those incidents gave him ammunition to demolish the Jenkins Jinx. He was definitely making progress. Wasn't he? Oh, man, he just had to be.

But Maggie was so…so fierce about the jinx, was determined not to fall prey to the belief that she could be the one to prove it untrue, to break the long cycle of disastrous marriages in the Jenkins family. No, she had said. No.

And little victories meant nothing if he didn't win the final battle. He couldn't bear that thought. He'd just keep on as he was, chipping away at that wall of Maggie's. He was going to conquer the demon that held her so tight.

He was going to marry Maggie Jenkins. She loved him, he believed that with every fiber of his being. And heaven knew that he loved her. That love would grow, become stronger, unbeatable, smash the jinx into dust to be blown into oblivion.

Luke nodded decisively, snapped off the lamp, then settled close to Maggie, his head on the same pillow as hers just as he'd promised.

But it was many hours before he finally slept.

Two weeks later Maggie and Luke stood in the honeymoon suite on the top floor of one of Phoenix's exclusive hotels.

"Luke, this is awful," Maggie said with a burst of laughter. "A heart-shaped bed? A color scheme of bright red? Velvet spread, upholstery, even the drapes? A shiny red hot tub? It's so tacky, it's beyond belief."

"Oh, I don't know," Luke said, grinning, "I guess it depends on how you feel about red. This place could sure turn a guy off Valentine's Day. Man, they went nuts in here."

"The manager said it's very popular," Maggie said, shaking her head. "That's a scary thought."

"Yep," Luke said, glancing around. "It's even worse than the one that had forty-two stuffed toy cupids. I counted them, you know, and there were actually forty-two of those chubby little guys ready to shoot arrows. That was a nightmare waiting to happen."

"Well, cross this one off the list of possibilities." Maggie looked at her watch. "I've got to rush. I'm meeting Janet and Patty at the bridal shop for the first fitting of their bridesmaids' dresses."

"Have you…um…looked at wedding dresses yet?" Luke said, sliding a glance at her.

"No, not yet. I'm sure the perfect dress for…for Precious is there because the selection is wonderful. That shop is where Ginger got her gown. They're terribly expensive, though."

"No problem," Luke said. "Don't even think about the money. The sky is the limit…or whatever. In other words, go for it."

"Right. Let's get out of here. All this red is giving me a headache."

"Are you sure you can't come to my place tonight?" Luke said as they started toward the door.

"No, I've got to go see my mother, Luke. You know, have dinner with her, chat, what have you. She's feeling neglected and I don't blame her. I haven't been to her house in far too long. I'll just go straight home from there."

"I'll miss you," he said. "I'm getting very spoiled having you next to me in my bed at night and seeing you when I open my eyes in the morning. It's nice. It's more than nice."

Maggie gripped the doorknob, then hesitated and smiled up at Luke.

"Yes," she said, "I agree. It's very, very nice." She laughed. "By the way, you know that superstition you laid on me last night? I want you to know that I purposely put on my left shoe before my right one this morning and I have not had one bit of unluck, if there is such a word."

Luke braced his hand flat on the door to prevent Maggie from leaving the brilliant-red suite.

"Well, now, aren't you turning into a risk taker?" he said, smiling.

"Not really, Luke. I mean, after all, these are just superstitions that I'm declaring to be untrue. You should be feeling a step-by-step sense of freedom as each one gets checked off your list. I don't think I'm taking any risks by doing that."

"Interesting," he said, frowning thoughtfully. "So you're saying that superstitions, old wives' tales, jinxes are based on a foundation of long-standing foolishness."

"Well, no, not entirely. I was referring to superstitions only. There are certain jinxes that have proven merit."

"So you say," he said thoughtfully. "Or could it be rather a long string of poor judgment? I had this friend in college who was convinced he was jinxed when it came to owning a car. Every used vehicle he purchased turned out to be a lemon. So he quit, gave up, said never again. He rode a bike, took buses and taxis. Man, what a hassle."

"But smart," Maggie said decisively.

"I didn't go with that theory. I convinced him to try one more time, run that risky risk. We went to a used-

car lot and he looked at a bunch of vehicles, then settled on the one he would buy if he was going to, which
he wasn't. We took it for a test drive and stopped to see
another buddy of mine who was a mechanic."

"And he said the car was a clunker. Right?" Maggie said.

"No, he declared it to be prime, good for another hundred thousand miles, so my friend bought it."

Maggie blinked, then frowned. "Really?"

"Really. The last time I saw him he was still driving that
thing. He said it gave him cold chills to dwell on the narrow existence he would have had if he hadn't sucked in a
deep breath that day and taken that risk, bought the car."

"But—"

"Think about it." Luke dropped a quick kiss on Maggie's lips. "Come on, let's go. You'll be late for the appointment for the dresses."

"The what?" Maggie said absently. "Oh! The dresses.
I've got to dash."

They left the suite and as Maggie hurried down the
hallway in front of Luke, he punched one fist in the air.

Yes! he thought. He'd scored some points—big-time.
The story he'd made up about the guy and car was genius-level thinking, especially since he had done it on
the spur of the moment because the opportunity had
been so perfect for it.

Maggie had heard every word he'd said, was digesting it in that mighty little mind of hers as evidenced by
the fact that she'd momentarily forgotten about the appointment she was almost late for.

He was folding his tent graciously and without complaint each time she declared one of his superstitions, albeit fictitious ones, as nonsense. All he was asking of her was to give up one jinx. One.

The one that would mean the difference between their having a future together or not. The one that would determine their entire lives. The one he had to defeat in the ongoing battle he was conducting to win the war and a forever with Maggie Jenkins.

"I'm just going to tape this hem in place for now," the seamstress said to Maggie, "until the actual bridesmaid is here for the final fitting."

"Oh, I wish it was really me," Janet said wistfully as the seamstress worked on the hem. "This dress is scrumptious. I love this color of green, Maggie. I want to own this dress."

"That's what Patty said before she left," Maggie said, laughing. She was seated on a velvet-covered chair, sipping a cup of tea. "She said this whole business is pure torture because she's had the dress on but it really belongs to someone else."

"She's right," Janet said.

"All set for today," the seamstress said, getting to her feet. "Let me help you take this dress off."

"No, I want to keep it," Janet said, then laughed. "Would it do me any good to throw a tantrum?"

"I'm afraid not," the woman said, smiling.

The dress was removed and the seamstress left the room. Janet began to pull on her own clothes.

"Janet," Maggie said quietly, "may I ask you something?"

"Sure."

"When you married Roger, did you believe that you would be the one to break the Jenkins Jinx, end it for all time?"

"Truthfully?" Janet said, sitting down next to Maggie. "I loved Roger so much, Maggie, that I blatantly ignored things about him that were red-alert signals indicating problems down the line."

Maggie set her teacup on the delicate table next to her and sat up straighter in her chair.

"Really?" she said. "I didn't know that."

"No one did," Janet said, sighing. "I thought I could change him, dum-dum that I was. He gambled far too much, hadn't held a job longer than a year in his entire life, thought money should be spent and enjoyed now with no thought given to the future.

"Even after the babies started coming he didn't get his act together. It was like having another child to raise. When I got divorced, no one asked me why, really. The family just assumed it was the Jenkins Jinx doing its thing."

"And Bill?" Maggie said, her heart racing. "What about your marriage to Bill?"

"Oh, sweetie, that was a joke. I was lonely, broke, scared to death of being a single mother, living paycheck to paycheck, and I latched onto Bill. Six months later I was sick to death of him cheating on me. Ta-da. Divorce number two for Janet the dunce."

"Why…why didn't you ever say that the Jenkins Jinx didn't have anything to do with your divorces?" Maggie said.

"It was easier that way, Maggie. Why tell everyone that I had such lousy judgment, had made such awful mistakes and was paying the price? The whole family felt so sorry for me because I was another victim of the jinx, so I let it stand, kept my mouth shut."

"Don't you believe there really is a Jenkins Jinx?" Maggie said, hardly breathing.

"I honestly don't know," Janet said, frowning. "Is it real? Does this family just have poor judgment in its choice of partners? Or did some of those marriages in our family tree collapse due to the jinx? I don't know the answer to that." She cocked her head slightly and studied Maggie. "Why are you asking me all this? It has been ages since you and I have talked about the jinx."

"I, um. Well, because… Yes, because of Roses and Wishes. I deal with happy brides all the time and…Mom thinks I made a mistake starting a business that only emphasizes what I'll never have because of the jinx. She really believes the jinx is true, you know. Having Roses and Wishes has made me think about it more than I normally would that's all."

Janet narrowed her eyes. "You never could lie worth a damn, Maggie Jenkins. Something is going on with you. Talk to me, little sister."

Maggie got to her feet. "There's nothing to tell you, Janet." She looked at her watch. "My, my, look at the time. I've got to go. I have so much to do. Details, details, details—the list is endless for a wedding."

"*Your* dream wedding," Janet said, rising. "That's what you're tending to."

"Well, it just worked out that way because of this unusual situation with Precious and Clyde," Maggie said. "I explained all that to you. So, yes, this is the wedding I would have if I was going to have a wedding, which I'm not because of the jinx…which you're now suggesting might not be real and…" She slapped one hand onto her forehead. "I'm getting a roaring headache, thank you very much."

"Maggie, there is no way to prove that the jinx is real, no matter what Mom says."

"But we've believed it ever since we were young girls, Janet. We can't pretend it isn't there. We lost count of the divorces in our family tree. There is not one happy Jenkins marriage in our history."

"And there could be an explanation for every one of those divorces just as there is for my two. As for Mom and Dad? The jinx? Come on, Maggie, it was a classic case of the guy who falls for his sexy secretary and thinks he can recapture his youth by dumping his wife and three kids and going off with a bimbo. That's not a jinx, that's a hormone rush or whatever."

"But—"

"I don't know," Janet said, throwing up her hands. "Someday maybe a Jenkins will stay happily married for fifty years and this jinx thing will be old news. Love is powerful when it's right and real. Will that Jenkins be one of my kids? Or will that someone be…you?"

"Me?" Maggie said, her voice a strange-sounding squeak. "Don't be silly. I'm not brave enough to test out the theory that the jinx might not be real. I'm not going to run the risk of having my heart broken to pieces. Nope. Not me."

"Oh?" Janet said, raising her eyebrows. "What happens if you fall head over heels in love?"

I already have, Maggie thought dismally. *And I'm not going to do one thing about it beyond accepting the fact that my time with Luke St. John is measured on the calendar.*

"Let's change the subject," she said. "Want to hear something funny? There's a superstition that when you see an ambulance you'll have bad luck unless you pinch your nose until you see a black or brown dog."

Janet laughed. "That's the silliest thing I've ever heard."

"I know. Try this one. If you have a goldfish in a pond at your home it's good luck, but a goldfish kept inside the house is bad luck."

"Where are you getting this stuff?" Janet said, shaking her head.

"And if the bottom of your feet itch," Maggie rushed on, "you're going to make a trip."

"I'm going to make a trip home right now," Janet said, smiling, "before you lay any more cuckoo stuff on me. Superstitions are nonsense."

"Are jinxes?" Maggie said, suddenly serious. "Is the

Jenkins Jinx as nonsensical as the superstitions I just rattled off?"

Janet sighed. "I don't know. I really don't know. Someone in this family is going to have to fall in love, listen to their heart for the truth, the honest-to-goodness truth of that love and— Good grief, look at the time. I've got to pick up the kids." She gave Maggie a quick hug. "Thanks for letting me play Cinderella in that gorgeous dress. 'Bye."

"'Bye," Maggie said, then sank back down on the pretty chair and stared into space.

Her mind was a mess, she decided. For as long as she could remember she'd believed that the Jenkins Jinx was real. But now? After discussing it with her sister? It was all so confusing, so muddled.

Yes, she was in love with Luke. But, no, she couldn't, just couldn't, run the risk of ignoring the jinx only to discover that it was a genuine curse that hung over her family. But Janet had said that her two failed marriages had nothing to do with a jinx. But then again...

"Excuse me," the seamstress said, coming back into the room.

"Yes?" Maggie said, relieved to be pulled from her jumbled thoughts.

"Time is passing and that wedding you're coordinating will be here before you know it," the woman said. "Are you going to look at our selection of exquisite wedding dresses today?"

"No, not today," Maggie said, an achy sensation gripping her throat as she got to her feet. "I'm suddenly exhausted, so very tired."

"I understand," the seamstress said. "But you will pick the bride's dress soon, won't you?"

"Yes," Maggie said softly. "I'll do it…soon, I promise. I'll have my Cinderella moment, then take the dress off and…and just be me again."

Just Maggie, she thought. Counting down the days until she said goodbye to Luke and was simply Maggie Jenkins. Alone and lonely.

Ten

During the next month Maggie came to feel as though there were two different people existing in her own body.

One was carefree, happy and deeply in love with Luke, enjoying every moment they spent together.

They ate out often, went to the movies, flew a kite in a grassy field, enjoyed a picnic and canoe ride at Encanto Park, shopped at various malls and attended several interesting lectures at Arizona State University. They cooked together—which was a hilarious disaster—tended to details for Precious and Clyde's wedding. And they made sweet, wonderful love.

The other Maggie was consumed by a breath-stopping chill each time she looked at the calendar and saw the time flying by. Summer had turned into fall, school had started again and Phoenix was buzzing with the success of the ASU football team.

They'd celebrated with a special dinner out when they'd finally reserved the honeymoon suite at the very hotel where the reception was to be held. It was perfect, they'd decided. It was decorated in good taste, had a marvelous view of the city lights, a hot tub in the bedroom area and a fireplace in the living room.

Maggie had told Luke that it would be impossible for Precious and Clyde not to like it, while her heart had ached because the honeymoon suite would not welcome Mr. and Mrs. Luke St. John.

Her life, Maggie thought at one point, gave a whole new meaning to the old phrase of laughing on the outside and crying on the inside.

The seamstress at the bridal shop left message after message on Maggie's answering machine, saying she must choose the wedding dress. Maggie created endless excuses why she couldn't get to the shop, as she was terrified she would weep the entire time. The mere thought of selecting that gown, trying it on while knowing it really wasn't hers, was just more than she could bear.

Ginger and Robert returned with glowing reports of their honeymoon in Greece, and the four of them often enjoyed a night on the town. The newlyweds literally shone with happiness, and Maggie had no choice but to sigh and admit to herself that she was green with envy whenever she saw them together.

When Luke announced that it was bad luck to set an empty rocking chair in motion, Maggie dragged him to a furniture store and gave each rocking chair a gentle push to get it going. They dissolved in laughter, apologized to the frowning saleswoman and beat a hasty retreat.

When October marched in and Halloween costumes were featured in every store, Maggie told Luke—again—that the invitations to Precious and Clyde's wedding had to be selected *now* so they could be printed, addressed and mailed.

"Luke," Maggie said one night as they watched a video in her tiny living room, "you keep saying you'll contact Precious and Clyde about the wording on the invitations, but you don't do it."

"I will," he said, his attention on the television.

"When?" she said. She really had no right to nag him because she still hadn't chosen the wedding dress. But, of course, Luke didn't know that. "Those invitations have to be mailed so the RSVP cards can be returned and I can coordinate the amount of food and drink for the reception." She paused. "Are you listening to me?"

"What?" he said, glancing over at her, then back at the screen. "Sure, I hear you. I'll take care of it. I'll call Precious and Clyde tomorrow…or the next day."

"Promise?" Maggie said.

"Hey, would you look at that car. James Bond has the greatest wheels, I swear. No matter how many times I see these movies, I go nuts for the vehicles. Whoa. That baby can really go."

"Mmm," Maggie said, narrowing her eyes.

"If Detroit ever produced one of those, I'd be the first in line to buy it," Luke went on.

"Luke," Maggie said quietly, "I'm beginning to have doubts about the validity of the Jenkins Jinx."

"Yeah, okay. I'd order my car painted in-your-face-red with chrome so shiny that…" Luke stopped speaking, stiffened, then snapped his head around to look at Maggie. "What? What did you say?"

"Nothing," she said, waving one hand in the air. "I didn't mean to speak aloud. It's just on my mind so much that it popped out before I realized that—"

Luke grabbed the remote, turned off the television, then gripped Maggie's shoulders.

"Say it again," he said. "Please, Maggie, say it again. You're having doubts about… Say the words so I can hear them loud and clear. Maggie, you have no idea how much I need to hear you say those words."

"It has become so confusing," she said, meeting his intense gaze. "Whenever I try to think clearly about the jinx, I feel like a hamster running around in one of those wheels and not getting anywhere."

"Go on," he said, not releasing his hold on her.

"My mother told us about the jinx after my father left us," Maggie said, her voice not quite steady. "I grew up believing in it, especially after we researched our family tree and… But I was talking to Janet about her marriages and for the first time in all these years she said she's not totally convinced there is a jinx.

"Maybe, she said, it's just a whole slew of Jenkinses with poor judgment. Or maybe there is a jinx that forces us to make bad choices, or… Oh, I don't know anymore. Janet feels that all it will take to prove there is no such thing as the Jenkins Jinx is for one of us to fall in love—real love, honest, true and for always love—and live happily ever after."

"Yes, yes. She's right. That's good. Great thinking," Luke said in a rush of words. "You have a very smart sister there."

"She said maybe it would be one of her kids that proved the jinx to be nonsense or perhaps it might be…might be…"

"Might be?" Luke prompted.

"Me," Maggie whispered.

"Maggie, yes, it's you," Luke said, his heart soaring. "Maggie Jenkins, I love you so damn much. I am totally, absolutely and forever in love with you. I want to marry you, have babies with you, wake up every morning and have you be the first thing I see. My wife."

"Ohhh," Maggie said, then sniffled as her eyes filled with tears.

"Maggie, do you love me? Do you?"

"Yes. Yes, Luke, I do, so very much. I didn't want to fall in love with you, didn't mean to, but I did. I'm still worried about the jinx because it's been drummed into my head since I was a little girl. One minute I think I don't believe in it anymore, but then I get so frightened and… I'm such a mess.

"But, Luke, do you know what I hang on to like a life-line to give me courage? It's you. It's you and your su-perstitions. Your family has believed in those things you've told me for years and years, yet you're so will-ing to let them go, run the risk of bad things happening because you put your shoes on wrong or forget to carry your acorn or…"

"You're so brave, so strong, so willing to move forward and dismiss those superstitions as nonsense and…"

The color drained from Luke's face and he dropped his hands from Maggie's shoulders.

"If you can have that kind of courage," Maggie said, an errant tear sliding down her cheek, "then I should be brave, too, not hide behind my fears, my belief in the Jenkins Jinx."

"Maggie, listen to me. Okay?" Luke said, his voice raspy. "I have to tell you something. But as you're hearing what I have to say, remember that we love each other. We do. We have a wonderful future together just waiting for us to step up and start living it as husband and wife. Will you do that? Remember that?"

"Yes, all right, but you're suddenly so… What is this thing you have to tell me?"

Luke got to his feet, walked around the small room, then sat back down, taking Maggie's hands in his.

"Maggie, my darling Maggie," he said, looking directly into her eyes, "I never…I never believed in any of those superstitions."

"Pardon…me?"

"I'd never even heard of most of them, had my secretary find them for me on the Internet."

"What? I don't understand."

"I was desperate, don't you see?" he said, giving her hands a little shake. "I didn't know how to get you to demolish that wall protecting you from the Jenkins Jinx.

I thought if you continually witnessed me dumping superstitions that I had supposedly believed in all of my life, you'd come to realize that you could do that with the jinx."

"You didn't believe that having goldfish in the house is bad luck?" Maggie said, her voice rising.

"Ah, Maggie, I had a whole aquarium full of goldfish in my bedroom when I was a kid."

"You—you lied to me? About the superstitions? All this time you've been telling me lie after lie, reciting one superstition after another?"

"They weren't lies, exactly. It was part of a master plan I had to win your love, your heart, to blow the Jenkins Jinx into oblivion so we could be together forever. My father helped me a bit. You know, that night in the pizza place with the acorn and—"

"I don't believe this," Maggie said, yanking her hands free. "What else, Luke? What else did you lie about?"

"I wish you wouldn't use that word," he said, grimacing. "It was a plan. The Plan—in capital letters."

"What else, Luke St. John," she said, her voice ringing with fury.

Luke took a deep breath, then let it out slowly, puffing his cheeks.

"The wedding," he said quietly.

"What wedding?" she said, totally confused.

"Precious and Clyde's."

"What about it? What kind of lies could you possibly tell me about their wedding?"

Luke cringed. "There is no…no Precious and Clyde, Maggie. I made them up. I needed a way to stay close to you after you knocked me over, captured my heart, at Ginger and Robert's wedding. The Plan—I bet you're getting tired of hearing those words—The Plan was for you to coordinate your own dream wedding with me next to you every step of the way.

"Then hopefully you'd fall in love with me, just as I already loved you, and everything would be ready for us to get married just the way you'd always dreamed of."

"That's why you kept hedging about the invitations to Precious and Clyde's wedding," Maggie said, nearly shrieking. "You couldn't ask them about the wording they wanted because they don't exist. And…and…we weren't picking out a honeymoon suite for them it was—"

"For us, don't you see? I wanted our wedding to be perfect for you, exactly what you yearned for. And it will be because you've seen to every detail just the way you want it. I did it for you. Us. You." Luke dragged a restless hand through his hair. "Ah, Maggie, please tell me that you understand that what I did was out of love for you."

"What I understand," she said, getting to her feet and wrapping her hands around her elbows, "is that you are a liar. You are despicable. You made a fool of me. Must have laughed yourself silly when you reported back to your father about the great progress you were making with your ever-famous plan."

"No, it wasn't like that," he said, throwing out his arms. "I had to have something to fight the Jenkins Jinx with because you had it wrapped around you like a fortress. And now you love me. And now you have doubts about there being a jinx on your family and—"

"No, I don't," she said, lifting her chin and ignoring two more tears that slid down her face.

"What?" Luke said hardly above a whisper as he got to his feet.

"I have no doubts whatsoever that the Jenkins Jinx exists, is very, very real, and I am its latest victim," Maggie said, her voice trembling. "I fell in love with a dishonest man, a liar, a schemer, a game player, a damnable *planner.*"

"No! You fell in love with a man who loves you so much he was willing to do anything within his power to win your love in return. Because of your belief in that jinx I had to resort to whatever I could do to accomplish that goal. Lies? No, not really. Well, sort of, but—"

"Get…out," Maggie said, tightening the hold on her arms. "Get out of my home and my life."

"Maggie, no," Luke said, "don't do this to us. Don't send me away. We're in love with each other, can have a wonderful life, have babies, grow old together. The superstitions aren't real, don't exist, and neither does the Jenkins Jinx. You're free to love…me."

Luke drew a shuddering breath and extended one hand toward Maggie. "Please, Maggie?" he said, his voice thick with emotion. "Marry me? Please?"

Maggie's trembling legs refused to hold her for another second and she sank onto the sofa, a sob catching in her throat.

This wasn't happening, she told herself frantically.

Oh, please, this wasn't happening. Luke had been playing games with her, with her emotions, her heart, her... There was no Precious and Clyde? How could people who had become so real to her not even exist? And all those dumb superstitions were part of a nasty, devious *plan* to...

How could Luke do this to her? Live a lie day after day, night after night as they made love? He wasn't remotely close to who she had believed him to be. She was a victim of his duplicity.

And she was the latest victim of the Jenkins Jinx.

"Maggie?"

"Leave...me...alone," she said, then covered her face with her hands.

Luke's shoulders slumped and he dropped his chin to his chest for a long moment before raising his head again to stare at the ceiling in an attempt to gain control of his emotions as an achy sensation gripped his throat.

He'd lost the war, he thought miserably. He'd fought the good fight, won some battles, but the ultimate victory was not his to claim. Maggie was sending him away.

She was once again behind the walls, clinging to the jinx, never wanted to see him again. There was nothing more he could do. The only woman he had ever—would ever—love was not his to have and he now understood what a broken heart felt like. This was the greatest pain, the most chilling loss, he had ever experienced.

"I'm sorry," he said quietly, looking at Maggie. "I never meant to make you cry. I never meant to hurt you.

What I did, I did out of love for you so we could be together forever. But I was wrong. I did it all wrong and I'm so damn sorry." He swallowed heavily. "Goodbye, Maggie."

Luke turned and walked slowly from the room, then down the stairs and out the front door of the Victorian house.

Maggie dropped her hands from her face and clutched them tightly in her lap as she gave way to her tears. She rocked back and forth, hardly able to breathe as the tears flowed and the sobs echoed in the silent room.

She finally shifted and curled into a ball of misery on the sofa, crying until there were no more tears to shed. Her head hurt and her heart ached for all that might have been but would never be.

Exhaustion finally claimed her and she slept fitfully, having taunting dreams of acorns, rocking chairs, goldfish and roses. Roses that died, their petals falling and disappearing into oblivion until there was nothing left.

Nothing.

Eleven

After three days and nights of weepy misery Maggie had had enough of her own gloomy company. On Saturday afternoon she called Patty and asked her if she was free to come over. Patty arrived an hour later, took one look at Maggie's pale cheeks and pink, puffy eyes and demanded to know what was going on.

"Tell all," Patty demanded, plunking down on the opposite end of the sofa from Maggie.

And Maggie told all. She sniffled her way through the tale of Luke's deception, of his diabolical *plan,* the endless string of lies he had told. She confessed her love for Luke and announced in no uncertain terms that she was the latest victim of the Jenkins Jinx.

Patty's mouth dropped open at times and she had to

tell herself to shut it as Maggie went on and on with her story.

"I know I have to cancel all the arrangements I've made for the imaginary Precious and Clyde's wedding," Maggie said, dabbing at her nose with a tissue, "but every time I pick up the phone I burst into tears. I'm a wreck. A mess. I may never recover from this disaster. *And I'm just so sad.*"

"That's very obvious," Patty said, nodding. "Whew. This whole thing is… Wow. Maggie, I don't think you're going to like what I'm about to say, but in my opinion this scheme, plan, whatever, of Luke St. John's has got to be the most romantic thing I have heard in my entire life."

"What?" Maggie said, jumping to her feet.

"Sit," Patty said, pointing to the sofa cushion.

Maggie sat. "How can you say that? Romantic? Ha! There is nothing romantic about lies, Patty. Oodles and oodles of lies. Luke doesn't have a superstitious bone in his body, but he made me believe that he… Romantic? Are you crazy?"

"Slow down. Calm down," Patty said, patting the air with the palms of her hands. "Let's back up here. You and Luke were very attracted to each other from the moment you met. Correct?"

"Well, yes, but…"

"If he had suggested at Ginger and Robert's reception that you two date each other, discover just how far that attraction might take you, you would have refused. Correct?"

"Yes, of course," Maggie said. "Something extremely intense happened between us, and I wouldn't have set myself up to have my heart broken by becoming involved with Luke, then falling prey to the jinx. No. No way."

"And Luke," Patty continued, "smart man that he is, realized that at some point and knew he had to come up with an untraditional way to continue to see you. He was determined to be with you, Maggie, no matter what. Think of the time and energy he spent putting his plan into motion and keeping it going."

"Those lies kept things going, all right," Maggie said, glaring at Patty.

"A hunk of stuff like Luke can snap his fingers," Patty said, deciding to snap her fingers, "and have just about any woman he wants. But he wanted you, Maggie Jenkins, and he worked very hard to get you. That, my dear friend, is romantic to the max."

"But—"

"Oh, Maggie, sweetie, the man is so in love with you it just melts my heart. You left him no choice but to be tricky, do anything and everything to be near you, and it was successful because you fell in love with him, too. And what did you do? You threw him out and declared him to be a jerk, or whatever choice description you nailed on him. You need your head examined."

"How can you say that? Whose side are you on?" Maggie said, nearly shrieking. "I thought you were my best friend, not Luke's. I'm talking about lies here, and deception and—"

"And love." Patty sighed wistfully. "Romantic love. Forever love. Will-you-marry-me love. Love in its purest and most beautiful form and—"

"You're getting gushy and mushy," Maggie mumbled. "Really nauseating."

"Well, what would you call it? Maggie, think about it. Really think about all that Luke did to win your heart. It just blows my mind. Good grief, the man was so desperate and determined he even asked his father to help him in his quest to… Oh, wow."

Maggie frowned and stared into space.

"Are you thinking?" Patty said, leaning slightly toward her.

"Yes, but… Well, he did spend a lot of time schlepping around with me to find the perfect honeymoon suite, despite his busy schedule. And he did memorize all those superstitions so he'd be ready to slip them in where he could. And he did keep telling me to plan the wedding of my dreams, all the details, details, details for Precious and Clyde because—"

"Because he was hoping and praying it would really be your wedding because you would be marrying him," Patty said, nodding. "Now you're getting it. Now you've got to admit that this whole thing is unbelievably romantic."

Maggie flattened her hands on her cheeks. "My gosh, Patty, what have I done? All I heard was that he lied to me, was playing a role to carry out his infamous plan and… In the very next second I was convinced that I had fallen prey to the jinx, was in love with the wrong man and… All I could hear was *what* he had done, not *why* he had done it. Then I tossed him out into the snow."

"That's a stretch," Patty said, laughing. "This is Phoenix, remember?"

"You know what I mean. Oh, Patty, I love Luke so much, and he loves me so much, and because of my life-long fears I lost him. I was so horrible to him, so nasty, so…despicable. It's over. Done. Finished. And I have no one to blame but myself. I'm so dumb."

"Yep," Patty said. "You've got that straight."

"Well, thanks a lot," Maggie said, narrowing her eyes.

"Well, for crying out loud, Maggie, you sit there like you're sentenced to weeping buckets for the rest of your days."

"I am!"

"Fine." Patty got to her feet. "One thing is very clear here."

"It is? What?"

"You don't love Luke as much as he loves you."

Maggie's eyes widened. "How can you say that?"

"Easy," Patty said, shrugging. "I opened my mouth and the words popped right out. What else can I think? Luke knocked himself out to win your heart. *The man made a plan.* You? You're just throwing up your hands and feeling sorry for yourself. He fought for you. You're resigned to going through life with a sinus headache from crying. Nope. You don't love him as much as he loves you. No way."

Maggie jumped up again. "I certainly do. I love him with my whole heart and soul and mind and body and…

Forget the body part, because some things are private. But I love him, Patty. I do. You think I can't come up with a *plan* to try to win him back, get him to forgive me? Well, ha! Just watch me. I'm leaping into action. I am woman. Hear me roar."

"Now we're getting somewhere," Patty said, settling back down on the sofa. "Okay, let's brainstorm. Your whole future happiness—and Luke's, too—is at stake here. Let's take it from the top. Think…*plan*."

"Damn that plan," Luke said. "I lost the woman I love because of The Plan, which I thought was so terrific, so brilliant."

"I tried to warn you that women are really touchy about duplicity, son," Mason St. John said, shaking his head.

The pair was having lunch at Mason's club at the same time Maggie was pouring out her heart to Patty. Luke had managed to choke down about half of his meal before giving up, his appetite gone.

"Yes, you did warn me," Luke said dully. "But did I listen? No, not me. I just plowed ahead with The Plan and now I'm paying the price. I am one very miserable man. The thought of never seeing Maggie again, not having a future with her as my wife, the mother of my children is… Hell, what a mess."

"Indeed," Mason said, taking the last bite of his lunch. "Dessert?"

"No, thanks. I'm not hungry. And I can't sleep at night and I'm aging before my very eyes. I'm a complete and total wreck."

"Mmm," Mason said, patting his lips with a linen napkin. "Care for some advice from your old man?"

"You actually have some for me?" Luke said, raising his eyebrows. "After the disaster I made of this situation?"

"Yep. My advice is…time. Give Maggie space and time to really think this through. Luke, women can run circles around men in the wisdom department. They think deeper, more detailed and emotionally than we do, God love 'em. Allow her to sift and sort what happened, what you did and why you did it. Be patient and wait."

"How long?" Luke said, his shoulders slumping. "Until Maggie visits me in a nursing home and tells me she still thinks I'm despicable?"

"Now that," Mason said, chuckling, "was funny."

"There's nothing funny about this, Dad. I've lost the woman I love!"

"So it would appear," Mason said, pointing one finger in the air. "But I'm not convinced of that yet. Time, Luke. Space. Patience. That's your new plan."

"The word *plan* should be banned from the English language," Luke said with a snort of disgust.

"Well, that's my advice, son. Oh, and do me a favor. Don't come back to the office this afternoon even though we decided we needed to work on that project we're facing. I don't think I can take any more of your sunshine mood. Go for a walk, take in a movie, get drunk, do something, but spare me."

"Thanks a bunch," Luke said glumly.

* * *

The following week went by so slowly, and Luke double-checked the date with his secretary so often that she was eyeing him warily and he decided he'd better knock it off.

In the early afternoon of the Friday following lunch with his father, Luke sat in his office staring into space, something he'd done a great deal the past few days.

He should fire himself for lack of productivity, he thought. He couldn't concentrate on anything but Maggie and that god-awful final scene in her living room. Time? Space? Patience? So far it was getting him zip. He hadn't heard one word from Maggie, and the knot in his gut continually reminded him he was terrified that he never would.

The intercom on the corner of his desk buzzed and he stared at it for a long moment, toying with the idea of ignoring it. It buzzed again. With a resigned sigh, Luke pressed the button.

"Yes, Betty?" he said to his secretary.

"There's a woman named Patty on the phone for you, Luke. She says that she's Maggie Jenkins's best friend and that it's imperative that she speak with you. Line one."

"Got it," Luke said, his heart racing as he snatched up the receiver. "Patty? Hello. This is Luke. Why are you calling? Is Maggie all right? Has something happened to her? Talk to me?"

"I would," Patty said, laughing, "if you gave me a chance."

"Oh. Yes. Sure. Sorry."

"Nothing has happened to Maggie, per se," Patty said, "except for the fact that she's terribly upset. Unhappy. Miserable. Sad. You know what I mean?"

"Yeah, I know what you mean," Luke said, squeezing the bridge of his nose. "There's a lot of that going around."

"But that's not why I called," Patty went on. "I'm at the bridal salon where Janet and I were fitted for the dresses that were supposedly for Precious's attendants at her wedding. I'm helping Maggie cancel all the arrangements, the bookings and what have you she made for Precious and Clyde, who don't need them because they aren't really real."

"And?"

"Well, the owner of the shop says these two dresses have to be paid for today, can't be canceled because…well, they're dresses just waiting for final fittings. I don't have enough money to pay for them and I know Maggie doesn't. I don't want to upset her more than she is by telling her I hit a glitch here. Do you think you could come down here and settle the account?"

"Of course," Luke said. "It's the least I can do. Give me the address." He paused. "Patty, I love Maggie, I truly do. Do you believe there's any hope of her forgiving me for what I did?"

"Gosh, Luke, I don't know what to tell you. I've never seen her so distraught, so… It's heartbreaking, just heartbreaking. It just breaks my heart because it's so…heartbreaking."

"Oh," he said, sighing. "That's bad. Very bad. Not good. It sounds like time is not doing the job."

"Pardon me?"

"Never mind," he said with another deep sigh. "Just give me the address of that store and tell the owner I'm on my way."

"Thank you, I'll let her know," Patty said. "I have to leave now because I have another appointment, but I'll assure the owner that you'll be here soon."

"I'll settle up with any of the suppliers that charge a fee for canceling orders. Man, I wish things were different. I wish... Never mind. This is all my fault. Call me if you run into problems."

"Okay. Sure. We may all end up eating a whole bunch of white-chocolate miniature roses that were to be in tiny baskets at each place setting at the reception."

"Roses and wishes," Luke said quietly.

"Yes. Well. 'Bye for now."

"'Bye Patty."

When Luke entered the bridal salon, a copper bell over the door tinkled to announce his arrival. A woman's voice came from somewhere in the distance calling out that she would be there in a minute. He wandered around the main area of the lushly decorated shop, his hands shoved into the pockets of his pants. He stopped in the middle of the room and frowned.

This was where an upper-crust bride-to-be came to select her attendants' dresses and to pick out her own wedding gown, he thought. With his damnable plan he'd forced Maggie to come here, make choices for her dream wedding while believing it was all for Precious and Clyde's extravaganza.

The same held true for the honeymoon suite, the menu for the reception dinner, every little detail, like white-chocolate roses in little baskets, that Maggie had had to deal with.

His plan hadn't been brilliant, it had been cruel. He, Luke St. John, was the scum of the earth and didn't deserve to be forgiven. Maggie must have daydreamed about those white-chocolate roses at some point in her life, had been in the process of making them a reality while thinking she would then watch Precious and Clyde's guests gobble up the sweet, pretty treat.

Yeah, he was definitely despicable. There wasn't a chance in hell that his beloved Maggie would forgive him for what he'd put her through, and he didn't blame her, not one damn bit.

"Sorry to have kept you waiting," an attractive woman in her forties said, hurrying toward Luke. "I'm Selina Simone, the owner of this salon. And you are?"

"Luke St. John."

"Ah, yes, Patty said you were coming. I trust you understand why I must be compensated for the dresses that Maggie selected."

"Of course," Luke said. "I'll write you a check. I'd like Patty and Janet to keep them. Could you see to that?"

"Yes, it will be my pleasure. They're gorgeous gowns. Maggie has such splendid taste and she was so excited when we found that exact shade of green she wanted for her—for the Christmas wedding she was coordinating. Well, I'm sure Janet and Patty will enjoy owning the creations."

"Right," Luke said gloomily. "It will be nice to know that someone smiled in the middle of this mess. Is there anything else I need to take care of here?"

"Well, yes, as a matter of fact there is," Selina said. "There are accessories, you see. The satin ribbons for the bouquets and what have you."

"Whatever." Luke nodded. "Sure."

"Would you mind coming into the back with me, Mr. St. John? That's where my records are, and it will be easier for me to check the order forms."

"That's fine. Lead the way."

"Well, I have something to tend to and will join you in a moment. Just go through that door over there and wait, if you would be so kind."

This was pure torture, Luke thought as he crossed the room. Every second he spent in this place pounded home the truth of how difficult all this had been for Maggie, how painful, how…heartbreaking, to borrow Patty's word. Yeah, well, he deserved to suffer, louse that he was.

He entered a medium-size room that had thick rose-colored carpeting. Cranberry-colored easy chairs were arranged in a semicircle in front of a white wicker arch with artificial greenery and flowers woven through it. A large three-sided mirror was on the opposite wall with additional chairs in front of it. Soft, dreamy music was playing.

Man, Luke thought, look at this place. It just got

worse and worse. Maggie had probably sat in one of those chairs and watched Janet and Patty try on the green dresses. The gowns of her dreams that she'd believed would be worn by Precious's attendants.

And a wedding dress? God, had Maggie been forced to select that already, too? Try it on? The wedding gown she'd wear if she was going to be the bride, knowing that Precious would walk down the aisle in it? He should be strung up by his rotten thumbs for what he'd done to his Maggie.

Luke jerked as the music became slightly louder. It was clearly the traditional wedding march.

Why were they playing that now? he thought, beads of sweat dotting his brow. He couldn't take much more of this. Maggie must have heard it at some point in this disaster and... Where was that lady, that Selina woman? He had to get out of here.

He looked frantically around, hoping that Selina Simone would appear, then a motion beyond the pretty arch caught his attention and he snapped his head back to see what it was.

Then he stopped breathing as he stared through the arch, finally taking a shuddering breath as a sharp pain shot across his chest telling him he was desperately in need of air in his lungs.

"My God," Luke whispered, his heart thundering. "Maggie."

She was walking slowly toward him, her fingers laced loosely at her waist. And she was wearing an incredibly beautiful full-length white wedding dress. It was an old-fashioned Victorian style with a high neck and a multitude of seed pearls on the bodice. It nipped in at her tiny waist, and the skirt swept to the floor in soft, luscious satin folds. The gossamer veil brushed her shoulders and was turned back to reveal her face.

And Maggie was smiling.

"Maggie?" Luke said, hearing the gritty quality of his voice.

She continued to approach with the measured steps of a bride walking down the aisle to meet her groom as the wedding march continued to play. She finally stopped in front of Luke and he swallowed heavily as he looked at her.

"Hello, Luke," she said softly.

"You are…" Luke cleared his throat. "Maggie, you are the most beautiful bride I have ever seen." He shook his head slightly. "But I don't understand what—"

"I'll explain," Maggie interrupted. "Let's sit down."

"Yes. Okay."

Maggie settled onto one of the cranberry-colored chairs, smoothing her skirt out around her. Luke pulled a matching chair in front of her and leaned forward, resting his elbows on his knees and tapping his laced fingers against his lips.

"Luke," Maggie said, looking directly into his dark eyes, "I hope you'll forgive me for the horrible things I said to you when you told me about your plan."

"Forgive *you?*" he said, splaying his hands on his knees. "I'm the one who wants to beg *you* to forgive *me* for being so—" he glanced around, then met her gaze again "—so cruel and heartless and thoughtless and for telling you all those lies and… The fact that I was desperate, so afraid of losing you, is no excuse for what I put you through. I thought I was being so clever, so… Maggie, I'm so sorry."

"Well, we're even as far as plans go," she said, smiling at him warmly. "Patty and Selina were in on *my* plan to get you here today."

"Oh?" he said, surprise registering on his face.

"Luke, I overreacted terribly when you told me about Precious and Clyde not being real people, about how you wanted me to organize *my* dream wedding and… All I could hear was that you lied to me, weren't who you had presented yourself to be. All I could hear was that I had made a horrendous mistake by falling in love with you and had become a victim of the Jenkins Jinx."

"No, I—"

"Please, just listen."

He nodded.

"I was feeling so sorry for myself," Maggie went on, "felt betrayed and… But Patty made me realize that what you had done wasn't despicable, it was romantic, it stemmed from your love for me and from your heartfelt desire to marry me and give me the wedding of my dreams."

"Yes, yes, that's it," Luke said, nodding jerkily. "That's why I did it. But it all blew up and I was convinced I'd lost you forever, that you'd hide behind those walls of yours and I'd never be able to get near you again."

"Luke, the walls are gone forever. After I talked with Patty, I went for a long walk and listened to my heart. I came to know that love, true love, forever love, is stronger than any jinx or superstition. I know that what you and I have together will withstand the good times, the bad, in sickness and in health, until death parts us and perhaps even beyond."

"Ah, Maggie," Luke said, his throat tightening. "I love you so much."

"I love you, too," she said, sudden tears filling her eyes. "I worked out a plan with Patty and Selina to get you here so you would see me in this wedding dress, the one I want to wear when I become your wife. I wanted to prove to you that I don't believe in the jinx or any superstition like the groom not seeing his bride in her dress before the ceremony. I wanted to prove to you that I'm free to live, to love, and that I want to spend the rest of my life with you as your wife…if you'll have me."

Luke stood and with hands that were not quite steady grasped Maggie's and eased her to her feet.

"Maggie Jenkins," he said, giving up any attempt to hide the tears shimmering in his eyes, "would you do me the honor of becoming my wife? Will you marry me, Maggie? Please?"

"Yes," she said, smiling through her own tears of joy. "Oh, yes."

Luke dropped her hands, framed her face, then kissed her so softly, so reverently, to seal the commitment to their future together.

Right on cue the music changed to a waltz—*their*

waltz. Luke drew Maggie into his arms and they danced around the room as though floating on clouds, looking directly into each other's eyes, seeing matching messages of greater understanding and forgiveness, of the love and happiness that would be theirs to share for eternity.

Several hours into the wedding reception of Mr. and Mrs. Luke St. John, the newly married couple had made their escape to the honeymoon suite.

"Oh, my," Patty said wistfully, "it was all so beautiful, wasn't it? Including me in this gorgeous dress. Just perfect. Every detail, detail, detail, as Maggie would say. Right down to those delicious white-chocolate roses. What a wonderful couple Maggie and Luke make. And happy? I think they give a whole new meaning to the word."

"Yes," Maggie's mother, Martha, said, "you're right. Seeing them together… Well, let's just say that there will be no more talk of the Jenkins Jinx in this family. Maggie and Luke have broken that nasty spell, I just know in my heart that they have."

"I agree with you, Mother," Janet said. "And I'd say that my cute brother does, too. He's danced all evening with that pretty girl he met here." She paused. "Didn't you love the wedding gifts Maggie and Luke gave each other? A tiny gold acorn on a delicate chain for Maggie, and she had gold acorn cuff links made for Luke. She told me it was their special way of remembering all that took place before this memorable night. Oh, God, that is so romantic I could weep."

"I already did," Patty said, laughing.

"No more jinx," Martha said, "and no more Roses and Wishes. Maggie has officially closed her business." She smiled. "She said that enterprise made all her wishes come true, so she's thinking of opening a baby boutique to see if that will hurry along the first little St. John bundle of joy."

"My goodness," Patty said, her eyes widening. "Does that sound superstitious to you?" She laughed. "Well, rest up, folks, because here we go again."

* * * * *

CHRISTMAS LULLABY

BY
CATHY GILLEN THACKER

This book is dedicated to Madeline Ruth Thacker

Chapter One

Amanda Witherspoon had heard Riley McCabe was returning to Laramie, Texas to join the Laramie Community Hospital staff, but she hadn't actually *seen* the handsome family
physician until Friday afternoon when he stormed into the
staff lounge in the pediatrics wing.

Nearly fourteen years had passed, but his impact on her
was the same. Just one look into his mesmerizing amber eyes
made her pulse race, and her emotions skyrocket. He had been
six foot when he left for college, now he was even taller. Back
then he had worn his sun-streaked light brown hair any which
way. Now the thick wavy strands were cut in a sophisticated
urban fashion, parted neatly on the left and brushed casually
to the side. His lanky body filled out his button-down shirt,
V-necked Fair Isle sweater and jeans in an exceedingly ap-
pealing way. He looked solid and fit, mouthwateringly sexy,
and every inch the kind of grown man who knew exactly who
he was and what he wanted out of life. The kind not to be
messed with. The sound of holiday music playing on the hospital sound system and the Christmas tree in the corner only
added to the fantasy-come-true quality of the situation.

Had Amanda not known better, she would have thought Riley McCabe's return to her life would have been the Christmas present to beat all Christmas presents, meant to liven up

her increasingly dull and dissatisfying life. But wildly exciting things like that never happened to Amanda.

"Notice I'm not laughing," Riley McCabe growled as he
stormed close enough for her to inhale the fragrance of soap
and brisk, wintry cologne clinging to his skin.

"Notice," Amanda returned dryly, wondering what the fa-
mously mischievous prankster was up to now, "neither am I."

Riley marched toward her, attractive jaw thrust out pug-
naciously, thick straight brows raised in mute admonition. "I
would have figured we were beyond all this."

Amanda had hoped that would be the case, too. After all,
she was a registered nurse, he a doctor. But given the fact that
the Riley McCabe she recalled had been as full of mischief
as the Texas sky was big, that had been a dangerous suppo-
sition to make. "All what?" she repeated around the sudden
dryness of her throat. As he neared her, all the air left her lungs
in one big whoosh.

"The practical jokes! But you just couldn't resist, could
you?"

Amanda put down the sandwich she had yet to take a bite
of and took a long sip of her diet soda. "I have no idea what
you're talking about," she said coolly. Unless this was the beginning of yet another ploy to get her attention?

"Don't you?" he challenged, causing another shimmer of
awareness to sift through her.

Deciding that sitting while he stood over her gave him too
much of a physical advantage, she pushed back her chair and
rose slowly to her feet. She was keenly aware that he now had
a good six inches on her, every one of them as bold and masculine as the set of his lips. "I didn't think you were due to
start working here until January 2," she remarked, a great deal
more casually than she felt.

He stood in front of her, arms crossed against his chest,
legs braced apart, every inch of him taut and ready for action.
"I'm not."

"So?" She ignored the intensity in the long-lashed amber eyes that threatened to throw her off balance. "How could I possibly play a prank on you if I didn't think you were going to be here?"

"Because," he enunciated clearly, "you knew I was going to start setting up my office in the annex today."

Amanda sucked in a breath and tilted her head back to glare up at him. "I most certainly did not!" she insisted. Although she might have considered a practical joke had she realized he intended to pick up right where they had left off all those years ago. Matching wits and wills. The one thing she had never wanted to cede to the reckless instigator was victory of any kind.

Riley leaned closer, not stopping until they were practically close enough to kiss. "Listen to me, Amanda, and listen good. Playing innocent is not going to work with me. And neither," he warned, even more forcefully, "is your latest gag."

Amanda regarded him in a devil-may-care way designed to get under his skin as surely as he was already getting under hers. "I repeat—" she spoke as if to the village idiot "—I have no idea what you are talking about, *Doctor* McCabe. Now do you mind? I only have a forty-five minute break and I'd like to eat my lunch."

He flashed her an incendiary smile that left her feeling more aware of him than ever. "I'll gladly leave you alone just as soon as you collect them."

Amanda blinked, more confused than ever. "Collect who?" she asked incredulously.

Riley walked back to the door. Swung it open wide. On the other side was the surprise of Amanda's life.

IF RILEY HAD GONE STRICTLY by the stunned and baffled look on his former antagonist's face, he would have thought Amanda Witherspoon was entirely innocent in the commotion that had just gone on down in the hospital's main lobby.

But four years of nonstop high school rivalry had taught him that no one could plan and execute a ruse better than the beautiful woman before him. Amanda stared at the triple stroller, currently being manned by two college-age hospital volunteers—Riley's twenty-one-year-old sister, Laurel, and her friend, premed student Micki Evans.

Amanda's glance moved over the three children ensconced in holiday clothing. "I take it these aren't patients?" Amanda guessed finally.

Riley gave a reassuring smile to the three kids. He had no idea who they belonged to, but they were incredibly cute, nevertheless. The infant—Cory—had short dark hair and inquisitive eyes so dark blue he knew they would eventually turn brown. Amber, the toddler, was practically bald; her thin blond hair barely covered her crown. But she had an infectious smile and a sunny, easygoing personality. Chloe, the preschooler, had a mane of wildly curly light brown hair that stopped at her shoulders, and light blue eyes that radiated more natural mischief than Riley's ever had in his prime. Riley had tried talking to them, to get to the bottom of whatever was going on here—to no avail. The baby merely cooed, the toddler babbled happily but incoherently, and the preschooler was so stubbornly mute it appeared they were playing a game Riley was not in the mood for. Scowling, Riley turned back to Amanda. He could understand her wanting to pick up the jokes again, even if they were a little old for such shenanigans. His life had never been more enthralling than when they had been testing each other's wills and skills. But this ploy was, in his estimation, way over the line of acceptable behavior. And he was determined to make Amanda Witherspoon understand that.

Micki Evans piped up nervously, "Laurel and I found them outside one of the entrances when we were coming in to volunteer this morning."

"There was an envelope addressed to Riley attached to the

stroller," Riley's younger sister, Laurel, quickly put in. "And for the record, I don't think you had anything to do with this, Amanda."

"Thank you," Amanda said.

"Well, I do," Riley groused. And he was damn furious about it. He didn't care how beautiful Amanda Witherspoon had become over the years. Or how sweetly sexy she looked in her pale blue nurse's uniform and white cotton sweater. She might appear innocent enough with her dark blond hair tucked into a casual ponytail at the nape of her neck, with sprigs of lighter blond hair escaping to frame her face in wispy strands. But Riley knew better. Her wide-set turquoise eyes radiated a spunk and daring that warned him not to be taken in by her soft feminine lips, stubborn chin and pert straight nose. Her fair skin might be lit with a glow that seemed to come from within, her cheeks a pale, becoming pink, but that did not mean she was the least bit trustworthy. Not when it came to him. Which was why, Riley schooled himself firmly, he could not let himself dwell on the new fullness of her breasts, the admirable slenderness of her waist, and the enticing curve of her hips. Never mind the lithe, graceful way she moved. Nor could he let himself wonder if her legs—now hidden by her uniform trousers—were as sexy and lissome as he recalled.

He was not here to woo her, but to call her to task.

Not that she looked ready to own up to anything she had done.

"May I read the note?" Amanda asked.

Curious to see how she was going to play this ruse out, Riley set his lips grimly and handed the red envelope over. Their hands brushed. He noted Amanda's hands were trembling slightly as she removed a Christmas card with a jolly old Saint Nick, adorned in cowboy hat and boots and holding a rope in his hand, featured prominently on the front of it. "I lassoed you a present," Amanda read out loud, before turning the page. Brow furrowed, she cleared her throat and continued reading out loud. "Dear Riley, Four-year-old Chloe, seven-teen-month-old Amber, and four-month-old Cory need the kind of love only a daddy with a heart the size of Texas can give. Please do right by them and see they have a very merry Christmas. Santa."

Amanda's lips formed a round O of surprise as she looked up at Riley. "You have three children?" she asked in amazement. "I didn't even know you were married!"

If Riley had been in a charitable mood, he would have given her an Academy Award for her acting. He was not in a charitable mood. "I'm not married," he told her flatly.

Amanda's eyes widened. "Wow. I mean, I remember you as being sort of irresponsible and joking around all the time, but…wow," she stammered again.

Temper surging, Riley turned to his younger sister and her friend. "Would you mind taking the children to the playroom down the hall?" he asked in a low, clipped voice, doing his best to keep his emotions under control lest he upset the children.

"No problem," Laurel said with a nervous smile. She wheeled the triple stroller around with Micki's help, and they all exited.

Once again, Riley and Amanda were quite alone. "Guess you've been a little busy since you left Laramie," Amanda quipped as she picked up her sandwich, slid it back into the paper bag bearing her name, and placed it in the fridge.

Not that busy, Riley thought. "Those aren't my kids," he repeated firmly.

Amanda tilted her head at him. "Tell that to the kids' mother," she suggested skeptically.

Riley planned on that and much more. An outrageous act like this would not pass without retribution. He promised Amanda Witherspoon that. "Which brings us to the next point," he continued calmly, looking deep into her eyes. "What kind of mother would let you use her children to play a joke on me?"

GOOD QUESTION, Amanda thought. Only she wasn't playing a joke on Riley McCabe. Which could only mean one thing— he had to be playing a joke on her. The kind that would break all records in the history of their long-running feud. "Forgive me for trying to get *you* to do the right thing," she said with a shrug, aware staff were gathering in the hall just outside the lounge.

"So you admit you're behind this!" Riley crowed, ignoring the implication that the trio of children was his.

"I admit," Amanda countered, as she stalked away from him and out into the hallway, "you're a fool if you think you can get away with trying to publicly embarrass me. And furthermore—" she whirled around to face him once again "—had I known when I accepted a position as pediatric nurse here two months ago that you were going to show up here, too, I would have found some other small and charming West Texas town in which to live and work!"

Riley studied the indignant blush warming her face and neck. "If I were you I would admit I was bested and call a halt to this right now."

"Hey!" Amanda angled an accusing finger his way. "I'm not the one with three children spirited away to the pediatric floor playroom."

Riley lifted a dissenting brow. The air between them practically sizzled with sexual sparks. "Aren't you?"

Oh, no, Amanda thought as dread spiraled inside her. She knew that look. The look that said Riley was about to do something even wilder and crazier than what had already been done.

"Is it true?" Meg Lockhart-Carrigan, LCH director of nursing, finally piped up. She and her husband, Luke, had a brood of four. Meg looked Riley in the eye. "Are those children yours?"

"Actually," Riley smiled, wrapping an arm around Amanda's shoulder. "They're ours."

A gasp went through the hallway as even more staff, patients and parents gathered to witness the unfolding scene.

Amanda could feel the blood first draining, then rushing, to her face. *Damn you, Riley McCabe.* She clamped her lips together and spoke out of the side of her mouth. "Stop. Teasing."

"Who's kidding?" Riley said, clearly enjoying himself. He slid his arm down to her waist and hauled her against his length. "I've been trying to get this woman to marry me for ages now. She won't do it. Not even after the two of us had three children in secret."

Amanda's fists curled at her sides. If ever she had wanted to knock someone's block off, it was now. Her eyebrows climbed higher. "Riley, cut it out," she ordered sweetly.

Riley grinned back at her mischievously. "Only if you agree to make an honest man of me."

"Now that would be hard to do."

"Not really," he said softly, his low sensual voice doing strange things to her insides. "Someone want to call the hospital chaplain?"

"Maybe he could help," Meg Lockhart-Carrigan said, already reaching for the phone at the nurses' station.

"I always knew there were sparks between the two of you," someone murmured.

"I didn't know they were this hot!" someone else chimed in.

The chaplain bustled into the throng. "Someone call?" Reverend Bleeker asked.

"Yes. I'd like to know if I can marry Amanda Witherspoon here and now," Riley said.

Reverend Bleeker's brow lifted. He had known them both since childhood, had borne witness to their youthful tomfoolery. "Is there a reason you're in such a hurry?"

Riley shrugged his broad shoulders. With maddening nonchalance, he clamped a hand on her shoulder and turned her back to face him. "It's the only way I can think to put an end to the scandal."

Amanda stared at him, her throat dry. She had to hand it to him. He was playing out this crazy hoax to the end.

Reverend Bleeker looked at Amanda.

All too aware of the warmth of Riley McCabe's strong, capable fingers radiating through her clothing to her skin, Amanda stated just as decisively, "I'm sure there's another way."

"I don't know how when the lives of our three unclaimed children are at stake," Riley countered with exaggerated sincerity.

Amanda started counting to ten. Slowly.

"Unless, of course, you're afraid to marry me," Riley continued. Leaning closer, he goaded Amanda relentlessly.

She shrugged free of his light restraining grip and propped her hands on her hips. "Why would I be afraid?" she retorted, telling herself she was not going to get roped into any wildly exciting romantic drama with him.

Riley lifted his broad shoulders in an indolent shrug. His eyes lasered into hers. "You tell me," he taunted.

"Actually, Riley, I'd love to marry you, right here and right now, in front of all these witnesses," Amanda fibbed, determinedly matching him jab for jab. "But it wouldn't be legal without a license."

Reverend Bleeker cleared his throat. "Actually," he corrected calmly, "it would be quite valid—as long as the two of you entered into this marriage in good faith."

Amanda did her best to retain her nerve. "Meaning?"

"You could get married right this very minute, if you wanted," Revered Bleeker reassured them with an encouraging smile.

Amanda's knees began to wobble. She struggled to keep a poker face. "What about a blood test?"

Reverend Bleeker spoke as much to the crowd gathering

in the hall of the pediatric wing as to the two of them. "None are required in Texas."

You're not helping me out here, Reverend, Amanda thought. "What about a license, then?" she asked, determined to find a face-saving way out of this mess Riley had gotten them into with his bravado. Not that she didn't deserve it, since years ago she had inadvertently pulled what had started out to be a peace offering and ended up being a very humiliating prank on him before she left town to go to nursing school in California, and he went off to college in Texas. She could hardly blame Riley if he didn't excuse her for embarrassing the heck out of him—she could hardly forgive herself.

"You have up to thirty days to apply for a license after you say your I Do's," Reverend Bleeker continued informatively.

Riley frowned, abruptly looking as concerned about the specifics of this mess they were suddenly in as Amanda felt. "Then what's that seventy-two hour waiting period all about?" Riley asked.

"That's how long it takes for the license to be valid, after the application is made," Reverend Bleeker explained.

And there was her out, Amanda thought. She wouldn't apply for a license. So the marriage would never be legal. Even if known prankster Riley goaded her into taking this ruse to the max. Which of course she hoped like heck he wouldn't. "Fine," Amanda said, looking at Riley and daring him to push her—and this farce—even one inch further, and see exactly what it got him. "Then let's do it!"

RILEY HAD EXPECTED Amanda Witherspoon to back out way before now. The fact she hadn't, impressed him almost as much as it irritated him. Not about to be the one to cry uncle in this battle of wills, he merely smiled, took her hand and said to Reverend Bleeker, "I'm every bit as ready to go through with this as Amanda."

Although Amanda's pretty smile stayed in place, Riley thought he saw her will falter just a bit as he looked into her eyes.

"Would you like to go to the chapel?" Reverend Bleeker asked.

And do this before all that was holy?

"No," Riley and Amanda said abruptly in unison.

"Here is fine," Riley stated, amazed to find the Reverend not harboring objections of his own. Instead, the chaplain appeared as if he had expected something like this from the two of them all along.

"Yes, let's do it right here," Amanda concurred. She turned to Riley and batted her eyelashes at him coquettishly. "So long as you realize, Riley, that I won't obey."

As if he were that crazy and naive! He had known, even as a kid, that Amanda Witherspoon was as headstrong as she was beautiful. "All I ask is that you honor me." Riley used his grip on her hand to tug her closer still. Damn, but she smelled good. More expensive, grown-up, and sexy than he recalled her in her youth, even with the hint of hospital antiseptic clinging to her clenched palm. "You can do that, can't you, Amanda?" he taunted.

Amanda replied with a delicate shrug and kept her eyes locked stubbornly with his. "Um. Sure." Her delicate brow furrowed. "I guess."

It was all Riley could do to keep from rolling his eyes as Revered Bleeker opened the small prayer book from the inside pocket of his blazer. "Very well," Reverend Bleeker said with a great deal less reluctance than Riley would have expected, "if there are no further objections…"

Unfortunately, Riley noted, there weren't.

"We are gathered here today to unite Riley McCabe and Amanda Witherspoon in marriage…Riley, do you take this woman…?"

For everything she's worth, including, and especially, her pride. "I surely do." Riley gave Amanda a crocodile smile and with great satisfaction saw her falter, just a little, again.

"Amanda, do you take this man…?"

Amanda flashed Riley a dirt-eating grin, that told him she was not, and had never been, a pushover. "Oh, I absolutely do," she agreed in a voice dripping with Texas sugar.

"Since we don't have rings we will dispense with that part of the ceremony," Reverend Bleeker said.

Thank goodness for small miracles, Riley thought, as he pushed away the unlikely but nevertheless sweetly lingering possibility of eventually getting Amanda in his bed. He didn't want this "union of hearts and souls" feeling any more real than it already did before he could get the deservedly embarrassed and humbled Amanda to cry uncle and legally undo it.

Out of the corner of his eyes, Riley saw hospital chief of staff, Dr. Jackson McCabe rounding the corner of the hall. Obviously, his uncle had been informed of what was going on and the talented surgeon looked none too pleased. Right behind Jackson was Riley's stepmother, Kate Marten McCabe, who was the hospital psychologist and grief counselor. She looked irked and exasperated as all get out, too.

"Riley, you may kiss your bride," Reverend Bleeker said.

And figuring it had to be better than the rest of the options facing him, Riley did.

Chapter Two

Amanda had figured Riley McCabe would kiss her. After all, it was the defining touch to his ridiculous prank. One, she knew, all of Laramie would be talking about for years to come. One that put her last accidental joke on him to shame.

But as he wrapped his arms around her in a straitjacket of warmth, tugged her close and lowered his lips to hers in a kiss that she knew darn well was all for show, all she could think about was how wildly sensual it felt to have his mouth on hers. Not in the hot, openmouthed manner she would have wished, had he been kissing her for real, but in the carefully close-mouthed variety popular on stage and screen.

A whisper of desire swept through her, followed swiftly by a flood of tingling. Her toes curled in her shoes. Her knees went weak. And she wanted more than anything to be able to kiss him back, really kiss him back. And that was when, of course, he let her go. Looking for a moment as oddly shaken and disturbed as she felt.

Which was, of course, ridiculous, Amanda reprimanded herself sternly, since all Riley had been doing was putting on a show for everyone around them who just happened to be there to unknowingly participate in this…sham!

As they stumbled apart, a cheer went up around them, followed by whistles and congratulations.

Riley dipped his head in acknowledgment, then took Amanda's hand firmly in his. Leading her through the fray, he dashed toward the elevator. Although Amanda had no desire to go anywhere with Riley right then, she did want to escape their audience. And that went double for Riley McCabe's stepmother, Kate, and the hospital's chief of staff, Jackson McCabe. Keeping a victorious smile she couldn't really begin to feel plastered on her face, she followed Riley into the otherwise empty lift.

As the steel doors closed behind them, Riley let go of her. Heart pounding, she leaned against the opposite wall, hands braced on the rail behind her. She glowered at him. "You know, I can believe you just seriously put a dent in *my* professional reputation. After all, you've had it out for me for years, Riley McCabe! But to use three unsuspecting little children and a hospital chaplain to do it…now that's low."

Riley punched in five and leaned back against the opposite rail. "I could say the same about you," he retorted evenly.

"You can't seriously deny you just set me up, but good!" Amanda admonished. "Pretending you and I were long-term lovers, with three illegitimate children to boot!"

Clearly aware he was annoying her terribly, he scanned her frame from head to toe, taking in the swell of her breasts and the curve of her hips before returning ever so deliberately to her face. He angled a thumb at his chest. "I don't deny employing my own particular brand of much-deserved payback on you just now."

"No kidding." Amanda continued to regard him accusingly. She had never been so embarrassed in her life!

"But I categorically deny setting you up," Riley insisted, as the elevator began to move and Christmas music filled the air.

Amanda felt herself flush self-consciously. She didn't know what her teenage nemesis was up to now, but she didn't like it one bit. And she especially didn't like the way he was continuing to look at her, as if he were imagining what it would be like to pick up where the chaste kiss had left off and make love to her here and now. Determined to irritate him as much as he was irritating her, Amanda blinked her eyes at Riley coquettishly. If he was pulling her leg, he was doing a damn fine job of it. "Then who did?" she inquired sweetly, wishing fervently all the while her heart would stop its telltale pounding and resume its normal beat. "Santa Claus?"

He tilted his head, gave her the kind of frankly male appraisal he had not been capable of in his youth. Back then she'd been dealing with a boy. Now he was all man. "Suppose you tell me. *Wife*," Riley commanded in a soft, derisive voice that did strange things to her insides.

If there was anything Amanda hated, it was being held accountable for something she did not do. That had happened to her a lot in the days she had been at "prankster war" with Riley McCabe. "I told you," she enunciated clearly, as another shimmer of awareness sifted through her, weakening her knees. "I. Don't. Know."

Steadfastly ignoring her goading manner, Riley moved so that he was towering over her once again. "Well, then," he countered grimly, "that makes two of us, because neither do I."

Amanda felt her pulse skitter and jump as shock set in. "You're serious!" She swallowed hard, still struggling to take it all in. "Aren't you?"

He nodded, "This once, yes I am."

Panic surged inside her and her heart began to gallop. This was like a bizarre dream! "Then if you really didn't do this… and I really didn't do it…" The blood drained from her face as she whispered tremulously, "Who did?"

Riley fell silent, shoved a hand through his hair, beginning to realize—as she was—the enormity of what had just happened. The elevator reached the top floor and the doors slid open. Riley took Amanda by the hand and led her to his office. It was in a state of disarray. Half-emptied boxes fought with diplomas ready to be hung on the wall. The only furniture currently in the room was a large desk and swivel chair.

"You promise me you don't know who those three kids are?" Riley asked yet again. He followed his question with a very sober, very probing look.

Amanda understood why he was having trouble believing her. There was little the two of them hadn't done to each other, back in their high school days. They'd covered every juvenile, teenage prank in the book, and then some, ending with Riley's managing to get a pet goat into her bedroom that had ended up eating the corsage from her senior prom, and her setting him up for what, she still suspected, had been the most humiliating, not-so-secret romantic rendezvous in his entire life.

"I would never use three innocent little children that way," Amanda reiterated emotionally. And she was beginning to realize, neither would he. Which left them where? she wondered. Another silence fell between them. They continued to survey each other, warily. "So who would have done something like this?" Amanda asked finally.

Riley's frown deepened. "I haven't a clue," he muttered.

"That Christmas card had your name on it," Amanda pointed out sagely. "Someone wanted those three children to end up with you."

"The question is why?" Riley mused, beginning to pace. He rubbed at the tense muscles in the back of his neck, looking more aggravated than ever.

Amanda hadn't a clue. She did know they were both suddenly over their heads. This was a situation for the professionals trained in such matters. "Maybe we should alert the authorities," Amanda suggested. "See what they can come up with."

Riley nodded his agreement, already reaching for the phone. "I'll put in a call to social services as well as my brother, Kevin.

He's a detective with the Laramie County Sheriff's Department."

"And while we're at it," Amanda said, quickly thinking ahead, relieved to have something else to focus on besides the two of them, "we better talk to the hospital administrator, too, since the abandonment happened on hospital grounds."

Riley nodded in agreement and he and Amanda made the calls from his office. As soon as they had finished, they went down to pediatrics. Mercifully, everyone who had witnessed their "wedding vows" seemed to have dispersed, including Riley's uncle, Jackson, and his stepmother, Kate. Amanda knew she and Riley were going to have to face up to what they had done—foolishly goading each other into a joke marriage—but that would come later, she decided firmly. After they took care of the children.

"I WAS BEGINNING to wonder when you were coming back," Laurel said as Amanda and Riley swooped into the pediatric playroom to claim the three children "left" in Riley's care.

"Or if," Laurel's friend, Micki Evans, added nervously. Unlike his little sister, who had a habit of getting in and out of all sorts of trouble, Micki was never one to cause anyone a moment's worry. Part of that was because Micki had been orphaned at fourteen, and only had a married older sister, who now lived in Colorado with her family, to rely upon. The rest, Riley supposed, was just personality. Laurel was dark haired and blue-eyed and so reckless and dazzlingly beautiful, guys couldn't take their eyes off her.

The petite Micki was red haired and freckled, and as serious about the future as she could be. The two young women were college roommates at University of Texas and best friends. Laurel had introduced her friend to Riley several years prior, and Riley had been mentoring the shy but studious Micki and helping her realize her ambition to attend medical school ever since. He'd even gone so far as to get Micki a summer internship in a Dallas hospital, where Riley had been on staff the previous summer, and then wrote a recommendation for her medical school applications earlier in the fall. Last he heard, she was still waiting to hear the result of her early-decision application to UT-Galveston med school.

"For all we knew, you two had left for your honeymoon already," Laurel said, only half joking, as she juggled the four-year-old Chloe on her lap.

Riley knew a veiled request for more information when he heard one. He had no intention of discussing his relationship with Amanda with his baby sister. "Amanda and I had a few things to discuss, about the kids," Riley said.

Micki was sitting on the sofa, with the infant Cory in one arm, the toddler Amber on the floor in front of her. None of the children were saying a word, yet seemed content as could be to simply hang out there. Which meant what? Riley wondered. Were the children used to being abandoned in strange places? Had this happened to them before? In their place, at their age, Riley would have been scared out of his mind. To the point that even Micki and Laurel, who were both great with kids and experienced babysitters, could not have calmed him. Yet these three children looked strangely accepting, almost numb.

"What's going to happen now?" Micki asked, as focused on detail as ever.

Riley hefted a diaper bag brimming with baby gear over his shoulder. "We're going up to my office to wait for the authorities and figure out what to do next."

"You're really concerned about them, aren't you?" Laurel marveled as they gathered up the children.

Riley knew his sister looked up to him, never more so than right now. For the first time in a long while, he didn't really feel he deserved it. "I'd be concerned about anyone in their situation," Riley said. "These three kids warrant better care." One way or another, before the day was done, he would see that they received it.

All three women looked uncomfortable at his blunt pronouncement. "Which is maybe why someone left the kids with you," Micki speculated after a moment as they crowded into the elevator. She maneuvered the stroller to the rear. "Because they knew what a good guy you were."

At the rear of the elevator, Amanda lifted a skeptical brow, but said nothing. It was clear she did not see him in quite the same way. Riley decided then and there to change her opinion of him. He didn't want Amanda thinking he was still the reckless, irresponsible, practical jokester she had known when they were teens. They were adults now. Hell, they were married—at least until they were able to correct their mutual foolhardiness. And they were going to have to work together at the hospital very soon. He wanted them dealing with each other from a position of mutual respect and maturity. The days of high emotion and impulsive behavior were past.

"Looks like your brother's here, at least," Amanda noted as the doors slid open and they moved out into the hallway once again. Riley followed her glance, catching sight of the tall, dark-haired man in the tan sheriff's department uniform and bone-colored Stetson. His youngest brother was an ace detective. Riley knew if anyone would be able to help them track down the origin of the children, Kevin would.

Kevin held the door for them, then followed them inside.

Finding a toddler wrapped around one of his legs, arms upraised, Riley reached down and picked her up. Aware how natural it felt to cradle the seventeen-month-old Amber in his arms, he asked, "Did you find out anything?"

"We don't have any reports of three children gone missing," Kevin stated grimly. Amber laid her head on Riley's chest. She put two fingers in her mouth and used her other hand to rub at the fabric of his sweater vest.

"I did, however, hear a report about two people getting married in a pretty big hurry, though." Kevin flashed them a teasing grin.

"Who told you?" Riley demanded irritably.

Immediately picking up on Riley's shift in mood, Amber frowned. It looked as if she might cry, so Riley widened his eyes and gave the little girl a great big smile to let her know it was okay. She relaxed in his arms once again, while Riley mentally reminded himself to watch his tone from here on out, lest he upset the kids.

Kevin touched the brim of his hat, pushing his Stetson farther back on his head. "It's all over town. And uh, just so you know, the news is sending pretty big shock waves through the family, too."

Riley could imagine. He hadn't faced off with Kate yet, but he figured he would have some more explaining to do as soon as his stepmother got hold of his father. When it came to family conundrums, Kate and his dad always handled things together. Which was probably why she hadn't chased him down thus far.

"Great," Riley murmured in an ultrasoothing voice at odds with the clearly exasperated content of his words. Out of the corner of his eyes, he caught Amanda's grin. "Now can we get back to the issue at hand?" he asked Kevin. "What are we going to do with the uh—you know?"

Kevin looked at Amanda, who had infant Cory in her arms, then back at Riley, who had toddler Amber in his arms, and over at Chloe, who was holding on to both Laurel's and Micki's hands for dear life. Kevin asked, "None of you have any idea who they are?"

At that, Chloe moved even closer to Micki and Laurel. The curly haired angel might not have said a word yet, but Riley was certain she hadn't missed one bit of what had been going on. The four-year-old absorbed words and actions like water into a sponge.

Riley shook his head in answer to Kevin's questions, while Amber sucked her thumb and laid her nearly bald head against his shoulder. "Aside from first names, no," Riley said, patting the toddler gently on the back.

Amanda looked serious now, too, as concerned and worried as Riley was beginning to feel. "I wish I did," she vowed, cradling Cory close to her chest. "But I can't remember ever seeing these children around the hospital or the community."

As Amanda was talking, social worker Felicia Winters joined them.

Amanda brought her up to date on everything that had happened thus far.

Felicia frowned. The plump gray-haired woman had worked for the county for nigh on thirty years. Her experience showed in the weathered lines of her face. "We have a real problem. There's no foster home available until mid-January, at the very earliest, that would allow us to keep them all together."

Big tears welled in the four-year-old's eyes. Noticing Chloe's distress, the toddler began to cry. Soon the infant and Chloe both joined in the cacophony of sound.

"You can't split them up," Amanda said to Felicia, over the din.

Riley agreed that would be too cruel, after what the children had already been through. "Their remaining security is tied to staying together," he said.

Felicia shifted the clipboard in her arms. "Believe me, I don't want to separate them but unless I get a suitable volunteer—a married couple—who can take all three children on an emergency basis, we'll have to place them in different homes."

At that, Chloe began to wail more loudly.

Amanda gestured for Riley to give her Amber, and swooped all three children into her arms simultaneously. "There, there, now," Amanda soothed firmly, patting them all on the back. "No one is going to make you leave each other. Riley and I are going to take very good care of you until we find your mommy and daddy."

Riley didn't know whether it was the conviction in Amanda's low, soothing voice or the tenderness of her touch that made the children calm down, but within a minute they were all quiet once again. She handed Chloe to Micki, Amber to Laurel, and Cory to Riley, then bent to rummage through the diaper bag and pulled out a bottle of formula. "Would you two please take the children down to the cafeteria for some lunch—and maybe stop by pediatrics on the way to warm this bottle for Cory—while we work on the specifics?" Amanda asked Micki and Laurel.

"No problem." The college coeds looked eager to leave the tense atmosphere of the room. Riley couldn't blame them.

"Riley and I will meet you there as soon as we are done here," Amanda promised, as Riley handed over the baby and then followed that with a crisp twenty-dollar bill meant to cover expenses.

"You-all take as much time as you need." Laurel smiled. "Micki and I can handle it." The girls put the children in the stroller and took off.

"You shouldn't have promised the children you and Riley would take them," Felicia Winters admonished as soon as they were alone again.

Riley hadn't intended to offer anything in terms of child care, and for good reason. He was a single guy, or at least he had been until an hour ago when his competitiveness and temper had gotten the best of him. He knew a lot about making sick kids well, and keeping children healthy, but nothing about how to take care of an infant, toddler and preschooler simultaneously. Furthermore, these weren't his kids. But the reaction of the children just now, coupled with Amanda's valiant offer, had changed all that.

"Amanda's right," Riley said. "The children are my responsibility. Whoever left them here today, left them with me." Like it or not, it was a task he couldn't abandon. "I'll take them."

"By yourself?" Felicia Winters blinked in surprise. Her expression turned skeptical. "Do you even have any experience with kids?"

Just the question he did not want to answer, Riley thought. "I'm a family doctor," Riley stated confidently. Looking over the petite Felicia's head, he saw the new respect in Amanda's eyes, found himself warming to it. "I can handle any medical issues that come up."

"Great," Felicia said dryly, as Amanda moved to stand right next to Riley, "but do you know how to change a diaper or make a bottle?"

"I'll help him," Amanda said, moving closer yet. "And I have plenty of experience with kids from newborn on up. I babysat my eight brothers and sisters as well as my nieces and nephews countless times."

Felicia exhaled. "I'd still feel better if I had a married couple."

"Actually," Kevin put in, looking eager to help, albeit in an ornery brotherly way, "Amanda and Riley are married as of noon today. In fact," Kevin continued with exaggerated seriousness, "they said their I Do's right here in the hospital's pediatric wing."

Thanks a lot, brother, Riley thought. He had been hoping not to bring their predicament into this. Too late, the county social worker was intensely interested.

Felicia looked at Amanda and Riley. "Is this true?"

Riley and Amanda nodded.

"So you're newlyweds—and you still want to do this?" Felicia asked in amazement. "Don't you have a honeymoon planned?"

Riley wished people would stop talking about that. It conjured up thoughts of hot, passionate lovemaking. And that was something that was definitely not going to happen between him and his temporary "wife." She'd caused him enough trouble already. If it weren't for her willingness to help him with the three abandoned kids he would have ended the farce of a union already. "Could we just go back to talking about the children?" he requested, making no effort to curtail his exasperation.

Felicia folded her arms in front of her and pressed her clipboard to her ample chest. "I'd prefer to talk about the two of you," she replied as Ted Keaton, the hospital's administrator, walked up. As always, the balding forty-something man looked as if he were in a hurry.

Caught up on what had happened thus far, the bespectacled five-foot-eight Ted said, "I can vouch for both of them. They're fine, upstanding people. Otherwise, they wouldn't work at this hospital. I didn't know about the romance." Ted paused to check the pager vibrating at his waist before turning it off. "Apparently, very few did, but that shouldn't make a difference, should it?"

"Not as long as it's a stable home situation," Felicia allowed.

"It will be," Riley promised quietly. He looked over at Amanda. She nodded her agreement, obviously as willing to put their personal issues aside as he was, in order to see Amber, Chloe and Cory's needs were met.

Felicia frowned before cautioning sternly, "If I agree to this, neither of you can bail out on me. I'd need your word you'll take care of the children until, at minimum, December 26."

With his brother on the case, there was no way it was going to take that long to find out where the kids really belonged, Riley thought. He looked at Amanda and shrugged. "You have it," Amanda and Riley said in unison.

The matter settled, Kevin left to file his report with the sheriff's department. Felicia Winters told them she'd start processing the paperwork and went on to her next case. As the hospital administrator was departing to answer his page, the phone on Riley's desk rang. He picked it up, listened, not liking what was being said on the other end of the connection. Finally, he exhaled. "We'll be right there," he promised.

"Right where?" Amanda asked curiously as Riley replaced the receiver on the base.

Beginning to feel as stressed out as Amanda now looked, Riley scowled and said, "The chief of staff's office. My uncle Jackson wants to see us." And that, Riley knew, could not be good.

"ALL RIGHT. Someone start explaining what's been going on here today," Jackson McCabe demanded as soon as the door was shut behind them. The talented general surgeon and devoted family man supervised Laramie Community Hospital's medical staff as smoothly as Riley's grandfather, John McCabe, had. Upsets like this were not encouraged. And as a new hire, with a previous reputation for playing way too many practical jokes, Riley knew it wasn't a conundrum he could afford to be caught in. Not if he wanted to be taken seriously as a family physician himself. Already regretting what his longstanding feud with Amanda Witherspoon had prompted him to do, Riley exchanged looks with Amanda. Neither knew exactly where to begin.

"Was the delivery of those three children a prank?" Jackson asked as Amanda eased into a chair.

Preferring to stand, Riley leaned up against a file cabinet. "Apparently not. Although we were both initially convinced that was the case."

Jackson rocked back in his swivel chair. "And then you blamed each other for their appearance?" he surmised.

Knowing this did not sound good, Riley folded his arms in front of him. He kept his voice even and matter-of-fact. "Yes."

"Whom do the children belong to?" Jackson asked as he picked up a pen and turned it end over end.

Delicate hands twined together in her lap, Amanda sat

stiffly in her chair. "We don't know. The police and social services are working on it. Meanwhile, Riley and I have been granted temporary custody of them."

Jackson's eyes widened. "You're sure you want to do this?" he asked.

Riley and Amanda looked at each other again. Realizing this was the one thing they agreed upon, Riley and Amanda both said in unison, "Yes."

Jackson set his pen down. "I'm surprised social services allowed that."

Riley shrugged. He slid his hands in the pockets of his slacks, and continued to lean against the file cabinet. "They didn't have much choice. All the foster homes are full."

Jackson mulled this over. "Was Felicia Winters's decision based in part on the fact you're married?"

"Yes." Amanda flushed.

"So it's a real marriage?" Jackson's brow rose.

Amanda swallowed and said nothing.

"I'm not sure how to answer that," Riley said finally.

"So in other words it is not," Jackson confirmed with a deeply disapproving look at both of them and a long disgruntled sigh.

Riley shoved a hand through his hair. He wished he didn't know his uncle so well, and vice versa. "Let's just say it's complicated," he said finally.

"Complicated?" Jackson echoed, looking even more outraged as he pushed his chair back from his desk. "Try disingenuous, at the very least."

What could they say to that? Riley wondered. It was true.

Jackson stood and flattened both hands on the desk in front of him. "Okay, then, here is what you two are going to do," he told them authoritatively. "You are going to collect those three children, go home with the three of them, and work this whatever-you-want-to-call-it out on your own time in your own way."

"But I have a shift to finish," Amanda protested emotionally. She rose to her feet, as well.

"Not anymore, Miss Wither—Mrs. McCabe. You're on an emergency leave for a honeymoon," Jackson said firmly. "Effective immediately."

Riley stopped slouching and moved away from the wall. He agreed they should be verbally chastised for the ruckus they'd caused earlier in the day, but an enforced leave was too much. "Don't you think you're carrying this a little too far?" he asked his uncle patiently.

Jackson turned his glare Riley's way. "I don't think so. And oh, by the way, you're on an emergency leave, too," Jackson told him. "Unless one of you wants to clear up any lingering misconception and tell everyone that you heartlessly used those children to further the longstanding feud between the two of you? And that your wedding was some big joke scripted strictly for the entertainment of the parents and patients in the pediatric wing?"

Riley wasn't going to confess to that and neither was Amanda since it could cost them temporary custody of the kids. And, like it or not, for the moment anyway, the welfare of the three abandoned children had to come first, before their personal comfort, even before their careers.

"In the meantime, I want you two to realize that everything you do reflects on this hospital," Jackson scolded. "Patients will not take you seriously unless you take yourselves seriously. And that goes double for the rest of the staff. You're not wild and crazy teenagers any more. You're married. You have three children who—thanks to your speedy nuptials— now have a home to go to for the Christmas holidays, so I suggest you take them there. When you are ready to apologize and make amends, call and make an appointment with my secretary. Then, depending on what you have to say, we'll go from there."

Chapter Three

Riley knew a golden opportunity to prove himself imperturbable when he saw it; he did his best to look as if the meeting with the chief of staff hadn't ruffled him in the least.

Amanda, on the other hand, looked as piqued as could be as they left Jackson McCabe's office. Her fair skin was lit with a riotous pink glow that matched the hue of her full soft lips. Her long-lashed turquoise eyes were sparkling with indignation. She had taken her hair out of its low ponytail just before entering Jackson's office and combed it with her fingers. Riley found he liked the way her dark blond mane looked, tumbling down around her slender shoulders, as much as he loved the way she filled out her nurse's uniform. Not that he could afford to be distracted by any of that just yet. Not while they were still technically married anyway…

"That went well, don't you think?" Riley commented as they took the fastest route to the cafeteria.

Amanda turned and shot him a drop-dead look, letting him know they were definitely not on the same page. Not now. Maybe not ever. "Just peachy. I always wanted to be put on administrative leave. Especially with you."

Okay, so maybe it hadn't gone so well. But griping and moaning about it wasn't going to change anything, Riley thought. The situation was what it was. The two of them were just going to have to deal with it. Given the fact his new "bride" slash partner in matrimony was not in the mood to discuss their punishment rationally, however, Riley decided a change of subject was in order. "Mind if I ask you a question?" he said casually, trying not to notice the provocative sway of her hips as she strode just ahead of him, trying her best to leave him in the dust.

Amanda exhaled, long and loud. She sent him another long-suffering glance over her shoulder. "If you feel you absolutely must."

Riley lengthened his strides to catch up. "Earlier, when we were talking to social services, why did you volunteer to help out like that?" He wouldn't have expected it from the Amanda he knew in high school. She never would have aligned herself with him, even momentarily, no matter what was at stake.

Amanda's shoulders stiffened. She refused to meet his gaze. "It wasn't for you."

Riley moved ahead to hold the door for her. "That much I gathered."

Her shoulder brushed his chest as she stepped past him into the stairwell. "It was for the children," Amanda continued as Riley shut the door behind them, closing them in the deserted passageway. Grabbing onto the railing with her right hand, she made her way carefully down the cement steps. "Their situation breaks my heart."

"Mine, too," Riley said, as he descended alongside her.

"And there's something else I noticed," Amanda said as they reached the first landing and circled around to the next set of stairs. She paused to regard him seriously. "In our line of work, you and I have both seen children who did not receive the care they should have had."

Sadly, Riley knew that was true.

Amanda swallowed and began climbing downward once again, slower now. "Those three kids do not act like children who have never known love."

Riley matched his strides to hers. Hands on her shoulders, he stopped her on the next landing, and turned her to face him. He surveyed the conflicted expression on Amanda's face that had appeared the moment they had both decided—impulsively, as usual—to jointly manage the guardianship of the children, even if it meant continuing their "marriage" a little while longer. "Meaning what?"

Amanda tilted her face up to his. "Someone out there obviously cares about them," she told him passionately. "Otherwise that person would not have left them with you, so they could have the kind of Christmas all children deserve."

"You think that person is going to come back for them?" Riley offered matter-of-factly, resisting what now seemed an ever-present urge to haul her in his arms and kiss her again. This time, without restraint.

Amanda nodded. "By December 26, if not sooner," she stipulated soberly. "When that person or persons shows up they are going to need our help. I want to be there when that happens. So," she released a long breath, and followed that with an equally telling look, before continuing in a determined voice, "if it means we stay technically married for the next week or so, before we undo what we so foolishly did a few hours ago, I figure we can soldier through."

Put it kindly, why don't you? Riley thought.

"So long as you understand," she went on firmly, as a fresh wave of color flowed into her cheeks, "this is merely a technicality to make social services—and the chief of staff—feel better about our situation."

Riley dropped his hands, stepped back. "So no sex, hmm?" No thinking about what it would be like to momentarily let their defenses down, and let the past be just that, and discover what it might be like if they were as well-matched in the bedroom as they had been in practical-joke-administration.

Suddenly seeming to be able to read his mind all too well, Amanda declared flatly, "Not even a whisper of it."

Riley would have liked to say the thought of making love to Amanda had never crossed his mind. But it had…. During the kiss, he had wondered if the rest of her was as soft and feminine as her lips. What would she do if he gave passion free rein and crushed that sweet mouth of hers under his? Would she be as feisty and unrestrained in her lovemaking as she had always been in her mischief? And how much longer before he found out?

"SO WHAT NOW?" Riley's baby sister asked moments later from her perch in the hospital cafeteria, after Riley had explained to Micki and Laurel what had transpired with the authorities.

"We're taking the kids back to my place for the time being," Riley said.

"And then?" Micki asked as she put the empty bottle back in the overflowing diaper bag.

"We keep looking for their parents or guardians, right along with social services," Riley said.

Micki and Laurel exchanged uncertain glances.

"But not to worry." Amanda smiled reassuringly. "I'm sure we'll be able to manage the three of them between the two of us. And regardless of how long it takes to get things—um—settled—Riley and I will see the children have the very best holiday possible."

Both young women relaxed visibly. "We'll be around if you need extra help," Laurel offered.

"Thanks." Riley smiled at his sister's typically generous offer. "But I think, right now anyway, that Amanda and I can take it from here."

They got the children's winter jackets, hats and mittens on. Then headed out, getting smiles and nods of approval from everyone they passed. Riley could tell from the way people were smiling at them that the rumor mill had been working overtime, and everyone thought the children were theirs. He considered correcting the misimpression, then decided against it. The truth—that social services and the sheriff's department were now involved—would get out soon enough.

"We've got a problem, Riley," Amanda said as he pushed the triple stroller out into the parking lot, toward his five-passenger SUV.

Actually, Riley thought, they had a bunch of them. He looked over at her in bemusement. "What's that?"

"We don't have car seats. And it's against state law to transport children in a vehicle without them."

"Good point," Riley murmured as he stopped just short of the driver's door. To his amazement, inside the vehicle, were two safety seats, and a booster seat. All properly installed on the backseat. He turned and looked at Amanda, not sure whether to feel relieved—that this major safety issue had been taken care of—or really aggravated. Truth was, he felt a little of both. He didn't like the feeling that some unidentified person was always one step ahead of him, manipulating and arranging. He was used to taking charge of his life, not feeling as if he was a victim of circumstances far beyond his control. "What the," he muttered in stunned amazement, loud enough for only Amanda to hear. "Who did this?"

Amanda stared at the rear seat. "I have no idea." She regarded him, clearly perplexed, then bent to lift Chloe out of the stroller. "Was your vehicle locked?"

"No," Riley admitted reluctantly as he picked up Amber. People in Laramie didn't have to lock their cars every second of every day.

Amanda set Chloe in her car seat, then turned to get baby Cory. "Maybe it was the same person who left the kids," she speculated.

More than ever, Riley wanted to know who that person was. "Do you know how to work these?" Riley asked, looking at the maze of straps and buckles on Amber's seat.

To his relief, Amanda did, and she leaned inside the vehicle to show him how.

Since it was located only a few streets away from the hospital, the drive to his house was accomplished quickly. Amanda took charge of baby Cory. Riley picked up Chloe and Amber and carried them both inside. All business, Amanda strode through the foyer, past the living room, to the kitchen. "We should probably do a quick inventory of your fridge and pantry and figure out what we're going to need to take care of them, and then go from there," Amanda said, over the infant's head.

"Good idea," Riley replied.

Amanda swung open the fridge and surveyed the contents—barbecue sauce and jelly, juice, milk, coffee, soda and beer. "Well," she drawled finally, shooting him a look, "you're definitely a bachelor."

Riley refused to feel embarrassed about the meager fare. "Give me a break. I just moved in a few days ago."

Amanda arched a delicate brow. "And yet managed to decorate the place from top to bottom?"

Riley followed her glance. The gray two-story frame house with the black shutters and doors was located in the historic section of Laramie. It had been built in the 1920s and lovingly maintained. "I bought it furnished, right down to the dishes and bath towels."

Amanda blinked. "You're kidding."

Did she really think he had selected the French chairs and settee in the formal living room, the gold-and-white toile drapes on the windows, and the antique Italianate dining room set?

Riley moved from the updated kitchen with cherry cabinets, stainless steel appliances and black marble countertops to the adjacent family room. The floor-to-ceiling windows brought in plenty of light. The brick fireplace made it homey, the large sectional sofa and entertainment armoire as comfortable as he needed it to be. This was the room where he hung out most of the time. The room, Riley couldn't help but note, that Amanda and the kids seemed to like the most.

"The woman I bought it from is a professional decorator and avid shopper," Riley continued, "and when I heard she was planning to auction off everything in here and start over in her new place, I made her an offer she couldn't refuse. Worked for both of us. I got a ready-made home and she got the funds to outfit her new place."

"Obviously, groceries didn't come with the deal," Amanda remarked dryly, walking back to eye his equally empty walk-in pantry.

"Sadly, no. Although I'm not sure that would have worked for both of us nearly as well, anyway. Mrs. Barker was heavily into macrobiotics and vegan. And I'm more of a meat-and-potatoes take-out kind of guy."

Amanda's glance briefly roved his tall, muscular frame. She seemed to find nothing to complain about there, Riley noted with pleasure.

"Heaven help us then," Amanda murmured as she propped the drowsy infant on her shoulder and patted his back until he uttered an adult-size burp.

"Want me to make a run to the grocery?"

Amanda nodded. "We're going to need diapers and formula and baby food—toddler variety—as well as foods suitable for a four-year-old."

Riley tried not to notice how maternal—and angelically beautiful—Amanda looked as she tended the children, even as he rummaged around for a paper and pen. Yet he sensed that she was still the same jokester she'd always been. A person couldn't change *that* much. He might be married to her—temporarily—but he wasn't in the market for a practical joker of a wife. No, when he married, he didn't want to be worried about what might be under his pillow or in his breakfast cereal. Nor did he want to have to be a continual court jester, there to provide maximum entertainment, the way he had been with Amanda years ago. Next time around…hopefully the last time around…he wanted to be free to be himself. Mature. Adult. Able to enjoy a good joke as well as the next person, but not constantly expected to deliver one. Their initial response to each other proved there was still plenty of "spark" between him and Amanda, in that regard.

"We'll also need plenty of whole milk, peanut butter, cheese and bread."

Riley had already forgotten the first few items on the list. He'd been too busy concentrating on Amanda, and his reaction to her. He jotted down what she had just said. "That sounds like a lot."

Amanda looked over his shoulder. "Or in other words," she guessed dryly, "too much for you to handle purchasing on your own."

Riley hedged, torn between pride and common sense. Grocery shopping usually took him a while, even when only a few things were on the list.

"Never mind, that look on your face is answer enough. Why don't we do some quick diaper changes and take Chloe to the bathroom, then all go to the store?"

That sounded like even more of an ordeal, Riley thought. Just getting them in and out of coats and car seats took a good ten minutes. "Shouldn't they nap or something?" he asked, beginning to understand what a huge task he had undertaken in volunteering to care for all three children at once.

Amanda's eyes glimmered with unchecked amusement. "Do they look sleepy to you?"

Anything but, Riley admitted reluctantly to himself, telling himself he was not going to get overwhelmed here.

"I think they'll be fine," she continued in a reassuringly matter-of-fact voice. "If not," she shrugged her slender shoulders affably, "we'll regroup, and come up with another plan. Besides, with the two of us there, it shouldn't take long."

The next few minutes were spent getting the children ready to go out again. Amanda put the sleeping infant back in the carrier and Riley carried the older children back out to the SUV. As Riley situated them in their safety seats, the two older children regarded him curiously. The four-year-old was seriously sucking her thumb, the toddler, her first two fingers. Neither was saying a word.

"So," Riley said, hoping now that she'd been around him a little more, Chloe would offer some helpful information. "Where are you kids from? Not Laramie, I know. If you were from around here, someone would have recognized you over at the hospital."

To Riley's mounting disappointment, she was as silent and uncommunicative as she had been when Kevin and Felicia Winters saw her at the hospital.

Riley could tell by the way Chloe was looking at him that she understood what he was asking, she just wasn't in a mind to cooperate with him. At all. Tamping down his frustration, his eagerness to get to the story behind the children's delivery to him, he tried again gently, "What's your last name? Where do you live? Do you have a dog? Cat? Grandma?" And who exactly was the Santa Claus in the note?

"They're not going to tell me anything, are they?" Riley whispered to Amanda, when the silence continued unabated.

"Give them time," she whispered right back, looking at that moment a lot more patient and understanding than Riley felt.

Time, Riley thought, was the one thing he did not want to surrender. It had only been a few hours, and already, he could feel himself beginning to feel somewhat responsible for the welfare of the kids. The McCabes were responsible stand-up kind of people who never turned their back on family or friends. Which meant that however these three kids had been delivered to his care, he had to see them through the Christmas holidays to safe harbor again. Period. He could not in good conscience do otherwise. Had they simply been pediatric patients of his, he could have kept a professional distance, while still caring for and about them. But he was assuming the role of "Daddy" here, however temporarily, a role that had much heavier emotional and psychological implications. And with Christmas Day still a week away…

What if the kids began to look at him as a parent figure instead of a guardian? What if they began to depend on him emotionally? Despite what the person or persons who had left them with him thought, Riley was not prepared to take on the three kids alone. Nor would it be fair to Amanda to ask her to help out indefinitely. Especially since Riley knew darned well that what worked in the short term might not be at all viable in the long run. No matter what happened next, Riley surmised grimly, the five of them were in one heck of a quandary.

"Wow. Three kids and a wife, all in one day. But then I guess you already knew about the kids, huh, Doc? I mean, there's no way you couldn't have," the young male clerk at the grocery store continued, suddenly looking as awkward and embarrassed as Riley felt.

Not about to get into the details of the children's abandonment while they were all right there, listening, Riley passed on the opportunity to correct the wrong assumption. The gossip mill would bring everyone up to date eventually. Soon everyone would know that the sheriff's department and social services were now involved.

Amanda looked at Riley. She was obviously thinking the same thing: it didn't matter what anyone else thought about them right now—they had to protect the children.

Riley turned back to the teenage clerk, "It's amazing. I'll tell you that." Hoping to discourage further comment, Riley turned his attention to the diapers and formula and baby food passing by on the conveyer belt.

Beside him, Amanda had her face nestled in the neck of infant Cory, while soothing Amber, who was buckled into the metal cart's toddler seat, with gentle strokes of her hand. Beside her, Chloe stood, an arm wrapped around Amanda's leg. As Riley paid for their purchases, he couldn't help but note how great Amanda was with the kids, and they with her. And he couldn't help but contrast the woman beside him with the Amanda he had known, years ago.

Without warning, his thoughts returned to the last prank she had played on him. It had been the night before he was set to leave for college, and she'd sent a note to him through mutual friends, telling him she was ceding victory of their four-year-long competition to him. Riley hadn't been surprised. Getting that pet goat into her bedroom without the cooperation or knowledge of any member of her family had been darned difficult. He felt he had won. Hands down.

So when she had sent him a note, asking him to meet her behind the bleachers of the high school stadium that night, saying she wanted to declare peace once and for all, he hadn't been averse to the idea. Something about the words she had written, and the way she'd been looking at him those last few weeks, had made him think—foolishly, he now realized—that Amanda had a giant crush on him. One that matched his secret crush on her. He'd gone to the rendezvous spot, and then waited and waited and waited. Predictably, Amanda had never showed, but unbeknownst to him, her friends had—and they'd snapped photos of him waiting wistfully in the moonlight, bouquet of wildflowers in his hands—with the long-distance lens from the school photography lab.

The photos—and the story of his foolishness—had made the rounds of everyone in the senior class by the time Riley and Amanda had both left for their respective colleges the next day. It had taken years for Riley to live that fiasco down. And now there was—albeit not by either of their doing—another chapter to add to the list. He had never expected to be involved with her again, never mind in quite this way. Although, Riley noted, as he wheeled the cart out to the lot, and hit the remote to unlock his SUV, she seemed to be handling the situation a lot better than he was. To his irritation, the more uneasy he became about the task ahead, the more relaxed she became. Maybe because—unlike him—she really seemed to be in her element here, as she simultaneously tended to all three kids.

Appreciating the way she looked with her dark blond hair tumbling over the cranberry-red muffler she had wrapped around her neck, he murmured, "This kind of responsibility doesn't throw you at all, does it?"

Amanda smiled back at him, looking trim and pretty in her long black winter coat, as she helped Chloe climb up into her safety seat. "I wouldn't think it would rattle you, either, given the fact we both grew up in large, chaotic families."

Riley lifted Amber out of the cart seat and carried her around to the other side of the vehicle. "We only had six kids in ours." Five boys, one girl.

"Only six," Amanda teased as she buckled baby Cory into his safety seat, too.

Riley shrugged as he struggled with the three-point restraint on Amber's seat. "Compared to your family's nine kids…" Six wasn't a lot.

Making sure everyone was in safely, they shut the doors and returned to the cargo area to load their groceries. "And now, temporarily, you and I are mutually in charge of three," Amanda asserted, briefly looking as astonished about that as Riley.

Riley liked their new feeling of camaraderie. But then, people always pulled together in a crisis. "Which perhaps wouldn't seem so difficult if I had any kind of babysitting experience at all," he continued affably.

Amanda's shoulder brushed his as they tossed diapers in next to the cans of formula. "Not to worry, Doc. I'll teach you everything you need to know."

Aware being this close to Amanda was putting all his

senses into overdrive, Riley forced himself to keep his mind on the task at hand instead of harboring fantasies of kissing her again. "You really enjoy being around kids, don't you?"

Amanda tipped her head back to look at him, but didn't move away. Obviously, she had no clue as to the direction of his thoughts. "I love it," she said softly.

"Which begs the question." Riley paused to search her face. "Why haven't you had any of your own yet?"

Riley saw her smile fade and her eyes go dark almost instantaneously. "The time has never been right," she said quietly.

Beyond that, she clearly did not want to discuss it. Realizing a change of subject was in order, Riley said, "The children seem to like you."

The sadness in her eyes fading only slightly, Amanda picked up a package of diapers and tossed it into the cargo area. Color filled her cheeks. "All children like me."

Abruptly, Riley felt as if she were pushing him away. The realization disturbed him. The last hour or so of mutual purpose had united him with Amanda in a way he had never expected. And it had made him realize something else. Something adult. He wanted to be closer to Amanda, to be able to look into her eyes and know their jokester past was just that, and she was as ready as he to move on to a more mature relationship. One that allowed them to talk intimately and honestly to each other, without always having to have their guards up. Right now, she was a mystery he wanted to solve. And the first step toward that would be to understand what was going on in that pretty head of hers and driving her actions. "You mean, because you're a nurse?" he asked.

To Riley's frustration, Amanda seemed to get even further away from him emotionally as she recited in a low, battle-weary voice, "Because I have the touch. I'm just a natural-born baby wrangler." She paused, her teeth raking the soft lusciousness of her lower lip. "It probably has something to do with growing up the second oldest of nine children. I spent my entire childhood helping take care of my younger siblings. It's only natural I would have picked up some skill at it along the way."

And now she thought he was using that skill—and hence, her—to his own advantage. Perhaps even being nice to her, just so she would help him. "I appreciate you helping me out here," Riley said.

Amanda sent him an even more skeptical look. "Sure."

Well, that certainly helped ease the tension, Riley thought dryly. But then he knew, as did she, that words were cheap. It was actions that counted. He would have to demonstrate to her that he had changed—just as he hoped she had—and that now that they'd put the mutual gags behind them, she could trust him again. And that was going to take time.

The two of them were silent as he drove back to his house. When they arrived, they discovered three large suitcases by the front door.

"Those wouldn't by any chance happen to be yours, would they?" Riley asked hopefully. Amanda shook her head, beginning to look as exasperated and wary as he felt. Feeling irked that the mysterious goings-on had not stopped, Riley parked and got out of the vehicle. He helped Amanda extricate all three children from their safety seats. Together, they headed for the front door. A quick peek inside the suitcases revealed the belongings of all three kids.

Amanda surveyed Riley over the tops of the children's heads. "You know what this is, don't you?" she commented softly. "Yet another sign that someone still cares, maybe more than that person would like to admit," she continued, speaking to Riley in a code the children were unlikely to be able to decipher.

Which meant that person or persons would eventually be back to claim them, thereby absolving he and Amanda of the responsibility for them, Riley realized slowly. Wondering why that idea wasn't as comforting as he would have expected, Riley helped Amanda get the children inside, then returned alone to unload the groceries. He was almost done when another car pulled up at the curb. Laurel and her friend Micki hopped out.

"I just thought I should warn you," Laurel told him hurriedly.

"Warn me about what?" Riley was about to demand when another car pulled up behind Laurel's and he saw the reason for his kid sister's concern.

NOT SURPRISINGLY, Riley's stepmother, Kate Marten McCabe wasted no time in getting to the point.

"Perhaps Laurel and Micki could watch the children for a few minutes while your father and I talk to you and Amanda," Kate told Riley, in the same direct, no-nonsense manner she had used on him and his brothers when he was an out-of-control teenager, dealing with his grief over his mother's death.

"I think Amanda can be excused from this," Riley said. He looked from his petite blond stepmother to his tall, fit father. It was one thing for his parents to be treating him as if he were still a kid, another thing for them to be addressing Amanda that way.

"Amanda needs to hear what we have to say, too," Sam declared. The owner of his own Dallas-based computer software company, he was as blunt and down-to-earth as he was successful.

"We'll just be upstairs, somewhere," Laurel announced discreetly. She took the infant. Micki picked up the toddler and took the four-year-old's hand. The five disappeared up the staircase. Seconds later, a door shut. Silence fell as Riley and Amanda sat down in the living room opposite Sam and Kate.

"I thought you two had outgrown pranks like this a long time ago," Kate said with a disapproving frown.

So had Riley. Until the moment he had dared Amanda to

marry him and she had upped the ante and actually gone through with it.

"It was one thing when the two of you were toilet-papering each other's houses and soaping the windows of each other's cars, all through high school," Sam added.

Riley thought about all the times he had "fixed" Amanda's locker so everything she owned would come tumbling out, and the time she had "jammed" his so all sorts of feminine hygiene products would come flying out, when he finally managed to get it open. She'd bested him on that one, too. But he'd gotten her good, a couple times. Most notably when he had her believing her favorite rock star had just been spotted in Greta Wilson McCabe's Lone Star Dance Hall, conferring with Greta's friend, real-life movie star, Beau Chamberlain. He grinned, thinking not so much of her star-crazed antics, as the temper tantrum—directed strictly at him—that had followed. Amanda was one beautiful woman when she lost her cool....

"But you're adults now," Kate continued sternly.

"One would certainly hope so," Sam frowned. "Your actions today would seem to indicate otherwise."

Riley knew his parents were upset and disappointed in him. On one level, he was disappointed in his own behavior, too. He should never have let Amanda get to him that way. Even if he had suspected—for one heated hour, anyway—that she was responsible for the appearance of the three kids. He should have let cool reason instead of his emotions prevail.

"And I'm sure your family would agree with me on that," Sam continued, all parental concern.

Amanda flushed, finally beginning to look as uncomfortable as Riley felt.

"Maybe they won't ever have to hear about it since they live in California now," Riley contended, doing everything he could to protect the woman at his side. "Especially if we're able to wrap it up soon and get the kids back where they belong, our hasty marriage will be declared null and void."

Amanda nodded and edged slightly closer to Riley. "I'm certainly not planning to tell my family about this," she echoed.

"You may not have to," Kate warned. "Your family still knows many people here in Laramie. And news like an impromptu marriage brought on by the appearance of three small children seldom stays quiet for long."

No kidding, Riley thought, in weary resignation. Word of their wedding in the hospital hallway had spread faster than a wildfire after a drought.

"We're going to sort this marriage thing out eventually," Amanda reassured his parents quietly.

"When the time is right," Riley agreed. Grateful his new "bride" was handling this uncalled-for intrusion so well, he reached over and briefly touched her hand.

"Meanwhile," Amanda continued with building confidence, "our plan is simply to care for the children to the best of our ability and wait for their parents or guardians to return." She shrugged and looked to Riley for emotional support. He gave it to her in spades.

"I mean, obviously the children have been well loved," Amanda continued matter-of-factly. "Sooner or later, someone has to show up to claim them and set the record straight…."

"And if they don't?" Kate asked bluntly.

"We'd obviously have to reassess our situation. But we're still days—maybe even weeks—away from that point," Amanda continued firmly.

"Did you mean what you said to my parents?" Riley asked Amanda seriously as soon as his parents had left.

Amanda released a short, impatient breath and continued to hold his eyes like a warrior princess in battle. "I didn't ask to be plopped into the middle of this mess, but I intend to do whatever is necessary to see these children's needs are met, even if it means voluntarily extending my leave from the hospital or taking vacation time. Although, obviously," Amanda continued fiercely, keeping her voice slightly above a whisper as she went to the kitchen to begin putting away the groceries they had brought in minutes earlier, "you and I can't stay married to each other indefinitely, Riley!"

Riley paused thoughtfully, then jumped on ahead. "Maybe we should."

Chapter Four

Amanda stared at Riley. She did not know how he could continue to look so cool, calm and collected after the events of the last four hours, especially when she felt so frazzled. She stepped closer so they were toe-to-toe. "Have you lost your mind?" she demanded, tipping her head up to his.

A slow, sexy smile crossed his handsome face. "Well, think about it," he drawled, in a husky voice that drew her even deeper into this escapade with him. "We're looking pretty foolish right now for having succumbed to our tempers and one-upped each other right into the state of holy matrimony. The chief of staff and my parents are right. If we back out we're going to look like a couple of reckless kids. On the other hand," he rubbed a hand across his close-shaven jaw, "if we stick with it, and pretend to give it a try—at least for a few months—our maturity would likely no longer be in question."

"Months!" Amanda echoed in disbelief. She couldn't pretend to be his wife for that long!

Riley rested his large, capable hands on her shoulders, keeping her in front of him when she would have pivoted—and run. He shrugged off her concern. Continuing to radiate a distinctly male satisfaction, he smiled at her reassuringly. "Once we've established to the community we are not still a couple of 'reckless kids,' then we can always say we gave it a shot and get a quiet, civilized divorce."

He really had covered all the angles. Except perhaps the most important one. "I don't want to be divorced again."

Riley blinked, dropped his hands and repeated in stunned amazement, *"Again?"*

Aware her shoulders felt cold and bereft where the warmth of his palms had been, Amanda replied in an embarrassed tone, "I really don't want to discuss this, Riley."

"Well, I do," he retorted, an emotion she couldn't define in his amber eyes. Riley paused, clearly caught off guard by her revelation. "You could have told me you were married before."

Amanda flashed him a sassy smile she couldn't really begin to feel, considering the mess they were in. "And when exactly would that have been?" she returned softly. "Before or after or perhaps *during* the interlude where you claimed those kids were mine as well as yours, hauled me in front of the hospital chaplain and demanded I marry you and make an honest man of you?"

Riley grimaced, conceding her victory. "Okay, point taken." He shoved both his hands through his hair.

Amanda noted the disarray his angst had brought to his rumpled, sun-streaked light brown hair, and wondered if the shiny clean strands were as soft and touchable as they looked. With effort, she forced her attention back to the subject at hand. "I'm glad you agree."

Another loaded silence fell between them. "Aren't you going to tell me about it?" Riley asked eventually, his curiosity unabated.

Amanda shrugged, her hurt and humiliation over that period of her life now a distant memory. She wanted to keep it that way. "There's not much to tell," she told Riley matter-of-factly. "I fell in love with a newly divorced doctor some ten years my senior when I was fresh out of nursing school, and married him. Five years later, he decided he had never loved me after all and went back to his first wife, who was also the mother of his two children. And you know what the worst part of it was? I knew it was a mistake way before that, but because of the kids, and the way they had depended on me to mother them whenever they were with Fraser, I stayed on anyway."

"Are you still in contact with the children?"

"No." Amanda swallowed around the lump in her throat. "My ex and his wife asked me to step aside and allow them to put their family together again, without reminders of the time they had spent apart. So I did."

"That must have been really difficult for you."

Amanda nodded, glad she hadn't had to explain to Riley how much the whole experience had hurt her, or how wary she was of letting herself get into such an emotionally devastating situation again. "Anyway, since then I've been a little more careful," Amanda said quietly. She hadn't dated anyone with children. Or continued seeing anyone who didn't seem thoroughly smitten with her from the get-go. Until now, anyway. "So what about you?" Amanda pushed her thoughts away from herself. "Is this…whatever it is we are in…your first marriage?"

Riley nodded, serious now. "But I came close to getting hitched two years ago," he told her, the walls around his emotions already going up. If there was one thing Amanda could identify from bitter experience, it was a man holding her at arm's length. Determined not to let Riley shut her out the way her ex had, she studied him. "I have the feeling there's more to this story." A reason why he had brought up his near miss to matrimony. "What haven't you told me?"

A troubled light came into Riley's eyes. His voice dropped a notch. "I've been thinking. There's no way on this earth Evangeline could have given birth to either the older or younger children and had them be mine. I saw her every week during the six years we dated—she was never pregnant. But the toddler was conceived about the time Evangeline and I broke up."

Worry swept Amanda that this situation they were in was all too real and potentially heartbreaking. "You think she might have had the baby and not told you about it?"

"It doesn't seem likely. But neither does the delivery of three children on my doorstep, so to speak." Riley paused, and looked all the more distressed. "What if one of the children is mine?"

Then Amanda was going to be the odd woman out again. But not about to admit to Riley that was how she felt, she forced a commiserating smile. "Then I'd say Evangeline has a heck of a lot of explaining to do."

"I agree." Riley looked Amanda in the eye. "Which is why I think the sooner we talk to her the better."

Aware they still had a lot of groceries to put away, Amanda went back to emptying sacks, while Riley attended to filling the fridge and cabinets. "Where is she?"

"Dallas. She's a physician at the hospital where I did my residency."

"Are you going to call her?"

Riley stood with a jar of baby food in each hand. "I think under the circumstances that this is a discussion better had face-to-face."

Amanda didn't know whether to be relieved or disappointed. "So, you want me to stay here with the kids?" she asked.

"No." Riley put the last of the supplies away, then turned to face her. "I want you and all three of the kids to go with me."

"SO HOW DO YOU WANT to do this?" Riley asked three and a half hours later as he parked in front of a contemporary seven-story condominium building in a trendy neighborhood of Fort Worth, Texas.

"I was thinking I'd just take Amber in and get their reaction to each other first."

For reasons she didn't want to examine closely, Amanda preferred not to meet the woman Riley had nearly married who might have borne his child.

"I'll just sit here with Chloe and give baby Cory his bottle," Amanda volunteered.

Unfortunately, no sooner had Riley left the car with Amber and disappeared into the lobby of the building, than Chloe began to cry. Her tears sparked wails from baby Cory.

"Riley and Amber will be right back," Amanda soothed.

To no avail.

Chloe became even more hysterical at the idea of being separated from one of her siblings.

With a beleaguered sigh, Amanda decided there was only one thing to do. Join 'em.

RILEY HAD LET Evangeline know he was en route to see her. When he had spoken to her briefly on the phone, she had reluctantly agreed to give him five minutes of her time if he met her at home this evening. Since they hadn't exactly parted amicably, Riley knew that was a major concession on her part.

Still, nothing could have prepared him for the sight of his ex-lover clad in one of the sexiest and most revealing negligees he had ever seen. Cut down to her navel in front, several inches below the waist in back, the black satin fabric clung to her hips and thighs before ending at midcalf.

Barefoot, with her inky-black hair tousled, she looked as if she had just crawled out of bed.

Taking a look at the toddler cradled in his arms, she frowned. "I hope you're not expecting me to babysit."

"Not unless Amber is your baby, too," Riley said.

Evangeline let out a peal of laughter that echoed in the elegant hall.

Behind Riley, the elevator doors opened on the sounds of two crying children. Amanda hurried toward him, staggering under the weight of the child in each of her arms.

Seeing Amber, Chloe wailed even harder. She held out her arms to her baby sister, who, seeing Chloe and baby Cory crying, began to sob, too.

"Darlin'," a low male voice called from behind Evangeline. A sexy, twenty-something stud wrapped only in a sheet, a cowboy hat tipped rakishly on his head, swaggered out to join them. "What's going on?" the young man asked.

Behind Riley, other apartment doors began to open. Irritated looks were thrown their way.

Evangeline rolled her eyes. "Come in here before I get a noise violation!" she demanded, ushering everyone inside her luxurious home.

Everything was white—furniture, drapes, rug. Even the Christmas tree that stood in the corner was a white-flocked artificial tree.

"What's this about?" the man continued, perplexed. "Who are these people?"

"A long and amusing story, I am sure." Evangeline patted her young lover on the arm. "Wait for me in the bedroom, hon. This won't take long."

"All right." The stud detoured to the bar, where he grabbed a bottle of wine. "But if you're not back in five, I'm coming back out to get you!" He disappeared around the corner.

Now that the children were reunited, they had all stopped crying.

"Well?" Evangeline looked at Riley.

Riley took Chloe from Amanda and cradled the four-year-old in his other arm, so Amanda was only holding the infant, Cory. "These three children were left for me at Laramie Community Hospital," Riley explained.

"What does that have to do with me?" Evangeline asked

with an accusing look. She looked irritated that he had bothered her. "They're not sick, are they?"

"They seem to be in fine health. The note stated that they needed me to be their daddy."

Evangeline paused to compute that information. Her precisely plucked eyebrows lifted in inquisitive fashion. "Why?"

Riley abruptly released his breath, his frustration mounting. "That's what I'm trying to figure out."

Evangeline tilted her head at him. She was still beautiful but also one of the most emotionally contained people he had ever met. Next to Amanda's fire and warmth, well…it was difficult for Riley to imagine what he had ever seen in Evangeline, aside from her considerable skills as a physician in a specialty most avoided, and the lack of emotional demands she placed on him at a time in his life when he had been so busy studying and learning he hadn't been able to handle any.

"Are you trying to tell me you cheated on me?" Evangeline continued.

"No. I'm trying to tell you that if one of the children is my child that you're the only possible mother, and only of Amber here." Riley gestured to the toddler cradled in his left arm. "Obviously, the time frame for four-year-old Chloe and baby Cory don't line up for us."

Evangeline looked at Amanda. "How do you line up in all this?" she asked suspiciously.

Amanda flushed. "I'm, uh, sort of temporarily, but not really his wife." The pink in her cheeks deepening, she waved off further inquiry. "It's a long and ridiculous story."

Evangeline burst into peals of laughter. "Oh, Riley, this one really takes the cake!"

Her reaction irritated the devil out of him. "You think I'm joking?" Riley demanded coolly.

Pity colored Evangeline's regard, as she shook her head at him. "I think you've had time to regret changing gears with me, and know the way you got into my life in the first place was through your very clever practical jokes on people. But I am not falling for this one, Riley McCabe." Evangeline shooed them all toward the door, disclaiming, "And I am not ever falling for you again."

"KIDS ASLEEP?" Riley asked Amanda an hour later.

Because it was too late to drive back to Laramie, they had checked into a three-bedroom suite, complete with kitchen, at an extended-stay hotel that was geared for families. Working as a team, they had fed and bathed the kids. While Riley gave Cory a bottle and put him down, Amanda tucked the older children in bed.

Amanda nodded. "Before I even finished the first story."

Riley peeked into the adjacent bedroom. Chloe was curled up in the double bed, the younger two were snoozing in portacribs lined up against the wall. As always, as long as the three could see each other, and knew they were together, they seemed content.

Reveling in the peace and quiet, Riley poured Amanda a cup of coffee and brought it to her. He sank down beside her on the sofa. There was a good six inches of space between them. They weren't touching in any way but it still felt intimate. Riley wasn't as opposed to that feeling as he figured he should be. "Sorry about what you witnessed earlier," he said, figuring they should talk about what had happened, rather than let it be the elephant in the living room all evening. "I had no idea Evangeline would be…entertaining."

"And then some." Briefly, Amanda looked as embarrassed as Riley had been to find his ex in such a compromising situation. Amanda sipped her coffee, avoiding Riley's eyes. "She's a very sexy woman."

Riley slouched down into the cushions and stretched his long legs out in front of him. "As well as a damned fine oncologist."

Amanda turned slightly to face Riley, her shoulder nudging his in the process. He noted with pleasure she made no attempt to draw away. "And practical joker, too?"

Riley thought he saw a fleeting glimpse of jealousy in Amanda's eyes. Aware he had jumped to conclusions and been wrong about Amanda's interest in him before, he pushed the tantalizing notion away and concentrated on answering Amanda's question instead. "No. Evangeline never played any jokes on me. She just enjoyed the ones I played on others." He paused, reflecting. "Her medical specialty is so emotionally grueling, the only way she survives is by blowing off steam during her time off."

Maybe because she was a nurse herself, Amanda seemed to understand how draining taking care of cancer patients could be. "So Evangeline is just living life to the fullest."

"Exactly," Riley acknowledged, knowing for a while that was all he had wanted to do, too—live his life in the moment, while having as little non-work-related responsibility as possible.

Amanda turned toward Riley even more, her bent knee brushing up against his thigh. She studied him intently, looking deep into his eyes. "What did you do to 'change gears' with her?"

Riley shrugged. "I asked her to marry me."

Amanda's soft eyes widened. "In a joking way—or serious?"

"I was serious," Riley admitted ruefully, recalling just how naive and shortsighted he had been about the dilemma facing them. "I thought it was time. I'd been out of residency a year. I wanted a family. Neither of us was getting any younger."

Amanda smiled and tucked a strand of dark blond hair behind her ear. "I hope you put it a little more romantically than that."

Riley tore his eyes from the soft spill of silky hair over her shoulders, only to find his glance at the even softer and more seductive curves of Amanda's breasts. She was wearing a red turtleneck sweater, with appliqués of Santa's workshop sewn on the front, jeans and a pair of red Western boots. Damn but she was pretty, he thought, even with her hair tousled and her lipstick long gone. He wondered if she knew how worked up he got just sitting next to her like this. Swallowing, Riley took another gulp of coffee. "That's about how I said it." He shifted restlessly in his seat, to ease the pressure starting behind the fly of his jeans.

Amanda ran a hand through her hair and rested her bent elbow on the back of the sofa. The unconscious movement gave him an even better view of her breasts. "I gather she turned you down."

Aware it was all he could do to avoid taking Amanda in his arms and really, truly kiss her this time, instead of pretending to do just that for the audience gathered around them, Riley nodded in acknowledgment. "And then she dumped me," he said matter-of-factly, recounting a disappointment he was long over. Nevertheless, it was nice to see the sympathy and understanding in Amanda's eyes, to know she felt for him, whatever he had been through. "Evangeline said we had come together for mutual fun and pleasure and she wasn't equipped for anything else. She could see that I was more than ready to settle down and have a family with someone, but she wasn't interested in kids or marriage—she had all she could handle with her oncology practice."

Amanda reached over and covered his hand with the softness of hers. "How did you take that?"

Enjoying the warmth of skin on skin, Riley turned his hand over, so his palm was against hers, their fingers loosely entwined. "My ego was hurt." He curved his hand tighter around hers.

"And…?" Amanda leaned closer still.

Drinking in the alluring clove and cinnamon scent of her

perfume, Riley shrugged again. "Deep down I was relieved. I think I always knew she didn't love me, as much as she liked spending time with me, and I don't think I ever loved her, either. 'Cause if I had I think I could have given up on the idea of kids and marriage and been content to just be with her. I think if I had loved Evangeline the way I should have, the two of us would have been enough."

"So now what?" Amanda withdrew her hand from the comfort of his. She looked as spellbound by him as he was by her. "You want to take the kids back to Laramie?"

"Eventually," Riley allowed, surprised at how protective he already felt toward the three little children. "But first I want to visit the family health center where I practiced for the last three years," he told her.

"More ex-girlfriends?" Amanda asked dryly.

Riley thought but couldn't be sure that he saw a glint of jealousy in Amanda's pretty eyes. He shook his head. "No. I'm a one-woman kind of guy, always have been." He looked deep into her eyes and winked. "I figure you should know that."

"I guess so, since I'm temporarily married to you," she bantered back, copying his comically exaggerated tone, some of the tension easing from her slender frame. "But back to why you want to go there…"

Riley covered her hand with his. "I'm hoping someone there will know who might have deserted the children."

Amanda lifted a curious brow as her fingers twined with his. "You think they might belong to a patient?"

Riley regarded Amanda, feeling a unity of purpose that was oddly soothing, as well as an indication of what a good team they made. "Maybe," he allowed quietly. He shrugged, his natural compassion coming to the fore. "It would make sense if the person responsible for the three kids was going through a rough time and thought they couldn't handle being a parent and looked to me—a family doctor—to take them in and care for them."

Unfortunately, a visit to the clinic early the next morning yielded nothing. None of the doctors and nurses there had recognized any of the children, and a search of the patient database yielded no matches either. Amanda was as disappointed by the lack of results as he was, and Riley thought about what to do next all the way back to Laramie.

As soon as they returned home, he put in another call to his brother Kevin. "Any news on the law enforcement front?" Riley asked hopefully.

"No," Kevin returned unhappily. "And no parents of three—male or female—have been reported missing either. We'll keep searching, but if we don't discover anything soon, you may want to go public with your search for their parents."

Riley guessed where this was going. "You mean call in the media."

"It is Christmas," Kevin countered hopefully. "And it's the sort of story national newspeople love."

Riley frowned and rubbed at the tension gathering in the back of his neck. "Stories like that also bring out every nut around."

"And you want to protect them from that."

"As well as whoever left them with me. Obviously, the kids' parent or caretaker had to be really desperate, and for whatever reason, that person trusted me to protect Chloe, Amber and baby Cory."

"I admire your tenacity even if I don't envy you the days ahead," Kevin said. "But I'll do my best to keep searching."

"Thanks, Kevin." Riley sighed.

"And in the meantime, you keep an eye out for any clues to their identity, too. Try to get the four-year-old to open up and start talking," Kevin advised.

Easier said than done, Riley thought, as he cut the connection and put the phone back on its charger base.

"No word, hmm?" Amanda said.

Riley shook his head and looked at Chloe. She was curled

up on the chaise lounge next to the living room window, fast asleep, her thumb in her mouth. Thankful he had bought this house with all sorts of comfort items he would never have thought to buy for himself, he went over and tucked the chenille blanket around her little shoulders. A wave of tenderness swept through him, as potent as it was unexpected. Although Riley loved kids and was used to caring for them, he wasn't accustomed to feeling such a strong parental pull. Yet there was no denying that the need to protect these children was as fierce as anything he had ever felt. The only thing that had ever come close to rivaling it was the attraction he felt for Amanda Witherspoon. He just hoped that the first wasn't destined to end as unsatisfyingly as the latter.

"Kevin thinks that the kids will help us figure out where they are from."

"Assuming we can get Chloe talking." Amanda smoothed Chloe's curls from her forehead and tucked the blanket in around her. She bent to kiss her cheek, then straightened, anxiety in her eyes. "She hasn't said a word yet," Amanda worried out loud.

Riley was concerned about Chloe's silence, too. He took Amanda's hand and led her across the room to the hearth. Behind the heat-tempered doors, a fire crackled. "Chloe probably hasn't spoken," Riley theorized, "because she is so traumatized by whatever happened to force the three kids' sudden abandonment."

Terrible possibilities filled both their minds. Amanda teared up. Before Riley knew it, he had put both arms around Amanda's shoulders and drawn her into a comforting hug. "I just can't imagine anyone leaving them at the hospital that way unless he or she were really in dire straits," Amanda said hoarsely, her face pressed against his chest. "The children are just so sweet and adorable."

And then some, Riley thought as he stroked a hand through Amanda's dark blond hair. He whispered back, "Never mind splitting them up."

Amanda tipped her face up to his. She looked so vulnerable. His heart filled with compassion and something else—something sweet and satisfying—he wasn't sure he was quite ready to identify. Hands splayed across his chest, she murmured fiercely, "We can't let that happen."

"No, we can't," Riley agreed, just as firmly. "We're just going to have to keep them with us until we discover who they really belong with."

"And yet," Amanda paused, distraught, "if we do that, they're going to depend on us," she cautioned, moving away from Riley once again. "Not just physically, but emotionally, as well."

Riley knew the dangers of that. They couldn't provide security for kids who had already been through heaven-knows-what, and then just rip it away. An action like that would leave them heartbroken, at the very least, and, at the worst, permanently mistrustful. It would be just as cruel to treat them in a methodical, uncaring way. "I know."

"They need a mommy and a daddy, Riley."

And Riley wanted to be there for them, in exactly that way. Surprisingly, Amanda seemed to yearn for that opportunity, too. Riley hadn't asked to be in this situation. Perhaps, neither had Amanda. Yet over the last twenty-four hours, the situation had evolved in ways neither had expected or could turn away from. He approached Amanda, hands outstretched. "Look, I know you nixed staying married to me simply for the sakes of our reputations and careers."

Her chin took on that stubborn tilt he knew so well. Amanda folded her arms in front of her, emotional armor back in place. "A decision I still think is the right one." She regarded him steadily. "Marriage is serious business, Riley."

He wasn't going to argue that. His mind moving ahead to what was best, not just for him or Amanda, but all of them, Riley pointed out calmly, "And yet we are married, Amanda." Up to now he had been fighting that fact, trying to ignore that aspect of the situation. But after a night spent tossing and turning alternately worrying about the children and fantasizing about her, Riley was beginning to wonder if that approach was even practical. Maybe instead of pretending there was no chemistry between them they should take the alternate path, explore it to its fullest, see where it led.

Amanda's fair cheeks flushed. "Married in name only," she reminded him.

Riley shot her a seductive smile, even as he cautioned himself not to move too fast, lest he jeopardize any passion they might feel in the future. "For now."

She whirled away. "Don't even think about seducing me."

"Why not?" Riley stepped in front of her and held his ground. He angled a finger at the region over her heart and continued with smug male satisfaction, determined to open her mind up to the possibilities the same way his was. "You're obviously thinking about it, or you wouldn't have brought it up."

Amanda tossed her head. Silky dark blond hair flew in every direction. "Only because you're looking at me that way," she accused, planting her hands on her hips.

Aware this was definitely not a conversation to be had in front of the kids, even if they were sleeping, Riley grabbed her hand and drew her into the adjoining dining room. He backed her up against the wall. "And what way is that?" he chided, liking the spark coming back into her turquoise eyes, the sassy, challenging spark she used to have whenever she looked at him.

Amanda looked at him warily. "The way that says you want to have your way with me."

Riley flattened his hands on either side of her, and leaned in even closer, until they were almost, but not quite, touching length to length. The playfulness that had livened up their youth was back, full force. "That is way too many ways in a sentence," he teased.

Amanda rolled her eyes, but to Riley's delight, didn't attempt to move away. "You know what I mean," she lobbed right back.

"I do." Riley straightened reluctantly, knowing he couldn't remain that close any longer without hauling her into his arms and kissing the socks off her. He regarded her steadily. "And I also know what I want—if the worst occurs and we aren't able to reunite these kids with their real parents, or get them back to their previous home."

Amanda paused. Her tongue snaked out to wet her lower lip. She regarded him with utmost caution. "And that would be—?"

"For all of us to become a family," Riley announced.

Chapter Five

Amanda swallowed. How was it possible that Riley McCabe had tapped into her secret Christmas wish for herself—the one she had foolishly penned in her "note" to Santa, that had been slipped, along with all the other letters from all the other pediatric patients and parents and staff, in the North Pole mailbox next to the Christmas tree in the pediatric playroom? Riley McCabe couldn't possibly know she had whimsically asked Santa for a husband and children of her very own....

Unless he had somehow seen her letter to Santa.

But that was impossible, wasn't it?

Whatever the truth of the situation, there was no clue on Riley's handsome face. "You can't be serious," Amanda allowed finally.

"Oh, but I am. Suppose no one comes to claim them. Or suppose someone shows up and says they can't or won't take care of them any longer, and they are 'giving' the kids to me, so to speak. I couldn't begin to do this alone."

Amanda did not doubt the truth of that. Struggling not to notice how good Riley looked, how handsome and ruggedly at ease, she fastened her gaze on the strong column of his throat, and the tufts of swirling dark gold hair visible in the open collar of his button-down shirt.

Hand to his chest, she pushed him back, knowing if there

was a point to be made this was the very best way to make it. "So hire a nanny."

Riley's amber eyes lit up. He leaned closer, his warm breath whispering across her ear. "You can't hire someone to love these kids, Amanda. It doesn't work that way." He paused to let his gaze rove her dark gold hair and the features of her face. "A mother's instinct is something a woman either has or doesn't have, and let's face it," he complimented her huskily, "you have it in spades."

Amanda tried—and failed—to remain impervious to his praise.

"Chloe, Amber and baby Cory have already been abandoned once." He paused to give her a guilt-inspiring look. "They don't need to be abandoned again. And the only way to ensure that they feel as loved as they deserve to be is if they have a mommy *and* a daddy in their life."

Without warning, Amanda recalled that Riley had lost a parent once, shortly before he and his dad and his four brothers moved to Laramie when Riley was fourteen. Her heart went out to him. "You really identify with these kids, don't you?" she commiserated softly.

Riley nodded. "I know what it feels like to lose a mom. I can't imagine being left with no one."

Amanda bit her lip. "They'd have you."

"A dad's important," Riley agreed candidly. "But there are things guys can't give that only women can. A certain...I don't know, softness and tenderness. Bottom line, women have a different way of looking at things than men do, and kids need both kinds of comfort." He tucked a strand of hair behind her ear before slowly, reluctantly, dropping his hand. "You're already giving them love and tenderness, Amanda." Riley searched her eyes. "They want to be with you."

Amanda couldn't deny that. She and the kids had bonded instantly. But she was good with all kids. To the point she had never met one she couldn't soothe. "They also deserve two parents who love each other deeply." A strong and loving marriage, her folks had often told her, was the foundation of every healthy, happy family. Amanda didn't see how you could have that when the union was fashioned strictly for convenience.

Riley challenged her with a look that was sexy, self-assured and faintly baiting. Amanda blushed. Being in such close proximity to him had left her feeling unaccountably jittery and excited inside. Unless she got hold of those feelings, who knew what might happen between them as the days and nights wore on.

"There are all kinds of love," Riley continued amiably.

Was Riley trying to tell her, just as Fraser had, that she wasn't physically lovable in an exciting or passionate way? That she lacked the siren gene that drove men wild? Having already endured one marriage that was lacking in the "bedroom," Amanda was not ready to sign on for another. And just because a mere kiss from Riley had thrilled her to pieces, did not mean that he felt the same. Men, she had belatedly discovered, were capable of viewing lovemaking as a physical release, instead of the blissful joining of hearts and souls she had always dreamed it could be. Amanda didn't want to find out Riley viewed relations between a man and woman as unemotionally and practically as her ex.

"We've been rivals." He traced the curve of her cheek with the pad of his thumb. "Why not friends and coparents, too?"

Amanda felt her knees weaken even as her heart began to pound. "Because if and when I ever hook up with a man again, I want it all, Riley," she told him fiercely. She dropped her glance to the strong column of his throat, visible in the open V of his shirt. "Physical passion. Deep abiding love. Laughs. Tenderness. You name it. I would think you'd want the same."

"I do. I just don't see why—with time—we couldn't have it all."

Amanda felt herself flush with an inner heat she could not contain. "I don't think real love works like that, Riley." They were vulnerable here. Both of them. They had to remember that.

Riley gave her a thoughtful once-over. "And I don't know why you're so determined to put the brakes on our undeniable attraction to each other without first figuring out where it might lead."

Easy, Amanda thought, as she swallowed around the sudden constriction in her throat and struggled to get air into her lungs. She didn't want to get hurt again and her feminine intuition was telling her Riley McCabe could break her heart, if she lowered her guard, even slightly. "We don't even know where the situation with the kids is going to lead," she continued.

"True, but I like to keep my options open," Riley returned meaningfully. "So should you."

Amanda glanced up at the ruggedly handsome contours of his face, appreciating his strength and determination as much as his irrepressible spirit. Independent in nature, she enjoyed being on her own. But single life could get lonely. Dull, even. With Riley as her partner, she knew she'd never have to worry about either again. And that was something to consider. Her days had been filled with work and little else since her divorce. Twenty-four hours with Riley and she felt as if she were living every moment to the fullest. It was a good feeling. One she didn't want to let go. She still needed some insurance against another failed romantic relationship. She needed to know he would be understanding and supportive either way. "And what if I decide an experimental fling with you is not what I want?" Amanda asked quietly. Would it cost them their newly blossoming friendship?

Riley lifted his hand and gently touched her cheek. "Then I'll respect that. And we'll go our separate ways, none the worse for having spent this time together," he promised, just as the doorbell rang.

Riley arched a brow, looking as annoyed by the intrusion as she felt. "You expecting someone?"

"No." Frowning, Amanda answered the front door and saw the family member she least wanted to see.

RILEY RECALLED Priscilla Witherspoon. Amanda's older sister had been the same age as his brother Will. His older brother had been a jock, prone to trouble, while Priscilla was an uptight bookworm, who now had a Ph.D. in quantum physics. Last he heard, Priscilla had been teaching at Stanford and living in California with the rest of Amanda's family.

"Honestly, Amanda, you could have let someone in the family know where you were," Priscilla began as she walked into the foyer. She was wearing a long tan raincoat and sensible shoes. Her dishwater blond hair was cut in an unflattering style that framed her thin face. "We've been calling and calling, ever since we heard the news about your latest 'mishap' with Riley McCabe from old friends here." Priscilla pushed her horn-rimmed glasses closer to her eyes and looked at the three children napping in the living room. "I must say it didn't surprise me to hear you had been sowing wild oats, Riley McCabe, but Amanda, I thought you knew better than to get involved with one of Sam's sons." Priscilla pursed her lips at Riley. "Especially this one."

Amanda pressed her index finger to her mouth. "Shh. Let's go in the kitchen," she whispered. "So we don't wake them."

"Well?" Priscilla demanded when they had retired to the rear of the house. She handed Riley her coat and he hung it on the decorative coatrack next to the back door. Looking as fashion challenged as ever in a red cord shirtdress and lime-green cardigan, Priscilla folded her arms in front of her and regarded Amanda with mounting exasperation. "What do you have to say for yourself?"

"I don't have to defend myself or my actions to you," Amanda said as she began to make coffee for the three of them.

Bravo, Riley thought, turning away to get out a cardboard bucket of holiday cookies they'd picked up at the market.

Priscilla regarded Amanda with concern. "You do if you don't want Mom and Dad and the rest of your siblings coming out here to talk some sense into you, too. Right now, I'm the emissary from the family, but it won't be just me for much longer unless you tell me something reasonable I can take back to them."

Riley noted Amanda was apparently too stubborn to explain anything to her interfering older sis, so he did it for her. "Three children I had never seen before in my life were abandoned to my care for the Christmas holidays. I am not the biological father of any of them. Obviously, I can't care for them alone so Amanda is helping me while we search for their real family."

Priscilla appeared only partially appeased. She narrowed her eyes suspiciously. "What does any of that have to do with the two of you getting married in the hallway of the hospital yesterday?"

Amanda winced and rubbed her temples. "It was a joke," she said.

Priscilla snorted derisively. "No one in the family is laughing, Amanda."

"Nor are the McCabes," Riley cut in amiably, hoping to divert some of the unwelcome "pressure" away from Amanda. He put his arm around her shoulder. "But that's life, Priscilla. What strikes one person's funny bone may seem completely humorless to someone else." Take this talking-to, for instance. He failed to see anything amusing about it at all.

His attempt to reason with Priscilla failed.

She glared at her younger sister. "I hope you have already taken steps to have it annulled."

Sparks of temper gleamed in Amanda's eyes as she poured mugs of coffee for all three. "Actually, we haven't."

"But you will," Priscilla pressured.

"Maybe." Amanda became even more tight-lipped as she set the cream and sugar on the center of the table with a resounding thud. "And maybe not. Frankly, I haven't decided what I want to do, and neither has Riley."

Shock warred with disapproval on Priscilla's face. "Amanda, you cannot seriously be thinking of continuing with this farce! Riley McCabe has always been the worst possible influence on you."

"Gee thanks, Priscilla," Riley said, helping himself to a couple of Christmas cookies.

Priscilla declined his wordless offer of a confection with a lift of her hand. "Well, it's true. Before you and your brothers moved to town, Amanda was a perfect little angel. She never got into trouble. She always did what she was supposed to do."

That didn't even sound like the woman he had married. Riley positioned himself next to Amanda, every protective instinct quickly coming into play. "Sounds boring," he announced lazily.

"Maybe to a bounder like you," Priscilla retorted archly. "But Amanda never played practical jokes on anyone, before or after you, Riley McCabe! Which leads us all to think—then and now—that you hold some sort of special power over her."

"Special power!" Riley echoed, not sure whether to be insulted or just amused. Beside him, Amanda rolled her eyes.

"And you continue to be a very bad influence on our Amanda, Riley McCabe!" Priscilla charged, even more disapprovingly.

Riley had to admit there was some truth to what Priscilla was saying. He hadn't ever matched wits and wills with anyone else the way he did with Amanda. Never found himself going over the line, to the point where his emotions were guiding his actions, rather than his intellect.

"Hello! I'm still here," Amanda interjected as she helped

herself to an iced butter cookie, too. Temper flaring, she glared at her older sister. "I am my own person! A mature adult who is perfectly capable of making her own decisions and living her own life, without the helpful advice of my family."

Priscilla scoffed. "There's nothing adult about a pretend marriage, Amanda. I assumed you would have learned that in your last go-round."

Riley winced as the color left Amanda's face. Darn that Priscilla. Amanda's older sister had drawn blood. Slowly and deliberately Riley put his coffee down. He wrapped his arm around Amanda's shoulders. "No one speaks to my wife like that," he warned, ready to throw Priscilla out bodily if need be.

"Amanda knows I didn't mean any harm," Priscilla declared with a frown. "I am just trying to talk sense into her." She gave Amanda an imploring look. "Let's go back to your apartment where we can talk in private, honey."

"No. Anything you want to say you can say in front of my husband." Amanda pressed intimately close and wrapped her arm around Riley's waist. Her head was resting on his chest. Riley knew it was just an act designed to get under her sister's skin, as much as Priscilla was getting under Amanda's, but he had never felt anything so good. So right. Maybe there was more to this marriage, and his relationship with Amanda, than he had realized....

It was Priscilla's turn to rub her temples and try again. "Look, Amanda," she said in a much softer tone, "I know how hard it has been for you since the divorce, especially since Fraser and his ex have refused to allow you to be part of your former stepchildren's lives. But you have eight nieces and nephews in California that would love to have you participate in their worlds. You could live with anyone in the family, look for a new job, babysit or nanny to your heart's content, and maybe eventually even find a new boyfriend." Priscilla glared at Riley, then turned back to baby sis. "Someone more suitable. Someone who doesn't think life is a joke."

"Hey, I never said that," Riley cut in, tightening his grip on Amanda all the more. He had a serious side. People, who had known him back when he was a reckless, fun-loving kid and hadn't been around to see his transformation into a responsible human being and family doc, just refused to see it. He had hoped coming back to Laramie as an adult, after such a long absence, would give him a fresh start. He could leave his jokester rep behind. The appearance of the three kids and his reaction to Amanda had blown all that. Once again he was trouble with a capital *T.*

"No, you just acted that way," Priscilla returned haughtily.

Amanda lifted her chin. Her soft lips compressed stubbornly. "Riley wasn't joking just now when he asked me to stay and bring up the kids with him," Amanda said, coming to Riley's defense as stalwartly as he had come to hers.

Priscilla paled. "You can't seriously be considering it," she breathed, distraught.

"Actually, Priscilla," Amanda paused to let the impact of her words sink in. "I think I just agreed."

"SURE YOU SHOULD BE sleeping with such a bad influence?" Riley asked drolly several hours later as he joined Amanda in the master bedroom and shut the door behind him.

Amanda was already clad in a pair of flannel pajamas that were the definition of sweet and innocent girl-next-door. And yet somehow they were damn near the sexiest nightclothes he had ever seen. Maybe because of the way she filled them out. Her dark blond hair was all tousled, her cheeks pink with agitation, her turquoise eyes glittering with fiery lights. She looked beautiful and kissable and ticked off as all get-out, and Riley couldn't say he blamed her. He wasn't happy about her sister's visit to them, either.

Riley crossed to the comfortable reading chair where Amanda was sitting, feet propped up on the ottoman in front of her, baby Cory cradled in her arms. They had discovered the previous night if they woke the four-month-old infant and gave him a diaper change and a bottle of formula at midnight, he would sleep until six or seven the following morning. It also helped to keep the bedroom lights low. Hence, only one bedside lamp was on. It illuminated the suite with a soft, romantic glow.

"I mean, I could thoroughly corrupt you or something even more than I already have," Riley teased, wanting to see more of the normal zest for life back in Amanda's eyes, instead of this roiling resentment.

Amanda finished giving the first half of the bottle and shifted the drowsy Cory onto her shoulder for a burp. "It's necessary—" Amanda stated firmly.

"Said Eve to Adam," Riley interjected pointedly, trying not to notice how the weight of the baby had pulled the fabric of her pajamas off one shoulder, exposing the shadowy hollow and the lusciously soft curves of her left breast. With effort, Riley returned his gaze to Amanda's face. It was a peculiar feeling, discovering they were both in the same boat. Riley was used to them being completely at odds with each other. To suddenly find they were facing the same dilemma—how to handle their families' mounting censure in addition to caring for the three kids together gave Riley a feeling of solidarity with Amanda he had never expected to have. And that, plus the increasingly intimate nature of their enforced cohabitation, was giving rise to all sorts of fantasies he knew he shouldn't entertain.

"I want to get my family off my case," Amanda continued as Cory, responding to her pats on his back, let out one—then two—man-size burps. Both of them grinned at the sound. "Which is why I invited my sister to spend the night with us before she flies back to California tomorrow," Amanda told

Riley seriously, looking so darn sexy at that moment he wanted to cross the room and take her in his arms and forget everyone and everything else. "Because I want her and the rest of my family to know that their days of pushing me around and telling me what to do are long over. I'm an adult. I make my own decisions. Ones that work for me and not them. Even when they make it clear they don't approve!"

Okay.... Glad we have cleared that up, Riley thought sarcastically to himself, a little disappointed he was being used that way but not exactly surprised. He had known from the moment his new wife had issued the invitation to her meddling older sister that Amanda had an agenda. He had just been hoping—foolishly, he saw now—that it hadn't all been to demonstrate her independence. But rather to open the door to romance, as well.

"And second, you and I are not really going to be sharing the sheets," Amanda said as she shifted baby Cory in her arms and moved gracefully to her feet.

Riley glanced back at the king-size bed that had been inspiring fantasies—however unrealistic—ever since he'd learned they would be hitting the sheets together earlier that evening. A fact that had incensed Amanda's meddling sister Priscilla to no end.

"You intend to sleep on the floor?" he teased, treading closer, aware of how much pleasure simply ribbing her brought. Although that was nothing compared to the intoxication he felt drinking in the alluring cinnamon and clove perfume she wore.

"No, silly." Amanda shifted baby Cory to Riley's arms and handed him the bottle, so Riley could get his baby-fix in, too. "I intend to devise a Great Divide."

"This, I've got to see." Riley settled down with baby Cory in his arms. He had held children dozens of times. Tiny patients. New members of the McCabe clan. But none of them had affected him the way these three kids did. He didn't know if it was the notion that they were meant to be with him, at least for now, the fact they were all so sweet and personable, or simply that they desperately needed parents to love and protect them. All he knew was that when they looked to him for comfort, food, shelter and every other necessity of life, he felt like a dad. And it was the best feeling he had ever had.

Well, maybe a close second best, Riley amended. The best thing he had ever felt was having Amanda in his arms, kissing him back, sending all his senses into overdrive. He had known her lips would be soft and warm and womanly. He hadn't expected her to taste so sweet, nor her lips to move in such a deeply sensual, evocative way. That one reluctant, ever so public kiss had conjured up the need to take that dangerous emotion and the white-hot bolt of desire and see exactly where it led them. Hopefully to bed. Not that, judging by her restrained expression, she intended to allow him to kiss her again anytime soon. Riley sighed, watching as she took a blanket from the cedar chest at the bottom of the bed and rolled it into a long cylinder. She then drew back the covers and tucked it between the two pillows.

"Nice," Riley said. Noting baby Cory had finished his bottle, he put him on his shoulder to burp. "But I fail to see how shoving a rolled blankie between our sheets is going to get your family to approve of our living situation." And that was exactly what Amanda wanted, whether she admitted it or not.

"Obviously, that isn't going to happen," Amanda said dryly. "But just the fact we're caring for the kids together, have been married, and are now sharing a bed is going to make it obvious that we are taking our quandary seriously and trying to lie in the bed we've made, so to speak."

"So perhaps that will encourage them to end the interference."

Riley rubbed baby Cory's back until another resounding burp filled the room. "Either that, or it'll have your parents even more upset and on the first plane out here, reading us both the riot act for acting so irresponsibly." From what he remembered of the elder Witherspoons, they were even more demanding and critical than Priscilla. Riley couldn't see them backing off in their demands. More likely, they would simply keep badgering Amanda until she caved.

Amanda's slender shoulders stiffened as she bent over the bed, placing the barrier just so. "There's nothing irresponsible about taking good loving care of these three children while we hunt down their parents," Amanda declared, taking the sleepy baby from Riley. Her expression so tender and loving it filled his heart, she laid the sweet infant down on the bed and swaddled him in a flannel blanket that would keep him warm and cozy through the night. Finished, she carried baby Cory to the borrowed crib in the children's room across the hall and settled him onto his back. His blue eyes shut, and his rosebud mouth worked as if still drinking the bottle before finally falling still once again.

With Riley beside her, Amanda checked on the other two children. Chloe was sleeping on her side, her teddy bear clutched in her arms. Amber was on her tummy, her knees drawn up beneath her, her diaper-clad bottom extended into the air. Amanda turned her gently, to a more comfortable position and tucked the soft blanket around her. She barely stirred. Riley took her stuffed animal and put it right beside her. They looked a moment longer, then left as quietly as they had come. Amanda noted the light in the guest room was off, which probably meant her sister was already asleep.

Appearing as relieved by the reprieve from Priscilla's nonstop lecturing as Riley felt, Amanda led the way back into the master bedroom. As soon as the door was shut, Amanda walked back to Riley. Hands on her hips, she looked him square in the eye and picked up where their conversation had left off. "I've been thinking, Riley," she told him soberly.

"Me, too," Riley quipped. *About taking a risk and kissing you again…*

"We established that I didn't play a prank on you and that the kids weren't left by your ex or any of your former patients in Dallas, but we really didn't take our search in the other direction. Is there anyone else—aside from me—who might feel he or she owes you a practical joke of this magnitude? Someone you've outpranked in the past, perhaps?"

Interesting point, Riley thought, and one he had yet to consider, probably because he'd been so focused on Amanda all along. He thought about it, then shook his head. "I see where you're going with this." He stripped off his shirt and walked into the adjacent bath. He left the door open and Amanda lounged in the doorway, watching, as he layered mint-flavored toothpaste onto his brush. He brushed his teeth, rinsed and spit. Aware this situation was beginning to feel almost too intimate, he wiped his mouth on a towel, then straightened, towering over her. "But this isn't the kind of joke a guy would play on another guy," he stated soberly.

Amanda knew she was reaching. In her heart of hearts, she sensed that the kids had been left out of desperation. Just as she realized she had to stop making this "marriage" of theirs suddenly feel so real. She needed to remind herself of his jokester past. Remind herself that Riley never had been the kind of guy she would pick to get involved with seriously. Because if she let herself think that way, if she let herself be seduced into thinking she could trust him, not just with her heart, but her long-held very secret romantic fantasies about him—or worse, gave in to the palpable sexual attraction simmering between them—she could be in a lot of trouble here. Big-time trouble. The kind of trouble a woman like herself did not recover from once the impetuous fling ended. And any involvement with Riley McCabe would likely end the moment the three children were removed from his care after Christmas.

"Trust me," Riley continued, simultaneously reading her wariness and looking irked that she had brought up the prankster side of him once again. "It's nothing any of my buddies would do."

Amanda edged closer, trying not to notice the stretch of satiny smooth skin over broad shoulders and muscular pecs, the washboard flatness of his abs, and lower still, where the arrow of dark gold chest hair disappeared into the waistband of his jeans. Was it her imagination, or was he beginning to be as aroused by their proximity to each other as she was?

"What about a woman, then?" Amanda directed her glance away from his beautiful body, back to his warm amber eyes. Was there someone else in his life uniquely intriguing in the way she had always been? Someone who had filled the years between his teenage rivalry with Amanda and his love affair with Evangeline, a woman he hadn't yet thought about?

"I don't play practical jokes on women." Riley returned the towel to the rack. He swaggered back into the bedroom and toed off his boots.

Amanda followed, heart pounding, aware their "marriage" had never felt more intimate or genuine than it did now. Which was ridiculous, she reminded herself sternly, since their union was merely a temporary solution to a very complex problem. "What do you call me then?" she demanded resolutely, keeping her eyes focused on his face.

"You," he tapped her playfully on the nose, "are the exception to the rule."

Amanda warmed beneath his teasing touch despite her strict admonition not to fall victim to his considerable charms. "And why is that?" she challenged softly. Letting him know with a glance that she had no intention of succumbing to the nonstop attraction simmering between them. No matter how much she wanted to discover what lay behind the fly of those snug-fitting jeans. Or just how he would kiss her if they had no audience.

"I don't know." He threaded a hand through the tousled layers of her hair. His glance roved her face and he looked as if he wanted very much to kiss her. For real, this time. "Maybe because you had a way of getting under my skin from the very first," he told her softly. "Maybe because you were such a good rival. And maybe just maybe because I've always had a little bit of a crush on you—" his voice dropped a seductive notch "—and just couldn't admit it to myself, until now."

His confession shook her to her soul. The next thing Amanda knew, his head was lowering over hers. If the first time he had kissed her had been unbelievably chaste, the second was passion defined. Before Amanda had a chance to do more than draw in a quavery breath, his arm was around her waist, tugging her close, and their lips were fused in a kiss that was more intimate and searing than anything she ever could have imagined. As his tongue tangled with hers, desire swept through her in hot, effortless waves. She felt so many things. Surprise. Heat. Want. Need. He tasted so good, so undeniably male. And as the fiery kiss continued, she found herself lost in the miracle of it. She had waited a lifetime to be kissed and held like this. She had waited a lifetime to feel like this. As if no one else, nothing else, existed in this moment of time but the two of them and the yearning deep inside them. And yet as he lifted a hand to unbutton her pajama top, his warm strong hands slipping inside her top to claim the silky softness of her breasts, panic engulfed her once again.

Fearful of making another mistake, of falling for a man who would never love her the way she yearned to be loved, Amanda finally tore her lips from Riley's and called a halt. "No," she said breathlessly, turning her head to the side, "we are not doing this just so I can get back at my family!" There were better ways to accomplish that, she knew.

"I agree," Riley said emphatically, picking her up in his arms and laying her down on the bed. "Our families have nothing to do with what is going on between you and me right here, right now." Riley stretched out beside her, tucked a hand beneath her chin and turned her face back to his. He looked deep into her eyes. He lowered his head, kissed her again, consuming her with his mouth. Lips, teeth, tongue, he used them all to maximum advantage as his hands returned to claim and caress her breasts. He was hard, relentless, irresistible in his pursuit of her. And still he kissed her, his lips warm and sure as he took every ounce of feeling that had been building between them for years and years, and used it to his advantage.

The kiss ended and his lips forged a burning trail down her neck, across her collarbone, the slope of one breast, then another. Amanda arched against him as his mouth circled each nipple, bringing them to taut aching peaks. Passion swirled and dipped around her, drawing her into its mesmerizing depths.

"What's happening now has to do with you and me," he told her as he made his way slowly back to her mouth. He threaded his hands through her hair, kissed her again, with even less restraint. He dragged her so close their bodies were almost one. Her senses spun as he sucked her bottom lip and touched the tip of her tongue with his own, then stroked his hands down her body once again. His warm palm slid lower yet. "This is about how we feel, Amanda. And what we want, which is to make love to each other, here, now."

Was that what she wanted? Amanda wondered shakily as Riley continued to inundate her with kisses and the overwhelming security of his tall, strong body? To make love without being loved? Realizing what was about to happen, what she had encouraged him to do, Amanda placed both hands on Riley's chest and pushed him away from her. "No," she said firmly, as the sensual mist faded and her sanity returned. "I don't care how good it feels," she told him fiercely, looking him straight in the eye. "We are definitely not doing this."

Chapter Six

"Are we going to talk about this?" Riley asked, as Amanda disengaged herself from his arms and rose from the bed.

"Isn't that my line?" Amanda replied as she plucked her pajama top from the floor and slipped it back on.

"We need to discuss why it happened," Riley continued, determined not to ignore the change in their relationship the way she so obviously wanted. "Where we go from here." He gave her a long, steady look. "We just very nearly consummated our marriage."

Amanda's hands trembled as she buttoned her shirt. "The reason we almost made love is we are living a fantasy life, pretending to be mommy and daddy to three children who are not ours. We need a dose of reality."

Reality, Riley thought, had been holding Amanda in his arms and kissing her without restraint, admitting that surrendering to their mutual passion had been what he had wanted from her all along. He closed the distance between them, not above using his superior size to inject some control into the situation.

"This mistake was just that," Amanda continued, plucking a brush off the bureau.

Riley tried not to take offense at that, even as he drank in her alluring cinnamon perfume.

Her hands trembled as she restored order to her hair. "And we made that momentary mistake because it's Christmas."

Riley lounged against the bureau next to her, his back to the mirror. He folded his arms in front of him. Reminded just how stubborn, strong-willed and defiant Amanda could be, he said, "I don't follow."

She lifted her chin, clearly trying for an air of cool challenge. "It's a well-known fact that romantically unattached people are lonelier and therefore more emotionally vulnerable during the holidays."

Riley arched his eyebrow deliberately. "So loneliness and a need for more holiday cheer drove you into my arms."

Amanda nodded. "And curiosity. I'm human. I like to have a little fun in the bedroom now and then."

Sure she was fibbing now, Riley demanded, "Since when?" The Amanda he recalled had been anything but interested in jumping from bed to bed. He sensed that was still the case, even if she wasn't quite ready to admit it to him.

Amanda crossed her arms stubbornly. "Maybe I've changed."

"And maybe you haven't." Riley put his hands on her shoulders and held her in front of him when she would have run away from what was happening between them. Again. "Maybe you only wish making love with someone could be an unemotional thing." Just as he had at one time when he had needed to protect himself from hurt and emotional demands he knew he would not be able to meet. That had all changed. He was tired of feeling so alone. He wanted the kind of emotional support and intimacy Kate and his dad, and all his married siblings, had. He suspected Amanda did, too.

Amanda blew out an exasperated breath and slapped both hands on her hips. She tossed her head at him, but made no move to extricate herself from his gentle, staying grip. "Since when did you know anything about me on such an intimate level?" she demanded, her lovely face gilded in the soft shadowy light of their bedroom.

Riley took her by the hand and led her toward the bench at the foot of the bed. The sudden cessation of their lovemaking left him feeling oddly bereft, and in some ways, lonelier than before. So maybe it was a good thing Amanda had pulled back at the last minute. If she hadn't, he might have really gotten in over his head. Picking up the threads of their argument once again, he said, "I know this. You spent more nights at home than most kids our age when you were in high school."

Amanda frowned, remembering. "I didn't have any choice about that." She sank down onto the padded seat. She looked down at her bare left hand that should have held a wedding band, proclaiming her as his new bride. "I was babysitting my younger siblings."

Riley regarded her empathetically. He sat down next to her and covered her hand with his. Delighting in the softness of her skin, he murmured, "I don't know how you did it, giving up nearly all your free time that way. I would have rebelled big-time."

Amanda's lower lip curved ruefully as she slanted him a sidelong glance, then stated in a low, matter-of-fact tone, "Ever stop to think my involvement with you was my rebellion?"

Riley paused, not sure whether that was a good thing or bad.

Her eyes sparkling at the memory of a very lively time in their lives, Amanda shook her head, continued almost shyly, "My parents hated my behavior when it came to you because it was so unlike me. And the more they tried to keep me home and out of trouble…"

Riley squeezed her hand companionably and looked her straight in the eye, remembering full well the ruckus they'd caused. "Not to mention, away from me," he interrupted softly.

"The more outrageous my jokes on you became," Amanda concluded.

Glad to recall a simpler time when one-upping each other was all that mattered, Riley wrapped a comforting arm around her slender shoulders. "I still haven't forgotten the time you turned all my science notes hot pink, right before semester exams. How'd you do that, by the way?"

She leaned against him, all the earlier contentiousness drained out of her. "Trade secret." She winked.

Liking the abruptly playful tone the evening had taken—it was a welcome relief after the stressful day—Riley shifted Amanda onto his lap and wrapped both his arms around her. "Come on. Spill." Riley prodded her with a look.

"We took all the paper out of your loose-leaf notebook and sprayed it with diluted fruit drink," Amanda confessed proudly even as she resisted cuddling against him.

Riley stroked a hand through the just-brushed softness of her dark blond hair. "Is that why the pages all had that sugary smell?"

Amanda nodded, still holding herself somewhat aloof.

Riley regarded her with respect, one accomplished practical joker to another. "Three hundred pages of notes must have taken a lot of time."

Amanda's eyes sparkled with merry accomplishment. "Yes, but it was worth it to see the look on your face when you opened your locker that morning and took out your science binder."

Riley chuckled softly. "Yeah, but I got you back by putting the green food coloring in your soda can." He recalled the excitement of those days. Always waiting, wondering, what she was going to do next…always plotting his next move. Knowing no matter what, he had to keep—and hold—her full attention.

Sort of like now.

Amanda shook her head in amused remembrance. She wreathed one arm about his shoulders, her fingers like silk against his bare skin, the other remained in her lap. "I had green lips for several days."

He stroked the pad of his thumb across the inside of her wrist, looked deep into her eyes. Knowing it was time their conversation took a serious turn once again, before she could avoid acknowledgment of what had just happened between them altogether, he continued softly, "And now you have a husband and a marriage you never planned on and dual responsibility for three kids."

Amanda stiffened, clearly as reluctant to get as emotionally entangled with him as ever. "It's more a convenient living arrangement than a marriage," she said defensively and moved to get off his lap.

Riley released her reluctantly. He stretched his long legs out in front of him and sat with his back against the foot of the bed. He watched as she stood and began to pace. "How do you figure that?"

She regarded him haughtily. "Because I have no intention of making our mistake a legal or in any sense a permanent one. Our marriage won't be a valid union unless we get a license before the thirty days are up. We both already agreed we have no intention of doing that."

Riley understood why Amanda was clinging to the initial agreement they'd made. She wanted to safeguard herself from hurt by not allowing herself to get emotionally involved with anyone again. He understood that. He'd done it himself. He also knew from experience that it didn't work. Avoiding meaningful emotional commitments only made you lonelier and more unhappy in the end.

He stood. More determined than ever to discover where this attraction of theirs was leading them, he took her weary, resisting body in his arms. "Forget the legalities of our predicament and the license, Amanda," he advised her gruffly. Cupping her chin in his hand, he lifted her face to his and scored his thumb across the softness of her lips. Ignoring the sudden wariness in her pretty eyes, he continued softly, "Let's talk about what's happening between us in this bedroom tonight."

UNFORTUNATELY, Amanda thought, that was exactly what she did not want to discuss. She tore her eyes from the bunched muscles of his chest and the whirling light brown hair that arrowed down and disappeared beneath the low-slung waist of his cotton pajama pants. "Mmm, no."

"No?" he asked, his sexy eyes glimmering mischievously.

Amanda closed her eyes against the memory of her response to the most masculine part of him. Her insides tingled as she recalled his kisses and what they had very nearly done.

"I don't know you well enough to talk about what's so obviously on your mind, Riley McCabe!"

Riley threw back his head. A deep male laugh, rich with irony, filled the cozy silence of the bedroom. The look he gave her was direct, uncompromising, confident. "You're something, Amanda Witherspoon McCabe, you know that?"

Hearing him add his name to hers made her flush with pleasure. When he looked at her like that, he made her feel beautiful. And that, too, was dangerous. "I know you think so," Amanda said, trying desperately not to think about the quivers happening in her tummy or the hope rising in her heart. "But in the meantime, you need to understand that despite what just happened here tonight that you and I are just... friends."

Riley groaned and pressed his hands to his ears, before fixing her with a comically exaggerated look as he declared, "Worst words a guy could ever hear! Particularly—" he paused, his glance sliding over the tousled strands of her silky blond hair and softly parted lips "—when the words come from his wife of only one day."

"Pretend wife," Amanda corrected, trying not to notice how handsome and sexy he looked in the muted light of the bedroom. "Temporary wife."

Riley looked as if he wanted to change her mind about that. At least long enough to get her in his arms again and make love to her. But she knew that would be a mistake. Their situation was complicated enough without bringing sex into the equation or allowing herself to think their marriage was anything but a temporary solution for the benefit of the children mysteriously left in Riley's care.

Taking her by the hand, he led her toward the bed. Noticing the rolled-up blanket had been knocked right of center during their hot and heavy make-out session, Amanda leaned over and put it back.

"We've really got to get some sleep," Riley said.

"No argument there." Talking intimately with Riley was only going to lead to other things she knew she should avoid, even if she hadn't managed to do so thus far this evening. Aware her heart was pounding and there was a telltale fluttering in her middle, Amanda slipped into her side of the covers, turned her back to the middle, and shut her eyes. She half expected Riley to kneel beside the bed, like the Prince in the *Sleeping Beauty* story, press home his advantage and give her a good-night kiss. Instead, he switched off the bedside lamp, walked around the foot of the bed, and climbed in the other side. Leaving her to deal with her disappointment and desire. Even though she knew he was only doing what she had firmly stated she wanted him to do.

"And speaking of good ideas…" Ignoring the practical aspects of their situation, Riley removed the rolled blanket and tossed it aside. Behaving as if he knew instinctively what was in her heart and on her mind, he pulled her into the curve of his body to sleep. Amanda knew she should resist cuddling now the same way she had resisted it when he had pulled her onto his lap. But it had been so long since she had been held like this, if she had ever been held like this, so warmly and tenderly.

"I think I just figured out what I want for Christmas," he murmured in her ear.

Probably the same thing she already had wished for, Amanda thought, sinking luxuriantly into the strong solid curve of his body. *Thank goodness Riley would never see the*

note she had written and slipped into Santa's mailbox, she
thought, already drifting off to sleep. 'Cause if he did, she
wouldn't have a chance at resisting him and the situation that
could still very well break her heart.

"LEAVING ALREADY?" Riley said to Priscilla Witherspoon the
next morning as she carried her suitcase into the upstairs hallway.

Priscilla set her bags down and marched into the "nursery"
where Riley was busy changing Cory's diaper. "If you were
any kind of a gentleman at all, Riley McCabe, you would end
this farce of a marriage and stay as far away from my sister
as possible."

Riley laid Cory down on the waterproof changing pad on
the center of the guest room bed. "Well, good morning to you,
too," Riley drawled as he unsnapped the legs of Cory's cotton
sleeper.

Arms folded militantly in front of her, Priscilla edged
nearer. A dour expression on her face, she watched as Riley
removed the sodden diaper, and pulled a baby cleansing cloth
out of the plastic holder. Holding the infant's legs with one
hand, Riley washed Cory's diaper area.

"We all tried to talk Amanda out of returning to Laramie
to work and live. She should have stayed in California, where
she could be close to all her siblings and their families, as well
as our parents. She doesn't need to do something like this to
have children in her life. She can babysit for her nieces and
nephews anytime."

So here was the rub. The real reason her family was so upset. "Was Amanda doing a lot of that, before she left?" Riley
asked, pulling a fresh diaper out of the box and sliding it beneath Cory's bottom.

"As a matter of fact," Priscilla returned coolly, "she was."
Riley stared at the diaper. Realizing the tabs were facing
the wrong way, he removed the diaper, turned it right side up

and slid it back under Cory's bottom. "To the detriment of her own social life?"

Priscilla paced back and forth beside the bed. "Amanda didn't want a social life after her divorce."

Riley found that hard to believe. He scoffed as he applied a bit of zinc oxide cream to Cory's tender skin. Finished, he frowned at the residue still on his hand. Then cleaned it off with another diaper wipe. "Everyone wants a social life whether they're looking for romance or not," Riley informed her as he threw the crumpled cleaning cloth into the diaper pail.

"Not Amanda," Priscilla declared.

No wonder Amanda wanted to leave California, Riley thought.

Amanda popped her head in the door. She had Chloe by the hand, and Amber on her hip. "Need any help?" Amanda asked her sister.

Priscilla shook her head, all tight-lipped disapproval once again. "I can manage my bag."

Amanda tensed, looking from Riley to Priscilla. "Everything okay in here?" she asked warily.

"I was just telling Riley to take care lest he have the entire Witherspoon clan to deal with," Priscilla said tartly.

Riley flashed a pained smile as he buttoned up the legs of Cory's diaper and ended up with one extra snap on each end.

"Hence, I think he knows what he has to do," Priscilla finished.

Amanda looked as uncomfortable and eager to get rid of her nosy older sister as Riley felt. "The girls and I'll walk you out," she said.

By the time Riley had refastened the snaps on Cory's sleeper and walked downstairs, Priscilla was driving away. A tense look on her face, Amanda led the two girls over to the scattered toys on the family room rug. They sat down and began to play.

"What did she say to you?" Riley asked when Amanda

walked over to the kitchen counter and plucked the breakfast dishes off the table.

Amanda shrugged her shoulders, a thoroughly dispirited look on her face. A remoteness he hadn't heard before crept into her low tone. "Apparently, my family sees similarities between my previous marriage and this one. They think I am just with you to have a chance at getting a ready-made family of my own. That without the kids, without the convenience of our living arrangements, and our 'marriage' giving me false security, I wouldn't even consider going along with you on this."

"And if what they think is true, what then?" Riley asked quietly.

"Easy." Amanda sighed. "They'll all be right there to say 'We-told-you-this-was-a-bad-idea.'"

Riley imagined that was all too true. Amanda's family had long blamed him for the disreputable turn in Amanda's behavior, whenever he was on the scene. It didn't, however, mean Riley agreed that he and Amanda were bad for each other. On the contrary, Riley felt he and Amanda brought out the vivaciousness in each other the way no one else did. "That's one way to look at it," he said, taking her in his arms. He held her close and tenderly brushed the hair from her face with the edge of his hand. "But suppose they're all wrong…."

IF NEARLY MAKING LOVE with Riley the night before had felt real, Amanda thought, it was nothing compared to the sensation of standing in the kitchen, their lower bodies pressed together, his arms wrapped around her waist. She wondered if he had any idea how easily she could lose her heart to him. Not just now, but forever. "And suppose I believe in Santa Claus, too?" she challenged with a sassy toss of her head, reminding herself they were still in a very fanciful situation that could conceivably come crashing down around them at any second.

"Hey, take it from someone who knows," Riley teased, giving her a once-over that stirred her secret desire even more. "Santa's been known to grant a wish or two or three."

If only old St. Nick could make Riley fall in love with her in a way that would last forever! But no one could do that. Riley had to come to feel that way on his own, or they literally had no future together, Amanda reminded herself sternly. She had married one man who cherished everything she did for him and his kids, but did not—had not—ever loved her the way he should have. She wasn't going to make the same mistake again. No matter how much she was beginning to feel…maybe had always felt…for her former nemesis, Riley McCabe.

Regarding him in a chiding manner meant to discourage such ridiculously impractical notions, she began, "Riley…"

"Gives us a chance, Amanda. Give this a chance." Riley's head lowered.

Amanda's traitorous heart filled with anticipation. The next thing she knew one hand flattened over her spine, bringing her close, the other was in her hair, tilting her face up to his. She had time to draw a quick excited breath, then his lips pressed against hers. Amanda tasted the masculine force that was Riley, felt his wildness in the unrestrained, sweeping motions of his tongue. She didn't want to surrender to him, but his will was stronger than hers, his embrace too full of sexual promise. With a low moan, she slanted her lips to better accommodate his mouth and twined her tongue with his. And even though she knew she should be resisting his incredibly tantalizing kisses, she couldn't seem to summon up the willpower to call a halt to the embrace, not when she was reveling in his tenderness and yearning was pouring through her in hot, potent waves. Amanda melted against him, acutely aware that she had never felt as sensual or been seduced quite so masterfully.

Riley had expected to kiss Amanda again. As soon as the opportunity presented itself and the mood was right. He hadn't figured she would respond quite so eagerly once her initial reservation was past. He hadn't expected her to mold her soft, slender body to his, wreathe her arms about his neck, go up on tiptoe and kiss him back passionately. Tormented beyond his wildest dreams—because now all he wanted to do was further the escalating desire and make her his—he drew back, breathing hard.

Amanda looked up at him, cheeks pinkening, her breathing as shallow and erratic as his. "The kids," he sighed, cursing his own restraint and bad timing. Had he known she was going to be this receptive to another kiss, he would have waited, picked a much better time. Like late tonight, after the children were all in bed for the night.

Amanda turned her head, noting at the same time as he that Chloe and Amber were still completely entranced by their play, and hence oblivious to the hot, passionate kisses between the two of them. A mixture of temper and chagrin sparkled in Amanda's eyes. "I thought we weren't going to make this mistake again!" she said.

Riley grinned, pleased by the indisputable fact she wanted him as much as he wanted her. "Hey," he protested in a lazy tone that brought even more indignation to her lovely eyes. "I never agreed to that."

"Well you should have," Amanda fumed, just as the doorbell rang and the two older children looked up from their toys.

"Saved by the bell," Amanda breathed. She gracefully extricated herself from his arms. "I'll get it."

Riley went to the door, too. His younger sister, Laurel, and her friend Micki Evans, were standing on the front stoop. Their noses and cheeks were red with the cold. Laurel held a fresh and fragrant evergreen wreath, strewn with red holly berries, in her hands. "Mom and Dad sent this over," Laurel said, helpful as ever. "They noted you didn't have one when they were here yesterday."

Micki smiled amiably as Riley and Amanda ushered the

young women inside and shut the door behind them, to keep out the cold wintry air. "We thought you might need some help with the kids," Micki said as she stood beside Laurel in the foyer.

Laurel's voice dropped to a conspiratorial whisper "We figured you might want to go shopping for a Christmas tree and presents and stuff."

Riley looked at Amanda. "Sounds like a plan to me."

"Me, too," Amanda replied.

"How long can the two of you stay?" Riley asked Micki and Laurel, aware the closest shopping mall and toy super-store was a good thirty minutes away, by car.

"As long as you need us to," Laurel said, already taking off her coat. "Micki and I are done with our final exams and home on break, so aside from the volunteering we're doing at the hospital, we're pretty much free to help you all the time."

"At least until Micki goes home for the holidays, too," Riley corrected.

Without warning, Micki got a pinched, unhappy look on her face.

"Actually," Laurel cut in as she wrapped a jovial arm around her friend's shoulders, "I've invited Micki to spend the holidays with us this year."

"You're not going home to Colorado to be with your sister and her family?" Riley asked, surprised. He knew from previous conversations with Micki that she and her sister were extraordinarily close, and had been since they'd been orphaned, years earlier. To the point that Micki usually spent every break with her.

Micki tensed and looked as if she didn't want to discuss it. "Not this year," she said finally, looking away.

Sensing he had touched a nerve, albeit unintentionally, Riley changed the subject smoothly. He knew if Micki and her sister'd had a familial disagreement it was none of his business.

Perhaps they'd patch things up on their own before Christmas actually arrived, in any case. "Any word from UT-Galveston medical school?" Riley asked Micki, changing the subject smoothly.

Micki grinned broadly. "Well, that's the other reason we stopped by." She literally exuded happiness. "I wanted to tell you that I got in!"

"Congratulations!" Riley said, genuinely pleased and proud of her.

"Thanks," Micki said. Tears of happiness glistened in her eyes.

Riley wasn't surprised the young woman was so emotional. He knew how much Micki wanted to be a doctor—it was one of the reasons he had written such a glowing recommendation for her.

Amber toddled over and wrapped her arms around Micki's legs. She looked up at her and babbled something unintelligible. Chloe moved toward Laurel and slipped in next to Micki. Standing between the two, Chloe wrapped an arm about each girl's knee and held on tight, still not saying a single word.

Laurel withdrew a piece of paper from her pocket and handed it to Riley, as concerned as ever about making everyone else happy. "Micki and I weren't sure what you guys knew about amusements for youngsters of a certain demographic, but we do because we've both done a lot of babysitting in recent years. So we sort of made a list of the t-o-y-s the k-i-d-s might like from S-A-N-T-A or you guys or whomever." She winked at Riley and Amanda. "It's a starting point, anyway."

As much as Riley hated to leave the three kids, even for a little while, he was glad for the time alone with Amanda. There was much they still had to deal with, to clear the way for them to pursue their attraction. He intended to see that happened. "Mind if we stop by the sheriff's department first and check in with my brother?" Riley asked as they headed toward Main Street, minutes later.

"I think it's a great idea," Amanda said as Riley turned his SUV into the parking lot. "The sooner we find out who the kids really belong with, the better."

Unfortunately, Riley and Amanda discovered to their mutual disappointment, Kevin did not have the answer yet. "We searched the database for missing kids nationwide," Kevin told them unhappily. "Nothing came up for any of them."

Amanda looked at Riley, the affection she felt for the children in her eyes. "I can't believe someone isn't missing the kids," Amanda murmured, tucking her hands in the pockets of her coat.

Feeling exactly the same way, Riley touched Amanda's shoulder reassuringly. "What about the note that was left with them?" Riley asked.

Kevin frowned. "There are fingerprints on it, aside from yours and Amanda's, but none that match anything in the system. Which means whoever left the kids with you does not have a criminal record."

"Well, that's good," Riley said, relieved. Aware Amanda was suddenly looking a little pale, he held out a chair and she slipped onto the seat.

"Isn't there some other way we could identify them?" Amanda asked, her initial distress fading as she focused on the task at hand. "Somewhere else we could look?"

Riley was eager to solve the mystery, too.

"We're trying the social service and charity agencies in the Dallas-Fort Worth area now," Kevin said. "Circulating the pictures of the kids, seeing if anyone knows of a family in trouble who also might have somehow come across your path, Riley, because whoever left the kids with you knows of you in some not so obvious way."

"What do you mean?" Riley asked.

"It could be someone who lived at the apartment complex

where you used to live, or someone who works at a restaurant or dry cleaners or grocery store you frequented. Or someone you ran across during one of your rotations during your internship and residency five, six, even seven years ago. And since Dallas is where you did your medical training and last worked, it seems the logical place to start."

"That's a lot of ground to cover," Riley remarked. "How soon do you think you'll have answers from all those places?"

"We'll hear back from law enforcement and social services in a couple of days."

"And if you don't find answers there?" Amanda asked, her delicate fingers worrying the strap of her shoulder bag.

"We'll gradually extend the search to the rest of the social welfare agencies in the state," Kevin said seriously. He went on reassuringly, "Plus, all the law enforcement agencies nationwide have now been notified, so should anyone report Amber, Chloe and Cory missing at any point in the future, those agencies will notify us immediately."

Amanda and Riley thanked Kevin and headed back out to the SUV.

"I don't know whether to feel elated or depressed," Riley said, opening her door for her.

Amanda snapped her safety harness while Riley climbed behind the wheel. "What do you mean?" she asked, appearing as if her emotions were as tumultuous and confused as his at the moment.

Riley frowned. "As much as I want the kids' family to be found, I don't want them going back into an unfortunate circumstance or being reunited with someone who doesn't want them, just because legally that's where they belong."

"Maybe whoever left them with you had good reason for doing what they did. Maybe they intend to leave the kids with you permanently, not just for the Christmas holidays. Maybe this was just a trial period or something. Kind of like a Christmas gift from the heart?" Amanda speculated, her soft lips taking on an optimistic curve.

Riley slanted Amanda an admiring glance. "You are romantic, deep down. Despite all your efforts to deny it."

"Hopeful," Amanda corrected, with an arch look, "that everything works out in a way that's best for all. In the meantime," she said, all business once again, "we better get on with the shopping."

The aisles of the toy superstore were packed with parents and shopping carts. En route, Amanda and Riley had narrowed the list of possibilities to two items per child, and two group gifts. A pink-and-white roadster-tricycle and a Talking Tammy doll for Chloe, a push-and-pull wagon and a Texas ranch toddler play set, complete with cowboys and animals, for Amber and a musical mobile and infant play gym for Cory. Riley added a huge tub of interlocking play blocks and several Educating Baby videos to the basket. He had just started for the checkout lines, when he went back and added a stack of storybooks—including several about Santa and the meaning of Christmas—that could be given to the kids and read now, to the cache. They made it another three feet, before he also added several wooden puzzles, which gave Amanda time to add a toy band and piano to the cart she was pushing. Riley grinned at her. "Do you think we're spoiling them?" he asked as Amanda selected three stuffed animals— a puppy for Chloe, a kitty cat for Amber and a teddy for Cory.

"I don't know. Maybe." Amanda appeared as if she was enjoying this as much as he. "But I so want them to have a wonderful Christmas, Riley."

"Me, too. And you know what that means?" he told her, enjoying the color in her cheeks and the sparkle in her eyes as they finally got in the long checkout line. "We've got to get a Christmas tree today, too."

An hour later, they were standing in the lot on the outskirts of Laramie. The local charity group had brought in Scotch pines that ranged from four to sixteen feet tall.

Riley grinned at her, looking happier than she had ever seen him. "You pick it out," he said.

Amanda knew this was all fantasy—the husband of her dreams and the kids she had always wanted, just in time for Christmas. But it was difficult not to get swept up into the dream nevertheless, if only for a short while. Doing her best to contain her emotions, she merely shrugged and said, "It's your house."

Riley took her gloved hand in his. "And you're my wife," he reminded her in a possessive voice. His grin widened playfully. "I have it on good authority that 'the wife' always gets the final say on decisions like this."

He was making her feel really and truly married to him. A dangerous proposition. Still tingling from the brief contact, she walked up and down the aisle of trees. The air was fragrant with the smell of fresh-cut pine and Christmas music played softly over the speakers mounted on tall, wooden posts. By Christmas Day it could well be seventy degrees outside, but for now the cold front sweeping the entire Southwest continued to immerse Laramie. Their breaths puffed in frosty circles in the damp wintry air. "How big a tree do you want?" she asked.

Riley shrugged. He tilted his head to study her, tucked a gloved hand just above her elbow. He came closer still, the warmth of his breath ghosting over her temples. "Show me what you want," he whispered. "It's yours."

Amanda blushed despite herself. She narrowed her eyes at him in exaggerated admonishment. "Getting a little racy there, aren't you, Doc?"

He waggled his eyebrows at her as they proceeded down the aisles at a leisurely pace, examining tree after tree. "Think so?" he asked cheerfully, looking more determined than ever to make her his—at least once—before this convenient marriage of theirs ended.

"For all the good it's going to do you," Amanda murmured right back, determined to be honest and let him know where they still stood. "Since—despite what my family thinks—I'm not one to repeat my mistakes." Except with Riley. With him, she was prone to letting emotion rather than cool reason rule the day. There was just something about him that brought out the reckless, restless, totally irresponsible side of her. Something about him made her want to throw caution to the wind and forget about putting on the brakes and make love to him, not just once, but again and again and again. And that would be a terrible move to make, since it would guarantee she would love him—and only him—forever. Regardless of how casually he felt about her and their current living arrangement.

Riley considered her for a moment, then leaned closer once again, bringing the tantalizing fragrance of his cologne with him. "What we started last night was not a mistake," he told her bluntly.

Amanda did not like the possessive look in his eyes or the presumption in his tone that said he was going to have his way with her again even if both their hearts got shattered all to pieces in the process. To have a dream just within your reach, and then have it yanked away, unfulfilled, was devastating, Amanda knew. She rolled her eyes. "Says you."

Riley chuckled as if he knew full well the reason behind her discomfort. He fingered the tag on a Christmas tree. "And so will you, one day soon," he told her gently, nudging the back of her hand with the back of his. He paused and looked deep into her eyes. "As soon as you admit we've got something special going on here. And agree to take it to the next step."

Suddenly, Amanda was having trouble getting her breath. "Third base?"

"Or fourth, if you need specifics." His voice dropped a seductive notch. "I want to make you mine, Amanda."

Amanda's pulse jumped. Leave it to Riley to lay it right on the line. "You mean have a fling," she said, marshaling her defenses and pivoting away from him.

Riley put his hands on her shoulders and gently turned her toward him. "Or a heck of a lot more."

"Depending?" Amanda asked.

"On how close you're willing to let us get," Riley replied seriously.

He was talking about joining more than their bodies now; he was talking about involving their hearts and minds. Unfortunately, as much as Amanda wanted to believe there was the possibility of a long-term future for them, bitter experience told her to be more than cautious where a man in Riley's situation, who simply needed a wife and mother for "his" children, was concerned. What seemed so right now might not appear all that perfect if the children were removed from the equation.

Slim Whittaker, the owner of the local hardware store and the president of the local Jaycees, came up to join them. "I hear congratulations are in order for you two," he remarked with a wink.

Amanda flushed self-consciously. Slim was in his sixties now, but she remembered darting in and out of his store a lot when she was a kid. Riley had done the same.

Riley let go of Amanda's elbow and shook Slim's hand. "No doubt about it," he said meaningfully, "I'm a very lucky man this holiday season."

As was she, in a way, since she had been dreading this holiday alone more than she could say. "Now if we could only pick out a tree," Amanda demurred, changing the subject smoothly.

"Well, let's see if I can assist you with that," Slim said.

Fifteen minutes later, a beautiful seven-foot Scotch pine

was tied onto the top of Riley's SUV. "What are we going to do about the presents?" Amanda asked.

Riley paused. "You're right. We can't let the kids see them before Christmas morning. It would ruin the surprise."

Amanda thought for a moment, glad to have something practical to focus on. "We could store them at my place in the meantime and pick up some decorations for the tree, while we're there. Unless you have some?"

Riley shook his head. "I've never even had a tree," he confessed sheepishly.

Amanda did a double take. "Never?"

Riley shrugged his broad shoulders listlessly. "It always seemed like too much of a bother for one person."

Unable to resist teasing him, Amanda said, "Did you say 'Bah, Humbug,' too?"

"Ha, ha, Miss Merry Holidays." Riley made a face and Amanda laughed.

Having gotten the reaction he wanted from her, he sobered once again and asked curiously, "So, when did you start putting up your own tree?"

Amanda's gaze drifted to his hands. Strong, capable, masculine. She was in awe of how gentle they could be. "From the time I had my first apartment in nursing school. Heck, even in the dorm, I put up a little tabletop tree and put lights up around my room."

"Somehow that doesn't surprise me," Riley drawled, parking in the space in front of her townhome-style one bedroom apartment. They carried packages to the stoop. While Amanda unlocked the front door, he went back for more. By the time he joined her with the last of the children's presents, she had slipped off her jacket, and turned the lights on the tree in the center of her living room. The evergreen tree was beautifully decorated, with white lights, colored glass balls and candy canes. An angel sat on the top. A single stocking hung on the mantel. "We're not going to have to undecorate your tree, are we?" Riley asked.

"Oh, no. I've got lots of decorations. I collect them."

Amanda disappeared up the stairs that led to the loft-style bedroom and bath upstairs. She returned with a large plastic storage bin. She opened it up and began to sort through the decorations she had collected over the years. "Let's see here. I've got colored lights, garlands, lots of red and green and gold velvet bows, and a star for the top. Do you think that will do? It's all pretty kid-friendly stuff."

"I think it will be perfect." With a frown, Riley glanced at his watch.

"I know." Amanda smiled in commiseration, feeling as reluctant to leave the intimate setting as he. She got the decorations ready to go. "We've got to get a move on," she said, as the phone attached to his belt began to buzz. "We told Laurel and Micki we'd be home before three o'clock, and it's almost that now."

Riley lifted the cell phone from its leather holster and glanced at the caller ID. "Speaking of Laurel," he drawled humorously, then hit the speaker-phone function on his phone. "Hey, baby sister. What's up?"

"Riley, you've got to come quick," Laurel said urgently.

"Why?" Riley demanded, suddenly looking as alarmed as Amanda felt, at the anxious tone of his sister's voice. "Nothing's wrong with the kids? Is it?"

"Oh, no," Laurel quickly confirmed, to Amanda's and Riley's mutual relief. "It's Mom and Dad," she explained nervously. "They're on the way over here."

Riley frowned, still perplexed. "And that is cause for alarm because…" Riley prodded his sister gently, while still holding Amanda's eyes.

Abruptly, Laurel sounded near tears. "They're going to yell at me."

Chapter Seven

"Since when have Mom and Dad ever yelled at you?" Riley asked, picking up the conversation with his distraught younger sister the moment he and Amanda walked in the door.

Laurel's lower lip trembled. She cast a look over her shoulder at Micki, who was playing with the two older children, while Cory sat beside her in the bouncy seat. "You know what I mean," she sulked, folding her arms in front of her, for a moment looking far less than her twenty-two years. "They're always so protective, and so darn nosy when it comes to my life!"

Barely able to contain his exasperation, Riley rolled his eyes. "I believe that's called being a parent."

Blue eyes spitting fire, Laurel continued to pout. She threw up her hands, all indignant fury. "When are they going to realize I'm an adult, capable of running my own life?"

This did not sound good, Riley thought. His parents did not lose their tempers with Laurel without a darn good reason. "What exactly did you do?" Riley demanded as a Jaguar sedan pulled up in front of the house.

"It's more like what I didn't do," Laurel mumbled. Peering out the window, she yanked open the front door and stepped out onto the front stoop. Riley took Amanda's hand, pulling her along with him and followed suit, shutting the door behind them. It appeared there was going to be some sort of showdown between his baby sister and their parents. Riley saw no reason to inflict it on Micki and the children. Amanda was a different matter. If she was going to be a part of his family, she needed to know what she was getting into. The McCabes were a close-knit bunch. If something needed to be said, it got said. Even if it hurt temporarily.

"You're not making any sense," Riley told Laurel as Kate and Sam marched determinedly toward them.

Laurel sighed loudly and shoved the wavy length of her dark hair away from her face. She looked at Amanda, who smiled at Laurel sympathetically, then turned back to Riley. "Mom and Dad saw my grades for fall semester."

"So what's the problem?" Riley asked, irritated by all the unnecessary drama in front of Amanda. "You're an A student."

"I thought we had a deal that you were going to be home to talk to us about this at three o'clock," Sam McCabe said as he reached the stoop.

Beside him, Riley's stepmother, Kate, looked equally upset.

Riley felt Amanda tense. He reached over and took her hand, not caring at the surprised looks that gesture generated.

"I was babysitting for Riley and Amanda's kids," Laurel said. She folded her arms in front of her aggressively as if prepared for battle.

Figuring a big brouhaha would help nothing, Riley did his best to ease the tension. "I didn't know anything about a family meeting or Amanda and I would have been here earlier and made sure Laurel was home on time," Riley said. "Although for the record, I think everyone is overreacting just a tad. What did Laurel do anyway? Get a B?" How big a tragedy was that? Geez. And he'd thought the Witherspoons were interfering and overprotective with their daughters!

"Try two Fs," Sam said grimly.

"What?" Riley and Amanda both did a double take.

"And two Cs," Kate added, equally concerned.

"Hey, let's not forget I got an A in my communications class," Laurel stated rebelliously.

"Unfortunately, that's not your major," Sam returned sternly. "And the grades in your area of concentration will determine what kind of job you can get upon your graduation in May. Employers are going to look at your performance in your business classes the last four months and wonder what in the heck has been going on with you."

"Do you-all really need to have this discussion here?" Riley asked in mounting exasperation. Wasn't this between Laurel and their parents?

Kate looked at Laurel with understanding. "Come home with us, dear."

Laurel moved so she was standing slightly behind and to the right of Riley and Amanda. "No." She regarded their parents stubbornly.

"At least give us an explanation then," Kate pleaded.

Laurel shrugged. "My grades are bad because I didn't have time to study."

"Why not?" Sam prodded.

"I was helping out a friend of mine who was in trouble," Laurel explained, stubborn as ever.

"For four months?" Sam asked disbelievingly.

"Yes," Laurel retorted, just as heatedly. "And for the record, if I had it to do all over again, I would—even knowing I was going to get such bad grades. Because that's just the kind of person I am!"

As her emotional diatribe concluded, Riley half expected his spoiled baby sister to say, 'So there!' and stick out her tongue, too. Fortunately, she did not.

"Is the friend still in trouble?" Kate interjected gently, using her skills as a gifted psychologist to inject tranquility into the volatile situation.

"Not so much," Laurel eventually allowed, a little less sullenly.

"Tell me the friend isn't male," Sam said, frown deepening.

Now that was like pouring gasoline on a fire, Riley thought. Thanks, Dad. Out of the corner of his eye he saw Amanda cast Laurel a sympathetic look. He followed with a warning look of his own. Laurel knew better than to talk back to their father.

"You've never liked any of my boyfriends!" Laurel returned furiously.

"Maybe because your boyfriends aren't on par with you," Sam agreed, not the least bit mollified.

Now that sounded like what the Witherspoons had to say about him, Riley thought.

Kate rolled her eyes as she stepped between father and daughter. "All right. Enough, both of you."

"Well, tell Daddy to stop being so mean to all my boyfriends," Laurel insisted.

"Well, start bringing home some that are worthy of you," Sam replied in the same contentious tone.

"How about we all just calm down and appreciate the fact that it's the Christmas season and we are all happy and healthy and here in Laramie together," Riley suggested.

Kate nodded in agreement. She turned back to Riley and Amanda in obvious relief. "Speaking of Christmas," Kate said, "the hospital has a favor to ask of you. It seems the person we had lined up to play old Saint Nick at tomorrow afternoon's pediatric party—as well as the person who volunteered to play Mrs. Claus on Christmas Eve—both have the flu. So, your names came up. I've got the costumes in the car. How about it? Either of you game?"

"Be happy to," Riley said, relieved at the change of subject.

"Me, too," Amanda said.

"In return," Riley continued, "Amanda and I would like you to do a favor for us."

"Name it," Kate said.

"Come in. Spend some time with the three kids. And tell us what you think…."

"They're obviously grieving," Kate concluded half an hour later as she helped Riley and Amanda prepare hot chocolate in the kitchen. In the living room, Sam had set the tree up in the stand and secured it to the ceiling with heavy-duty twine that would keep it from tipping over. Micki and Laurel were stringing it with lights, while Amber and Chloe watched intently, and Cory slept in the portable bassinet nearby.

Amanda got out the mugs and lined them up on the counter. "Well, that's to be expected, isn't it?" she asked Kate. "Since they're separated from whoever it is who normally takes care of them?"

"And yet," Kate pointed out, "the children aren't frantic, the way you would expect them to be if they had been ripped from their caretaker's arms, only a few days ago."

Riley went back to stand beside Amanda, so close their shoulders were touching. "You think the children should be crying under the circumstances."

Kate nodded, her expression solemn. "Amber and Chloe are definitely old enough to suffer from separation anxiety, but instead of sobbing constantly for their mommy and daddy, and running to the window and looking out, they just look sad and sort of resigned."

"Like the abandonment has been going on for a while?" Riley presumed.

Kate added marshmallows to the mugs lined up on the counter. "It's as if they are used to attaching themselves to whatever kind adult is handy. That's not a good situation. It doesn't bode well for what's happened in the past, or what might happen in the future."

Amanda reached over and took Riley's hand. He squeezed

it, hard, letting her know whatever happened, they were in this together, and they would move heaven and earth to protect and care for those kids. It wasn't a task Riley would have asked for, but it was one he had been given this Christmas season and took very seriously.

Amanda squeezed Riley's hand in return. She met his eyes, letting him know with a single glance they were of one mind on this, then moved to get a tin of Christmas cookies.

"I'm especially worried about Chloe," Amanda told Kate. "Amber babbles constantly but Chloe hasn't said a word since she was left with us."

"And yet you can tell Chloe understands everything that is being said because if you ask her to do something, she knows what you mean and she's cooperative in the extreme," Kate observed.

Which meant what? Riley wondered. That Chloe was afraid of being abandoned? Again? And was trying to do whatever she could to prevent it from happening? The worry over what the kids had been through, and might still be facing, brought an ache to Riley's heart. Resolve to his gut. "What can we do to help Chloe feel better and start talking again?" Riley asked, no longer surprised by the fierce protectiveness he felt for the children.

"For starters," Kate advised, "make life as normal for the children as possible. Have Chloe and Amber do things that might seem familiar to Chloe, like help put the ornaments on the tree, once Sam has the lights all the way on, or bake Christmas cookies. Take the kids to the pediatric party tomorrow and let them sit on Santa's lap. Who knows? If it is exciting enough, Chloe may forget her grief and her anxiety and start telling us what's on her mind. Or at least ask Santa for the help she wants…"

"WANT TO HELP ME put the star on the tree?" Riley asked Chloe.

Chloe looked at Riley shyly. Her wildly curling light

brown hair bobbing, she nodded her head ever so slightly and put her tiny hand on a point of the star, next to his. Riley boosted her a little higher in his arms, and hoisted her so she was within reach of the top of the tree. Amber sat on the sofa, sucking her first two fingers while Amanda climbed onto the step stool positioned on the other side of the tree and helped guide the star in Chloe's hand onto the top branch. Chloe grinned, her light blue eyes radiating both satisfaction and excitement, as the star settled into place.

"It's pretty, isn't it?" Amanda smiled.

Chloe smiled back and gave another little head bob, but still didn't say a word.

Amanda went back to the sofa and lifted Amber so she could see, too. The toddler's brown eyes widened. She began to babble incoherently. Occasionally, they heard "pretty" but could not comprehend anything else of what Amber was saying.

Riley stepped back and plugged in the lights. The tree glowed with colored lights and pretty velvet ribbons. On the lower branches were child-safe figures—elves, Santa and Mrs. Claus, reindeer, snowmen and gingerbread men. All were within reach of the two children, and could be taken off and then replaced on the lower branches of the tree as much as the children desired.

"Pretty," seventeen-month-old Amber said again.

Chloe remained silent, but spellbound.

"I hate to say it, kiddos, but it's time for bed," Amanda said gently. "So what do you say? Shall we go upstairs, get into our jammies and read a Christmas story?"

She held out her hands. Chloe and Amber each took one.

Happier than he could recall being in a very long time, if not ever, Riley went along to help tuck them in. Twenty minutes later, all three children were sound asleep. Riley and Amanda were back downstairs. The rest of the evening stretched ahead, intimate and inviting.

Amanda smiled, admiring their handiwork from the doorway of the formal living room. "I'm glad we got the tree."

"Me, too," Riley agreed. It looked as perfect in front of the bay picture window as the fire did roaring in the grate, on the other side of the room.

Riley walked over to add another log to the fire. "I just worry we might be going overboard," Amanda said after a moment.

Riley shut and locked the glass doors that kept the children safely away from the flames. He regarded Amanda, noting how beautiful she looked with her dark blond hair casually upswept, and her thin-wale cranberry shirt untucked. "Overboard in what way?" he asked as she neared.

Amanda ran her open palm down the side of her form-fitting black slacks. She raked her teeth across the softness of her lower lip. Worry lit her pretty blue-green eyes. "When we tucked them in just now, it felt like they were ours."

To Riley, too. "And that's a bad thing?" he teased, knowing where she was going with this, even as he wished she wouldn't.

Amanda swallowed hard, abruptly looking as if she might cry. "What if Kevin finds out whom they really belong to and that person wants them back?" she asked, stubbornly voicing the thoughts he refused to think. "What if this was all a way to give the kids a happy Christmas their own parents couldn't manage, financially or otherwise?" Amanda paused, shook her head. "I've been down this road before, Riley," she continued in a low, choked voice. "I've taken children into my heart, made them my own and had them ripped away. It hurts more than you could ever imagine."

Riley was beginning to—it had only been a few days, and already he felt as much a daddy to the children as Amanda did their mother.

"And even if no one comes to claim them or we discover their parents have permanently abandoned them," she continued, "there's no guarantee that social services would approve our request to adopt them, given the tenuous state of our marriage."

She had a point there, Riley knew. He wrapped his arms around her and held her close. "I'm concerned too," he told her tenderly, pressing a kiss on the top of her head. "I promise you we'll do everything we can to protect them," he murmured, rubbing a hand reassuringly down her back.

Aware they were getting used to touching each other this way, to behaving very much like a couple, he gazed into her eyes. "And we'll start," Riley continued determinedly, "by getting some expert legal advice."

"THANKS FOR COMING OVER this evening," Riley told his aunt, family law attorney Claire McCabe Taylor.

"No problem." Claire allowed Riley to take her coat and hang it up. She ran a hand through her short auburn hair, and carried her briefcase into the living room, where Amanda already had coffee and cookies waiting. "I was working late tonight anyway. What's up?" Claire focused her intelligent dark green eyes on the two of them.

They all sat down. Amanda and Riley on the sofa together, Claire in the club chair opposite them. Briefly, Riley explained the situation while Amanda poured them all a cup of coffee.

"Okay, let me get this straight," Claire said, pausing to sip her coffee and take a few notes on the legal pad in front of her. She pushed her reading glasses farther up on the bridge of her nose. "When someone left Riley the three children, you both thought it was a practical joke. And you continued to think that when you said your I Do's in the hospital hallway."

"Right," Riley said, regretting that more than he could say. He knew now he should have believed Amanda when she first denied having anything to do with the appearance of the children instead of goading her into a prank-marriage both of them were still trying to live down.

"Has anything happened to change that?" Claire tugged at the hem of her discreetly tailored suit jacket. "Have you taken out a license or taken steps to make your union a real one in any way?"

"Are you asking if we have consummated our marriage?" Riley said.

"Not to put too blunt a point on it, but yes," Claire replied matter-of-factly, all lawyer now, "I am."

Amanda and Riley both flushed self-consciously. "Does it make a difference?" Riley asked, hoping it didn't. When he made love to Amanda, and he was determined now that he would, he wanted it to be for all the right reasons. Not as a means to an end.

"It depends." Claire sat back against the chair cushions, looking more concerned about the legal facts of the situation than the emotional ramifications. "If you two are planning to stay married, sleeping together certainly validates the union in the eyes of the court."

And it would certainly bring them closer, Riley thought. Which was exactly what Amanda seemed to fear.

Amanda's eyes darkened unhappily. "Even if we don't have a license?" she asked, avoiding Riley's eyes.

"You still have time to get one." Claire gave them both a pointed look. "And I would advise it if you want to stay married, just because it will makes things simpler in the long run, to have all the loose ends tied up. But," Claire stipulated clearly, "*not* having a license won't invalidate your marriage, since you have said your vows in front of the hospital chaplain and a myriad of other witnesses, are currently living together under the same roof and at least have the opportunity—if not the will—to consummate your union."

Make it as unromantic as possible, why don't you, Riley thought disparagingly, even as he knew this was exactly why he had called the straight-talking Claire over there to meet with them, so they would know exactly where they stood from a legal viewpoint.

"What happens if—at some point—we decide we don't want to stay married after all?" Amanda asked in a low, choked voice. Her hands were trembling slightly as she lifted her coffee cup to her lips. "Can we legally end it without getting a divorce?"

Riley understood why Amanda didn't want a second divorce. Her first had been difficult enough. What she didn't yet realize was that he was beginning not to want an end to their hasty union, either, albeit for totally different reasons.… He wanted to see where this attraction of theirs would lead. Find out if it was as powerful and inevitable as it seemed.

Claire studied them, then said finally with a great deal of lawyerly care, "The fact you two are continuing to live together certainly makes it harder to ask the court for an annulment."

"But not impossible?" Amanda concluded, zeroing in on all Claire hadn't yet stated with obvious relief.

Claire made a seesaw motion with her hand. "You'd need to have grounds, be able to prove that you did not enter this marriage in good faith."

"For example?" Riley questioned, not sure what she meant.

"If you were not of sound mind because you were inebriated," Claire explained. "Or were fooling around, playing a joke on each other. Although personally, I wouldn't go into a court of law and tell a judge that, because the judge would likely think the two of you did not respect the sanctity of marriage, and that could get you into trouble with the court." Claire paused. "So what's going on here? *Are* you two planning to stay married or not?"

Amanda and Riley looked at each other. Were they?

Tension sizzled between them. Try as he might, Riley could not figure out what was in Amanda's heart or on her mind. She seemed as confused about the situation as he was.

He knew she was drawn to him, that she wanted only the best for the children. She also did not want to be hurt and the deeper their involvement with each other became the more potential there was for heartache, if everything did not work out as flawlessly as Riley hoped.

"Would our being married make a difference if we moved for custody of the children, if it turns out they don't have a home or other family to take care of them?" Riley asked.

Claire didn't even hesitate. "The state of your marriage will make a big difference, either way," she advised firmly. "Being part of a union that is a joke, even temporarily, would make you both look unreliable to the court. On the other hand, if you have a solid, committed relationship, and the children are doing well under your care and want to be with you, that will go a long way in your favor, should you request to adopt them."

RILEY WALKED his aunt Claire out to her car. When he returned, Amanda was in the kitchen. She had the can of powdered formula and the jug of sterile water out and was busy assembling all the bottles for the next day. She looked rumpled and tired, and worried to her bones.

Riley felt exactly the same way.

He walked over to lend a hand by assembling the plastic components that went inside the bottle and kept baby Cory from imbibing too much air during feedings. "About what Claire said," Riley started.

"Your aunt is right about one thing," Amanda returned, before he could even attempt to persuade her that they had done the right thing in letting their growing feelings for each other practically lead them into bed. "We never should have gotten married the way we did with both of us thinking—erroneously, as it turned out—that it was all a practical joke that had gotten way out of hand. Had I even suspected," Amanda continued grimly," that our behavior could hurt our chance at an annulment later on, I never would have said 'I do.'"

"But we did say 'I do,'" Riley reminded her.

"And now," Amanda worried out loud, "we're living together, which only adds to the public perception that our marriage is a real one."

Sometimes it felt like one, Riley thought. To Amanda, too, it would seem. Was that what was really bothering her?

Riley took her hands in his. They were soft and silky and very feminine. "Claire didn't say our situation was hopeless, Amanda."

A distant look came into her eyes as she shrugged off his assertion. "Of course not. She's much too tactful to tell us what a mess we've made of our lives with our reckless behavior."

Taking in the tension in Amanda's slender frame, it was all he could do not to take her in his arms and kiss her until she went limp with longing. Keeping his eyes locked on hers, he continued, "But you obviously think we have done just that. Don't you?"

Amanda extricated herself from his grip and went back to putting the nipples and lids on the baby bottles. "I think our playing house this way has unnecessarily complicated our situation, and may get in the way of our getting a simple annulment as opposed to a divorce."

She sounded more the dispassionate attorney than his aunt had, Riley noted, as he helped her put the assembled bottles into the fridge. "And if you have to get another divorce you're going to feel like a two-time loser," he guessed.

Amanda shut the door with more force than was required. As she swung back around, she favored him with an unappreciative smile. "Be blunt, why don't you?" she said sweetly.

Riley backed her up against the appliance, not above reminding her that she was still his wife, still the woman—the only woman—he wanted in his life. He flattened his arms on either side of her, caging her in with the length of his body. He let his gaze drift over her in the same dispassionate way she was regarding him. "Is that the only reason why you don't want a divorce from me?"

Amanda's eyes sparkled and her deliciously full lower lip slid out in a kissable pout. She lifted her hands in an indifferent gesture and let them rest against his chest, carefully keeping him at bay. "What other reason could there be?" she challenged.

Riley sifted his fingers through her hair, loving the silky feel of it. The way her body shuddered and softened toward his, even as temper flashed in her eyes. "The difference in connotation between the two ways to end a marriage, perhaps?" he answered as she slipped beneath his outstretched arms and danced away from him. "A divorce indicates the people were married and they tried to make it work and failed. Whereas an annulment," Riley specified brusquely, "seems to imply they were never *really* married at all."

Amanda gave Riley a deliberately provoking look. Smiled with all the resolve of a born-and-bred Texas belle. "Which is why I would prefer to have one," she stated resolutely, as they continued their breathless two-step around the kitchen until her back was to the wall and he was in front of her once again.

"But it's not really true, is it?" Riley retorted, just as determinedly. Excitement building inside him, he struggled to examine his own emotions. "Especially when you consider we have been taking care of the kids together, have been behaving as husband and wife, slept in the same bed, and have nearly made love—"

Pretty color flooded her cheeks. "One night, Riley! And we did not finish what we started!"

Riley let his glance rove slowly over Amanda from head to toe, taking in her long, lithe legs, slender waist and generous breasts. "Only because you called a halt."

Her glinting eyes were hot with temper, her chest rising and falling with each breath. He braced a hand on either side of her and held his ground, all the while cautioning himself not to move too fast. His voice dropped another intimate notch. "If it had been up to me we would have risked it all then, and we still would."

Exasperation hissed through her teeth. She kept her gaze level with his as she continued to study him. "You're impossible."

Riley grinned and reminded himself to be the gentleman he had been raised to be. "I'm realistic." He looked at her sternly. "Bottom line, we want to take care of these kids, Amanda. Our best shot at doing that is by staying married. And if we're going to stay married, sex is going to have to come into the equation somewhere, given the fact we are both young healthy adults who clearly have the hots for each other. Even if you're too stubborn to admit it."

Amanda raised her delicate brow in pointed disagreement. "Whether we desire each other is irrelevant. We don't love each other, Riley!"

"That doesn't stop a lot of married couples I know," he insisted, determined that someway—somehow—they would handle this without sacrificing the passion they'd discovered but had yet to fully experience.

Amanda gave him a censuring look.

"Okay, bad joke," he apologized calmly, resisting the urge to take her all the way into his arms and kiss her, only because he was afraid she would take any move at this juncture the wrong way.

"Thank you." Amanda paused. "Besides, we haven't discussed every way of keeping the kids, assuming they have no other home or family. You could adopt them as a single parent, Riley, and hire a nanny or a housekeeper."

Riley knew that but the option did not appeal to him. He wanted to continue this arrangement the way it had started, with he and Amanda caring for the children together. "Where would you fit into their lives if I did that?" he asked softly, knowing she had to be as aware as he what a good team they made.

A troubled look came into her eyes. "I could still be their friend or mother figure."

Now who was kidding themselves! "And you'd be satisfied with that?" he prodded gently. A silence fell that told him she would not. She was simply looking for a way out of their increasingly complicated connection to each other. Guilt washed over Riley, for ever putting her in such a convoluted situation.

"Anyway," Riley continued, doing his best to put a practical spin on their situation that Amanda could accept, "a housekeeper slash nanny is out. I've already been there, done that, the year after my mom died." He had never had a more miserable existence. Nor had the rest of his family. He would not inflict it on the three innocent babes sleeping upstairs.

"That's right," Amanda recalled thoughtfully. The tension in her slender shoulders eased once again. "You and your siblings had a whole series of nannies before your Dad moved you all back to Laramie."

"Ten of 'em, in six months, and they were all awful." Riley pulled a ladder-back chair out from under the table and sank into it. Taking Amanda by the wrist, he guided her gently onto his lap. "If Kate hadn't agreed to step in and help out for a few weeks—as a favor to my grandparents—I don't know what we would have done."

Amanda settled more comfortably on his thighs and wreathed her arms about his neck. "Look, just because your dad hired some bad nannies doesn't mean that there aren't any good ones out there."

Riley supposed that was true. It wasn't the point.

"You really want to put these three kids through a trial-and-error process while we search for the perfect Mary Poppins after all they have already been through?" He swallowed hard around the sudden lump in his throat. "Do you really want to deny them your tender loving care?"

Amanda raked her teeth across her lower lip. It was obvious to Riley how much she already loved them. "I guess that doesn't make sense," she admitted finally.

"You're darn right it doesn't," Riley agreed without hesitation.

Worry lit her eyes. "But neither does pretending to have a real marriage just to be able to adopt the kids!"

Riley shrugged and, his mind already racing ahead, asked point-blank, "Who says we have to pretend?"

Chapter Eight

"The fact we're not in love with each other?" Amanda guessed, citing the most obvious deterrent to their staying hitched that came to mind.

"But that doesn't mean we will never be in love," Riley argued in a low practical tone. "When Kate Marten moved in with my dad and my brothers and me, she and my dad didn't even like each other. In fact, the two of them irritated the heck out of each other."

Amanda tapped her chin in a parody of thoughtfulness. "I see that similarity."

Riley ignored her droll remark. His amber eyes took on a persuasive gleam. "Plus, Kate was engaged to be married to some other guy."

Amanda drew in a bolstering breath. She had feared all along the intimacy of their situation would be too much for them. She had counted on the kids to serve as distraction, chaperones and all-around energy sappers. Instead, their mutual love of the children was drawing them inexplicably closer. Which meant it was up to her to keep a cool head. Amanda favored Riley with an artificially bright smile. "Except I'm not engaged to someone else."

"Yes, that is one thing in our favor," Riley acknowledged in the same droll tone, before turning serious and shifting her closer, once again. "The point is," he continued gently, searching her eyes, "both Kate and my dad cared about all of us kids. And that shared concern brought them closer and closer, until there was no longer any denying the fact that the two of them had fallen in love with each other and wanted to spend their lives together, taking care of us."

Amanda swallowed around the sudden lump in her throat and tried not to think how handsome Riley looked in his sweater-vest, pin-striped button-down shirt, and faded jeans. "You think because it happened to them it could happen to us?" Despite her efforts to keep her emotional distance, she could feel herself being drawn in.

"Yes. But even if it doesn't happen in that same way, I think you and I and the kids have what it takes to make a happy family. Think about it, Amanda." Riley cupped a hand over her knee, the warmth of his palm spurring her heart to beat a little faster, even before he gave her a companionable squeeze. His eyes darkening with possessive intent, he shifted his grip from her knee to her hand and affably continued making his case. "You and I have always gotten each other and known what makes each other tick, otherwise we never could have kept our long-running practical jokefest going all through high school."

That was certainly true, Amanda thought, feeling the warmth and tenderness of his comforting presence all the way to her soul.

"We share a common concern and affection for Chloe, Amber and Cory. We both want to be their parents, if it turns out they are as 'genuinely orphaned' as they appear." Riley ticked off his reasons, one after another. "We share a love of medicine and healing others. We work well together as a parenting team. Plus—" he paused to let the weight of his words sink in "—we both decided—separately, but at the same time in our life—that we wanted to return to our roots and make our home in Laramie."

These were all good reasons. At one very naive time in her

life, Amanda had imagined they were all reason enough to make a marriage last. A heart-wrenching loss of the husband who never really loved her, the kids she had come to call her own and a painful if matter-of-fact divorce had taught her otherwise. She wanted it all. She wanted to know, if she ever committed herself heart and soul to a man again that he would love and cherish her and stick with her through thick and thin. She did not want to live the rest of her life waiting for Riley to figure out, as her ex-husband had, that he really loved and wanted to be with someone else.

"And then of course," Riley teased in a low, risqué voice, "there is the sex. I think we've got real potential there, too."

There it was, the trademark orneriness, the inability to be serious for more than five minutes at a time, that she had been expecting from Riley all along. "I knew you were going to bring that up," Amanda declared hotly. She wished she didn't want him to kiss her again, but she did. And judging by the way he was looking at her, he wanted to kiss her again, too. She tried to get up off his lap.

He wouldn't let her. So she tried again. And this time he did let her go. "I know we haven't actually made love yet—at least not all the way," he said as he followed her to the adjacent laundry room, "but I think when we do it's going to be amazing."

Amanda flushed self-consciously despite herself. She opened the lid of the washer and began transferring wet baby clothes into the dryer. "Plus we get each other, Amanda. And we share the same sense of humor. Many an arranged marriage has started—and succeeded—on much less." Riley stood close enough to be able to see her face, but not so near he was in her way. His voice dropped a compelling notch. "Given the right conditions, the love between a man and woman can grow as easily and completely as the love we already feel for the kids."

Wordlessly, Amanda shut the dryer door and switched it on.

She took a load of pastel bath towels and receiving blankets and stuffed them into the well of the washer.

Riley picked up the pink-and-white bottle of laundry detergent specially formulated for young children's tender skin and removed the cap. "I know there are no guarantees, Amanda," he said as he filled the measuring cup to the line and handed her that, too. "There never are when it comes to relationships." He paused as she poured in liquid detergent, handed the lid back to him and added fabric softener to the dispenser. "But don't you think we at least deserve a real chance at making this work—in every way—instead of arbitrarily setting limits on our feelings that may not hold in any case?"

Amanda set the dials and hit the on button, then turned, resting a slender hip against the machine. She folded her arms in front of her, doing her best to hide the hurt and disappointment she felt, at having been proposed to in such an unemotional way. "I think you missed your calling," Amanda returned dryly, wishing fervently that Riley could love her the way she was beginning to love him, with all her heart and soul. But he didn't and she needed to force herself to remember that before she found herself becoming a "convenience" in lieu of a "wife" once again. "You should have been a salesman," she told him admirably, pretending a joking ease she couldn't begin to really feel. "Because with a silver tongue like that you could probably sell anything."

Riley ignored her attempt at levity. He let his glance rove her face before returning with laser accuracy to her eyes. "Does that mean you agree?"

"It means…" Amanda drew a deep breath and forced herself to hold her ground, even as she protected her heart, and the hearts of the three children involved. "I am seriously confused." *And so seriously in lust with you, Riley McCabe, that I can't stand it.*

Something flashed in Riley's eyes. He began to relax. "You don't have to decide anything now," he reassured her softly, lounging back against the opposite wall. He slid his hands in the pockets of his jeans and continued talking to her as casually as if they were discussing the weather. "All you have to do is leave yourself open to the possibility that this current conundrum of ours might actually turn out to be the best thing that ever happened to us."

And what if it was just another road to heartache and misery? Amanda wondered.

Riley straightened, a confidence-inspiring smile on his face. "We can do this, Amanda," he told her, abruptly leaving all traces of the reckless side of him behind. "We can make our marriage a real one in every way if we remove the self-imposed limits and just allow ourselves and our imaginations free rein."

FIGURING HE HAD PUSHED as hard as he dared for one night, Riley said good-night to Amanda and let her go on to bed—alone—in the guest room while he stayed up late with Cory, giving the infant his last bottle of the night and rocking him back to sleep, before turning in himself at midnight.

He figured he almost had Amanda agreeing with him, but by morning he could see her guard was up once again. Which meant he was going to have to use every weapon in his romantic arsenal to get her to open up her heart to him as readily as she had already done with the three kids. Riley figured, with a little help from family and friends, he could do it. Because now that he knew what he wanted—a relationship with Amanda every bit as strong and enduring and unexpected as Kate and Sam's—failure simply was not an option.

In the meantime, he and Amanda had the task of playing Santa and Mrs. Claus for the kids in the hospital. Riley was going to be up first. He knew it was a long shot, but he hoped the Christmas ritual would spark something in Chloe, help her start talking again. He wanted the little girl to feel secure enough to speak again. Riley knew Amanda harbored the same hope. Hence, their spirits were high as Riley, Amanda and the three kids met up with Micki and Laurel at the pediatric ward the next afternoon, in advance of the big event. Instead of their usual pink-and-white volunteer aprons and white shirts, both young women were dressed like Santa's elves.

Laurel winked at Riley and swiftly gave him the info he needed. "Santa is going to be joining us in the pediatric playroom for our staff and patient Christmas party at two this afternoon."

Riley glanced at his watch. That gave him approximately thirty minutes to get dressed. "I'll be in my office, taking care of something," he said.

Micki stepped into his path. "Before you leave, you have to write a letter to Santa," she interjected with a smile.

Riley took the holly-green paper and envelope they handed him. He looked over at Amanda. She looked pretty in a trim black wool skirt, white turtleneck and dark green Christmas cardigan, embroidered with gaily wrapped gifts, decorated trees and candy canes. Opaque black tights made the most of her slender, showgirl legs. "You, too," he said.

Amanda smiled and ran a hand through her straight and silky hair, pushing it away from her slender shoulders. "I already mailed my letter to Santa weeks ago," she said with a mysterious grin.

Noting the pinkness of her cheeks, Riley wondered what she had asked Santa to bring her. But figuring she wasn't about to tell him, at least not here and now, he held the paper so only he could see and quickly filled in his yuletide request.

Finished, he slid the paper into the envelope and sealed it. "Put it in the mailbox." Laurel pointed to the box on the post next to the Santa's Workshop in the corner.

Riley walked over and slid it into the slot.

Still wondering what was in Amanda's letter to Santa, he kissed the kids goodbye and squeezed Amanda's shoulders. Ignoring the mixture of caution and desire in her eyes that had been there ever since they got up that morning, he brushed his lips against her temple, too, then headed to the parking garage to pick up the garment bag containing the borrowed Santa suit and went on up to his new office space.

It was just as he had left it the other day, with diplomas half-hung, and boxes of belongings scattered among the utilitarian office furniture the hospital had supplied.

Feeling a little blue that chief of staff Jackson McCabe hadn't yet seen fit to reinstate him and Amanda, Riley switched on the office intercom. "Silver Bells" filled the air as he stripped down to his boxers and T-shirt and pulled the pants up over his legs. The first thing he noticed was that the pants were way too short, the second was that the waist was about a foot and a half too large for his belly. A fact that would have been no problem, had the wide black belt been notched to fit him, but it was cut to wear with the pants.

Riley searched through the rest of the costume. There was no stuffing for his waist. He picked up the phone and asked the hospital operator to page Amanda Witherspoon. Seconds later, her voice came on the line. "Amanda speaking."

Warming at the sound of her sweet, melodious voice, Riley replied, "Hello, Amanda. This is your husband speaking."

A slight pause in which she seemed to be thinking a moment. "What's up?" she asked finally.

"If you're not that busy, could you bring me a pillow?"

She laughed, a soft silky sound. "Is this a trick question?"

Riley sighed and took another look at the pants hem hovering just below his calves. Good thing those boots were nearly knee-high. Or should have been knee-high if he weren't so tall. "The only trick involved is how I'm going to keep these pants up without something to hold them up. And since I can't exactly run around the hospital half-dressed without spoiling the surprise for the kiddos…"

"I'll be right there." Click.

Suddenly feeling a little happier and a lot more optimistic, Riley sat down to wait. To his pleasure, Amanda wasn't long in getting there. She breezed in, two pillows in hand. "Just in case we need to make you a little rounder than one pillow will allow," she said.

"I thought these suits came with special padding," Riley said.

Her expression softening compassionately, she tossed him one fluffy white pillow. Riley caught it one-handed. "Maybe whoever wore it last didn't need the extra, um, girth," she speculated cheerfully.

"Good point." Glad he had her help, Riley slid the padding into the front of his pants. The pillow kept going until it hit the seam at the base of the zipper.

"I think you're going to need to put the jacket on before we can secure it, since the belt goes over the jacket." Her expression as serious as the task of creating a viable St. Nick for the kids, Amanda handed Riley the coat. As Riley released his grip on the waistband of his pants and dutifully slipped the jacket on, his pants and the pillow both fell down to his knees. Amanda's soft laughter filled the air.

Had they been anywhere else, had Riley been able to take advantage of his unexpected disrobing and make love to her then and there, or at the very least get in a few passionate kisses, he wouldn't have minded the situation one bit. As it was, he just felt ridiculous. "Oh, man, this is just not going to work," Riley said, embarrassed. Though he didn't necessarily mind being indisposed around Amanda, being so around the kids and their parents and staff and having a wardrobe malfunction was another matter indeed.

"Sure it will, we just have to figure it out," Amanda said confidently. Her lips curving determinedly, she searched through the garment bag and pulled out two suspenders. "For starters, these will help," she said, holding the black elastic aloft.

Riley looked skeptical. "It will keep my pants up, but it won't keep the pillows in place."

Amanda grinned. "Give me a chance to work some magic here."

While Riley held his pants at waist height, Amanda stepped behind him and snapped on the suspenders, front and back, then helped adjust them so they fit over his shoulders. She slid two pillows in front of him. They filled in the space created by the extra fabric at Riley's waist. Riley looked and felt ridiculous. "I look about nine months pregnant," he quipped, trying not to think about what her nearness was doing to him. "Which wouldn't be bad if I were a woman and expecting, but…"

Amanda studied him while he thought about kissing her again. "Maybe we should put one in front and one in back," she said. No sooner had she tried it, than she clapped her hand over her mouth and burst into giggles. "Um, no."

"A little too roly-poly?" Riley asked, wondering even as he spoke how it was possible for her to get prettier every single time he saw her. Amanda had been a real looker when she was a teenager, but that was nothing compared to how gorgeous she was now.

She shook her head, explaining merrily, "A backside that's just too oddly shaped."

"Well, we wouldn't want that," Riley drawled.

"Let's try this," she said, and put the pillows side by side on his chest, instead of one on top of each other. The fluffy white cushions wrapped around his sides, but kept the girth more barrel shaped and hence like Santa.

"Now if we can just figure out how to keep the pillows from slipping around," Riley lamented.

Amanda snapped her fingers. "We'll use surgical tape!" She went into the supply cabinet in one of the exam rooms, and returned to the private office where Riley was dressing.

Now they were talking, Riley thought. "So what did you ask Santa for Christmas?" he asked Amanda curiously as she secured the pillows around his midriff. He had to admit he liked it when she put her hands on him like this and acted all wifely. Maybe because such moments gave him a glimpse of what it would be like to really be married to her, heart and soul.

She slanted him a flirtatious look. "If I tell you, it won't come true."

"Sure it will," Riley declared with a wink, "since I'm Santa."

She straightened, the silk of her honey-colored hair brushing against his chin, and flashed him a lofty smile. "Not the real one."

Riley liked matching wits with Amanda. It made him feel as if he was in one of those old Tracy-Hepburn movies Kate and his dad liked to watch on TV. "There is no real Santa," he said.

"Sure about that?" Amanda taunted with exaggerated certainty. She moved away from him, offering him a great view of her stunning backside as she put the tape and scissors away.

Riley followed her lazily. He put his hands on her shoulders and brushing the silky curtain of hair aside, gave in to temptation and pressed a fleeting kiss on the nape of her neck. Her skin was silky and warm. "I can give you whatever you want, you know."

She quivered at his questing touch and turned to face him. Splaying both hands across his chest to hold him at bay, she tilted her head at him and gave him one of those imperious looks that made him want to haul her against him and kiss her until all pretense between them faded and she went weak in the knees. She shook her head at him in an indifferent gesture. "I don't think that would be prudent, do you?"

Riley wrapped both arms about her waist, regretting the layers of cotton that kept them from really touching, middle to middle. "Since when have you ever wanted to be prudent, Mrs. McCabe?"

"Since forever," Amanda said.

Riley grinned. The one thing Amanda was not was a good fibber. Smiling his satisfaction, he looked down at her tenderly, amazed at how much he liked seeing her like this, eyes sparkling feistily, her deliciously full lower lip sliding out in a kissable pout. "Then how about you give me what I want?"

Her eyes shimmering with an unmistakably aroused light, she regarded him in a deliberately provoking manner. "And what would that be, Doctor McCabe?"

You, Riley thought. "This." Riley planted one hand at the base of her spine, the other at her nape. Hauling her as close as the pillows would allow, he dipped his head and, ignoring her soft gasp of surprise, delivered a searing kiss. To his deep contentment, Amanda did not even try to draw away, and he let all he wanted come through in another long, deep kiss.

With an immediacy that stunned him, she confirmed her acquiescence with a soft sigh. Her fragrance waltzed through his system, inundating him with the sweetness of desire. He shuddered as her tongue swept into his mouth, hotly and voraciously, and she threaded her fingers through his hair, bringing his mouth closer still. Her passionate response was all the encouragement he needed. With a low groan, Riley twined his tongue with hers, drinking in the sweet peppermint taste of her lips, and the sweetly feminine fragrance of her skin and hair, making no effort at all to disguise how much he wanted and needed her, and was beginning to realize now that he always would. He wanted to be a husband to her in every way. Starting now. Today.

She groaned as his hands moved to her breasts. "Riley…"

"That's it." He cupped the soft weight in his hands, felt his own body—and hers—tauten in response. He sensed the need pouring out of her, mingling with the desire and the temper. "Say my name," he whispered huskily against her throat. Unable to help himself, he delivered another stolen kiss, this one sweeter, more drawn out than the last. His need to be close to her as overwhelming as it was inevitable, he tipped her head up to allow him greater access, and kissed her long and hard and deep. Soft and slow.

"This is not what you were brought here to do this afternoon," Amanda protested, even as she kissed him back, more tenderly and rapaciously than before.

Eager to please her, knowing it couldn't be done here, now, Riley reluctantly broke off the kiss and lifted his head. "You're right," he told her, still struggling between his desire to protect her and his desire to make mad, passionate love to her, damn the consequences to their lives, their careers. Desire thundering through him in waves, he stepped back, very much aware what the self-imposed restraint was costing him. "We shouldn't start something we can't finish here and now."

Amanda pressed a hand to lips that were wet and swollen from their kisses. Her eyes glowed with a soft, ardent gleam, even as sanity returned and she hitched in a short, worried breath. "Or ever, if we're going to be bluntly honest."

Riley wasn't that gallant. He sensed, in the end, she wouldn't be, either, as a passion like this was too strong, too powerful, to resist. But for the moment, he realized reluctantly, there were other yuletide promises to keep and wishes to fulfill. So they'd just have to concentrate on that.

AMANDA WAS NOT surprised the kids in the pediatric ward welcomed "Santa" with shouts of glee and excited smiles. The holiday was always a particularly emotional time for their young patients. Being in the hospital just made it more special. And, gold-rimmed Santa glasses disguising his lively amber eyes, Riley did not disappoint.

"Ho, ho, ho, and what would you like from Santa this year, little boy?" he asked the six-year-old patient, who was still recovering from an automobile accident.

"A pony," the child said enthusiastically.

Amanda watched his parents wince.

"'Cause I want to ride it," the little boy continued, settling as comfortably on Riley's lap as the plaster casts on his arm and his leg would allow.

Riley removed the pipe from the corner of his mouth, then asked in a low, thoughtful voice, "Do you have a barn for the pony to sleep in and a grassy pasture where the pony can eat?"

The little boy shook his head.

Riley stroked his beard. "Hmm. Well," he allowed in a gravelly voice that could very well have belonged to the legendary St. Nick, "a real live pony needs both to be happy. But a stuffed toy pony—now that can stay in your room and even sleep in your bed at night. Would you like that?"

"But I want to ride it!" the little boy pouted.

Riley tilted his head, considering. "Santa's workshop has toy riding ponies," he allowed finally. "The kind that you rock back and forth on. Is that what you mean?"

The little boy nodded. His parents relaxed into smiles. This, apparently, was something they could handle, giftwise. "Well, I'll talk to the elves and see what I can do," Riley said. "In the meantime, you keep on taking your medicine, and do what the nurses and doctors and your folks tell you to do, okay?"

The little boy nodded. He wrapped his uninjured arm about Riley's neck as the photographer took their picture. "I love you, Santa," the child whispered.

Riley smiled as he patted the child's thin shoulders. "Love you, too, son."

Next up was an appendectomy patient, still sore from surgery, who wanted a dollhouse. Then a four-year-old recovering from a tonsillectomy, and an eight-year-old who was undergoing chemotherapy. Finally, it was Cory, Amber and Chloe's turn.

Cory went first. As soon as the infant looked up at Riley's beard, he burst into tears. "Santa" was unable to comfort him, even when he whispered in the infant's ear. Perhaps spooked by her baby brother's reaction, Amber cried, too, and squirmed to get off Riley's lap the moment she was set down. Finally, it was Chloe's turn. Suspicious and uncooperative, she sat with her arms folded in front of her and refused to acknowledge "Santa's" presence, even when Amanda, Micki, Laurel and some of the other "helper elves" coaxed her to do so.

Amanda could tell Riley was bummed about it, and remained so through the rest of the day. By the time they had put the kids to bed for the night, she'd had enough of his pensive mood. It was so unlike him.

"How much longer are you going to continue worrying about what happened today?" she asked as the two of them met up in the family room to clean up the play area. She knew the rest of the day had been difficult for all of them. The kids had wanted Amanda, not Riley, and remained out of sorts all the way to bedtime. It hadn't mattered how Riley had tried. He had remained a persona non grata to the kids, who seemed to resent the fact he hadn't been there to comfort them, along with Amanda, when they had needed him.

"I'm not worrying," Riley declared as he picked up colorful interlocking blocks and tossed them into the plastic carrying case.

Amanda rolled her eyes as she bent over to pick up the storybooks, lent to them by the extended McCabe family. "Ha!" she said as she organized them and put them into a neat stack on one of the end tables.

Riley scowled as he got down on all fours to retrieve the

blocks sticking out from beneath the bottom of the sofa. "Well, maybe I am feeling a little disappointed the kids did not sense they could trust me, costume or no."

And therefore, Amanda guessed, been happy to sit on Santa's lap and confide all. Instead, unlike the rest of the children in the pediatric ward who had greeted Riley's Santa Claus enthusiastically, all three of the children in Riley's care had given him their own version of the heave-ho. "That booming baritone you were using and your costume probably just scared them." She slipped off her black suede flats and wiggled her stocking-clad feet in the carpet. "After all, you were wearing two pillows, a beard, wig and glasses!"

Riley took a moment to admire the view of her legs from down there, before shifting his gaze to his knees. "Kids have a sixth sense about who they can trust and who they can't. That's obviously why they naturally go to you more than me," he ventured with a disgruntled sigh.

Amanda couldn't argue that; the parenting, post-Santa, had been a little one-sided. Not because Riley hadn't been available, but because for whatever reason the three kids had wanted her. And only her, for the rest of the day. To an embarrassing degree. Furthermore, she was as frustrated by the current situation as he was. Doing her best to soothe his wounded feelings and ease the concerned look in his eyes, Amanda said, "They were probably still just a little freaked out by seeing Santa."

Riley winced as he tossed a toy school bus into the storage bin. "I think you just made my case for me."

"Maybe they had never seen a fat man in a hat and beard before," she theorized helpfully, noting Riley did not feel as confident caring for the three children as prior circumstances dictated.

"And maybe," Riley retorted sharply, then softened the effect of his words with a commiserating smile, "all kids need a mother's love more than a father's, especially at times when they are upset or sad or scared, or simply not feeling all that secure."

Able to see he was mentally kicking himself for what he perceived as his failure on the parenting front, Amanda faced him. "Are we talking about Amber, Chloe and Cory?" she asked gently, knowing there had to be more here than what was visible on the surface. "Or you and your siblings after your mom died?"

Riley lifted his shoulders in an indifferent shrug. A brooding look was on his face. "Dad tried, but he just wasn't much comfort," he allowed brusquely.

Amanda could see Riley was worried about following in his father's footsteps. Worried about parenting the kids on his own. Worried about somehow not being up to the task if the kids remained in his care. But she didn't want to be his wife—or their mother—just for that reason. And she feared that was where this assessment on his part was leading. "That was your father's fault, not yours," she stated firmly.

"Whereas Kate—a stranger—was a huge help to us," Riley continued with a sigh.

No surprise there, Amanda thought compassionately as she trod closer. She knew what it was to doubt yourself, feel you had failed, or worse, impulsively gotten yourself into a situation you should have avoided at all costs. It wasn't fun. "Kate's a psychologist and a grief counselor, Riley. And a very talented one at that," she soothed with a sympathetic smile. "Of course she could help you more than your Dad. Kate wasn't grieving your mother. You and your sibs and your dad were. And as for the kids, they wouldn't have responded to me any better had I been the one wearing the Santa suit today."

Riley lifted a skeptical brow. "Care to put that to the test when you wear the Mrs. Santa suit on Christmas Eve?" he challenged mildly, a hint of the old sparkle coming back into his eyes.

Not if it proved the theory he was currently espousing, Amanda thought. Hands spread wide, she inched even closer, and looked at him with exasperation. "It's not a fair comparison, Riley. That will be three days from now. The children will have a lot more time with us, between now and then, than you have had with them thus far and that will in turn give me an unfair advantage over you."

"Meaning what?" Riley scoffed, deliberately weighing every word she said. He took her hand lightly in his. "That you think they'll not just warm to your Mrs. Claus the way they didn't warm to my Santa, but will probably even tell you what they want for Christmas? Not that Cory can do anything but coo yet or we're likely to understand Amber's babbling, mind you."

"But it's the attempt that counts." Amanda guessed where he expected things to go. "Especially if Chloe were to pick that opportunity to speak for the first time."

Riley's fingers tightened over hers. "Right," he said.

Reveling in the warmth of his tender touch, Amanda offered playfully, "And if they want to run in the other direction when they see me in my costume? What then, Riley Mc-Cabe?"

He gave her the lazy once-over. "Then I owe you anything you want for Christmas, Mrs. McCabe."

Amanda's heart rate kicked up another notch. She liked the sexy turn the conversation was taking almost as much as the sound of his low, husky voice. "And if they don't, what then?" Amanda asked.

"Then *you* owe *me* anything *I* want," Riley murmured, his eyes glowing with a determined sensual light as he took her all the way into his arms.

"And what would that be?" Amanda asked, splaying both hands across his chest.

"Guess," Riley lowered his mouth to hers. His lips were warm and firm against hers, sweetly coaxing, loving. And in that moment, everything stopped. The world narrowed to just the two of them. Amanda had waited a lifetime to be kissed and held like this. She had waited a lifetime to feel like this, she thought, as she wreathed her arms about his neck and threaded her fingers through his hair. And she'd be damned if she could stop it. She kissed him back thoroughly, loving the way his tongue stroked hers, once and then again...and again.

Amanda had never been a particularly sexual person, but Riley McCabe made her feel white-hot. All woman. As in need of the emotional comfort and physical reassurance he offered as she was eager to give it, in return. She moaned low in her throat and drew closer yet, swearing as her knees gave way as swiftly as her will to resist. Their coming together like this had been inevitable. She had known that from the very first, which was why she had fought so hard against it. Because she had known making love with Riley would change her forever. As he continued kissing her persuasively that no longer seemed like such a bad thing.

The next thing Amanda knew, Riley was drawing her over to the large sectional sofa. He shut off the lights in the room, stripped off his clothes in the moonlight filtering in through the drapes, then wordlessly helped her out of hers. Another shiver of excitement swept through her. "Beautiful, so beautiful," he breathed as he took her in his arms again and kissed her as if he were in love with her and would be for all time. Aware she had never felt desire like this before, fearful she never would again, she clung to him, returning his caresses eagerly. He guided her down to the sofa, turned her onto her side, facing him and stretched out beside her. Amanda's heart raced as his mouth moved on hers in a kiss that was shattering in its possessive sensuality. His manhood pressed against her inner thighs, hot and hard, as he molded her breasts with his hands, circling the aching crowns, teasing the nipples into tight buds of awareness. Coupled with his wanting, it was enough to drive her toward abandon. She arched against him, murmuring her need low in the back of her throat. "Riley—"

He chuckled softly, pressing his lips against her throat in a series of hot, wet kisses. "We're getting there in due time, I promise." He kissed her again, then his mouth was moving to her ear, the nape of her neck, sending her into a frenzy of wanting once again. Engaging every sense he made his way slowly down her body, patiently exploring, fulfilling every wild and wanton fantasy she had ever had. Shifting from passion to tenderness and back again, until there was only the driving need, only this moment in time, the throbbing of his body and hers. Amanda hitched in a breath, aware he was making her feel so warm and safe, even as she was trembling and falling apart…. "Riley, oh Riley," she whispered as he filled her heart and sent her soaring.

For Riley, their coupling had been years in the making. Aware she had never looked more radiant than she did at that moment, color blushing her cheeks, dark golden hair tumbling over her bare shoulders, he tunneled his hands through the smooth strands and moved upward to once again capture her soft, parted lips. Yielding to him with the sure sensuality of a woman who had secretly been his to take for years and years, she clasped his shoulders and trembled as he kissed her, their bodies taking up a primitive rhythm, until there was no doubting for either of them how much they needed each other, needed this. Not that Riley was really surprised. Amanda had been his obsession all four years of high school. And she had remained in his thoughts every year thereafter. He had told himself he could handle coming back to Laramie, knowing all the while that she was living here again, too.

Now, as she surrendered herself to him completely, the soft whimpering sounds in the back of her throat a counterpoint to the lower, fiercer sounds in his, he realized that Amanda was precisely the reason why he had come back.

Not, as he had first thought, because he wanted to be taken seriously by those who had known him in his teens.

But because there had been something unfinished between them, he realized as he shifted her over onto her back, parted her knees and stroked the delicate insides of her thighs. Because she had haunted his dreams and made him feel alive.

Never more so than right now, Riley noted ardently as he moved to make her his in the most intimate way possible and she arched to receive him. Unable to delay their joining a second longer, he stretched out over her. He slid his hands beneath her, lifted her to him, driving deep, kissing her hotly all the while.

Until that moment, Riley hadn't recognized the difference between making love to someone, versus simply having sex. Now, he knew, and he realized, as both shattered and reached for the edge of oblivion, he would never go back again.

This was what he wanted. What he had always wanted. Amanda.

In his arms. In his bed. In his life.

"I CAN'T BELIEVE we just did the one thing we're not supposed to do!" Amanda lamented as soon as they'd both had a chance to catch their breath. Extricating herself from Riley's embrace, she moved away from the sofa and began hurriedly getting dressed all over again.

Riley would have preferred to stay naked. Unfortunately, he knew she wouldn't be comfortable unless he were wearing something, too. She needed to relax if they were going to have the conversation they needed to about what had just happened between them, so he reluctantly pulled on his boxer briefs and slacks. He shrugged on his shirt and, leaving it open, walked over to stand beside her. He was stunned by the swift change in her mood—from passion to regret—and yet he wasn't. Deep down, he had known she wasn't as ready for this as he was. Yet he had seduced her because he had seen that as the quickest path to Amanda's heart.

Trying to inject some levity into the situation, to lighten the mood between them, Riley quipped, "What I can't believe is that it took us so long to do what we're not supposed to do." Especially since both of them had a long colorful history of doing just that.

Amanda threaded her fingers through her hair. Her palms trembled as she pushed her silky mane away from the flushed contours of her face. "You wanted this to happen all along," she accused, looking as near tears as he had ever seen her.

Riley knew he was supposed to feel thoroughly chastised, but he didn't. She might think they had just gone too far, too fast. He didn't. "You want the truth?"

"Of course!"

Her increasingly emotional state made it easier for him to remain calm. Riley shrugged. "Then yes," Riley admitted frankly, "I did."

Exasperation hissed through her teeth. She balled her fists at her sides and looked at him as if she didn't know whether to slug him or kiss him again. "Riley, we just had sex," she told him miserably. "We consummated our marriage!"

Riley knew it hadn't been simple sex. That left you physically drained but feeling nothing inside, not wanting or needing more. Knowing he had to touch her again, he took her stiff, resisting body into his arms, and sifted his fingers through her hair. "So what?"

"So it makes things a lot more complicated."

"I've got news for you, Amanda. Things were already complicated and they're going to get more so."

Amanda pushed herself away from him. "Not if I have anything to say about it," she remarked, giving him a killer look. "We made a mistake, Riley. It doesn't mean it has to happen again."

Riley grinned, and though he was very tempted to prove

her a liar here and now, thought better of it as she picked up her shoes and stormed toward the stairs. "We'll see about that," he promised lazily.

Amanda swung around to face him. She planted both hands on her hips and glared at him, her eyes gleaming like polished stones. "What is that supposed to mean?" she demanded.

Riley sauntered closer, not stopping until they were nose to nose. He studied her closely. Her lips were still swollen from their kisses. Her full, luscious breasts were rising and falling with each rapid breath she took.

Her hair was tousled and sexy. She looked so ripe and ready to go back to bed, in fact, it was all he could do not to let his baser instincts get the better of him and seduce her all over again. "It means we both know now exactly what it is we've been missing." He paused to let the weight of his words sink in, then continued in a soft serious voice that promised them a future every bit as exciting and satisfying as their first bout of lovemaking had been. "I'm not going to forget," he told her frankly. "And neither, Amanda, are you."

Chapter Nine

The phone rang at shortly after five the next morning. Riley groaned and reached for the receiver. "McCabe here," he muttered drowsily.

"Hi, Riley. This is Meg Lockhart-Carrigan. Sorry to wake you so early, but is Amanda there, by chance? I tried to get her at her apartment and there's no answer."

"Hold on." Riley looked up to see a sleepy Amanda coming out of the guest room across the hall. He motioned her in and passed the receiver over to Amanda.

She perched on the edge of his bed, still rubbing her eyes. Riley noted Amanda looked none the worse for their night spent apart, whereas he'd been so lonely for her he'd had a hard time falling asleep.

"Hello?" She listened intently.

Knowing it must be important if the director of nursing at Laramie Community Hospital was calling at this time of day, Riley switched on the bedside light. He surveyed her patiently as he lounged against the pillows, waiting for her to finish.

Amanda was clad in an old-fashioned pink-and-white-striped flannel gown that had a high collar and a row of buttons down the front. Tiny pleats brought the soft fabric close against her breasts. Beneath her sternum, the fabric was loose and flowing. She looked as pretty and sweetly satisfying as their lovemaking had been. It was all Riley could do not to take her in his arms and make her his all over again.

"No. It's not a problem," Amanda was saying as she brushed the hair from her face. "Does this mean…? Right. I understand." Disappointment permeated her low tone. "No. Of course. We'll talk about that later."

In the bassinet at the end of the bed, Riley heard Cory begin to stir. He went to get the drowsy infant. "What's up?"

Amanda picked up her brush and ran it through her hair on her way to the bathroom. "One of the nurses on the day shift for pediatrics has come down with food poisoning. Meg asked if I could come in at six-thirty for the patient status report, and work from seven to seven today. I said okay."

"Does this mean you're off administrative leave?" Riley asked as he gently laid Cory down on the bed. He unsnapped the legs of his sleeper and took off the damp diaper.

"Unfortunately, no." Amanda's tone went from matter-of-fact to tense and out of sorts in an instant. "Meg made it clear that this was just an emergency request. To be reinstated, you and I still have to get our situation straightened out and talk to her and Jackson McCabe."

Riley knew Amanda was as frustrated by their predicament as he was. And yet, she knew, as did he that there were no easy solutions, save making and keeping their marriage a real one. Something she was not yet inclined to commit to, although Riley still had hope this would happen, sooner rather than later, despite her generally cautious approach. "You're upset to still be on leave?"

Amanda shrugged and avoided his eyes as she reached for the uniform—since laundered—she had been wearing the day they had gotten the kids and been married. "The only time I haven't worked as a nurse, since earning my B.S.N., was when I was married to Fraser and taking care of his kids."

Riley put a clean diaper on Cory then discovered he needed a dry sleeper, and T-shirt, too. "Was that what you wanted?"

Amanda stepped into the bathroom to dress. Completely oblivious to the impact her slender curves were having on him, she spoke around the door that blocked her from his view. "I would have preferred to pull two or three twelve-hour shifts a week, and spend the rest of the time mothering, but Fraser didn't agree that was wise, so…I put my own ambition on hold. And stayed at home."

Riley finished dressing Cory, and noting the room had gotten a little chilly overnight, wrapped him in a blanket. "If we're able to adopt the kids, as we both hope, I think you should be able to work, too."

"Right now that's a pretty big *if*, Riley." Amanda accompanied Riley to the kitchen. She took a bottle out of the fridge, added a premeasured amount of water to the baby warmer, put the bottle in and switched it on. Finished, she turned to Riley and held out her arms for Cory. Burying her face in the infant's dark hair, she pressed a kiss to his crown, cuddled him close. "I know the circumstances don't really seem to warrant this opinion, but I still think whoever left the kids with us really loves them and is going to change his or her mind and want them back, once the holiday has come and gone."

Riley was afraid of that, too. It didn't mean he was going to hold back on anything while he waited to find out what December 26th would bring.

"All the note specifically asked you to do was see the kids had a merry Christmas. It did not ask you to keep them permanently."

"The part about them needing a daddy to love them seemed to imply that."

"I agree. And that's the way I want to read the situation, too, but we have to keep in mind—for all our sake's—that this may not be the case," Amanda cautioned.

Noting the bottle warmer had switched off, Riley removed

the bottle and tested a drop of formula on his wrist. Finding it to be just right, he handed the bottle to Amanda. She sank into a chair, while he set about pouring Amanda some juice and making her a couple of slices of toast. "Well, regardless how this eventually turns out, or what happens, the kids still need all our love, Amanda. And the promise of a safe and loving future, no matter who they are with. Us, or other family."

Amanda sighed as she lovingly cuddled the infant in her arms. "I want that for them, too," she said wistfully. "But no matter what happens, I still need a job to go back to, and a life. So, in that sense," she admitted, her lips taking on a troubled slant, "maybe this request from Meg, along with the conditions she and Jackson McCabe have put upon either of us going back to work full-time at the hospital, is just the reality check we need."

"TELL ME YOU NEED OUR HELP this morning and you'll be saving my life," Laurel said, three hours later, when Riley opened the front door to find his baby sister and Micki standing on the front stoop.

The evening before Riley couldn't have imagined he would be able to handle all three kids by himself all day, but the children seemed to have gotten over their pique with him. It was as if their post-Santa discontent had never happened.

Being able to parent as efficiently as he and Amanda did together, however, was another matter entirely. Chloe and Amber had been up since six, but thus far Riley had managed only breakfast for all three, clean diapers for the two younger sibs and an assist in the potty for Chloe. However, no one was crying and everyone's hands and face were clean, so Riley considered that a victory, albeit a small one. "You heard Amanda got called in to work?" he asked.

"No. I'm just trying to duck another lecture from Mom and Dad," Laurel said. Shivering in the brisk morning air, she rushed past into the house, Micki on her heels.

The friends smiled as Chloe and Amber padded out into

the foyer, in their footed sleepers. The two little girls beamed up at the two pink-cheeked college coeds. It was almost as if, Riley thought, the four of them spoke a language he had yet to master—female!

"What are Kate and Dad lecturing you about?" Riley asked, shifting Cory to his other arm.

Laurel heaved a huge sigh. "The same thing." She threw up both hands, the moment she took off her coat, and looped it over the rack in the hall. "My poor grades. Dad still wants to find the person responsible for distracting me from my studies, like that's going to help anything. He's been quizzing Micki every chance he gets for info on my latest guy friends."

Micki made a face, looking as though she wanted to be any-where but Laramie while all this was going on. Riley felt for the premed student. Always so serious about the direction she wanted her life to take, Micki never seemed to get in any trou-ble at all. He only wished he could say the same thing for his impetuous baby sis. Riley took Micki's coat and hung it up, too. "*Was* it a boyfriend's fault?" Riley asked Laurel, point-blank.

Laurel gasped in dismay. "Not you, too!"

Looking increasingly uncomfortable with the private, fa-milial direction the conversation was heading, Micki took the hands of Amber and Chloe and slipped off into the family room, where an Educating Baby video was playing on the television. She sat down in the middle of the toys spread out over the rug and was soon joined by the other two.

Laurel held out her arms, and Riley handed Cory over. He walked into the kitchen to get another cup of coffee for him-self. "Maybe if you told Kate and Dad the whole story, they would understand why you did what you did and ease up on you," he suggested.

Cuddling Cory nonstop, Laurel followed Riley into the sunlit kitchen. "Oh, they would not."

Riley paused to offer his guests coffee. When they both refused, he poured himself a cup and put the pot back on the warmer. "Are you still involved with this person or persons?" he continued his inquisition.

Suspicion tautened her features. "Why does that matter?" Laurel demanded, even more upset.

Riley prayed for the patience he didn't usually have for Laurel's self-generated predicaments. "I think it would be re-assuring to the folks to know the crisis—whatever it was—that caused your grades to nosedive last semester is over. So—" Riley lifted the mug to his lips "—is it over?"

Laurel shrugged and held Cory all the closer. "Sort of."

Riley lifted a brow.

"Well, I hope so," Laurel amended hastily. "At least I *think* it is."

"That's not very comforting, Laurel."

"It's the best I can do at the moment," Laurel announced airily. "And anyway, it'll all work out eventually even if I *haven't* found a permanent solution to all the problems quite yet."

If only he had that kind of confidence about his own situation with Amanda and the kids, Riley thought.

"My doing poorly first semester is no reason for me to spend the spring in Laramie," Laurel continued haughtily.

Riley paused. "Mom and Dad want you to do that?" he asked in surprise.

"Yes," Laurel tossed her mane of dark hair, "and all because I won't promise them I won't help this friend of mine anymore!"

"Well, maybe they're right, maybe this friend of yours is a bad influence on you," Riley speculated bluntly.

Laurel's voice dropped to an accusing whisper. "And maybe my friend isn't any more of a bad influence on me than Amanda Witherspoon is on you, big brother!" Seeing she had struck a nerve, Laurel backed off, slightly. Then asked slyly, "How are things going between you and that new wife of yours, any-way?"

Was there no end to his family's nosiness? Riley won-dered. "None of your business."

"Did you hear that Micki?" Laurel yelled into the adjacent room. "Riley won't tell me what's going on with Amanda. That means he's sweet on her."

Riley shook his head, sipped his coffee, said nothing.

"You are, aren't you…?" Laurel persisted, edging closer. Her dark blue eyes glittered with excitement that reminded Ri-ley how young—and naive—Laurel still was. "Will you stop matchmaking for me and my wife and worry about your own problems?" he asked, making no effort to hide his exaspera-tion.

"Why, when yours are so much more interesting?" Grin-ning, Laurel shifted Cory to her other shoulder. "So what did you get your wife for Christmas and when are the two of you going to give it up and start wearing wedding rings?"

Yet another question his family shouldn't be asking. Ri-ley gave her a quelling look. "When we feel like it."

Pique turned the corners of her lips down. "At least tell me that you've gotten Amanda a Christmas present," Laurel said.

He said nothing.

"Riley." Disappointment echoed in Laurel's low voice. "How can you expect to woo Amanda into staying married to you if you don't even cover the basics?"

Because he was wooing Amanda in other more important ways by making love to her and making her his, Riley thought. Not that his approach seemed to be working all that well in retrospect. When Amanda had left for the hospital this morning, she had just about seemed "reality-checked" into leaving this tenuous life they were building for themselves. And all it had taken to make her feel that way was a little ad-mittedly precipitous lovemaking with him and a few honest but direct words from the hospital's nursing supervisor. Being back at the work Amanda loved—even temporarily—would probably only cement those feelings.

Aware the college girls were waiting for his confession, Riley said drolly, "I hate to break it to you two hopeless romantics, but it will take more than a present to make Amanda want to stay married to me."

Micki joined them. She looked as curious now as Laurel. "Why do you say that?" she asked softly.

Riley had been thinking about that all morning. Amanda did not have a mercurial personality. She was at heart as steady, practical and efficient a woman as he had ever seen. Except where he was concerned. He alone seemed to have the ability to drive her crazy and push her to do things no one else could even hope to see. Part of that was the sizzling physical attraction between them they were just now acknowledging. The other half was the combination of suspicion and one-upmanship their "war of pranks" had built up over their teenage years. That four-year contest had lain an underlying foundation of distrust between them that Riley was having a hard time erasing.

"It's complicated," he muttered finally in frustration.

"Tell us!" Laurel practically shouted since she was so irritated with him.

"It's because of a lot of stuff that happened when we were kids," Riley explained finally. And because, bottom line, Amanda didn't quite trust him or her feelings for him, or his for her, any more than she trusted that the children might very well be permanent fixtures in their lives if no one came back to claim them. It was because Amanda kept waiting for the other shoe to fall, just as he sort of secretly was. It was because this all seemed a little too good to be true. It seemed like a TV movie about Christmas, rather than their own actual lives. Hell, it seemed like a dream from which he never wanted to awaken.

"So? Can't you go back and fix it?" Laurel persisted.

"Yeah," Micki put in, unable to see what the insurmountable problem was, either. "Why don't the two of you just agree to go back to the point where everything went terribly wrong and start over from there?"

THE FIRST THING Amanda noticed when she walked in the front door at seven that evening were the five Christmas stockings attached to the fireplace mantel. The second thing she noticed was Laurel and Micki sitting in the living room with all three children, reading bedtime stories, instead of Riley. She slipped off her coat and hung it on the rack next to the door.

"Riley's not here," Laurel volunteered.

"He had to go out for a while," Micki added.

"But there's something upstairs on your bed," Laurel continued.

"He said you should look at it right away," Micki agreed.

Amanda went in and kissed and hugged each of the three children. They all looked happy to see her, but content to be where they were, too.

"Long day, hmm?" Laurel said.

Amanda nodded. It wasn't the work that had worn her out so much as the endless questions about Riley and their marriage and what the future held for them. Smiling and pretending to shrug off such serious questions had taken its toll on her. The truth was, she wanted to know where they were headed, as well. Was Riley in the process of falling in love with her the way she was falling in love with him? Or was it more a convenience and casual sex sort of thing?

"Well, maybe what Riley left for you will cheer you up," Laurel stated slyly.

"Only one way to find out," Micki agreed.

Her interest definitely piqued, Amanda walked upstairs to the master bedroom. She had half expected the bunches of mistletoe hanging from every conceivable arch and doorway.

The stuffed goat standing on the center of Riley's king-size bed was something else. The goat was surrounded by a circle of green plastic Easter grass and what looked like a half-eaten prom corsage. Hanging out of the goat's mouth, was an envelope.

Stymied and smiling in bemusement, Amanda picked up the envelope and took out the note inside. It was yellowed with age. And bore her juvenile handwriting, not his. It said,

Okay, smarty-pants, you win. I can't compete with a goat. Nor do I want to. I've always had the hots for you and tonight I'll prove it to you. Meet me behind the high school bleachers—home side—for a make-out session you'll never forget. Your rival, XXXOOO, Amanda.

A line had been drawn though *Amanda* and *Riley* had been substituted. By his signature—and it was definitely his signature, she would recognize that handwriting anywhere—was a crudely drawn heart with an arrow through it, and a Christmas wreath.

"Very funny, Riley McCabe," Amanda whispered as she sat down on the bed and stroked the stuffed goat's whiskers. So they were back to playing pranks on each other again. The question was, what did *she* do next?

RILEY STOOD, waiting in the cold. Beyond the Laramie high school stadium, he could see the Christmas lights blinking in the dark, starry night. Eight o'clock, he figured Amanda'd had enough time to get home, talk to the girls, see the goat and the note, change clothes and head this way. The cell phone in his pocket vibrated. He plucked it out and answered on the second ring. "This better be good news," he warned.

"Operation Win Her Heart is well under way," Laurel reported merrily.

A wave of relief flowed through him, followed swiftly by impatience. "Did Amanda say she is coming to meet me?"

Laurel scoffed. "Well, no. But she did say she was going out and might be kind of late, and asked us to stay until one of you showed up again."

Now, that sounded promising, Riley thought, eager to pick up where they had left off the evening before. Though not necessarily here, out in the cold. "Are the kids in bed?"

"Yes," Laurel replied smugly. "Sleeping soundly, I might add."

Riley looked out at the parking lot, which was empty save for his SUV. A mixture of disappointment and unease flowed through him. "You're sure Amanda didn't give you a clue what she was going to do?" She couldn't have taken the goat and the note the wrong way…could she? Oh, hell, what if those particular symbols of their tempestuous past had made her mad instead of eager to see him?

"I thought you had this all worked out," Laurel persisted.

Heaven knew Riley had tried. He heard rustling noises and muffled voices on the other end of the connection, as if Laurel was covering the mouthpiece with her hand, while she talked the situation over with her coadvisor to the lovelorn.

The transmission cleared up again. Laurel's petulant voice came through clear as a bell. "I knew you should have let us help you with whatever you set up for her, Riley! Who gives the woman they love a stuffed goat, anyway?"

Who indeed? Riley wondered. Had he been nuts to think he and Amanda could go back? Pick up where things had taken a really wrong turn and make them right again? So they'd have a foundation of trust beneath their relationship, instead of wariness and mutual double crosses.

"Whatever you do, when she does show up, don't try to be funny," Laurel advised in a low serious tone. "Because she didn't look like she wanted funny when she left here."

Great, Riley thought. Since funny had generally been his strong suit with the ladies.

"Be romantic," Micki chimed in, even more helpfully.

Footsteps sounded on the paved path behind him.

Riley turned, saw Amanda coming toward him. He was used to her being gorgeous, but she blew him away tonight in a red chenille turtleneck sweater, sheepskin-lined suede jacket, skintight jeans and bright blue-and-red Western boots. Her silky-straight hair was loose and flowing, framing a face that couldn't help but make angels sing. "Gotta go." He cut the connection, folded the phone in half, and put it back in the pocket of his leather bomber jacket.

"Talking to your little helpers?" Amanda teased, her long legs eating up the ground between them. She stopped just short of him.

Riley's pulse jumped as he took in the sophisticated cinnamon fragrance of her perfume.

"If you mean Micki and Laurel…"

She sent him a look that was at once skeptical and amused. A little too wary and cool. As if she had gone all the way back to high school, to the beginning of their relationship with each other, when she had to keep her guard up and her sense of humor at the ready at all times. He swore silently to himself.

Amanda tipped her head up and searched his eyes. "They seemed very eager for us to get together tonight."

Maybe because they knew how much was riding on this, Riley thought. As well as how very bad I am at telling this woman what I feel. "I guess you got my note," he said inanely at last, wondering where all his own devil-may-care-cool had gone.

"Actually," Amanda corrected as she came one step closer, "it was my note to you." The lights in the parking lot illuminated the area behind the bleachers. It was light enough for him to see the regret in her eyes, dark and deserted enough to still feel somewhat intimate and cozy. She paused, confusion reflected on her face. "You kept it all these years?"

He took her hand, and walked along the back of the bleachers, all the way to the other end. "It was in my high school yearbook."

"And it never occurred to you to take it out?" Amanda said, as they moved across the front, to the middle of the bleachers. "Why didn't you throw it away?"

"I don't know." Riley led her toward the top of the bleachers, where the view of the Christmas lights in town was best. "At first I was just so furious at being taken in by such an obvious ploy to humiliate me." He settled on the cold metal seat, his back to the home team press box.

Amanda settled close beside him. She propped both boots on the bench below them. "You thought I was serious."

Riley shrugged and took her leather-gloved hand in his. "I'd had a secret crush on you for what had seemed like forever." He figured he might as well confess. Maybe if he bared his soul to her, she would start believing she could trust him. He turned and gave her a sidelong glance. "It stoked my ego to think the same might have been true for you. Then, when I found out it wasn't…"

"Actually," Amanda interrupted, "it was." Her thigh brushed up against his as she turned toward him, too. "I had a secret crush on you, too, Riley." She shook her head, recalling. "Why else do you think I kept up the practical joke war?" Color came into her cheeks. "It was the only way I knew to get and keep your attention."

Her confession sent his spirits soaring. "You had that, all right," he told her. So much wasted time. So much they still didn't know and understand about each other. "So what made you write that note to me in the first place?" he asked her curiously.

"The goat." Amanda took his hands in hers. "And the fact we were both heading off to college and might never see each other again, since my family was also moving to California. I knew by fall break that 'going home' to me would mean hopping a flight to San Francisco, whereas you would still be driving home to Laramie to see your family."

Riley struggled to understand the episode that had caused such pain. "So you wanted one final chance to humiliate me in front of your friends?"

Amanda ducked her head, embarrassed. "I didn't think my friends knew about it. I wrote the note to you in secret! And told everybody I knew that I was done playing pranks on you. And I meant it. Unfortunately, my girlfriends didn't believe it for one red-hot minute and they followed me here to the stadium that night, camera in hand. I was about to run off to meet you behind the bleachers when they ambushed me, and figured out enough about what was going on to put two and two together. I was so embarrassed, and afraid I was the one about to make a total fool out of myself by throwing myself at you, that I saved face and let them think I had meant to stand you up all along." She swallowed hard, shook her head, and Riley could have sworn there were tears shimmering in her eyes as she said thickly, "It broke my heart to see you standing out here, all alone."

It had been no picnic for Riley, either. The hurt and humiliation of that one night had stayed with him for years. "Where were you?" he demanded gruffly.

Amanda raked her teeth across the seductive softness of her lower lip. "In the visitor stand press box."

He shook his head, recalling full well the disappointment, knowing he never wanted to experience it again. "You broke my heart that night, Amanda Witherspoon." Worse, she had the ability to do it again, even more thoroughly, if this marriage of theirs did not play out the way he wanted.

"I broke mine, too." She cuddled closer, tightening her grip on his hands. "It took me years to get over what I had done." She leaned forward persuasively. "I still feel bad about it."

Riley could see that was true. "So make it up to me," he

said with an offhand shrug, letting the last of his anger and resentment drift away.

Amanda blinked. "How?"

Riley grinned and rolled lithely to his feet. "Like this." Ignoring her soft "oh" of protest, he took her by the hand and led her back down the bleachers, the way they had come.

"Riley—"

Ignoring the low note of warning in her voice, the one that said she did not do anything she did not damn well want to do, Riley guided Amanda willy-nilly down the stairs, behind the tall metal stands. They were breathless as they reached his destination. "You owe me a make-out session behind the bleachers."

Amanda laughed and kept her gaze level with this. "If we get caught…" she warned, excitement gleaming in her eyes.

Riley caught her around the waist, and backed her up against a tall support post. He positioned his body possessively close to hers. "We're married," he told her huskily, ready to be as mischievous as their mutual reputations warranted. He tilted his head to one side. "Who's going to get us into trouble for doing what married people do?"

"That," said a low voice behind them, "would be me."

Chapter Ten

Riley turned to see his brother Kevin standing there in his sheriff's deputy uniform. The shortest of the five McCabe brothers, at five foot eleven, he was also the scrappiest of the brood. He had been in countless fights in high school, while standing up for others who were unable to defend themselves, until he learned to channel that energy and redirect his gallantry. Now, he was as law-and-order a guy as they came. And Riley respected his youngest brother immensely.

Which didn't mean that he was always glad to see Kev.

Riley let out a frustrated sigh, aware this wasn't the first time Kevin had interrupted Riley's interaction with Amanda. Back in the days when they had all been kids, Kevin had seemed to have an instinctive sense of when to come crashing onto the scene…just in time to ruin everything. "Anyone ever tell you that your timing is the absolute worst?" he demanded grouchily

"Everyone," Kevin agreed with a smug grin on his boyishly handsome face. He tipped back the brim of his hat, to get a better look at their faces. "Although you *might* thank me for showing up since the school grounds security guard is about to make rounds through here in five minutes."

Riley blinked. Tucking an arm about Amanda's waist, he brought her in close to his side. He loved the way she felt, cuddled against him in the cold, facing down "the law." "The high school has security now?"

Kevin nodded, sober as ever. "The sheriff's department patrols through here, just to make sure kids aren't up to any mischief."

Riley sighed, disappointed he was not going to be able to continue with his juvenile but oh-so-sexy plans for the evening. "All right. We're leaving," he stated reluctantly.

Kevin held up a palm. "Not so fast. I tracked you down here for a reason. I wanted to give you a progress report on the attempts to identify the kids. We've gotten return e-mails from every Texas child welfare agency."

Riley and Amanda tensed simultaneously.

"And?" she asked in a low, breathless voice.

"Nothing." Kevin frowned, his disappointment apparent. "No one has been able to help."

Not sure whether he was happy or sad about that, Riley asked, "What next?"

"We're sending out similar bulletins with the kids' photos to the social services agency in all fifty states. We're asking the head offices to forward the e-mails to every child welfare office in their jurisdiction, in hopes someone will see it, recognize the kids and lead us to their family, or at least tell us what happened to put them in this situation."

Sounded like a plan, Riley thought, admiring his brother's tenacity and willingness to help. "And if that doesn't work?" he asked.

Kevin shrugged. "We could put the kids on one of the morning shows on TV that is broadcast nationally and ask the viewers for help. But that tends to bring out all the nutcases, as well as people who genuinely want to help, and it would force the Texas Department of Children and Families to get involved and take custody of the children before Christmas. Right now, things are operating under Laramie County jurisdiction, and since we are a rural operation with limited funding, we have more leeway in what we do than they do at the state level."

"In letting them stay with us, for instance," Amanda said softly.

"Right." Kevin mulled over their options. "The state might do that, too, but there is also the possibility that they might not. There's no way to tell until it happens, and then it's too late. Decisions are made. The kids might be split up, at least for a while."

"That would devastate them," Riley said.

Amanda wrapped her arm around Riley's waist, demonstrating how much a team she and he had become. "And us," she said.

Kevin studied them. Admiration and respect shone in his eyes. "You two have really fallen in love with those kids, haven't you?"

Riley looked into Amanda's face. They nodded at each other, then turned back to Kevin. "Let's just continue to take it slow," Riley said. "Until we see what happens after Christmas, if someone comes back to claim them or not, and go from there."

Kevin tugged the brim of his hat low across his brow once again. "The sheriff's department is okay with that, if you are."

"We are," Amanda and Riley said in unison.

Kevin grinned, all brotherly mischief once again. "I'd tell you to get back to what you were, ah, doing, but…"

Riley censured his baby brother with a look. "Enough said."

Grinning, Kevin shook his head. "You married folk." He chuckled as he strode away.

Riley and Amanda were left alone once again. "So much for best-laid plans," Riley grumbled. "Not that interference or delay has ever stopped me." He tilted his head and slanted his lips over hers.

Amanda had figured Riley would want to pick up where they'd left off. She wasn't prepared for his kiss's impact on her. The depth of their combined passion rippled through her in long, shimmering waves, until she wanted to touch him everywhere, kiss him everywhere and never stop. She shuddered at the heat and pressure of him where he surged against her, hip to hip. She reveled in the comfort of his arms around her. And as he continued to kiss and hold her, something inside her melted and the barriers around her heart, everything that had been keeping them apart, disappeared. As all the feelings they had for each other manifested themselves in kiss after steamy kiss, Amanda realized she was tired of protecting herself, tired of shutting herself off from even the possibility of love. She wanted to make love to Riley more than anything, and if it hadn't been for the sweep of a flashlight catching them in its bright yellow arc—and the discreet cough behind them—who knew what might have happened, she thought ruefully as she and Riley broke apart.

"Looks like we've been busted." Riley flashed the stadium security guard an apologetic grin. He took Amanda's elbow. "Guess we better head home," he drawled.

Amanda waggled her eyebrows at him. "Not necessarily," she whispered as they strolled off.

"THIS HAS TO BE ONE of life's great mysteries," Riley mused half an hour later as he and Amanda sat on the floor of her tiny apartment, surrounded by the presents they had bought for the three kids.

"What?" Trying not to be affected by the husky timbre of his voice—they'd never get done here tonight and they needed to get this yuletide task accomplished—Amanda selected a roll of pretty red-and-green wrapping paper.

He sighed his impatience. "Why the manufacturers don't make paper to fit the sizes of the toy boxes for kids."

Amanda lounged on the carpeted floor, admiring the way

he looked in her apartment. So at home, so big and sexy…and male. "Do you want me to try and wrap that one?" she offered sympathetically.

The testy tone returned to his voice. "No, no. I've got it."

Wasn't that just like a man to never admit defeat or an inability to do something. "Okay," Amanda allowed with a shrug. "But if you need help…"

He scoffed at her. "Oh, ye of little faith."

His expression more determined than ever, Riley cut a length of paper and flattened it on the floor in front of him. Amanda had only to look at it to see they had a problem. She cleared her throat. "Um, you know, Riley…"

Riley held up a silencing palm, cutting her off in midsentence. "I realize I've got to turn the box on its side." He set it down in the middle of the paper. Pulled the paper up around the box. It didn't begin to reach.

She started to speak.

He shot her a look.

She restrained herself from offering more advice but couldn't quite suppress an amused smile. Riley turned the box yet another way. And another, and another. Seeing he couldn't cover it all in any direction, he frowned.

Amanda finished wrapping another package and put it on the pile of already wrapped presents. "Care for some help?"

He shook his head, frowned again. "I'll just save this piece for another box," he said.

He cut another length of paper. This one was way too long, but still fell short of covering the entire girth of the box, no matter how he tried to position it. As his engineering efforts failed, one after another, his easygoing smile fell victim to a heartfelt glower. "All right, come and help me," he said finally, with a grim expression and beleaguered sigh.

"Since you asked…" Amanda murmured, a little amused that a man who was so talented in almost every other aspect could let such a small thing annoy him so much. But then, she thought, maybe that was the point. Riley didn't have to struggle to be wonderful at other things; he just was.

Heart racing at the proximity of their bodies, she knelt beside him and showed him how to position the box so the sides were covered.

"That still leaves the ends," Riley said, as she secured the paper with strips of tape.

Amanda's knee nudged the hard musculature of his thigh as she moved around. Another thrill swept through her, threatening her concentration even more. She ignored the tightening of her nipples beneath her sweater and forced herself not to think about how wonderful and right those same legs felt draped over hers. They weren't here to get distracted by their desire for each other and make love, they were here to wrap presents for the kids, while they had the opportunity to "play Santa," unobserved.

"I know." It took every ounce of willpower she possessed to concentrate on the task at hand. And that meant not noticing the telltale fluttering in her tummy or how good he smelled, like a wintry mix of pine and spice. Never mind how the blinking lights on her Christmas tree and the soft lamplight in her apartment brought out the gold streaks in his thick brown hair.

"We're going to have to cover the ends separately with additional squares of wrapping paper, cut to fit," she continued to explain. "And slide the 'patches' up underneath the existing wrapping paper, like this, so it's not so obvious it's a piecemeal job."

Less clumsy, now that they had a workable plan, Riley helped her secure the paper on one end, then the other. They set it upright, labeled it for Chloe, put a big red bow next to the tag and set it next to the roadster-tricycle they had purchased already put together.

"Maybe you should do all the big packages from now on," Riley said, his voice relaxing into a deeper baritone.

"Why don't we do them together?" Amanda asked. "It's easier."

"Okay." He smiled at her with lazy familiarity.

"Especially when we make such a good team," Amanda continued before she could censor herself.

The minute the words were out, a self-conscious blush moved from her neck to her cheeks. "Careful now," he teased her lightly, no doubt about what was on his mind, either. "Those are kissing words."

She grinned as he leaned over and lightly touched his lips to hers. "Work first," she commanded, although deep down she yearned to surrender everything to him.

Riley sighed and leaned back obediently. "Somehow I knew you were going to be quite the taskmaster this evening," he told her ruefully.

Amanda rolled her eyes, pretending she hadn't been thinking about making out with him ever since she'd read that note he'd left for her. Having to leave the stadium after indulging in only one very hot and steamy kiss had been torture. And yet she knew they needed to establish far more than sexual compatibility to make their relationship a real and lasting one. Friendship and emotional intimacy, an ability to work together on common goals, were important components of successful unions, too. Not that they would actually stay married to each other unless she thought Riley could love her, too. Swallowing around the sudden tightness of her throat, Amanda batted her lashes at him coquettishly and picked up the banter every bit as casually as he had left off. "And here you thought I only invited you back to my apartment for the…um…"

Devil-may-care lights flashed in his amber eyes as he picked up where she had flirtatiously left off. "Nooky?"

Amanda reveled in their spirited wordplay. She told herself there was nothing wrong with either kissing or flirting as long as they continued to build the rest of their relationship, too. She favored her husband with comically exaggerated re-proof as she picked up another present and selected a roll of gift wrap they had yet to use. "Now, that's a word I haven't heard in a while."

Riley filled out a name tag for the present he had just wrapped. "Well, brace yourself, woman, because more oldies but goodies are coming up as soon as we get our Santa's Workshop chores done this evening."

They continued to wrap. The silence that fell was comfort-able. Amanda realized they were having a good time, just be-ing together, working on something for the kids.

"You know, you haven't told me what *you* want for Christ-mas," Riley said absently.

Easy, Amanda thought. She wanted their marriage to be real. She wanted the children to be theirs. She wanted the life they were playing at now to be theirs forever. But afraid to say that for fear of tempting fate and ruining everything, she avoided his searching gaze and answered only, "I don't know. I have everything I need. In terms of material stuff."

"Well, that's a big help," he muttered.

Amanda shrugged. She figured he was smart enough to come up with something on his own, if so moved. Not that she wouldn't like *anything* he gave her. Curious, she asked him, "What do you want for Christmas?"

He replied without hesitation. "I want the kids to be happy and safe and loved."

Good answer. "I want that, too," she said softly.

"And even though it's selfish of me, if their family can't be found or can't take care of them, I'd like you and me to be the ones doing the parenting of them." He met her eyes calmly, casually assessing her reaction to his words. "What do you think of that?"

Was he putting her through some sort of test here? If so, it was only fair, since, in her own way, she had been testing him all evening. She only knew if his protectiveness toward the kids was a character flaw, she shared it, too. "I don't think it's selfish," she said, her tone as guarded as his had been.

Riley shrugged stubbornly, not as willing to let either of them off the hook. "It sort of is," he stated, as they picked up bits of ribbon, paper and tape, and stuffed them in the garbage sack she had brought out. "Getting a ready-made family this way is almost cheating. It's as if all the hard work has been taken out of it, and the two of us just get to step in and enjoy."

Put that way it did sound a little self-serving, Amanda noted uncomfortably. She knew, even if he didn't, that their actions had been propelled by kindness. Sure, they were benefiting from the situation. The love they were giving the kids and getting back in return was making their Christmas season much happier and more emotionally fulfilled than it would have been otherwise. But that was just the way things were working out. They hadn't asked for any of it.

Aware Riley had never opened up to her this way before, and shown her the inner workings of his heart and soul, she guessed quietly, "Sort of the way you purchased your house, completely furnished and decorated, and ready to move in?"

"Right."

And because it had been so easy, he didn't quite trust it all to work out. Amanda knew exactly how that felt. Nothing wonderful had ever come all that easily to her, either.

Silence fell between them, and with it the understanding both had sought.

Riley kneaded the muscles in the back of his neck. "Although," he admitted in his soft Texas drawl, "not everything about getting the kids has been as easy as purchasing the house was."

Hearing the hint of Riley's generally humorous outlook back in his voice, Amanda smiled. "What hasn't been?" She tied the sack closed and took it to the front door, to take out as they left.

Riley stood, working out the kinks in his long limbs. He picked up the rolls of wrapping paper and stacked them neatly by the stairs. "Winning your heart and your trust," he told her with a rueful grin. He closed the distance between them, wrapped his arms around her waist. "I think I'm still working mighty hard on both of those."

Not so hard, Amanda thought, considering the fact she had already fallen head over heels in love with him. Even if she hadn't dared tell him yet.

"But seeing as Determination is my middle name," he teased, raining kisses down the side of her neck, then giving her a long thorough kiss meant, she was sure, to shatter any lingering resistance she might have.

So what if none of this was going to be easy, Amanda thought, as Riley swept a hand down her spine, urging her closer yet, so her breasts were crushed by the hardness of his chest, the depth of their need for each other no longer secret. The two of them could make this hasty marriage of theirs a real one if they wanted it badly enough. She already loved Riley. He was close to falling in love with her, too. She could see it, feel it, taste it. Now all she had to do was make him realize it, make him see that she was the only woman for him, the only woman who could give him what he needed and wanted. If she were as resolute as he, if she dared risk all, maybe they could make it happen.

"I plan to achieve those things, too," Riley continued, kissing her as if there was no tomorrow, until she had never felt sexier in her life.

"Maybe you don't have to work for any of that," Amanda said softly, caught up in the intensity of what she was feeling. Daring to put her feelings on the line, more than she ever thought she could, she whispered without an ounce of pride, "Maybe you already have everything you need from me to make our relationship work over the long haul." Riley lifted his head, grinning as if he had just won the million-dollar lottery. She swallowed hard. Bypassing any discussion of her heart, she continued swiftly, wanting him to know this much, "I know I've already gotten what I really want for Christmas."

His eyes darkened even more. A sensual smile tugged at his lips. "Which is…"

"This." Amanda went up on tiptoe, putting everything she had into the impromptu kiss. Fitting her lips to his, slanting her head to just the right angle as she stroked his tongue and lips, all the while caressing the hard musculature of his shoulders with slow, seductive strokes. "You."

His arms tightened around her, strong, insistent, cocooning her with warmth. And just like before, he knew with damning accuracy just how to get to her. Her senses spun as he sucked at her bottom lip and touched the tip of her tongue with his own. Her excitement mounted, fueled by the rasp of their breath, the torridness of their kiss, the promise of the hours ahead. She arched against him, just as relentless in her pursuit of him.

Eventually, they had to come up for air. When they did, slowly, inevitably, he lifted his head. "Mrs. McCabe!" he chided playfully, as ready to be seduced as she was to entice. "Are you flat-out coming on to me?"

Wanting to make this an evening he would never forget, Amanda moved away from him. "Yes, I believe I am." Deciding if she was going to do this, she was going to do it all the way, Amanda went over to put on some music. Off went the more pedestrian Christmas carols. On came the sexy, sultry strains of "Santa Baby." "Got a problem with that, Doctor McCabe?" she asked, for the first time in her life feeling beautiful inside and out.

Riley couldn't hold back a smile as Amanda took off one Western boot, then the other. Wiggled her way out of her jeans. "Not a one," Riley said hoarsely as her red chenille turtleneck came over her head. She sashayed toward him in a lacy see-through red bra, matching thong, and…the obligatory Christmas socks. He grinned, aware he was already hard as a rock. "I like your style."

"Good. I like yours. And I especially like you stripped down." She picked up the remote to her stereo, pressed play. The song they had been listening to started all over again. She lounged against the side of the sofa, arms crossed in front of her. "Your turn, Santa."

Trying hard not to notice how her posture plumped up her breasts and had them spilling out of the tops of her décolleté bra, lest he get ahead of where they both wanted him to be, Riley drawled right back, "I knew you had a wicked streak."

"So?" Amanda vamped. "Show me yours."

Never one to pass up an opportunity to clown around, Riley put some hip action into it as he unbuttoned. Opening the edges of his shirt wide, he showed off his chest and shimmied around in his best parody of a male dancer. Amanda was laughing softly as he slipped his shirt off, and swung it around, lasso style, over his head. It hit the banister. His T-shirt followed suit. His boots and socks came off, too.

Riley decided he liked the excited glitter in her eyes as she watched him unbuckle, unzip and peel down. He also liked the way her chest was rising and falling with each ragged intake of breath, the way she couldn't seem to take her eyes off the bulge behind the fly of his Christmas boxers, even as she tilted her head in a way that dared him to take this particular brand of love play any further.

So, of course, he did.

Her breath caught as she saw how very much he wanted her.

Had always wanted her.

"Got a problem with not making it all the way upstairs to my bed?" Amanda asked in a hoarse voice.

Riley noted the way her nipples were poking ardently through the lace. "You had somewhere else in mind?"

Amanda took the quilted lap rug off the back of the sofa

and spread it out across the floor. She dropped down to her knees. "How about right here, next to the tree?" Her eyes darkened ardently. "I've always wanted to make love in the glow of the Christmas lights."

"I think that can be arranged," Riley promised, already turning off every other light in the room.

Wanting to remember every moment of this night, Riley let his glance sift slowly over her. Amanda was gorgeous no matter what she was or was not wearing. But she had never looked more radiant than she did at that moment, with color blushing her cheeks, her hair tumbling, straight and silky, over her shoulders.

He dropped down beside her, taking in her long slender legs and smooth thighs, the shadowy vee visible through the lace of her thong. "Tell Santa what you want, Mrs. Claus…." he encouraged, already divesting her of her lingerie.

She trembled as he bent and kissed her budding pink nipples one by one. She clasped his shoulders and sighed as his mouth moved urgently over her breasts. "Peppermint kisses…"

He slid down, kissing the hollow of her stomach, stroking the soft insides of her thighs. "Like this?" He traced her navel with his tongue, then dropped lower still, to deliver the most intimate of kisses, until she was overcome with pleasure, shuddering.

"Oh, yes…" she whispered.

"And this." He stretched out over her, fit his lips to hers, and let her lead him where she wanted to go.

"Definitely yes." Amanda groaned as their tongues twined urgently and his body took up a primitive rhythm all its own, until there was no doubting how much he wanted her.

"How about this?" He eased her knees apart, lifted her up. She gasped as he plunged into her, deliberate and slow.

Her eyes widened as she stretched to take him inside her. "That's nice, too."

He kissed her slowly, thoroughly. Sliding an arm beneath

her he coaxed her to take all of him, again and again, until she was moaning, moving against him. What few boundaries existed between them, dissolved. She was his. He was hers. He pressed into her as deeply as he could go, and then they were lost, all coherent thought spinning away in ribbons of endless pleasure.

Afterward, they lay wrapped in each other's arms. His body still humming with the aftershocks of passion, Riley felt a fierce wave of possessiveness.

He still did not know what was going to happen with the three kids, but he knew this: he could no longer imagine his life without Amanda.

"DID KEVIN FIND YOU?" Laurel asked, the moment Riley and Amanda walked in the door, shortly after midnight.

"Yes, he did," Amanda replied.

Riley helped Amanda with her coat, took off his own.

"Any word on the kids' identity?" Micki asked, looking equally concerned.

He shook his head, not bothering to mask his discouragement about that. "The sheriff's department is still looking but nothing yet."

"Well, maybe the person or persons responsible for this will contact you after Christmas is over, to talk or something," Laurel said hopefully. "You know, once the kids have had a merry holiday and all that."

Looking as though she were trying—and failing—to figure out a way to comfort them, Micki finally nodded her agreement. "Maybe you should just enjoy Christmas with the kids and not worry about it so much."

"That's kind of hard to do when we don't know if we're going to be able to keep them or not," Riley returned with a frown. He walked to the fireplace and warmed his hands on the flame. He glanced over at the TV. The weatherman for the late news was on the screen, predicting a white Christmas in

Laramie County—something that happened only once every decade or so—to the skeptical guffaws of his news show colleagues.

"But if you could, you would adopt all three of them?" Micki said.

Riley and Amanda nodded in unison, very much in agreement about that. "We have no intention of splitting them up, or allowing anyone else to do so, either," Riley said firmly.

"That's good." Micki's shoulders sagged in relief. She looked at Riley and Amanda earnestly. "Because Laurel and I have both noticed the three of them are happiest when they are together. And I wouldn't want what happened to me and my sister when our parents died to happen to them."

Amanda stepped closer to the fire, too. "Did you and your sibling get split up?" she asked softly.

Micki nodded, sadness in her eyes. "Social services couldn't find a placement to take both of us for almost a year and we were put in different foster homes. Losing each other was almost worse than losing our parents. And if that's how my older sister and I felt, at eight and fourteen," Micki recollected sadly, "I can't imagine how Chloe, Amber and Cory would feel."

Riley wasn't surprised Micki and his sister were so protective of the three children—the two college girls had spent almost as much time with the children as he and Amanda had. Plus, they probably felt some responsibility because they had been the ones who had found the kids by the hospital's employee entrance. "You don't have to worry," Riley told them both firmly, taking Amanda's hand in his. "Amanda and I are going to do whatever it takes to protect the kids."

"Even if it means staying married?" Laurel asked curiously.

"Even then," Riley said.

"I'm not sure you should have promised them that," Amanda

said after the girls had left. She stood before the fire, shivering, rubbing her hands together.

Although he was almost overly warm in the heat of the room, Riley moved to stand next to her. He, too, looked into the licking flames behind the safety glass. "Why not?"

"Well—" Amanda shrugged as she turned toward him "—we haven't been together all that long yet and…"

"And?" He reached out and touched her face.

"…and we don't know what's going to happen between you and me." Worry was back in her eyes.

Riley figured she was thinking about what had happened in her previous marriage. "I'm not going to fall in love with anyone else, or leave you for them," he told her, knowing on this subject she had her own demons to wrestle. That it might take her a while to believe.

A tremulous smile crossed her lips. She didn't quite meet his eyes. "You never know. Love is a funny thing," Amanda said softly, stepping closer, and resting her head against his shoulder.

"The emotion may be unpredictable," Riley agreed, doing his best to erase her insecurity as he wrapped a comforting arm about her waist. "I'm not." He lifted her chin and waited until she looked him in the eye before he continued persuasively, "You can count on me, Amanda. I promise you that." And to prove it, he took her to bed and made slow, thorough love to her all over again.

"ARE YOU SURE YOU DON'T mind watching the kids by yourself all day?" Riley asked Amanda over breakfast the following morning, marveling that she could look so pretty and pulled together after so little sleep. Fifteen minutes in the shower, another ten with her blow-dryer and makeup, and she looked good enough to grace the covers of a magazine. "Laurel and Micki aren't going to be able to help," Riley continued, moving his gaze away from the shimmering softness of her hair. "They're slated to volunteer at the hospital today."

Amanda looked up from the pancakes she was cooking. She flashed him a confident smile. "I can handle it."

Riley quirked a brow, recalling how difficult the previous morning had been for him, when she had been gone. "All three of them at once?"

Amanda gave him an indulgent smile. "Sweetheart, you're talking to a woman who was handling a minimum of four of her siblings at a time, from age twelve on. Believe me, it will be a piece of cake."

"I wish I had some of your multitasking skill," Riley murmured admiringly. He could change diapers and prepare bottles, and ready-made toddler and preschool meals easily enough. He couldn't manage to do dishes or laundry or even get all three of them dressed in addition. The very basics, keeping everyone happy at once, was all he could manage. And that took every ounce of energy he had.

Amanda favored him with a sexy wink. "You have plenty of talent, in many areas." She paused to press a kiss on his brow before setting his plate in front of him. "As for the rest—" her hand trailed lightly across his shoulder "—the more experience you have, the easier it will get."

Riley dug into his expertly prepared breakfast. "I'll take your word on that, although if things work out the way we hope, and all our Christmas wishes come true," he continued, speaking in a code Amanda would understand and the children wouldn't. "And we both go back to work, we're going to need to get some household help or at the very least arrange for a sitter."

Amanda's eyes darkened seriously. "Don't forget the hospital has a childcare center for employees that is open twenty-four hours a day, seven days a week. It's nice, because you can use your breaks to go down and visit with your kids."

Riley paused, realizing again how much he had to learn. "I hadn't thought of that."

"It'll all work out." She held his eyes deliberately. "Promise."

Riley hoped so. He wasn't sure what he would do without Amanda and the three kids. And he wasn't so sure, after what she had said the evening before about love being unpredictable, that she would stay forever if the kids weren't there.

Amanda looked as if she were having the same disturbing thought. She cleared her throat, took a sip of coffee, changed the subject every bit as smoothly and politely as he had come to expect. "So what's on your schedule today, Dr. McCabe?" she asked pleasantly.

Riley rocked back in his chair. "It's a secret."

Amanda lifted a brow, her interest piqued, as she forked up a bite of pancake with blueberry syrup.

"I could tell you," Riley teased, reaching over to take her hand in his and give it a tender squeeze, "but then you wouldn't be surprised. And Santa wants you to be surprised."

At the mention of jolly old St. Nick, Chloe and Amber looked on with interest. Only Cory, who was seated in his bouncy chair, sleepily sucking on a pacifier, looked oblivious.

Amanda rolled her eyes. "Well then by all means, go ahead," she counseled dryly. "Just be sure and save some time for me, 'cause I've got some personal shopping to do before tomorrow, too."

By the time the breakfast dishes were done and Riley had showered and dressed, Amanda had Cory asleep in the bassinet in a corner of the kitchen. Chloe and Amber were wearing aprons, humming "Feliz Navidad" right along with her, and "helping" Amanda make cookie dough.

The scene was so cozy and familial—so reminiscent of the happiest days of his own childhood—he couldn't help but linger. "Now, I don't want to leave," he grumbled, wrapping his arms around her slender waist.

Amanda turned and splayed her hands across his chest, her touch as warm and inviting as the look in her pretty eyes. "You can help us when you come back," she said.

"Promise?" he said softly, affectionately tracing her face with his hand.

She rose on tiptoe to give him a sweet, exceptionally gentle kiss on the lips that brought an answering fullness to his heart. "It wouldn't be Christmas without you," she murmured.

Chapter Eleven

"You wanted to see me?" Laramie Community Hospital chief of staff, Jackson McCabe, asked.

Riley nodded as the two men shook hands. In his private life, Riley knew his uncle appreciated a good joke as much as anyone, but when it came to the hospital the talented general surgeon was all business. "First, I want to apologize for the ruckus earlier in the week," Riley said as they continued on into Jackson's private office and shut the door behind them. "And second, I want you to stop holding Amanda accountable for any part of it and reinstate her immediately."

Jackson quirked a dark brow now threaded with silver. "What's changed from the last time you two were in here?" he asked, as blunt and to the point as ever.

Everything, Riley thought, as he dropped down into a chair in front of Jackson's desk. "We're still married, for one thing."

Jackson cast a wary look at Riley's hand. "I don't see a wedding ring on your finger. Nor did I see one on hers when I ran into her yesterday."

"That's being taken care of, as soon as I finish here today."

Jackson frowned at Riley. "In what sense?"

"In the sense that I'm getting her one for Christmas," Riley told his uncle seriously.

Jackson's features softened in relief. "Then you're planning to stay married?"

"Yes." Even if he hadn't yet gotten Amanda to agree to it. The hard edge was back. "Why?"

Riley did his best to curtail his frustration. He wasn't used to being grilled about his private life by his superiors. But then, he wasn't used to being embarrassed at his workplace the way he had been the day the kids had been mysteriously delivered to him, either. "Isn't it obvious?"

Jackson shrugged. "Maybe I want to hear you say it."

"We've discovered we like being married."

Jackson gave Riley a stern look. "Being married or playing house?"

Riley recognized the tough love approach for what it was. It didn't mean he had to like it. "You're crossing the line," he warned.

Jackson shrugged his broad shoulders nonchalantly. "Then that makes two of us, doesn't it?"

Tension stiffened Riley's frame as the conversation veered into dangerous territory. "What do you want from me?" he demanded.

Jackson refused to relent. "Probably the same thing your wife wants."

"Which is—?" Riley returned evenly.

Jackson regarded Riley for a long moment. "Oh, for starters, a declaration of your undying love."

Riley hadn't felt like this since he'd been called in to the principal's office, for chastisement about one of the many practical jokes he had played on Amanda. Problem was, he was no longer a mischief-prone kid, Amanda no longer his teenage rival. "Amanda and I haven't…that's not our style."

Jackson shook his head in silent reproach. "So you don't love her," Jackson surmised with a scowl.

As a matter of fact, Riley did. But not about to tell his uncle that before he'd even had a chance to tell Amanda, he curtailed his resentment and returned mildly, "My feelings and hers are irrelevant to this discussion."

Jackson leaned forward and rested his forearms on the desk. "I don't think so." His penetrating gaze narrowed even more. "And I don't think Amanda would think so either if she were here."

"Look." Riley returned his uncle's unrelenting judgment with a warning gaze of his own. "All I want is for you to stop taking your disappointment in me out on her."

"What about the kids?" Jackson waited, letting his words sink in before he continued. "What happens to them if no one claims them?"

That at least was easy. "Then Amanda and I have agreed we're going to adopt them and bring them up ourselves."

Another lift of the brow. "That's quite a commitment."

"And one we would not undertake lightly," Riley underscored, just as firmly.

Jackson nodded. "I respect you for that." He sighed, shook his head. "Even though I think you're a fool for staying married to a woman you can't even say you love."

Riley was going to say it. But on his own time, in his own way, when the moment was right. Not when someone was thinking the usual worst of him and demanding he do so. Ignoring that part of the lecture, Riley pushed on for the answer he had come to get. "So will you let Amanda back on staff?"

Jackson pushed his chair away from the desk. "I'll let you both back on staff as soon as Christmas is over and we find out what is going to happen to Amber, Chloe and Cory."

"What do they have to do with this?" Riley asked. He got to his feet, too.

"Everything, apparently." Jackson walked him toward the door.

Riley stared at him in confusion. "I don't get it."

"The kids are obviously the glue holding you together. If

the situation changes, if that is no longer the case, your relationship with Amanda could change," Jackson explained, not particularly happily.

Riley thought about the way Amanda had returned his kisses and caresses, the way she looked at him, the love he felt flowing through her, even though she hadn't come close to saying the words to him, either. "No, it won't," he returned stubbornly.

The skeptical look was back on Jackson's face. "Well, let's be sure." He frowned. "I want your marital situation resolved one way or another before either of you comes back to work."

RILEY LEFT his uncle's office. He wasn't sure how that meeting could have gone any worse. He was glad he hadn't mentioned it to Amanda, though. "Hey, Riley," director of nursing Meg Lockhart-Carrigan intercepted him in the hall. "Since you're not working, how about doing the pediatric floor a favor?"

"Sure," Riley said.

Meg steered Riley into the staff lounge. She picked up a bulging laundry bag, handed it over.

Riley was all for doing penance, if it got him what he wanted—a life with Amanda and the kids, and both their jobs back, but this was ridiculous. He looked askance at Amanda's boss. "You want me to do your wash?"

"No, silly," Meg whispered, leaning close, laughter in her eyes. "I want you to answer the letters to Santa so 'Mrs. Claus' can pass them out to the letter writers on Christmas Eve."

"Sure," Riley agreed readily. "I'll get Amanda to help me with that tonight. But in return you have to do a favor for me and get Amanda's ring size."

Meg's eyes twinkled with approval. "I already know it. It's a six. She tried on the ring Luke gave me for my birthday, last month. We're the same size."

"Thanks."

"No problem." Meg regarded Riley slyly. "You getting her a wedding ring?"

Riley just smiled. "Do not tell her I asked. Not even a hint," he warned.

"Okay, but just so you know, she likes diamonds."

"Don't you all," Riley tossed back, knowing a diamond was exactly what he was in the market for.

Whistling, he headed down the hall, stopped when he saw Micki standing at one of the playroom windows. She appeared to be wiping tears from beneath her eyes. Concerned, Riley went over to her. He rested a hand on her shoulder. "Hey. Everything okay?"

Micki started, then seeing it was him, relaxed slightly, even as she brushed fresh tears away. "Fine."

She didn't look fine, Riley thought. "Did something happen?" he asked her gently.

"No." Her freckles stood out against the paleness of her skin.

"Then why are you crying?" Riley persisted, aware in all the time he had known the young woman that he had never seen her tear up like this.

Micki shrugged, refusing to meet his eyes. She ran a hand through her red hair and didn't answer.

Riley wanted to respect her privacy as much as he wanted to be her mentor. He sensed right now she just needed a friend. "Are you homesick?" he guessed at the reason behind her unhappiness. "I know you're not going home to Colorado for Christmas this year…." Riley paused, unsure how much to push, knowing he had to offer something. "It's probably not too late to change your mind, you know," he told her helpfully. "You could still get a flight."

"No. I'll be okay." Micki shook off her tears determinedly. "I'm just…I don't know." She smiled at him bravely. "Feeling overly sentimental or something. I'm okay. *Really.*"

Then why, Riley wondered, didn't he believe it?

RILEY DROVE UP just as the Overnight Delivery truck was pulling away from the curb. He waved a cheerful hello at the driver, parked his car, grabbed his gift-wrapped packages and walked inside. Pausing only long enough to tuck his Christmas presents for Amanda in the bottom of her stocking, he headed for the rear of the house.

Chloe, Amber and Cory were all napping in the family room. Amanda was standing at the kitchen window, talking on the phone. An opened blue-and-white cardboard envelope was on the kitchen table. She appeared to be holding an airline ticket in her hand.

"I know it is nonrefundable, Mom. And I appreciate it. But you and Dad should have talked to me before you purchased it." She sighed loudly. "I can't." Exasperation crept into her low voice. "Okay, then, I won't. No." Panic edged her tone. "Now, don't do that, either. Priscilla should enjoy the holidays with all of you." Amanda rubbed her temples. "Mom, I mean it," she warned. "Don't. Do. This."

Amanda pulled the receiver away from her face and stared at it. She sighed again and clicked the End Call button.

Fairly sure it was safe to enter her domain, Riley slowly closed the distance between them. As he neared her, he saw tears glistening in her eyes. He didn't even have to think about what to do next. Wanting her to feel as cared for and loved as she made him feel, he put his arms around her, held her close and stroked her hair.

Amanda's voice was muffled against his shirt. "You're not going to believe what my family is doing now," she told him in a low, miserable voice.

Riley looked at the airline ticket she still clutched in one hand. He took a wild guess. "Trying to get you home for the holidays?"

"They're just doing this to try to break us up," Amanda sniffed, indignant.

Riley shrugged, not so surprised about that after Priscilla's visit. Nor could he really blame the Witherspoon clan, given all they didn't know. "Well, it won't work, even if you do go home to California for the holiday," he soothed.

Amanda lifted her head from his chest. She looked deep into his eyes. "You'd really be okay with that?"

Riley nodded, almost as surprised by his unselfishness as she was. "If it was what you wanted and needed to do? Sure. Which isn't to say I wouldn't miss you like hell. I would," he told her wryly. He wrapped his arms more tightly around her. "But I'll always be supportive of you, Amanda. That's what husbands do for their wives." And McCabe men had a long tradition of treating their women with the respect and consideration they deserved.

Amanda sighed and dropped her head back down to rest on his chest. She let him protect her the way Riley had always wanted to protect her. "I wish my family could see and hear this."

He stroked a hand through her hair, loving the silky softness of the honey-colored strands. "You could invite them all here."

Her answering laugh had a hollow sound. "Be careful what you wish for," Amanda told Riley sadly. "Besides, there is no way they could afford that, any more than they could afford the nonrefundable ticket they just bought for me."

Riley refused to let her take responsibility for a situation not of her making. "It's not as if the ticket has to go to waste. You can always change it for a later visit if you pay the change fee."

Amanda wrapped both her arms around his waist. "That's not the point."

"I know." Riley enjoyed the feel of her soft slender body cuddled close against him. He tucked a hand beneath her chin and lifted her face to his. "But it's the reality of the situation. They gave you a wonderful gift. It's up to you to decide how to use it without allowing them to make you feel guilty."

Her lips took on a rueful curve. "You sound like you know something about that."

Riley acknowledged this was so with a dip of his head. "It's true. I've fought my own battles on that score."

"When?" Amanda asked, wanting to understand him the way she never had in the past.

"After my mom died," Riley said quietly. He looked deep into Amanda's eyes. He had never talked about this to anyone. Now he found himself wanting to lay bare his soul. The gentleness and understanding in Amanda's expression encouraged him to go on. "My mom had been ill for a long time, but it was still a shock when she finally lost her battle against breast cancer. We were all so devastated. I can't even put it into words. She was more than just a mom, she was the heart and soul of our family. And when we lost her…" Riley's voice caught. For a moment he was so choked up, he couldn't go on. "Anyway, my dad was a wreck." Riley let go of Amanda and moved about the kitchen restlessly as he continued to recollect, "It seemed the only way he could cope was by burying himself in work, which left the rest of us to fend for ourselves."

Amanda's heart went out to Riley. She hadn't expected Riley to confide in her this way, but she was glad he was. It made her feel closer to him. It made her feel as if he was at long last letting her in. "That's when you had that whole series of housekeepers, right?" she prompted, recalling.

Riley nodded, his expression sad but accepting. "Yep. Anyway, to say we kids were resentful is the understatement of the century. We gave every one of those housekeepers pure hell. And Kate, too. Our acting out was the only way we could cope with the loss. For Brad, that meant dating every girl in sight. Will began sneaking drinks. Kevin stopped communicating and kept trying to climb out on the roof, even after he fell off and broke his arm. And Lewis was sensitive to a fault."

Amanda recalled hearing all about the McCabe family shenanigans—back then, Sam's motherless brood had been the talk of the town. "What about you? What did you do?" Anything she didn't already know?

"Got myself into more mischief than any kid had a right to pursue." He paused, shook his head. "Luckily, most of it was harmless. But I know that my constant joking around really bothered the rest of my family. You could see they were all grieving in one way or another. It looked like I didn't care at all. Or feel any loss. And of course I did. I just couldn't admit how miserable I was. Knowing what people thought about my pranks made me feel guilty. The more guilt I felt, the more I acted out."

"A vicious circle," Amanda summed up, commiserating with him.

"Yep."

Amanda angled a thumb at her chest. "And here I thought I was the inspiration for all your jokes."

"Are you kidding?" Riley flashed her a sudden grin, which she promptly returned. "You were my saving grace. Had I not focused on you and tried so hard to keep your undivided attention all through high school, who knows what kind of pranks I might have cooked up to distract myself from my loss."

"When did the guilt stop?" Amanda asked softly, closing the distance between them once again.

"That's the hell of it." Riley inclined his head. "With families it never really does. At least not in my experience. 'Cause you always know when you have disappointed your loved ones, just as you know what you have to do to redeem yourself in their eyes."

"Like going home for Christmas," Amanda said.

"Or taking marriage seriously," Riley replied. "Which is what both our families seem to want for us. They're only irritated with us because they think we still see our situation as a joke. Once they realize that has changed," he told Amanda confidently, "they will all not only forgive us, they'll approve of what we've done here. You'll see. In the meantime…how long have the kids been asleep?"

"Thirty minutes, tops."

"How long do you expect them to nap?"

"Another hour, minimum. Why?"

"Let's turn the baby monitor on down here and head upstairs."

Before Amanda could do more than gasp, Riley had swept her up into his arms and was heading for the stairs. Her heart pounded in her chest. "I can't believe we're actually going to do this in the middle of the day," she said breathlessly.

A mischievous grin tugged at the corners of his lips as he headed to the master bedroom. "Why not?" Riley whispered playfully as he carried her sideways through the door. "It is nap time, after all." He flashed another smile as he deposited her ever so gently on the bed. "And I did ask you to open your heart and mind to the possibility of us making our relationship a real and loving one in every way. It seems to me love-making is very much a part of a real and viable marriage."

Amanda hitched in a breath as she raised herself off the pillows as far as her elbows would allow. Detecting a change in his attitude, she demanded huskily, "What are you saying?" She stared at him, aware he was already yanking off his sweater vest, pulling it over his head, dropping it on the chaise in the corner. The devil-may-care look she recalled so very well from their youth was etched on his handsome face, along with a seriousness that spoke to her soul.

"I'm telling you I am tired of playing house," he said, ever so softly. Dropping down to sit beside her, on the edge of the bed. "I'm telling you I want us to be for real. And that telling each other everything that's in our hearts and making love is the best way I know of to get where we both want to be. So unless you tell me to scram…"

But he didn't want to, Amanda noticed, as he sat there, waiting for her decision. And neither, if she were being truthful, did she. "Oh, Riley." She let herself fall back against the pillows and draped her forearm across her brow. "You really are so very bad for me," she whispered tremulously.

"In that case," Riley leaned forward as the staticky silence of the baby monitor filled the room. Planting a hand on either side of her, he caged her with his arms. "Let me attempt to live up to my very wicked reputation."

Amanda wrapped her arms around his neck. "And me, mine," she whispered right back.

His head lowered. She shut her eyes, ignoring the fact that he had yet to say the words she most wanted to hear. Surely one day Riley would tell her that he loved her as much as she loved him. And until then, it was Christmastime, after all. And being with Riley was her most fervent wish. She hadn't wanted to fall in love with him, hadn't wanted herself to be that vulnerable. But she already knew in her heart it was too late. She did love him heart and soul and always would. Even if the worst happened, in the end, and their marriage didn't last, and the cautious side of her kept telling her it most surely would not, she would have these precious moments to remember from this day forward. Short of having a family and husband of her very own, the kind that would be hers forevermore, making love with Riley was the very best thing.

The last of her doubts slid away as his lips met hers in a scorching kiss that brought with it the fulfillment of every sexual fantasy she had ever had. Her hands moved from his neck to his chest, where she busied herself opening up each one of the buttons, one by one, laying bare the inviting hardness of his chest, the satiny smoothness of his skin and the springy tufts of masculine hair. Without breaking off the kiss, she helped him out of it, let it fall to the side of the bed.

Riley's lips left her mouth, forged a burning trail across her cheek. "Are you undressing me, Nurse McCabe?" he whispered in her ear.

"Why yes, Doctor McCabe," she whispered right back, lowering her hands to his belt. She batted her eyelids at him coquettishly, then indulged in a kiss that was deeply passionate. "I believe I am."

"Did I give you my permission?" he asked, slanting his mouth across hers, devouring her with a boldness that was as heady and new as her own.

Noting he had already taken off his shoes, Amanda worked his trousers, and boxers, down his legs. She paused to kiss the insides of his knees, his calves, as she knelt before him and removed his socks. There was something so wonderfully wanton, being fully dressed, while he was splendidly naked and handsome as could be. Something so unlike her…and yet so right, nevertheless. She had always wanted to be free in the bedroom. Riley made her feel as though she could do and say and want anything and it would be okay. More than okay.

"Because," he continued teasing her playfully, looking his fill of her, too, "I don't *recall* giving it."

Running her palms along the gloriously muscled insides of his thighs, Amanda trailed kisses over his knees, higher still, as she murmured, as innocently as she could, "It was implied."

"Oh…really?" Riley tangled his fingers in her hair.

Already so needy and hot she ached, Amanda nodded, "In that kiss."

"Mmm." Riley caressed her shoulders, the slope of her neck. "What else was implied?"

"Maybe a little of this," Amanda whispered, daring more than she had ever dared in her life.

Riley sucked in his breath.

Smiling at the pleasure she was giving, Amanda murmured lovingly, "And this." She explored the muscular perfection of his body, the throbbing desire, the need. "And this," she whispered, even more tenderly.

"Amanda," Riley moaned, letting her command his surrender, in the same way he had first commanded hers. He let her have her way with him until it was suddenly all or nothing and he could stand it no more, and then Amanda found she was lying back against the pillows once again.

"My turn," he whispered, easing the zipper down on her skirt.

Amanda lifted her hips off the bed as he relieved her of her skirt, cardigan and turtleneck. Reclining in nothing but her bra, opaque black tights, and panties, she managed, "I don't think I can wait much longer."

Riley stopped her from removing her bra just then. He draped his naked body alongside hers, in no hurry to rush the pleasure along. He turned slightly to face her, the hardness of his thigh pressing up against hers. "Sure you can."

Amanda trembled as he ran his lips across the tops of her breasts and the U of her collarbone, the side of her neck, the inside of her ear. She trembled as he found her mouth again, delved deep, luxuriating in the feel of his warm, callused hands caressing her skin. "Says who?"

His arousal pressed against her, creating an ocean of warmth inside her. "Your very own St. Nick." He shifted her closer, his tongue parting her lips, touching the edges of her teeth, and then returning in a series of deep, mesmerizing kisses that robbed her of the ability to think past that moment, and the inevitable continuing consummation of their marriage.

"Christmas after all," he said, continuing on his sensual quest, finally taking off her bra and teaching her pleasure in ways she had never imagined, "is something that should be enjoyed to the absolute limit." Hands hooked beneath the elastic of her panties and tights, he pushed those down, too.

Amanda drew in a shaky breath as he settled between her thighs and sought out the most feminine part of her. "I think you're doing that, all right," she moaned, as he pushed her to the absolute limit, until at last there was no more waiting, no more denying the passion that had taken hold of them both, and they were both gasping. She wanted him deep inside her, and he gave her that, and so much more, drawing her into a realm of sensation that had them both reaching the outer limits of their control. Holding tight, they soared into soft, sizzling love and shuddering pleasure.

They stayed like that, for long moments after. Feeling exhausted and replete, Amanda turned blindly into Riley's arms and buried her face in the hair on his chest. Heart brimming with tenderness, loving the gentle way he held her close, she snuggled closer. "Riley?"

He stroked a hand through her hair. "Hmm?"

I love you. So much. But as much as she tried to form the words, they would not be said. Not now. Not yet.

He waited. When she still didn't say anything, he unwrapped his arms. Releasing her reluctantly, he shifted onto his side, bent his elbow and propped his head on his hand. An awkward silence fell between them as he searched her face and asked quietly, "What did you want to tell me?"

Needing to reassure herself by touching him, she stroked a hand across his chest. Knowing it was too soon, that she could ruin everything if she declared her feelings for him this quickly, she pushed away the impulse to share everything with him, and said only, "I just wanted you to know that—" she paused to take a bolstering breath "—this was the best Christmas present I've ever had."

He looked deep into her eyes. A slow sexy smile crossed his face as he took her hand and lifted it to his lips. The tension in his shoulders eased. "For me, too." He winked. "Not that we're through yet…"

Amanda had only to look down to see the proof of his desire, feel her own body quicken in response and know that her longest-held wish—to be cherished, body and soul—was finally coming true. "Again?"

"This is the season for giving, you know." Riley clamped an arm about her waist and drew her closer, looking at her in a way that made her feel beautiful and wanted in a way she had never been. His voice dropped a husky notch. "And I want to give you so much joy, so much pleasure…."

Her head swam with the scent and feel of him. "You are

one very hard man to resist," she murmured as he laid claim
to her mouth with fierce possessiveness.

Riley smiled. Rolling onto his back, he pulled her on top of
him and wrapped his arms around her. "Keep thinking that
way, Mrs. McCabe, and we will have a very merry Christmas
indeed."

"THE CUFF LINKS ARE certainly very nice," the salesclerk told
Amanda.

One hundred stores in the mall, and where had she ended
up? The jewelers. "I don't know." Amanda hesitated, feeling
more foolish and uncertain than she could recall in a very long
time. "It seems sort of…"

"Impersonal?" the expensively dressed brunette asked.

"Yes."

The clerk slid the velvet-lined tray back in the glass case.
"How long have you and your man been dating?"

A self-conscious flush warmed Amanda's cheeks. "We're
not really dating."

"Of course," the clerk agreed readily. "A passé tradition for
women our age."

At what age, Amanda wondered, was dating no longer acceptable? The clerk had to be at least ten years older than she
was. And she wasn't wearing a wedding ring, either. But
then, she probably wasn't married to anyone, technically or
otherwise.

"I just meant we're not in high school anymore," the clerk
amended hastily, seeming to think she had offended Amanda
on some level.

Amanda realized it wasn't really the clerk bugging her—
it was the situation, and the uncertainty that went along with
it. And the wariness her mother had engendered in one long-

distance phone call. Amanda was thirty-two now. A grown woman who had been married and divorced. She was a registered nurse. And yet, the last few days around Riley had made Amanda feel as if she was an emotion-driven, lust-filled, mixed-up, crazy-in-love teenager!

She wasn't used to that.

Wasn't sure she wanted to get used to that!

Without Riley her life had been dull and, with the exception of the work she enjoyed, absolutely passionless. Now she had passion, but along with that came worry and uncertainty, two things Amanda felt she could happily do without.

"So is this a long-term relationship?" the clerk asked delicately, bringing out a tray of elegant diamond and gold rings.

Amanda couldn't see Riley wearing one of those, either. They were simply too fussy and flashy. She shook her head, even as she answered the clerk's question with a mumbled, "It's supposed to be."

The clerk's elegant brow arched. "You don't sound sure."

"A lot is involved," Amanda said stiffly.

"Of course." With an indulgent look, the clerk brought out a tray of gold chains, suitable for a man.

Again, no.

"We have these children," Amanda explained, as the clerk slid yet another tray back into the case.

"Oh!" A wealth of understanding in a single word.

"They're not ours. Not yet anyway," Amanda amended hastily.

"Oh." More subdued.

"If we continue stewardship of them, then I believe we will stay together," Amanda explained. If only because Riley couldn't handle all three of them alone, and—having lost his own mom at the tender age of thirteen—firmly believed all kids needed a mother and a father.

The clerk's brows knit together. "So it's not really a romantic involvement, then, between you and this gentleman you wish to purchase a gift for?"

Actually, Amanda thought wistfully, their love affair was highly romantic, which of course made the cautious side of her mistrust the longevity of her impetuous but passionate romance with Riley all the more. If only he'd said he loved her, maybe then she'd feel secure. But he hadn't and neither had she, so all she knew was that he was crazy in lust with her and that he wanted to make their marriage a real one in every way, and so did she.

"Or is it a romance?" the clerk inquired, abruptly looking as flummoxed as Amanda felt.

Not sure how to answer that, but certain she didn't want to try and put it in words, Amanda merely shrugged off the question.

"The thing is," she said finally, swallowing hard and turning her attention firmly back to the task at hand. "I've never really seen Riley wear a shirt that required cuff links, or any other kind of decorative jewelry, either. He's more of a button-up and button-down kind of guy, if you know what I mean."

"Are you absolutely certain he wouldn't like a ring?" the clerk asked, determined, it seemed, to get her sale and commission. "We have some that are very understated."

The only ring Amanda wanted to see on Riley's large, capable hands was a wedding band. Again, she shook her head. "Riley's not really a ring kind of guy, either."

"How about a watch, then?" the clerk suggested brightly. "We have wrist or pocket. Both styles are excellent, elegant gifts as well as practical timepieces."

Time, Amanda thought, as the clerk brought out yet another velvet-lined tray, was the one thing running out. In two days, Christmas would be over. Whoever had left the children might very well show up to claim them. Or the police might track them down. When that happened, Amanda and Riley would meet the person or persons responsible for the abandonment face-to-face and they would know whether or not the children were being put up for guardianship and/or adoption. And that, more than anything, would determine the future between them.

"BAD SHOPPING TRIP?" Riley asked when Amanda strolled in the door, close to dinner time. She brought with her two pizzas and a garden salad.

"Why would you say that?" Amanda asked brightly.

He looked at her, his expression vaguely suspicious, his lips set in a thoughtful line. "The glum look on your face before you adjusted it." He took the cardboard boxes and take-out sack from her hand, then sauntered closer still.

"Don't mind me." Amanda wrinkled her nose in aggravation. *I've just been busy wishing for the best and expecting the worst.*

Still studying her, he braced a hip against the kitchen counter and crossed his arms. The pleasure he felt at seeing her again was in his amber eyes. "Stores crowded?" he asked her coyly.

Aware there was very little space between them now, she matched his provoking grin. "Oh, yes."

His eyes lit up with a teasing glow. He hooked an arm about her waist and brought her all the way against him. The warmth of his body, where it pressed up against hers, gave new heat to hers. Amanda caught her breath as he rubbed his thumb across her lower lip, tracing its sensual shape. "Buy me something wonderful?" he murmured in her ear.

Amanda trembled in a way that let him know just how sensitive she was to his touch. "I never shop and tell."

He peered at her argumentatively. "How about kiss and tell then?"

"Not that, either."

"Hmm." He acknowledged her confession with a wry smile,

then leaned over to kiss her cheek. "Guess I'll have to wait then."

That was the problem, Amanda thought, she didn't want to wait for anything. "I guess you will," she flirted back. Their eyes locked. The familiarity and ease between them deepened. Another silence fell between them, happier this time, and fraught with tension.

Chloe and Amber burst into the room. Amanda knelt, giving both little girls the perfect proximity to hug her fiercely. "I missed you," she said, kissing them both.

Amber drew back. She touched Amanda's face with the flat of her hand. "Pretty," she said, repeating the one and only word she could pronounce intelligibly.

"I think so, too," Riley winked.

Amanda flushed self-consciously. "Thank you," she told Amber. "I think you're pretty, too, sweetheart."

Meanwhile, Chloe held on tight, her little face buried in Amanda's neck. Realizing some extraspecial attention was needed for the oldest child, Riley swooped seventeen-month-old Amber up into his arms. Chloe kept right on hugging Amanda. "Everything okay this afternoon?" Amanda asked Riley.

He nodded. "We've been singing Christmas carols. Or rather, I have. I keep hoping someone will join in, but so far…"

His voice trailed off as Chloe finally drew back. She looked into Amanda's eyes. For a second, Chloe's mouth worked, her eyes grew intense, and Amanda thought she was at long last going to speak. She knew for certain the little girl wanted to communicate something to her, but…the moment passed, and Chloe's face relaxed, and she withdrew into herself again.

Amanda kissed Chloe's cheek, hugged her tight, then swooped the four-year-old up into her arms and carried her into the kitchen, where Cory was sleeping in his bassinet. "I was telling the kids that we're going to bake those Christmas cookies after dinner tonight," Riley said. "Is that okay with you?"

Enjoying the sweet sense of family, Amanda smiled. "As a matter of fact, that is exactly what I had planned."

"Maybe doing the familiar," Riley continued as he helped both girls into their seats, "will spark something verbal from someone, if you know what I mean."

Amanda nodded, easily understanding Riley's coded message. "If not right away, then soon," she said.

"Because Christmas is all about wishes coming true."

The question was, Amanda thought, what exactly were Riley's? The same as hers? Was he searching for a forever kind of love, too? Or something a lot more casual?

Chapter Twelve

"What's so funny?" Amanda asked, catching her husband's amused smile, as they surveyed the damage done during an hour of gleeful cookie baking and decorating with the kids. All of whom had since been put to bed.

"You." Riley tapped Amanda playfully on the nose. "You've got red sprinkles on your eyebrow, green frosting on your cheek and flour in your hair."

Amanda studied him as a kaleidoscope of emotions twisted through her. "Ha! You're one to talk. You've got confectioner's sugar on your temple, and pizza sauce on the back of your neck."

He raised a quizzical brow.

"From dinner." Amanda got a clean cloth out of the drawer and dampened it beneath the faucet. "Those kisses and hugs the kids gave you left their mark, too."

Riley stood still while she dabbed at the offending marks on his skin, then took the cloth, cupped her chin in his hand and did the same. "That makes us two of a kind, then."

Amanda melted under the gentle ministrations of his hands. The next thing she knew, his head was dropping. His lips were on hers in a sweet, sensual kiss that stole her breath away. "You taste like cookie," she murmured.

"So do you." He steered her beneath the mistletoe hanging from the entranceway to the kitchen and delivered another kiss. She melted into it, thinking all the while this was her merriest holiday ever.

"Want to…?"

"Yes," she said softly, looking deep into his eyes. "But we can't. Not yet anyway. We have to answer those Dear Santa letters for the kids in pediatrics, remember?"

Riley nodded, a faint smile curving his lips. "I've been putting it off."

"Hard to know what to say," Amanda agreed.

He retrieved the wicker basket at the end of the counter. "Meg gave me a list of possible replies, as well as Christmas cards and envelopes to write on, so if you'll help…we can get it done and get to the good stuff."

"You're incorrigible."

Riley winked. "Never more so than when I'm around you."

They cleared the table of just-frosted cookies and wiped it down. Riley began opening envelopes while Amanda loaded the dishwasher and turned it on. She wiped her hands on a towel and sat down to join him, just in time to see him slipping an envelope into his sweater vest. "Ah ah ah!" Knowing full well by the sly expression on his handsome face that he was up to no good, she made a grab for the pilfered letter. "What's this?"

"Nothing you need to see," he declared.

She wrested it from him anyway, noticed his handwriting on the front. "That's your letter to Santa! Which must mean mine is in here, too."

"Yep." Riley pointed to another envelope right in front of him. "All the other staff letters seem to have been removed."

"They were probably forwarded to the appropriate spouses and significant others," Amanda murmured, taking charge of her letter. "What did you ask for in yours?"

Riley held his just out of reach. "I'm not telling—until you let me in on what you asked for," he teased.

Did she want him to know what she had wished for?

"I'll show you mine if you show me yours," he persisted.

Amanda had the feeling that despite his outward bravura that Riley was a little embarrassed about what he had written, too. "Mmm. I need to think about it," she allowed finally.

Mischief tugged at the corners of his lips. "Your request was that racy, hmm?"

"You never know," Amanda fibbed, feeling a self-conscious flush warm her cheeks.

He rubbed the inside of her wrist. "You do constantly surprise me."

Ribbons of sensation flowed through her. She looked deep into his eyes. "I gather your request was rather tame?"

"Maybe." He favored her with a smile that was rife with sensual promise. "And maybe it was as wild as can be. There's only one way to find out, and that's to open them both on Christmas Eve."

AN HOUR LATER, they were at the end of the letters. Most had been easy enough to answer. A few were not. Figuring they needed to warm up to those, Amanda and Riley saved the most difficult ones for last.

Amanda reported, "Shelby Huff wants a kitten for Christmas."

Riley frowned. "She's in the hospital because she had a severe asthma attack."

"Right. Which makes a cat impossible for her." Amanda paused thoughtfully. She rested her chin on her upraised hand. She liked the cozy feel of doing a yuletide task with him. "Should Santa offer Shelby a stuffed kitty cat or a book or DVD about felines?"

"Probably," Riley allowed, already pushing back his chair and headed for the phone, "but let's call her folks and see what they want to do first. They may have a better idea."

Mr. and Mrs. Huff were in favor of a stuffed toy kitten and

a movie about a kitten that runs away from home with several dogs. Both presents had already been purchased. So Riley and Amanda wrote a letter that said,

> Dear Shelby, I know you can't be around cats because of your asthma so I am sending you two very special presents that will let you love kittens without getting sick again. Love, Santa.

"That ought to do it," Amanda said as she addressed and sealed the envelope that had already been stamped with a return address of Santa's Workshop, The North Pole.

Riley continued sorting through the letters that were left. "Here's one from Laurel."

Curious, Amanda put down her pen. "What does it say?"

Riley opened it up. He read out loud,

> Dear Santa, Please give my friend everything my friend needs for a very Merry Christmas. Love, Laurel.

The mystery remained. "Still no boyfriend's name?"

Riley drummed his pen on the tabletop. "She was probably worried Mom or Dad would get handed this note, or somehow learn of its contents."

"And yet she wasn't worried enough not to write it."

"I guess there's a little belief in Santa's miracles in all of us."

Amanda knew that was certainly true of herself, given what she had written in her letter to St. Nick.

Riley sighed. "If Laurel has a flaw, it's identifying too much with other people's problems. Of course, that's not surprising since one of her parents is a psychologist and grief counselor who devotes herself to helping others."

"You'd think your parents would be more understanding of her," Amanda said.

"Well, you know parents." Riley shrugged in obvious regret. "They want to protect their children first, and worry about everyone else later. No good parent puts their own child at risk so they can help someone else, especially when the action required is to their own child's detriment. Unfortunately, Laurel seems unable to protect her own interests the way our folks would wish."

Amanda got up to pour them both a glass of milk. "What do you mean?"

Riley's gaze followed her as she moved about the kitchen, preparing them a bedtime snack. "When Laurel was eight, she sold her brand-new bicycle for five dollars because her best buddy had lost his lunch money and was too embarrassed to tell his parents or the teacher and she didn't want him to go hungry." He helped himself to one of the sugar cookies when Amanda brought a plate of them back to the table.

"She got put on academic probation in high school when she tried to help a football player who was really struggling academically to write an essay, and he took her sample draft, slapped his name on it and turned it in."

Amanda sat down and took a cookie, too.

"Her apartment at UT has been a revolving door for friends who need a place to stay but never contribute financially," Riley continued grimly, shaking his head, "so Laurel's always running out of money for food, rent, gas and utilities, and that was never truer than this past fall." He paused to take a drink of milk to wash down the cookie he had just eaten. "Mom and Dad don't mind her helping people. In fact they applaud it. They just wish Laurel would watch out for herself in the process. And not let others constantly take advantage of her."

Amanda bit into a delicate spritz cookie, with green sprinkles. "Helping out others is a good thing, though," Amanda argued, thinking Riley was being a little hard on his only sister. "Laurel's certainly been a good friend to Micki. Inviting her for Christmas."

Riley leaned back in his chair, stretching his long legs out in front of him. They brushed hers under the kitchen table. "That's something else that bothers me," he remarked, snapping the head off a butter-cookie reindeer.

Amanda sipped her ice-cold milk and waited.

"I've known Micki for four years," Riley said. "Granted, our relationship was totally geared around Micki's desire to go to medical school, but she always spent her holidays with her sister and her family in Boulder, Colorado. She never would have missed a Christmas with them."

Amanda shrugged, and still thirsty, got up to retrieve the bottle of milk from the fridge. "Maybe Micki's sister went on holiday elsewhere this year."

"Maybe. But wouldn't she at least have invited Micki to go with them, given the fact Micki has no other family?"

"Maybe she did. Maybe Micki didn't want to intrude," Amanda speculated. She'd been a fifth wheel enough times in her own siblings' lives to know how that felt.

"And maybe Micki and her sister had a fight," Riley speculated boldly, "and Micki refused to go home for the holidays or something like that."

Amanda paused. "You think that's why Micki was crying in the hospital earlier today?"

"Maybe, and maybe something else is wrong. Something her sister should know about."

"Like what?" Amanda asked, wondering where Riley was going with this.

"Well...what if Micki were pregnant or sick or just plain broke or something? Isn't it possible that Micki's family sent her money for a plane ticket home and Micki spent it on Laurel's latest charity case instead? And now is afraid to say so, lest her sister and her sister's husband react the same way my mom and dad have to Laurel's recent activities? You know how close the two girls are, how much they want to help people."

Yes, Amanda did. She knew Riley had a point. It was good to help others, but every person also had a responsibility to see to their own needs, too. She lifted a brow. "You thinking about interfering?"

Riley rubbed his fingertips up and down the outside of his empty glass. "I've been wrestling with my conscience all day." He paused to look Amanda in the eye. "Part of me knows that Micki is a grown-up and capable of making her own decisions, and certainly, at age twenty-one, entitled to her private life. The other part says if it were Laurel in this situation, upset and possibly hiding something and not coming home for the holiday, and someone else were in a position to help reunite Laurel with the family that loves her, I'd want that person to intervene."

"Do you have Micki's sister's number?"

"No," Riley allowed, with another frown, "but I know her sister's name is Adelaide Rowan, and her husband's name is Wiley."

"So, look them up, call to wish them a merry Christmas and tell Micki's sister how happy you are that Micki was accepted to UT-Galveston med school. Scope things out that way."

Riley paused. "You think it'd be okay?"

Amanda shrugged, no more sure than her husband was. On the other hand, Riley's instincts in situations like this were usually good. "If you're right, it might be just what Micki needs to reunite her with her family in time for Christmas."

With a decisive nod, Riley went to his computer and looked up the phone number. Using the speakerphone function so she could hear, too, he dialed it and got the automated message, "This number has been disconnected." No new number was listed.

Scowling, Riley called the phone company, to see if they had an updated listing. They did not. Further searches on the Internet also proved futile. "Well, what now?" Amanda asked. "Are you going to ask Micki?"

"Eventually," Riley said. "But first, I'm going to see if Kevin can help us."

Still using the speakerphone, Riley telephoned Kevin. He was pulling a double shift in order to be off the next evening for the McCabe Open House at Sam and Kate's home. "Sure I can look into it," Kevin said, while Amanda and Riley both listened. "Got a couple things going right now, though. Is tomorrow soon enough?"

"Sure," Riley said. "Thanks." He hung up the phone and took Amanda into his arms.

He felt so warm and strong. "Feeling better?" she said.

Riley nodded. "You know what would make me feel even better, though?" he whispered, as he tunneled both hands through her hair.

Amanda grinned, guessing lightly, "The same thing that would help me?"

Riley swung her up into his arms. "Time's a wastin' then." He carried her up the stairs, down the hall.

"This is becoming a habit," Amanda teased, already trembling with need, as he deposited her on the bed.

"Gotta work off those cookies and milk somehow," he joked right back, in a voice that melted her reserve and appealed to her heart all the more. The next thing Amanda knew, Riley was stretched out beside her, one leg draped over hers. She lost her breath as his gaze lovingly roved her face and his lips covered hers once again.

They might not have everything worked out just yet, she thought dizzily, as she kissed him back as deeply and tenderly as he was kissing her, but right now, she didn't care. All that mattered to her was the chance to be with Riley like this. She knew he was the love of her life and if she didn't take advantage of this opportunity to be with him she would regret it forever, and she didn't want regrets where the two of them were concerned, only sweet, wonderful, blossoming love. The future, she was sure, would take care of itself. All she had to worry about now was the holiday ahead, and the hot, sizzling pressure of his mouth moving over hers. She moaned low in her throat, feeling everything around her go soft and fuzzy as he caught her lower lip in a tantalizing caress.

His expression fierce with longing and the primal need to possess, Riley stopped long enough to undress them both. Sensations ran riot through her, thrilling, enticing. Trembling, they climbed between the sheets and Riley took her in his arms again. He cupped her face, whispering her name, angling her head so he could deepen the kiss even more. Another shiver of excitement went through her. Heart pounding, the yearning in her a sweet incessant ache, she arched against him. Moving restlessly. Feeling the fullness of him straining against her thigh as he bent his head, his lips tracing an erotic path across her rosy-tipped breasts.

The hot slow strokes of his tongue across her nipples, the gentle suckling, was unbearably tender, intimate, seductive. Helpless to resist, Amanda closed her eyes. Pleasure drifted through every inch of her. Lower still, she felt a melting sensation, a weakening of her limbs. Her back arched, her thighs parted. They had barely started, and already she was on the edge of blissful oblivion. Loving the fragrance of his after-shave, so brisk and wintry, the sandpapery feel of his evening beard as it sensually abraded her skin.

"I want you," she murmured, as his hands and lips and teeth and tongue, found her there and there and there. "So much," she said as he shifted upward, fitting his mouth over hers once again.

He shifted onto his back, pulling her over him.

"I want you, too," he murmured, filling his hands with her breasts.

Eager to please him as he was pleasing her, Amanda caressed the smoothly muscled skin of his chest and shoulders, loving the way his flat male nipples pebbled beneath her questing palms. Lower still, the unmistakable evidence of his arousal nudged the softness between her thighs. Determined to give as much as she got, she worshipped him with her lips and tongue. She worked her way downward, past the silken hair and flat muscular abdomen to his abundant sex, even as she trembled with a fierce unquenchable ache. Wanting him to want her as fervently as she wanted him, she cupped the fertile part of him with one hand and stroked the length of him with the other, until he was quivering with need, repeatedly saying her name.

She slid upward once again, straddling his thighs. And then he was lifting her, positioning her just so. Amanda opened her legs and took him inside her, pulsing, aching, searching for pleasure and release. She had never felt as close to anyone as she did to Riley at that moment. She surrendered to him completely as their lips met in another searing, endless kiss. Trembling, they moved together, loving each other with every fiber of their beings, connecting as one heart, one soul, in a way that felt as real and indisputable and enduring as any marriage vow. And when they lay quietly, when they were still snuggled close, wrapped in each other's arms, Riley looked at the clock, and saw—as did Amanda—that it was just past midnight. And no longer December 23.

"It's Christmas Eve," he said, looking happier—more content—than she had ever seen him.

Amanda grinned, knowing this was her best holiday ever, too. "Well, then, Merry Christmas," Amanda responded right back, able now to envision many more blissful yuletides with Riley and the kids.

Riley planted a kiss on her brow and held her all the tighter. Tenderness radiated in his voice. "Merry Christmas indeed."

RILEY AND AMANDA were finishing the breakfast dishes the next morning when they heard a soft, musical sound. Both abruptly stopped what they were doing and looked in the direction of the adjacent family room where the two older children were sitting on the floor, playing with their toys. "Is that… 'Feliz Navidad'?" Riley asked, his eyes lighting up with amazement.

"It certainly is!" Amanda smiled. Edging surreptitiously closer, they strained to listen. Chloe was indeed humming her version of the popular Christmas song. "This is a good sign," Amanda whispered happily.

Riley nodded and leaned down so his face was next to hers, his lips close enough to kiss. "Maybe Christmas will be what it takes to have our little angel talking again," he murmured softly, shooting an affectionate look at Chloe and her siblings.

"We can hope," Amanda said, her mood as festive as the song.

He steered her beneath another sprig of mistletoe, and they kissed, sweetly and tenderly. "You sure you're up for playing jolly old Mrs.-You-Know-Who for the kids at the hospital and the kids at the McCabe family's annual Christmas Eve Open House?" Riley teased.

Amanda nodded, warming at the intimacy in his voice and eyes. "Absolutely positively." She winked.

He waggled his eyebrows at her playfully. "If you want some help getting into the costume…"

Amanda splayed her hands across his chest, as eager as Riley to make wild, wonderful love again, and further the emotional bonds between them. "You just worry about watching the kids and helping Kate and your dad get ready for the party this evening," she instructed.

"You sure?" His heartbeat picked up beneath her palm. He bragged with macho self-assurance, "I'm very good with buttons and zippers."

"You can show me later," Amanda promised. She massaged the brawny width of his shoulders, let her hands ghost all the way down his muscular arms to his wrists. "Much later, when it's time to put on our kerchiefs and nightclothes and climb into bed and await the sounds of the sleigh bells on the roof."

Riley looked out the window. He looked handsome and re-laxed in a burgundy pullover sweater that brought out the am-ber lights of his eyes. "You know the weatherman keeps insisting there's a chance of snow."

Amanda couldn't help but admire the way he filled out his gray gabardine dress slacks. The man had one nice backside. "They say that every year," she acknowledged as she moved closer yet. "It only happens once a decade or so."

"Well, maybe this year is the year," Riley hoped out loud.

"It certainly is the year for a lot of things," Amanda agreed, aware she had never felt happier.

Riley helped her into her coat. She went in to say good-bye to the kids, promising to meet up with them later at Kate and Sam's. Amber gave her an enthusiastic hug. The drowsy Cory cooed up at her from his bassinet. Chloe stopped hum-ming to herself when she saw Amanda had her coat on and was getting ready to leave. As Amanda knelt to embrace her, the little girl held tight to Amanda's neck, drew back to look into Amanda's eyes. The old anxiousness was back, Amanda noted sorrowfully. "I promise. I'll see you later," Amanda re-assured Chloe firmly. "We're all going to be together for Christmas, I promise."

For a second, Amanda thought Chloe was going to say some-thing in return. But the moment passed, and the four-year-old merely offered a faint smile and hugged Amanda fiercely again.

RILEY THOUGHT ABOUT Chloe's reaction to Amanda's leave-taking the rest of the morning, into the afternoon. Sadly, he knew exactly how the little girl felt. There was so much he wanted to say, too, so much he feared, too. What he had found with Amanda was a once-in-a-lifetime love and happiness. He could only hope Amanda felt it, too. One way or another, he would find out on Christmas Day.

In the meantime, he had three children to get ready and transport to the McCabe family gathering. And this time he would be doing it without Amanda's help. Fortunately before she left, she had helped lay out the clothes each child was to wear, readied the bottles of formula and packed the diaper bag with essentials to take along. So Riley's exit from the house went much smoother than it would have had he been left to his own devices. Eager to see his brother and find out if there was any new information on the children's identity, Riley sought out Kevin as soon as he arrived. "Got a minute?"

"I want to talk to you, too," Kevin told Riley. Kevin glanced at Micki and Laurel, who were seated on the floor, playing with Chloe and Amber. "But we should do it privately. Let's bring some more wood in for the fire," Kevin said.

Riley handed baby Cory to his brother Will. "Watch him, for a minute, would you?"

Will—the oldest of Riley's brothers and the most determinedly unmarried—looked as if he had been handed twelve pounds of dangerous material, instead of a baby. But he concurred nevertheless.

Riley and Kevin donned jackets and walked out back to the woodpile. The sky was a wintry gray overhead. The air felt damp and cold, ready for snow. Riley's hopes for a magically white Christmas intensified. "So what's up? Did you track down Micki's sister and brother-in-law for me?"

"No," Kevin frowned. "And I have to tell you why…."

Riley was still numb from what he had just learned when he and Kevin walked back inside. He knew what he had to do as he walked over to where Micki was playing with the kids. "Micki, could you help me with something?" Riley said.

Micki looked up. Once again, Riley was fairly certain, from the residual puffiness of her eyes, that Micki had been crying. Now, sadly, he finally understood why.

Micki looked surprised, but as willing to help out as ever. "Sure."

Kevin winked at Micki as he sat down next to Amber, Chloe and Laurel. "I'll keep your place," he teased the youthful group around him lightheartedly. "I'm more fun anyway!"

"Ha!" Laurel said, in response to her brother's teasing, as Riley and Micki walked toward the front of the big Victorian.

"Let's step into my dad's study," Riley said. It was the one place he knew they wouldn't be disturbed.

Micki began to look alarmed as Riley shut the double doors behind them. "Is something wrong?" she said.

Riley rested a hip against his dad's massive desk. "I thought maybe you could tell me."

Silence fell. Micki's lower lip began to tremble.

So much made sense to Riley now. "You're the one who left those kids for me," he said slowly. "Aren't you?"

Tears flooded Micki's eyes. "Please don't be mad at me," she begged. "I just didn't see any other way."

"Why don't we start at the beginning?" Riley suggested kindly.

Micki swallowed hard. "My sister and her husband were killed in a car accident last September. I was named guardian of Chloe, Amber and Cory. So I brought all three kids back to Austin with me and they moved in with me and Laurel."

Which explained a lot, Riley thought. Laurel's disastrous grades, her defiant proclamation she'd do it all again, the nonstop requests for more money from Kate and his dad.

"I tried—I really did—but even with Laurel's help I couldn't be both mother and father to them." Micki's chin quivered. Tears dripped down her face. She scrubbed them away with her fingers. "I knew I was going to have to find someone else to take them, someone who loved kids, somebody who wanted a family of their own but didn't have one yet."

"Why didn't you just ask me then?" Riley said gently, struggling to understand why the two young women had felt such an elaborate ruse was necessary to get him involved in the situation. Hadn't he gone all out to help Micki secure a position as a premed summer intern and written her a stellar recommendation to medical school?

"Because Laurel and I both figured you'd say no if we did, because you weren't married yet and you were starting a new job and you didn't yet have any experience being a daddy. On the other hand—" Micki paused and shrugged "—we decided if we left you the kids as kind of a Christmas gift and asked you to give them the holiday they deserved, and we stuck around to see you got a lot of help taking care of them, that everything would be okay. You would get to know them, and once that happened, we figured you'd love them, too, as much as we do, and want to keep them. We never imagined you'd think Amanda dropped off the kids as a joke on you or demand she marry you as a result!"

Riley ran a hand across his jaw, smiled ruefully. "That was a little dramatic, wasn't it?"

"No kidding!" Micki enthused. "People at the hospital are still talking about it. But even that seems to be working out all right." Micki paused to search his face. "Because you do love her, don't you, Riley," Micki noted with an emotional satisfaction that matched Riley's own. "You love both Amanda and the kids."

AMANDA COULDN'T SAY WHY, but she just knew something important had happened between the time she had left the house and arrived at the McCabe family gathering. Micki looked different. So did Riley. But she had no chance to speak to either of them privately as she walked in, a big basket of presents over her arm. Speaking in a jolly bass tone, Amanda Ho-Ho-Hoed her way through the throngs of family and friends, passing out envelopes from Santa to those who had written him and dropped their letters off at the hospital pediatric wing mailbox, and distributed gifts provided by Kate and Sam McCabe to all of the children.

"Want to sit on Mrs. Claus's lap?" Riley asked Amber when Amanda took the chair of honor before the fireplace.

Amber gleefully complied. Struggling to stand up, she patted Amanda's face with both her tiny palms, running her fingers through the strands of curly white hair framing her face, examining the gold-rimmed glasses perched on the edge of her nose, and the velvety fabric of her costume. Finally, Amber patted Amanda's rouged cheeks and pronounced her, "Pretty!"

Everyone roared with laughter.

Riley winked. "I agree."

Next up were Brad and Laney's two preschoolers. Their older brother, Petey, also played along.

Several more cousins took their turns.

Then baby Cory.

Finally, it was Chloe's turn. Expression serious, she climbed onto Amanda's lap, looking soberly into her eyes.

Amanda adjusted her gold-rimmed Santa glasses. "And what would you like for Christmas, little girl?" Amanda prodded in the most compelling Mrs. Claus-voice she could manage.

Chloe looked at Amanda.

Then Riley.

Back at Amanda again.

There was no clue as to whether Chloe recognized Amanda or not. And to Amanda's disappointment, Chloe still didn't speak.

"It's just going to take time for the communication with you-know-who to be ongoing again," Riley said, hours later, as he and Amanda drove the short distance back to his house. "It will happen."

Amanda certainly hoped so. She couldn't help but feel a little like a failure. She had been so certain than Chloe's Christmas gift to them was going to be to start talking again.

Or at least communicating more openly in some way. Instead, the self-protective wall remained up, strong as ever.

Although no one would ever know it from Riley's behavior. He hadn't been able to stop smiling whenever he looked at her or the kids all evening. Micki and Laurel had seemed to be extraordinarily relaxed and joyful, too. For the first time, Micki's face had lost that pinched, way-too-serious expression she wore whenever she thought no one was looking her way.

"Let's get the kids in their pajamas and tuck them in, and then we'll…talk," Riley said.

Amanda lifted a brow.

Riley flashed her a sexy things-are-so-good-you-just-don't-know smile again. It was the kind of grin someone had when they just knew they had gotten you the perfect Christmas present and couldn't wait to give it to you, Amanda thought. Which in turn made her wonder what Riley was going to think of the rather lame—but nice—wristwatch she had selected for him. At the time, she had felt it appropriate.

Now, it didn't begin to relay all she felt in her heart for him. She could only hope he would understand that so much had changed between then and now. And would continue to do so.

By the time they had the kids ready for bed, another half hour had passed and baby Cory was already sleeping soundly. Riley deposited him in his bassinet then joined Amanda, Chloe and Amber on Chloe's bed. Chloe was clutching a copy of *'Twas The Night Before Christmas* in her hand. She thrust it at Amanda. "You want me to read this?" Amanda asked. And thought, but couldn't be sure it wasn't her imagination, that Chloe nodded ever so slightly in response.

"Pretty!" Amber said as she scooted over onto the right side of Amanda's lap.

Chloe took up residence on Amanda's left side.

Riley sat against the headboard and stretched his legs out in front of him. "Sounds good to me," he said.

Achingly aware of how much a family they felt at this moment, Amanda opened the book and began to read. Amber was nearly asleep when she finished; Chloe, spellbound. Amanda closed the book. "You know Santa is going to come here tonight and leave you a present under the tree. And one for Amber and baby Cory too, but he can't come until you're asleep."

Chloe's eyes sparkled with excitement.

"We're pretty sure you're going to be happy with the presents Amanda and I have for you this year, too," Riley said.

Chloe's smile broadened slightly.

"Ready to go to sleep?" Amanda asked, gently ruffling the little girl's curls.

And this time Chloe did nod. Quickly, she scrambled to her feet, wrapped her arms around Riley's neck and hugged him hard. Kissed his cheek. Then hugged and kissed Amanda just as enthusiastically. Amanda and Riley kissed and hugged her right back. Amber joined in. And there was so much excitement it was another fifteen minutes before they had them settled into their beds. "Meet you downstairs in five?" Riley whispered at the bedroom door.

Amanda nodded.

She stayed nearby, until she was sure all three children were sleeping soundly and went back downstairs, her present to Riley tucked into the pocket of her red velvet jumper.

He had the Christmas tree lights on, and the rest of the living room lights off. A cozy fire burned in the fireplace. A bottle of wine sat open on the coffee table, along with two long-stemmed glasses. Amanda's heart took a little leap as she joined him on the sofa. "Looks like we're celebrating," she said lightly.

His eyes darkened. "You have no idea," he said dryly, taking both her hands in his, squeezing them affectionately. "I have so much to tell you I don't know where to begin."

Amanda'd heard an opening statement like this once before, the night Fraser had told her he wanted to reconcile with his wife, so he was divorcing her and taking his kids with him. But this couldn't be the same, she told herself sternly. For one thing, Riley looked happy with whatever it was. "So what happened today?" she asked, unbearably curious. "What haven't you told me?"

"I found out who the kids are, Amanda," Riley announced proudly. "I know who left them with me."

Chapter Thirteen

"How? When?" Amanda asked, looking every bit as shocked and wary as Riley had felt hours earlier.

Riley took both of her hands in his. Briefly, he explained what Kevin had found out about Micki's sister and her husband. "They were killed in a car accident in September," Riley related sadly, his heart going out to his young protégée and her two nieces and nephew. "Apparently, Micki was given custody of her sister's children and she took Amber, Chloe and Cory back to Austin with her. They moved in with her and Laurel and, with Laurel helping her every step of the way, Micki made every effort to be a good guardian to them."

Amanda sat back against the cushions of the sofa, still struggling to take it all in. "Which explains why Laurel's grades went down," she theorized, slowly extricating her hands from his.

Riley nodded. "Apparently, Laurel figured it wouldn't matter what GPA she graduated with, but they knew Micki's grades had to be excellent if she wanted to get into medical school, and she did."

Amanda laid a hand across her heart. "And no one knew?"

Riley shrugged. "Micki didn't want anyone finding out, for fear that her custody of the three kids would somehow keep her from achieving her long-held dream of becoming a doctor. She especially didn't want me to know, since she had already asked me to write a recommendation for her, which I had done."

Amanda rose from the sofa and began to pace the room restlessly, her mood remote and tense. "So the two girls kept it a secret."

"Until they realized they were in over their heads. Micki wanted to come to me then and ask me to adopt the kids, but Laurel wasn't sure I would take it on alone, if they simply asked me."

Amanda paused in front of the fireplace. She ran both her hands through her silky hair. "So instead they hatched the plan to pretend the kids had mysteriously been left at the hospital for you."

"Right. Knowing all the while the two of them would be there to lend a hand and see the kids were all right. They didn't figure on you being made mother." Restless now, too, Riley stood and crossed to Amanda's side. He lounged opposite her, thrusting his hands in his pockets, leaning one shoulder against the mantel. "But they couldn't be happier about the way things have turned out."

Amanda tipped her head up to his. Some of the light left her blue-green eyes. "What do you mean?"

Riley smiled at Amanda determinedly. He looked deep into her eyes and cupped her shoulders warmly. "I told them both that I'm going to stay married to you and we're going to raise the kids together." He paused, aware the words weren't having the effect he had hoped, given the passionate and romantic turn their relationship had taken the last few days. Her unexpected reserve confused and frustrated him. He had been certain from the way Amanda had been behaving toward him, that this was what they both had been hoping would happen—that the kids would be theirs, and the way would be clear for them all to be together in the traditional family way. Yet Amanda was behaving as if he were backing her into a corner against her will.

Out of nerves or simply the traditional premarriage doubts and fears?

Figuring if ever there was a time to be presumptuous, this was it, he continued with a bolstering smile. "Micki and Laurel couldn't be happier."

To Riley's consternation, Amanda looked even more nervous and on edge. She backed away from him once again. "So everyone at the party—your whole family—knows this?" she questioned him, incredulously.

"No." Riley paused, searching her face. He knew everything was happening very quickly. It had been a shock to him, too. "Just me, and Laurel and Micki, and Kevin and now you. Micki was adamant we not sadden everyone's Christmas with the news of her tragedy." Riley closed the distance between them once again.

"Micki is ready to move forward on the adoption immediately," he told Amanda seriously.

Twin spots of color appeared in her cheek. "I see," she returned in a brisk, emotional voice.

"Assuming," Riley continued gruffly, "you still want to be a mother to the kids and stay married to me." Right now, he noted, as dread filled his soul, she did not look as if that were the case.

Amanda tossed her head. "You think there's a reason why I shouldn't?" she asked, testy.

Riley sighed. Still eyeing her determinedly, he released a short, impatient breath. "I think that you think there's a reason why we shouldn't." And he didn't like that at all.

IT WAS THE MOMENT OF TRUTH, Amanda knew. Riley was offering her all she had ever wanted. Yet something about his matter-of-fact recitation rang hollow with her. And the emptiness of his words echoed the void deep inside her. "You know that I love the kids with all my heart," she started thickly, achingly aware of all he hadn't said. That he loved her, that she was the only woman for him and always would be. That the two of them had what it took to build a lasting marriage that would serve as the solid family foundation needed to adopt the three children and see them through to adulthood and beyond. This was a lifetime commitment they were about to make, yet it didn't seem as if Riley were thinking much past the immediate future. And while Amanda appreciated his gallantry, she knew they couldn't pretend that passion, friendship and mutual concern about the children was enough to hold a marriage together. Bitter experience had shown her that was not the case, that without a deep and abiding romantic love between husband and wife a family could not survive over the long haul.

"And yet…despite this love…?" Riley prompted, sauntering closer.

Amanda swallowed as he advanced on her slowly, his eyes holding hers. She had to make him see the truth of their situation. Trembling at his nearness, Amanda held up her hands. Heart breaking, she paced away from him once again. "What did your letter to Santa say, Riley?"

Riley blinked and regarded her cautiously. "What does that have to do with this?" he demanded.

"Bear with me," Amanda replied in the same short tone. She retrieved both letters from the antique writing desk by the window and handed the one she had written to him. Struggling with all her might to hold back her tears, she commanded, "Open it."

Riley shot a curious look at her, tore the seal.

"Read it," Amanda ordered.

With a frown, Riley complied, reading the first five words that were there for everyone participating in the letter writing activity and then the ones that were handwritten on the blank line provided.

Dear Santa, Please give me the loving husband and children I have always wanted. This time, for keeps.

Riley looked up, as if not sure what her point was. "So we're on the same page," he said with an indifferent shrug. "So what?"

But Amanda knew, and she didn't much like the unwelcome truth that was staring them both in the face. She regarded him politely. "Now may I read your letter to Santa?"

He stood, legs braced apart, arms folded in front of him. Looking increasingly disillusioned, he ordered tersely, "Go ahead."

Amanda carefully slid a delicate finger beneath the seal, loosened it, and withdrew the letter without ripping the envelope. She read the scripted words out loud. And then the ones he had written in his commanding scrawl,

Dear Santa, Please give me a family. And Chloe, Amber and Cory one that loves and cares for them, too.

Riley started toward her impatiently. "Now that we know we both ultimately want the same thing…" he said, handing over the offending paper.

"Don't you see?" Amanda waved the letter in front of him, like the red flag it was. Emotion choked her voice so she could hardly speak. "We both want this to work out so badly we're willing to convince ourselves of darn near anything."

Riley stared at her, his jaw hardening to the consistency of granite.

Knowing it sounded like the cruelest kiss-off possible, Amanda forced herself to forget her own selfish ambitions and do what was right nevertheless. "Our shared affection for the children is not enough to build a family on, at least not one that will last," she said as a heartrending silence fell between them.

She shook her head, feeling unbearably weary. Resigned. "Divorce is really hard on kids, Riley," she told him emotionally. She couldn't bear to knowingly hurt the three children they already loved so much. "Chloe, Amber and baby Cory have already been through so much, losing their folks, living with Micki and Laurel, being dropped off with us." Amanda's voice broke. She shoved both her hands through her hair. "It wouldn't be fair to let them think we were in a situation that would last forever if it isn't going to last forever."

Hurt and anger faded, to be replaced by an icy resolve that chilled Amanda to her soul. A stoic look in his amber eyes, he asked her calmly but brusquely, "Are you telling me you don't want to be married to me?"

Under these conditions? "This is exactly what I'm telling you," Amanda told him firmly but sadly. As difficult as it was for both of them, she knew she was doing the right thing.

RILEY KNEW he was supposed to bow out like a gentleman and let her go. Trouble was, he had never felt less gallant in his life. "I don't get it," he told Amanda angrily.

Shaking her head in futility, she brushed past him and headed for the rear of the house. "I know that you've wanted a family for quite a while. So have I. And I know how you like to fast forward your way through all things domestic."

He followed her out the door into the garage. "Speak your mind, why don't you?"

She paused next to the trunk of her car. There was no missing the mounting disappointment and resentment in her eyes. "Listen to me, Riley. You bought this house because it was already furnished right down to the dishes and you didn't have to do a thing but move in. Granted, you didn't plan or even ask for any of this, but the end result was that you got three kids and a wife practically the same way. Boom. One minute you're a single guy. The next you're both a husband and a daddy to three gorgeous kids."

Riley watched as she unlocked the trunk, then pushed it

open for her. "I didn't hear you objecting all that much at the time," he said, staring down at the presents heaped inside.

"Because, as these letters just demonstrated, it was my fantasy, too." Amanda brought out several gaily wrapped packages. Riley followed suit. "But we have to be realistic," she continued stalwartly. "If these three kids hadn't been dropped into our laps, we would most definitely not be married today."

He followed her inside. "You don't know that."

"I know this." Amanda set the packages down underneath the tree, then whirled to face him. She tapped a finger against his sternum. "Sex, fun, domestic compatibility and a shared love of practical jokes is not enough of a foundation for a marriage."

He followed her back to the garage to get more presents, his actions as deliberate as hers. "I thought we were doing pretty good."

She stalked across the cement floor of the garage, the long feminine skirt of her red velvet dress swirling around her shapely calves. "Really."

"Yes."

She whirled to face him. "Riley, we've been playing house."

He ignored her withering glance. "I haven't been *playing* anything."

"You're right," Amanda returned bitterly. "You've been honest. You never pretended to be doing this for anything other than your desire to give the kids security."

Riley's heart slammed against his ribs. "I told you how I felt about you," he reminded. It had been in every look, every action, every kiss, every time he made love to her.

Amanda pressed her lips together grimly. "Sex is not love, Riley."

What they had experienced could not be faked. "Says who?" Riley volleyed right back.

"Says me!" Amanda cried emotionally. "And every other adult who has fallen into the trap of making love for all the wrong reasons, the way we have been, and then gone on to regret it." Her turquoise eyes glimmering moistly, she turned away from him.

"Like you are now," Riley guessed, watching her rummage blindly through the presents still in the trunk.

"Yes." She finally picked up two of the lighter ones.

"Why?" Riley grabbed the heaviest packages.

Amanda drew a stabilizing breath. Spine stiff, she headed back into the house again. "Because the fact that we are very good together in the sack muddles things terribly," she whispered.

Riley waited until they had set their presents down in front of the tree. He took her by the shoulders. "You're wrong, Amanda. The fact we are good together clarifies everything."

She wrested free, stepped back with dignity and grace. "It certainly shows just how vulnerable we both have been," she observed quietly.

"So you're saying you bedded me because you were lonely?" Riley snapped, folding his arms and assuming a militant stance.

"And because it's Christmas," she retorted, just as fiercely. "And because we've been caught up in the spirit of the season. And we wanted to be able to stay together for the kids," she concluded miserably.

He stared at her in frustration. "We still can."

Cupping a hand around the back of her neck, he tried to make her look at him, but she wouldn't and she wasn't listening, either. "Riley, I can't be married to you without also knowing we have the kind of love that lasts a lifetime." She speared him with a censuring gaze.

"And you don't think we do." For him, her actions were a bitter replay of the past. Evangeline had turned down his marriage proposal because she didn't want marriage, love or kids.

Amanda was turning him down because she did. She just didn't trust him to be able to give them to her, not in any lasting fashion anyway.

"Sadly, no," Amanda stated carefully. "I don't."

"So what was the last week about, then?" Riley asked angrily. "The ultimate in practical jokes? An extension of the one you last tried to play on me?" Had all of this, the lovemaking, the sweet words, the confidences, been nothing more than payback for past jokes? he wondered.

Amanda tried to go around him. "This is nothing like our meeting in the high school stadium that night."

He moved to block her way to the garage. He knew they still had more presents to bring in, but that could wait—this truth-telling session couldn't. "Don't you mean the meeting that didn't happen?" he asked her silkily, ignoring the killer look she aimed his way. "Will your friends be laughing with you over this one, too, Amanda?" he continued cynically, feeling like the biggest chump there ever was. "'Cause I know it's something everyone in Laramie won't soon forget."

Amanda stood as still and lifeless as a statue. "It doesn't matter what other people think."

"Maybe it didn't before," Riley differed curtly, "when we both left Laramie and headed off to college. Now things are different." He struggled to regain control of his emotions. "Now we are both going to stay." And he would forever be labeled as Amanda Witherspoon's fool.

The phone rang. Almost grateful for the interruption—anything had to be better than this misery—Riley stalked over, picked up the receiver and barked into it. "McCabe here."

"Riley, Jackson."

Riley quickly noted his uncle was using his chief-of-staff tone.

"Someone put tainted eggs into the nog at First Baptist's Christmas Festival this afternoon. We've got a hundred people here at the E.R., all sicker than dogs, and more arriving by the moment. Can you come in and help us out?"

As ready to roll in an emergency as ever, Riley said, "I'll be right there." He hung up the phone, turned back to Amanda. "I've got to go to the hospital."

She looked at him, composed, matter-of-fact once again. "What are we going to do about tomorrow, the kids, Christmas?"

Riley shrugged and didn't reply. Too hurt to even think about it, too choked up to get a single word out, he went to grab his coat.

"I'll stay with the kids," she offered.

But not with me, Riley thought, heartbroken. He swallowed hard around the gathering lump in his throat. Reminding himself that the kids' needs still required attention, Riley tabled his own anger and hurt and made his tone as cool as hers. "Thanks." With a growing sense of helplessness, he was out the door.

Over at the hospital, things were even worse than what Jackson had described on the phone. People of all ages were reaching for basins, or running for the bathrooms. The children and the elderly were particularly hard hit. It was nearly midnight before they had everyone treated and either released or admitted to one of the rooms upstairs.

Riley had never been partial to nog, but he knew he would never be drinking it again. Nor would anyone he cared about, unless he was certain it had been made with pasteurized egg product instead of raw eggs.

"Can I talk to you for a minute?" Jackson asked as he and Riley headed out to their cars in the physician's parking lot.

"Sure." The cold air felt good. Riley looked up. He still didn't see any snow. But the air was so damp it almost stung against his face.

"Thanks for helping out tonight," Jackson said, their low voices and footfalls the only sound in the otherwise silent night. "I'm aware you didn't have to give up your holiday to come in, under the circumstances."

Riley shrugged. He watched their breaths turn frosty in the winter air. "I wanted to help. I'm a doctor. This is what I do."

"I know that." Jackson paused as they leaned against Riley's SUV. He looked Riley straight in the eye. "I think I misjudged you, earlier in the week. When those kids were delivered to the hospital—"

Riley held up a hand. "I reacted badly, I know."

Jackson shook his head, disagreeing. "You reacted admirably under the circumstances," he corrected. "After your initial shock, anyway. Taking charge, making sure the kids had a good holiday. Even your relationship with Amanda was a lot more complex than I first thought."

"And maybe not," Riley sighed. He thrust his hands in the pockets of his coat.

Jackson's glance narrowed. "What do you mean?"

Riley knew he had to confide in someone. "I asked her to stay married to me tonight." He sighed his frustration and

regret. "She said no."

Jackson blinked. "Why?"

Riley shrugged and ran the toe of his boot across the blacktop. "Beats the heck out of me. None of her reasons made a whit of sense."

"Doesn't she love you?"

"I thought she did," Riley replied shortly.

Jackson paused. "She knows how much you love her, doesn't she?"

Riley frowned. "She certainly should. I've shown her in every way I could think."

"And of course," Jackson returned with a dry look, "you've said the words out loud, too."

It was Riley's turn to pause.

"Oh, man. Tell me you didn't neglect to do that!" Jackson shook his head.

Riley threw up his hands and defended himself hotly. "I was working up to it."

"Well, I wouldn't stay married to you either under those circumstances!" Jackson retorted.

"Thanks ever so much for the support." Riley turned away.

Jackson slapped a familial hand on Riley's shoulder, turned him back. "I know your pride is hurt by the rejection, Riley. And victory in this competition or whatever it is between you and Amanda has meant everything to you, up to this point. But maybe it's time that changed."

AMANDA HAD JUST CORKED the wine and was putting away the unused glasses when the phone rang again. It was her sister, Priscilla. "You have to know we were all very disappointed you didn't get on that flight this evening and come back to California, Amanda."

Amanda released a long, slow breath and said calmly, "I told you I wasn't going to do it." Her days of dancing to her family's tune were over.

"For a change fee, you could still come home early tomorrow and be here for Christmas Day. I checked. There is space available on the 7:00 a.m. flight out of Dallas."

Amanda frowned. Had it only been a few hours since Riley had left to go to the hospital? It felt like a lifetime. "Priscilla, I appreciate all you and everyone else including Mom and Dad have done for me over the years. I'm happy you want me in California for the holidays. But my home is here in Laramie now and so is my family," she finished, before she could stop herself or think about the enormity of what she was saying.

Priscilla gasped. "You can't possibly be thinking of staying married to that troublemaker Riley McCabe!"

Was she? Amanda had gone into this relationship with

him more on a lark or a dare than anything else. But all that had changed in the time they had spent together. She had never dreamed she could have it all with him. But Riley had stormed through the walls around her heart and shown her that she had never lost the potential to love or be loved in return. He just hadn't loved her. At least not in any conventional way. And yet what they had shared had been so much better and more fulfilling than anything she had ever had, because she had paid less attention to what other people thought she should do and had instead done what felt right to her in her heart. And that had been to love Riley with every fiber of her being, without worrying what he might or might not give her in return. And they had done the same for the children. To Amanda's surprise, giving of herself so freely and unconditionally still did not feel like a mistake. What was it people said about love? That it was the gift that kept on giving?

Aware her sister was waiting for her response, Amanda said firmly, "Whether I stay hitched or not is my business and my decision and no one else's. Please send everyone my love and tell them Merry Christmas for me." Amanda hung up the phone. Her heart felt lighter than it had in years. And at the same time, heavier.

Hearing baby Cory begin to stir upstairs, Amanda put a bottle in the warmer, and went up to get him. She eased him out of the bassinet, paused long enough to check on Chloe and Amber—both were still sleeping soundly—and, clean diaper in hand, carried Cory back downstairs. As she walked through the foyer, she heard a car door outside.

Riley! Amanda thought hopefully. Her heart sank as she saw Micki stepping out of the car. Amanda had the front door open by the time Micki reached the stoop. She ushered her inside.

"I'm glad you're still up," Micki said.

Amanda noted it looked as if Micki might have been crying again. "I had a chance to talk with Riley," Micki rushed on, slipping out of her coat. "But I didn't get to speak to you. And there's so much I want to say."

"I've been wanting to talk to you, too," Amanda told the young girl gently. "You've really had a rough time." Amanda laced her free arm around Micki's shoulders. Together they walked into the kitchen.

"You don't know the half of it." Micki wiped fresh tears away.

Amanda plucked the bottle from the warmer. Still cradling Cory in one arm, she tested it on her wrist, while Micki talked about the accident that claimed her sister and brother-in-law's life, explaining about the will that left all three children to her.

"I had doubts all along about whether I could do it or not," Micki confessed, "especially when Chloe shut down and just stopped talking and withdrew into herself, but I knew I had to try. So I took the kids back to Austin with me, and Laurel was great about letting them all move in with us and helping me take care of them, to the detriment of her own grades."

"I understand Laurel helping you," Amanda said. "Why didn't she tell her folks?"

"Because I asked her not to." Looking more stressed out than ever, Micki rubbed at the tense muscles in the back of her neck. "I was still trying to get into medical school under early admission, and I had asked Riley to write a recommendation for me." Micki paused, bit her lip. "I was afraid if he knew I had custody of three children that he would feel I had too much on my plate to undertake physician education and training in addition to parenting. I know it's selfish, but I didn't want to be refused my dream for that reason."

Amanda looked at Micki with understanding. "When did you decide you wanted Riley to have the kids?"

Micki rested her chin on her upturned hand. "I knew I had to find a family for them by early November, but I didn't want them to go to just anyone and I knew from my sister's and my own experiences that once you become a ward of social services that things happen under their rules and guidelines. The person giving the children away doesn't get to say who they end up with. I had heard from Laurel how much Riley wanted a family of his own, how impatient he was for that to happen. I figured if I brought them here, and Riley adopted them, that he'd have his whole family—all the McCabes— to help him. I never figured on you and Riley falling in love, but I have to tell you," Micki confided earnestly, "that made my giving the kids to him all that much easier."

Amanda shifted Cory to her shoulder for a burp. "Why didn't you just tell him outright what you wanted him to do?"

"Laurel thought Riley would refuse, without really even considering it, because he was going to start a new job and he hadn't had any experience being a daddy. We also both knew what a softie he is, deep down, and we sensed that if he was around them that he would love the kids as much as we did."

"Well, convoluted as your plan was," Amanda said kindly, "it did work. Riley and I both love the kids dearly." To the point Amanda did not want to give them up, any more than she wanted to give up Riley—and their marriage.

"And they love you, too. I can tell. In fact, I think Chloe's about ready to start talking again. She was on the verge of blurting something out several times today."

Amanda smiled, agreeing. "I've had that feeling, too."

Micki watched as Amanda continued giving Cory his bottle. "It's because you and Riley make her feel safe in the same way her parents did, the way I just can't, no matter how hard I try." She shook her head in obvious frustration, then went on frankly, "I mean, I know all three kids love me and like spending time with me, but it's as an aunt, not a mommy." Micki paused, looking relieved she had gotten that off her chest. "Riley said if you adopt the kids I can still see them a lot and be an aunt to them. Do you feel the same way?"

Amanda nodded emphatically. "I think you should be in their lives, Micki. I think they'd miss you terribly if you weren't. And the same goes for me."

Fresh tears appeared in Micki's eyes. She got up and came over to give Amanda a hug. "You're the best," she said thickly, wiping her eyes. "Riley and the kids are so lucky to have you in their lives. Riley knows it, too. Everyone was talking about it at the party after you guys left. They said they'd never seen Riley look at anyone the way he looked at you tonight."

Hope rose in Amanda. She knew she had never looked at anyone the way she looked at Riley. Was it possible…?

"No one thought your marriage had a chance, especially 'cause of the way it all started, but now…" Micki hesitated. "You are going to stay married to Riley, aren't you?"

Was she? An hour ago Amanda would have said unequivocally no, she was not. Now…now she wasn't so certain. And it had to do with so much more than what was best for the kids in the here and now. Or even the distant future. It had to do with what was in her heart.

Chapter Fourteen

Tiny snowflakes, almost too little to see, were filling the air as Riley parked his SUV in front of his house. The night sky had taken on the soft white glow of a winter storm. Down the street, many of the residences had gone dark except for the festive Christmas lights. Inside his home, the upstairs windows were dark, but the lights downstairs—including those on the Christmas tree visible through the sheer draperies—were still burning bright.

Did that mean Amanda was still up?

And if so, was she waiting for him, or waiting for him to arrive and take charge of the children so that she could pack her bags and leave?

Figuring it didn't matter what Amanda had planned, so long as she heard him out, he stepped out of his SUV and headed for the door. Heart thudding with anticipation of seeing her again, Riley unlocked the front door and walked inside.

Amanda was where he had left her.

Only this time her hair was swept up on the back of her head and she was wearing a pair of red flannel pajamas festooned with ribbon-wrapped candy canes and reindeer-drawn sleighs. Riley wasn't sure what was sexier, the soft warm fabric over softer, warmer skin, or the fact she was ready for bed and waiting for him. All he knew for certain was that she had never looked more beautiful—nor more determined—lounging on the sofa, a book in her hands. He took off his coat, and headed in to join her by the fire.

"We need to talk," she said simply, turning her eyes up to his. She tossed the velvety lap robe away from her knees, swung her legs gracefully off the center cushions of the sofa, and shifted her feet onto the floor. After a moment in which she stared long and hard at the fire, she turned back to him and forced herself to go on. "I think I was too hasty before," she continued introspectively as she motioned for him to sit down beside her.

"I think so, too," Riley said quietly. He dropped down next to her and turned, one leg angled toward her, so they were facing each other. Draping an arm along the back of the sofa, he made himself comfortable and waited for her to go on, his gut twisted into a knot of apprehension. He wanted so much for them—a happy marriage, raising the three children together…everlasting love. But she had to want those things, too.

Amanda swallowed. Turquoise-blue eyes shrewdly direct, she reached over and took his hand in hers. "We shouldn't end things this way."

"Also agreed," Riley told her solemnly.

She squeezed his fingers affectionately. "Christmas is a time for giving."

Riley turned in the direction of her gaze and for the first time noticed two gift-wrapped boxes on the coffee table, one small and square, the other rectangular and about the size of a shirt. He felt his hopes rise another notch.

"And although I wasn't initially at all certain about the gifts I selected for you," she said in a low, tremulous voice, "now I think they are exactly right."

Riley knew his were the correct gifts, too. The challenge would be in convincing her of that.

As she looked over at him, Riley thought, but couldn't be sure, there was a telltale sheen of emotion in her eyes. There was no doubt there was plenty of remorse. She paused, shook her head, "I thought I needed romance to be happy, Riley."

Knowing he'd never had so much at stake in his entire life, afraid she was going to tell him straight out that she didn't love him and never would, Riley cut her off with a recitation of his own regrets. He wanted her to know he was to blame for what had gone wrong between them, too. "And I thought I needed an immediate solution to our dilemma of where we go from here." His voice caught. It was a moment before he could go on in a voice anywhere near cool, "I don't."

She regarded him, perplexed.

"I denied you a proper courtship," Riley explained, achingly aware he had moved way too fast for Amanda's comfort, in an effort to make her his. "I thrust you into the mother and wife role you weren't prepared to take on and then made the case that just because we could live together harmoniously, loved the kids and had great sex that we could live happily ever after. You told me it wasn't enough, and you were right, Amanda. It's not. But at the same time, just because you don't love me…yet," he told her hoarsely, "is no reason to call it quits."

Amanda blinked. And this time there was no doubt, Riley noticed. Her eyes were full of tears. "Wait," she said thickly. "What did you say?"

"Just because you don't love me…" he repeated gruffly.

"But I do!" Amanda protested.

Riley inhaled deeply. He let his breath out slowly as the first glimmer of hope rose in his chest. "Say that again?" he asked.

Amanda shifted over onto his lap, wreathed her arms about his neck. She smiled at him, all the joy he had ever wanted to see on her beautiful face, and looked directly into his eyes. "I. Love. You. Riley McCabe."

Joy filled Riley's heart. He could only stare at her in wonderment. Hot damn, this was one great Christmas! "I love you, too, Mrs. McCabe," he told her in a low, rusty-sounding voice.

"Well, why didn't you say so?" Amanda demanded, clinging to him as if she never wanted to let him go. Her eyes were overflowing, her voice was clogged with tears.

Riley held her closer still, loving the way she felt in his arms. Wondering how he had ever managed without her, glad he was never going to have to do so again, he told her softly, "I thought I had told you." He paused to search her face. "Every time I kissed you or held you or made love to you, I thought you knew." He tunneled his hands through the silk of her hair, loving the way she felt cuddled so close against him. "I thought words were cheap, that it was actions and intent that counted. But now I know words are every bit as necessary as deeds." He caught the shimmer of happiness in her eyes and couldn't help but grin. "So plan on hearing those three words from me every day for the rest of our lives."

Amanda kissed him sweetly. "I promise to say them, too. Because I do love you, Riley, so very much."

They kissed again, even more passionately. "Speaking of love," Riley said, when the languorous caress finally came to a halt. "I have two gifts to give you that speak to what is in my heart." He handed over two boxes.

Amanda noted that both looked as if they had contained jewelry. Could they be…? With shaking hands, Amanda opened the smaller one first. She caught her breath at the sight of the sparkling marquise diamond.

"Oh, Riley," she breathed, so moved she could barely speak.

He looked deep into her eyes. "This is the engagement ring you should have had if we'd done things properly," he told her in a gruff, tender voice.

He slipped it onto her finger.

Amanda admired the exquisite jewelry against her skin. It was perfect. He was perfect. "It's absolutely beautiful," she said softly.

Grinning, Riley drawled, "I'm glad you think so." He handed her the next gift. Her hands still trembling, she opened it, too.

Inside were two matching gold bands.

Before she could take the smaller one out and slip it on, he cautioned her, "I don't want us to wear these just yet."

She looked up, disappointed.

He told her in the firm masculine voice she had come to love, "I want to wait until we've said our vows again, in front of family and friends, so there won't be doubt in anyone's mind that we are really married this time. I've already spoken to Reverend Bleeker. He's ready to do it any time we are."

"The sooner the better," Amanda vowed, knowing Riley was right—they needed to wait to wear these rings until they said their vows. For real, this time. It would mean more.

She handed him the large box. "And how about opening this?"

Riley picked up the box. She had an idea what he was thinking—it was surprisingly light. To the point it felt almost empty. He unwrapped it, took off the lid. Inside was a single printed page. Across the top it read, Application For Texas Marriage License. Amanda's section of it had already been filled in. "I know we have thirty days, but I thought—hoped— we might want to make it indisputably legal."

Once again they were on the exact same page. "You thought right." Riley brought her closer for another searing kiss.

"And the last one." Amanda gave him the smaller gift.

Riley opened it and saw the watch inside.

"At first I thought it was a lame gift," Amanda explained, as she took out the expensive, elegant timepiece and helped him put it on his equally elegant and masculine wrist. "But then I began to really think about what it meant." She paused, looking deep into his eyes. "Me giving you the gift of time. From here on out."

The grin on his face was as wide as the Texas sky. "I can't think of anything I'd like more. Except this." He stood and led her to the stairs and their bed, where they came together once again, loving each other, body, heart and soul.

THE KIDS WOKE at six o'clock Christmas morning and were as delighted as Amanda and Riley to find a blanket of pristine white snow covering the ground.

"Guess who came to our house last night?" Amanda said as they waited for Riley—who had gone down to put the coffee on and turn the lights on the tree—to come back and join them.

Chloe's eyes sparkled with excitement as she jumped up and down on the bed.

"Pretty?" Amber said, jumping, too.

"Santa Claus," Amanda confirmed, catching them both in her arms for a hug.

Chloe's eyes got even bigger.

"Everybody ready?" Riley appeared in the doorway, looking sexy and handsome as could be.

"We sure are," Amanda said. She handed Amber to Riley, picked up the cooing Cory from the bassinet and took Chloe by the hand. "Let's go downstairs and see what's under the Christmas tree."

Chloe gasped in delight when she saw the presents. Letting go of Amanda's hand, she ran right over to them. Amber soon joined her.

Together, they unwrapped the gifts.

It was hard to say who was happier, Amanda thought, the kids or she and Riley.

"Looks like we scored a hit," she said as Chloe sat on her pink-and-white roadster-tricycle, and Amber toddled around with her push-and-pull wagon full of blocks.

Riley took Amanda's hand and kissed the back of it, everything he felt for her reflected in his tender gaze. "In every way," he promised.

"I love you," Amanda whispered, her heart filling with joy.

"I love you, too," Riley whispered back.

Hearing, Amber perked up. "Wuv!" she shouted, dropping her wagon handle and toddling over, showing off her new plush toy kitten.

"I think we've got a new word here," Amanda said happily.

"Wuv!" Amber repeated jubilantly again. Lacing her arms around Amanda's neck, she kissed her, then turned to Riley and did the same.

Chloe turned and stared at them both for a minute. Then she slid off her roadster-tricycle and came over to join them, too. Once again looking desperate to communicate, Chloe smiled at Amanda and Riley shyly.

"Did Santa bring you what you wanted?" Riley asked.

Chloe nodded. Imperceptibly, but it was a nod.

Amanda could barely contain her excitement. "What do you like best?" Amanda asked her.

Chloe smiled. Broadly. She took one of Amanda's hands and one of Riley's. And then she did what they had been waiting for—for what seemed an eternity—she spoke. "My new mommy and daddy," she said.

ONCE CHLOE STARTED talking again, it seemed she couldn't stop. The four-year-old chattered all morning, whispered through service at the church and continued talking at the family gathering at Sam and Kate McCabe's.

Micki—who had been unable to keep her secret any longer—had gone ahead and confessed to the McCabes the tragedy that had befallen her family. Sam and Kate had made her an honorary member of their family on the spot, a move seconded by one and all. Kate had offered unlimited grief counseling. And Sam and Kate made up with Laurel, now that they finally understood why her grades had taken the nose-dive the previous semester.

It seemed to Amanda the holiday simply could not get any better.

Until, that was, they heard the clomp-clomp of horses and the ringing of bells at four that afternoon.

The kids all ran to the window. "It's Uncle Travis!"

"And he's got a sleigh!"

Travis McCabe came in, stomping the snow off his boots. Travis looked at Riley. "We're all set," he said.

"For what?" Amanda asked.

With a grin, Riley reached over and squeezed her hand. "The wedding we should have had," Riley said.

Twenty minutes later, they were all back at the church. Reverend Bleeker was waiting for them. And this time he looked very happy to be presiding over the ceremony that would join them together forever as man and wife.

Amanda placed the wedding ring on Riley's hand. "I promise to love you unconditionally…respect you…laugh and cry with you…"

He put the wedding ring on hers. "…comfort and encourage you…and stay with you for all eternity…"

Reverend Bleeker smiled as he completed the blessing and said, "I now pronounce you husband and wife. Riley—"

"I think I know what to do next," Riley cut in playfully as everyone laughed.

And he did.

* * * * *

MISTLETOE MANOEUVRES

BY
MARGARET ALLISON

Margaret Allison was raised in the suburbs of Detroit, Michigan, and received a BA in political science from the University of Michigan. A former marketing executive, she also worked as a model and an actress. The author of several novels, Margaret currently divides her time between her computer, the washing machine and the grocery store, she loves to hear from readers. Please write to her c/o Silhouette Books, 233 Broadway, Suite 1001, New York, NY 10279, USA.

For my sister, Jenny, with love

One

It was nearly midnight, two weeks before Christmas, and for the first time in months they were alone. As if anticipating what was to come, Rick grinned, silently daring her. Tall and ruggedly handsome, with thick black hair and piercing blue eyes, Rick Parker was the type of man who was accustomed to getting what he wanted. A modern-day pirate, he traveled the world collecting beat-up hotels, jewels in the rough, turning them into luxurious resorts.

It was now or never. Lessa took a breath of courage, determined to say the three words she had wanted to say for years. She was so close she could smell his expensive aftershave, so close she could smell the minty freshness of his breath.

"You're fired, Rick."

The muscles in his jaw tightened and his eyes darkened as the impact of her words sank in. "I'm not going to let you take this company away from me," he said.

A flicker of apprehension coursed through her. After all, this was the man who had orchestrated a corporate mutiny, betraying his own mentor. Since then his domineering style of management had turned Lawrence Enterprises into a behemoth of a company, earning its fearless leader his pirate nickname along the way. What, she couldn't help but wonder, would he do to her?

But if he thought a threat would help save his job, he was wrong. She had promised her father on his deathbed that she would get revenge on the man who had stolen his company. That she would one day fire Rick Parker.

Since she had returned to the business six months ago, Rick had only added to her determination. He had done his best to thwart her path, treating her more like an annoying schoolgirl than an accomplished businesswoman. He fought her on every aspect of her agenda, from the color of the new logo to the direction of the company. It was as if he still considered her the same girl who had suffered a crush on him so fierce that a mere glance in her direction could cause her heart to soar. He should've realized he had lost his power over her long ago. He couldn't make her walk the plank any more than he could swindle her out of the company. "There's nothing you can do," she said. "I am chairman of the board."

"A situation that has everything to do with stock and nothing to do with expertise."

"My father had always intended for me to run this company. I've worked long and hard for this moment, Rick. I own a majority and I'm qualified. I've paid my dues."

"Your father may have started this company but I am the one who made it what it is. This company needs me."

"No, Mr. Parker. This company does not need you. Neither do I."

He leaned backward, crossing his arms. "The board is in agreement?"

In fact, she had had to struggle for the board's approval to fire Rick. Ultimately, they had had no choice but to agree with her. After all, as Rick had just said, she owned two thirds of the stock. "Yes," she said.

There was no mistaking the glimmer of anger in his eyes. He stood up and turned his back on her as he walked to the window. From their vantage point on the top floor of a New York City high-rise, he had a bird's-eye view of the twinkling city, lit up for the impending holiday.

"I don't want to hurt you, Alessandra," he said, referring to her by her full name, which was seldom used.

"Hurt me?" If she wasn't mistaken, she was the one who had fired him.

"I guarantee you, if you go through with this, you'll regret it." He turned around to face her.

"I don't think so," she said. Who did he think he was anyway? She stood up and straightened her suit jacket. "I've read your contract. You have a noncompete clause. Due to your work and contributions to this company, I will grant you some of the dignity you did not extend to my father. You have until the end of the day tomorrow to clear out your office."

"So this is your revenge, is it?" he asked. "You should know I didn't have anything to do with the way your father was fired."

"You may not have pulled the trigger but you were the one who loaded the gun." Bravo. That was a line she had worked on, one she never actually thought she would say. She gave him a quick, curt nod. "Goodbye, Rick."

She could almost feel his eyes watching her as she walked out of his office. She shut the door behind her and let out a sigh of relief as she leaned up against it. She had done it. She had fired Rick Parker and lived to talk about it. She had expected a bloody uprising, a long and drawn-out war. But in one anticlimactic moment, it was over. All of her years of study and work had paid off. Rick Parker would not be a part of her life or her father's company anymore.

Rick's secretary stepped off the elevator and smiled at Lessa. Betty had worked at Lawrence for years and had been Rick's secretary ever since he had arrived. "Hello, Lessa," she said cheerfully.

Lessa felt a pang of guilt. Unlike her boss, Betty was kind and good-hearted. For some reason that Lessa couldn't fathom, she was also devoted to her boss. She knew Betty would be upset to hear that her longtime boss would not be working there anymore.

"What are you doing here so late?" Lessa asked.

"Rick had some research he wanted ASAP," Betty said, rolling her eyes. "Some people have no respect for the Christmas season. I've only got half of my shopping done. Have you started yet?"

Lessa was finished with her Christmas shopping only because there was just one person on her list—Gran. Almost eighty years old, Gran was her great-aunt, her only living relative and her best friend. Lessa had always been close to her aunt and had grown even closer after her father had died. Gran had been awarded custody and Lessa had moved into her small condo in a Florida retirement community. Years later, when her aunt sustained an injury, Lessa had repaid the favor, moving Gran into her New York apartment so that she could care for her. Although her aunt was healed and could have moved back into her old condo, Gran had made it clear that she liked staying with Lessa. And Lessa preferred it that way, too. After years of living by herself, it was nice to have some company. "I'm done with my shopping," Lessa said.

"Oh, lucky girl. How do you have time? You're here around the clock."

"The Internet."

"Ah. I still like to shop the old-fashioned way. I love being in stores during Christmas. There's an excitement in the air, don't you think?"

"Yes," Lessa said, suddenly realizing that she was still leaning up against Rick's door as if blocking Betty's path. She stepped away from the door and took Betty's hand. "I just want you to know that regardless of what happens to Rick, you have nothing to worry about." She would take care of Rick's secretary. The only person she planned on getting rid of was Rick. Leaving a confused Betty, she hurried to the elevator, stepping inside just as Betty opened her boss's door.

As the elevator doors closed, Lessa caught a glimpse of Rick. He was staring straight at her, and the look in his eyes gave her pause. It was not the look of a man who had just lost his job. It was a look of pity. Of regret.

But why would he feel sorry for her?

* * *

"That was odd," Betty said as she walked into the room. "I wonder what she meant by that."

Rick glanced at the stack of documents in her hand. "Is that my research?"

She nodded as she gave him the papers. "She said that no matter what happens to you, I don't have anything to worry about. Do you know what she was talking about?"

"I've just been fired," he said casually, thumbing through the documents.

"What?" she exclaimed, the surprise registering on her lined features. "That can't be."

"Alessandra has decided that she's ready to take over Lawrence Enterprises."

"That's ridiculous. She's too young."

"She's the same age her father was when he started the company."

"But you *are* the company. If it wasn't for you, the stock would be worthless."

"I don't think she realizes that. She feels that this is her rightful place. It was her father's company, therefore it's owed to her."

Betty sank into a chair, stunned. He used the momentary silence to his advantage, quickly scanning the document. It was a list of all the companies that had purchased Lawrence Enterprises stock in the past two weeks. Alessandra's mismanagement had weakened the company and the stock value considerably. Gossip surrounding the tension in his relationship with the chairman of the board of Lawrence Enterprises had been circulating for months. Industry insiders knew that

Rick's departure would make the company a prime target for a takeover. And, from the evidence before him, several ambitious corporate vultures were already hungrily gobbling up stock.

As he glanced over the names of the buyers, several in particular stood out. They were all companies owned by a woman he'd once dated, Sabrina Vickers. Sabrina owned many different companies, each under a different name. And there was only one reason she would be buying so much stock under all those different names: She didn't want anyone to know what she was up to. Sabrina, it appeared, was planning a hostile takeover of Lawrence Enterprises.

He had no doubt that Alessandra had scoured over this very same data, looking for signs of exactly this. But there's no way she could've figured it out yet.

In a small voice, Betty said, "I assume I'll be next?"

"I thought she just told you not to worry," he said.

"Don't worry? I've got two kids in college. I've worked here for the past thirty years. I can't imagine finding another job." She breathed in deeply and said, "Two weeks before Christmas and she's firing people. It's not right. You're going to fight her on this, aren't you, Rick?"

"Alessandra Lawrence is not gunning for anyone else. Believe me, she could barely fire me." He was an expert at reading his opponents. He had heard the hesitation in her voice and seen the anxiety in her eyes. At least, he thought, she had enough common sense to be frightened.

"Rick," she said, leaning on his desk, "what are you going to do?"

He glanced up, meeting her eyes directly. "Absolutely nothing. If Miss Lawrence wants this company, she's going to get it."

"But I thought you said I didn't have anything to worry about? We all know what's going to happen with her in charge. The stock's been plummeting ever since she became chairman of the board."

"I assume Alessandra thinks that it will all blow over once she proves herself."

"By the time she figures out what she's doing, there won't be any company left." Betty shook her head. "To think I knew her when she was just a girl. I remember her father bringing her to work. He was so proud of her. She was a big tennis player, remember?"

"Not really."

"She won the NCAA and a bunch of other competitions. Her matches were even on TV a couple times. We all thought she was going to turn pro. She was a nice girl, always so quiet and polite. She had such a crush on you back then. She used to hang around that drinking fountain right outside your office. You have to remember that, don't you?"

"I think you're mistaken, Betty." His memory of Howard Lawrence's daughter back from those days was foggy at best. The Alessandra Lawrence of today was a beautiful woman, with long, curly red hair and sparkling green eyes. He remembered when he'd first laid eyes on her after not seeing her for years. He'd had no idea who she was and couldn't help but feel an immediate attraction. She'd been dressed conservatively in a fitted green suit that outlined her lithe figure. His attraction for her had dimmed when he'd discovered that the office visitor was none other than Alessandra Lawrence. Even if she weren't the most insufferable woman he had ever met, he would never get involved with her. He had no intention of having an affair with the largest shareholder.

"Who would think that she would come back and destroy us all?" Betty shook her head.

"Let's not get carried away. The fight is hardly over. In fact, it's just beginning." He grinned. "Now go grab your briefcase. We're going to move operations to my apartment for a while."

After Betty left, Rick began packing files. He had expected this moment for quite a while. Although he had hoped that, for her sake, Alessandra would change her mind, he was not surprised. She had made it clear she was out for revenge from the first moment she had come into her stock. At the time, he had paid little attention. He knew she was attempting to get on the board, but he couldn't imagine the board would vote her on, much less hand her the chairmanship on a silver platter.

After all, what were her qualifications? A fancy degree and a couple of years experience at a rival firm. But the board had been sympathetic to her cause. She wanted to run the company her deceased parents had begun.

Unfortunately, everyone was overlooking the fact that it had not been Howard Lawrence's company for a very long time. It was Rick's blood and sweat that had made the company into what it was today. When he'd first started working at Lawrence, it had been a small firm, desperately in need of change. The woman he loved and planned to marry had just died, and Lawrence Enterprises offered him a chance to travel the world. For the first few months he functioned on automatic, working to escape his pain. And every time he returned to

New York, he couldn't wait to escape once more. He worked twenty hours a day. One month he'd be in South America, the next in Asia.

But his newfound peace was short-lived. Howard Lawrence soon took the company public and the new board was concerned that he was not capable of taking it to the next level. When they first approached Rick about taking it over, he was hesitant. He knew how much the company meant to his boss. But, as they reminded him, they had already made their decision. Howard Lawrence was out. Rick had assumed the presidency and all the trials and tribulations that came with it. He had paid a steep price, devoting one hundred percent of his time and energy to making it a success.

Not that he minded. He had not met anyone since Karen who had inspired him to miss a meeting in Singapore or a hotel opening in Rio. His family had grown used to him missing birthdays and holidays. But if Alessandra had her way, that would all change very soon.

It was not anger he felt, however, but pity. He was not about to be cast aside by a woman who had anointed herself heir apparent. He had no choice but to teach her a lesson she'd never learned in all of her graduate programs.

He was going to destroy her, Rick Parker style.

Two

If Lessa had expected an easy transition to CEO of Lawrence Enterprises, she would've been greatly disappointed. But she had been a competitive athlete, a top junior player with a big serve and an even bigger return of serve. And although she was used to charging out to a big lead, not every match went that way. She knew that no matter how many hours she spent on the court practicing, there were times when her serve would be off, or her return would be shaky, and her opponent would be the one in command. Then she'd have to play from behind. It wasn't her first choice, but in a way, it had been good for her. It proved to people she wasn't getting by on talent alone, that she could gut out a match with the best of them. Since she'd started at Lawrence Enterprises, she'd likened her struggle to a rough match. She might be in a hole, but she knew she'd dig herself out. Somehow.

But now, less than twenty-four hours after firing Rick Parker, she was beginning to think she had underestimated her opponent.

She had arrived at work that morning to find out that the company was under threat of a hostile takeover by Sabrina Vickers, heir to the Kato Resorts family fortune. Sabrina was known for taking over corporations and breaking them up, selling off the properties one by one. If she succeeded in taking over Lawrence Enterprises, the company would be ripped apart in a matter of months.

"You must be exhausted," her aunt said when Lessa finally made it home that night. "You've been at work since five this morning. And I bet you haven't had anything decent to eat all day." Her aunt shook her head as she walked over to their small galley kitchen. Their apartment was located on the top floor of a brownstone in midtown Manhattan. It was a simple two-bedroom with a living room and a small dining room. But it had one luxurious feature: an old, original wood-burning fireplace complete with a marble mantel. Lessa would often come home to find her dinner on the table and a roaring fire in the fireplace. Tonight, although it was nearly ten o'clock, was no exception.

Lessa pleaded with her aunt not to hold dinner for her, but her aunt was determined to do just that. "What else have I got to do all day?" she'd asked in her usual cranky tone.

"How could I not have seen this coming?" Lessa said after she told her aunt the news.

"She was too sneaky," Gran said.

Although Sabrina had bought stock through her various companies, never using her own name, Lessa blamed herself for not being more diligent. After all, she knew that a hostile takeover was a threat during any period of turmoil. "But she's been buying stocks for weeks. I should've been more thorough."

"Stop beating yourself up, Lessa. You know what your father always said. Don't waste time thinking about what you should've done. The question is, what can you do now?"

"The board wants me to bring back Rick." That was putting it mildly. Although the majority had voted to fire Rick, news of the takeover had sent her supporters running for cover. Everyone was pointing a finger and most were aimed directly at her. They considered Rick the one person capable of saving Lawrence Enterprises.

Her aunt sat down at the table and raised her eyebrows as if to say, "Well?"

"I've tried to call him to discuss it but he hasn't returned my calls." Lessa knew this was just part of his mind game, psyching out the opponent, but it still unnerved her. "You should've seen how smug he was last night. How cocky. I'm certain he knew about this takeover when I fired him. It was like…like he knew I would be forced to ask him back."

"So you've decided to give him back his job?" her aunt asked.

"I don't know what to do. I'd prefer to fight this myself. It could be an opportunity to win not only my company but the respect of everyone who works there."

"Sounds like a good idea. Now eat your dinner."

"Unfortunately," Lessa said after she dutifully took a bite, "the cons are enormous. I stand a very good chance of losing everything. I'm taking a gamble not only with my career but also with the livelihoods of everyone associated with Lawrence. If I lose, a lot of people will suffer." She didn't mind gambling with her own future, but she did not feel right risking the livelihoods of so many others.

"You think Rick can save the company?" her aunt asked.

"Maybe. He's well respected inside the company and in the industry. I think his presence alone would soothe stockholders." Once again she saw him standing in his office, his handsome blue eyes twinkling with arrogance. "Rick outplayed me. He'll get a new contract and be able to demand more money."

"*If* you take him back."

She set down her fork. "Oh, Gran, I've made a mess of things."

"Nonsense. I've never been more proud."

"How can you say that? Look what I've done. If Sabrina gets this company, she'll destroy it. She'll sell it off piece by piece."

"I hate to see you like this," her aunt said. "I don't think your father realized what a burden he presented you with."

"No," she said, shaking her head. "I was given a wonderful opportunity."

"Wonderful? Look at you. Twenty-six with the weight of the world on your shoulders and more than a thousand people's livelihood dependent on your decisions. It's Christmastime. You should be out celebrating with friends, drinking eggnog and kissing under the mistletoe. Instead you're staying up all night worrying about this company."

"Dad was my age when he began Lawrence. He had the same responsibilities."

"Your father was already married when he and your mother bought that old inn. And there was another big difference. This was his choice. His dream. It was your mother's dream as well."

"It's my dream too."

"Is it?" Her aunt sighed. "I loved your father dearly but sometimes I wish he was still here just so I could wring his neck. How could he do this to you?"

They had been over this so many times before. "Gran…"

"All I know was that he wasn't thinking straight. I know in my heart that he would not be happy to see that you had tossed aside your dreams just to fulfill his. No parent wants that for his child."

Lessa knew her father had loved her dearly. No one had been prouder of her tennis success than him. He had given her her first racket and had been her original coach. But things had changed after he'd taken the company public. She'd rarely seen him and when she had, he'd been too exhausted to do anything but read. She had been as surprised as anyone when he'd called her into his hospital room and had asked her to win back his company. But she had loved her father dearly and would've done anything to help him. She had made him a promise that she intended to keep. "But I like this business," Lessa said.

"Let's be honest," her aunt said. "If you hadn't made him that promise, would you be sitting here today fretting over the status of this company?"

Would she? She honestly didn't know. But it made

little difference. Lessa did not believe in wasting time thinking about what could have been. Her tennis career had ended long ago. Keeping Lawrence Enterprises out of the hands of Sabrina Vickers was what mattered now.

"I know I want this company to survive. More than I've ever wanted anything," she said.

"Then I have no doubt you'll succeed. You had the courage to go up against Rick Parker. Not many people would dare such a feat. Your father did, of course. And we all know what happened to him." Her aunt smiled. "You're a very determined girl. You always have been."

She smiled appreciatively. "Thanks, Gran. I don't know what I'd do without you."

Her aunt walked over to the kitchen counter and grabbed a small brown bag out of a cardboard box.

"What's this?" Lessa asked.

"It's a little something to cheer you up."

Lessa opened up the bag. "Mistletoe?"

"I thought it might help you enjoy the season."

"Thanks, Gran, but I don't think I'll be doing much kissing this Christmas."

"Both the Vikings and the druids believed there were special powers associated with mistletoe. That it was capable of miracles."

"You've been talking to Mr. Chapman again, haven't you?" Mr. Chapman was the owner of Chapman's Market, where they typically did their shopping. He was an amateur historian and every time Lessa's aunt went shopping, she returned home with a story. "It would be a miracle if I actually had someone to kiss this Christmas."

"Make a wish and we'll see if it comes true," Gran suggested.

Lessa laughed for the first time that day. "I wish for my own company. A successful company with employees who actually like me."

"Now it's my turn," her aunt said, taking the mistletoe and closing her eyes. She opened her eyes back up and said, "There."

"You're not going to tell me what you wished for?" Lessa asked.

Gran shook her head. "No. Now help me decide where I should hang this."

"How about in the closet?"

"Now, that's not optimistic of you."

Lessa smiled. She appreciated her aunt's enthusiasm. Usually, she loved Christmas, but this season was proving to be especially difficult. The stress of work was getting to her.

"What else is in that box?" Lessa asked, spying the small black writing on the side. As she walked toward it, the words came into focus: Christmas Ornaments. She suddenly remembered that she had promised to pick up a tree on her way home.

"We were supposed to have our tree-trimming party tonight," Lessa said apologetically. Every year she and her aunt celebrated the season by decorating the tree together. Lessa had been so distracted by work that she had completely forgotten.

"We'll do it another time."

"I'm sorry, Gran. I feel terrible. I know how much you were looking forward to putting up the tree."

"Oh, please," her aunt said, brushing it off. "I don't care about a silly tree. What I care about is you." Her aunt sighed. "I'm worried about you, Lessa. You're young and beautiful. There's no reason you shouldn't have someone to kiss under the mistletoe."

"Maybe next Christmas," she forced herself to say. She didn't want to disappoint her aunt but she knew the possibility of her having a boyfriend next Christmas was the same as it had been this year and the year before—slim to nil. As much as she might like to have someone special, it wasn't in the cards anytime soon. How could she get involved with someone when she typically worked thirteen hours a day, six or seven days a week? "Not this Christmas, I'm afraid." She absent-mindedly picked up the mistletoe as she thought once again about her situation at work. "This Christmas I'll be lucky to still have Lawrence Enterprises."

Her aunt sighed. "Well then, go do what you need to do. Go confront this Rick Parker in person."

"Go to his apartment?" She didn't like the idea of going to see him in such a personal location. She had been there once before, a decade earlier, when her father had sent her to deliver some files. She remembered how nervous she had been, remembered the way her heart had jumped into her throat when he answered the door. He had just returned from a trip and his shirt was untucked and halfway unbuttoned. Stubble of a beard along his jaw added to his dangerous charm.

Although Rick had been twenty-seven years old, eleven years her senior, she had fantasized about being invited inside. "I know you're young," he would say, "but I'm willing to wait." And then he would take her in his arms and give her a kiss she would remember for years. But in reality, he barely looked at her. He took the files and was perusing the information when she heard a woman laugh. She looked around Rick and saw a woman leaning against the couch. She was wearing a long, silky robe and thumbing through a magazine. She reminded Lessa of a gangster's moll, with tousled platinum-blond hair and bright pink lipstick. Rick had signed the papers and Lessa had left, feeling envious of the woman wearing the beautiful lingerie. Lessa thought her the luckiest woman in the world.

"I don't know that I can go there without an invitation."

"What choice do you have?" Gran asked.

Her aunt was right. She didn't have a choice. As much as she hated to admit it, she had a feeling the board was right. Only one man could save Lawrence Enterprises. Rick Parker.

Rick was not surprised to hear that Alessandra was waiting in his lobby. In fact, he had been expecting her. After all, forcing a personal meeting was exactly what he would've done under similar circumstances. What else was there to do when your nemesis refused your calls?

The truth of the matter was that he had been too busy to speak with her. His phone had been ringing all day. The stock had dropped significantly, and board members, furious with Alessandra, had been pleading with him to come back. But it wasn't the loquacious board that had prevented him from speaking to Alessandra. It was the fact that he himself was one of those gobbling up discarded stock for a discounted price—all under various business ventures, never his own name. By firing him, Alessandra had given him the power to do what, as CEO of Lawrence, he was legally forbidden—buy stock.

It was all part of his plan to regain power and rid himself of Alessandra Lawrence for once and for all. The plan was simple. He would purchase stock without Alessandra's knowledge. When she was forced to ask him back, he would negotiate a deal in which she gave him whatever stock he still needed for a majority. Once he had a majority, he could do whatever he liked. And his first order of business would be to fire Alessandra.

The elevator doors opened and Alessandra stepped into his apartment. He had to give her credit. In spite of the hellish day he knew she must have suffered, she looked remarkably composed. Her long red hair was pulled back in a ponytail and she was wearing a gray overcoat. She held her head up high, making her look like a regal queen who was blessing him with her presence.

"Hello," he said as she walked toward him. "This is a surprise."

"Is it?" she replied, meeting his gaze directly. "I would've assumed that you knew very well this meeting would happen."

He held back a grin as he motioned toward the couch. "Please," he said.

"What are your terms?" she asked quietly, standing right where she was.

"Terms?"

"I'm not here to play games, Rick. I assume you knew about the hostile takeover. You orchestrated your own firing yesterday simply to terminate your contract in the midst of a corporate upheaval. You knew that I would be forced to rehire you on your own terms."

"And are you?" He knew better than to waste his time

by attempting to deny the accusations. She wouldn't believe him anyway. And he cared little what she thought.

She snapped open her briefcase. "I'm prepared to give you a ten-percent raise and a one-year extension on your contract."

She handed him the contract but he didn't accept it. "I'm not interested."

"What do you mean?"

He could hear the nervousness in her voice and see the fear in her eyes. Without realizing it, she was giving away her hand. She knew she needed him.

"Ten percent and a one-year extension are not enough."

She swallowed, taking a deep breath. "What do you want?"

"I want the raise, the extension, and…" He paused, noticing the way the her slender hands clutched the papers. "Half of your stock."

The color drained from her face. No wonder. It was an outrageous request. So outrageous that he had not even pondered it. But since she seemed so desperate to have him return, why not?

"No," she said.

He took another step toward her. He was so close, he could smell her slight flowery scent. "Well then," he said in a soft whisper, "I don't think we have anything to talk about."

Her eyes were full of fire as she tightened her lips. "This was my father's company. He always intended that I would one day be at the helm."

"And maybe you will. In the meantime, I'll own half of your stock. We'll be partners."

"Partners?" she asked quietly, her voice ragged.

It was obvious that she was hesitant to give up hope that she might one day regain the company. But it was difficult to feel pity for her naïveté. She should've known better than to challenge him. He had warned her and she had no one but herself to blame for the consequences.

Still, this interaction was making him uncomfortable. He would have an easier time of this if she were defiant and narcissistic. He walked back toward the elevator and pressed the button. As the doors opened he said, "Feel free to take some time to think about my offer. But the bottom line will not change. You need me if you're going to save your father's company. You and I both know I'm the only one capable of accomplishing this. If I don't come back, try as you might, I can guarantee you that Sabrina Vickers will take over the company. And when she does, she will do what she has always done. She will break it up into little pieces, selling off the properties your father and I have worked so hard to build. By next year Lawrence Enterprises will be nothing but a memory. Is that what your father would have wanted?"

He could almost see the inner machinations of her brain. She had no choice but to accept his terms, however audacious they were. "I've worked very hard for this company, Alessandra. I've given it fifteen years of my life. I don't want to see it destroyed. But this is your decision."

"I'll agree under one condition," she said after a moment's hesitation. "That I give you my shares only when the threat of a takeover is alleviated."

"Fine," he said, holding out his hand. "So we have a deal."

"I'm willing to put past grievances behind us in order to save the company," she said. With what appeared to be a supreme amount of effort, she accepted his hand.

"I'm very happy to hear that, Lessa," he said, squeezing her hand gently. "Because in order to save this company, you're going to have to forget what you learned in grad school. Now," he said, letting go of her hand, "can I take your coat?"

"What do you mean, forget what I learned?" she asked, shrugging off her coat and handing it to him.

"Sabrina Vickers is simply the first in a long line of companies waiting to steal Lawrence Enterprises," he said, hanging up her coat. "The problem is not Sabrina, it's the perception that Lawrence Enterprises is a company in turmoil. All the Sabrinas have crawled out of the woodwork. And there's only one way to get rid of them."

"Let's hear it," she said, taking a seat on his leather sofa.

He sat across from her and leaned forward. "We need to convince Sabrina and everyone else that my job is intact. That our…union is secure."

"What are you suggesting?"

He paused, almost enjoying the look of anticipation in her eyes. "We're lovers."

He watched as the surprise in her eyes gave way to indignation.

"No," she said.

"Just for show, of course. It's the only way. We need to prove to Sabrina Vickers and the rest of the world that we're together. That my firing was simply a lovers' quarrel. If you and I are united, in both power and money, they'll know better than to attempt another takeover."

"That's ridiculous," she said, standing. "This is business, not make-believe."

He stood up so that he was towering over her. "If Sabrina thinks for one moment that you asked me back only because of her takeover bid, she's going to know that my stay is only temporary. She'll know that, sooner or later, you're going to fire me again. The end result is that she will never give up her shares. She will simply wait it out and strike when the timing is right."

"This ridiculous scenario is the best you can offer? I don't think so. We'll win this company back the old-fashioned way. By proving that we're stronger than her."

"But we're not. In the past year, stocks have fallen considerably. Stockholders are aware of the turmoil at Lawrence and are anxious to shed their shares while they're still worth something. You got us into this mess, Miss Lawrence. I think you owe it to everyone to do whatever you can to get us out." He could almost see the disdain in her emerald eyes.

"What does this…plan of yours entail?" she asked.

"We meet with Sabrina and do our best to convince her that we're in love…or at least, you're in love with me. We'll explain my departure as your reaction to a lovers' quarrel. That you would never really do anything to harm me or the company."

"I'm not an actress, Mr. Parker. And I'm not a hysterical woman." He didn't doubt it. She looked as icy as princesses come. But beneath the veneer he could swear he saw something else. Perhaps, he thought, she was one of those women whose prim visage was a mask for the fire and passion beneath.

"How long will it take you to draw up the contract?" he asked.

"I have to have it approved by the board first."

"That shouldn't be a problem. Meet me at Teterboro Airport tomorrow at eight in the morning. Bring the contract with you. I'll sign it before we leave."

"But that's less than ten hours from now."

"I guess you should get going, then," he said, taking her coat out of the closet.

"I have not agreed to do this."

"You'll do it, Miss Lawrence. You have no choice." As he hung her coat around her shoulders, his fingers brushed the skin of her creamy-white neck. She jerked forward, touching her fingers to the spot as if burned.

Her eyes narrowed and he could see the hatred burning inside. She took a step toward him and for a moment he thought she might slap him. Finally she bit her lower lip and turned away with her head held high, as regal in defeat as she was in victory. He couldn't help but smile as he shut the door.

He was going to enjoy this.

Three

Lessa sat beside Rick in the limo, determined to maintain her composure. She forced herself to focus on the laptop screen before her, trying to forget that she and Rick were getting closer to Sabrina Vickers by the minute. That Rick had just signed a deal in which she gave him half her stock, essentially making them partners, paled in comparison to the task at hand. But she had no choice. After all, to bow out was to admit defeat. And she was not defeated. Not yet anyway.

She had, however, suffered a professional setback that was so severe many at the office were already planning her retirement. The rumor mill had been working overtime ever since she'd arrived. Everyone knew she would not be the chairman or even on the board if she didn't own a majority stake in the company. The most recent rumor had her paying off the board members to

get her post. Her efforts to win the employees over—
starting a day care in the office, increasing benefits,
even supplying coffee and doughnuts in the morning—
were ignored.

Time, she reminded herself. She needed to be patient.
After all, her father had been just as beloved as Rick.
Rick had had to work hard to turn the tide of sympathy,
but he had done such a good job that the employees
seemed to have forgotten all about her father. The fact
that she was Howard Lawrence's daughter and the rightful heir to Lawrence Enterprises meant little. The only
thing that mattered from now on was how well she got
along with Rick.

They were no longer opponents but partners. Her
new strategy revolved around winning Rick's respect.
She had a hunch that if she won Rick over, she might be
able to win over everyone else. It was a strategy that held
little appeal, but she had no choice. She had made a deal
with the devil and now she had to make the best of it.

Lessa glanced at Rick. He was talking on his cell
phone, laughing as he spoke to a colleague. The crin-
kles from his laugh lines only made him look more
handsome. Wearing an open-neck business shirt and
khaki slacks, he looked relaxed and in control, totally
at ease with the caper they were about to attempt.

Once again panic gripped her heart as she thought,
What am I doing?

Could she really pull this off? What did he have in
mind? Holding hands and kissing? Or just exchanging
knowing glances?

She took a deep breath and closed her eyes. She had
to approach this just as she would a tough match. Like

the one she'd played against Korupova, the tall Russian girl with the black hair, in the NCAAs her sophomore year. Korupova was a lauded champion and Lessa began the match determined that the only way to win was to hit every bit as hard as her opponent. But it soon became obvious that she was outmatched. Korupova was a better and stronger athlete. Since Lessa could not win the match on the strength of her strokes, she had to come up with a new strategy. She switched from offensive playing to defensive, hoping that through sheer determination and patience she could outlast her opponent. In the end, Lessa had squeaked out a victory. She counted that win as the best of her career because it made her think she could get into something completely over her head and somehow, someway, get her feet under her and win. Just like now. Rick may be a superior player, but by staying in the moment, by not letting her fears get the best of her, she would get her feet under her again. And she would be victorious.

"Are you ready?" he asked, snapping his phone shut.

She glanced at him and nodded.

He smiled and took her hand. His touch sent a bolt of electricity running through her. So surprised was she by her reaction to him that she yanked her hand away.

"Now, now, Lessa," he said, purposely referring to her by her nickname. "Is that a way to respond to a lover's touch?" He shook his head, still holding her captive with his eyes. She couldn't miss the twinkle of mischief there. It was obvious he took pleasure in her discomfort. She was certain it was a different experience than what he was used to. When he held a woman's hand, he probably expected a sigh of delight.

"I suggest you swallow back whatever revulsion you feel toward me and focus," he said sternly. "When I touch you, do not grimace or make an effort to get away. Remember your mission and do your job."

He was right. She had agreed to this; now she had no choice but to give it her all. After all, if they were successful with Sabrina, they could single-handedly thwart all other takeover attempts. Maybe. At the very least, they could buy themselves some time to prevent this from happening again. She took a deep breath and picked up his hand. Still staring into his eyes, she brought his hand to her mouth and kissed it.

His eyes softened and he smiled. "That's better," he said. "I knew you could do it if you put your mind to it." Then he pulled his hand away and opened his cell phone, making another call and going back to business as if nothing had happened.

She rolled down the shaded limousine window, welcoming the bright sunshine. They were meeting Sabrina at one of her most famous resorts. Located on Paradise Island in the Bahamas, it was one of the most romantic resorts in the world, catering to honeymooners. Lessa breathed in the warm, tropical air. New York had been dark and overcast with the forecast of another day of freezing rain. She reminded herself that this was one of the things her parents had loved about this business. Whenever one world became unpleasant, they could escape to another.

She kept reminding herself how fortunate she was as the car pulled into the gated resort and stopped in front of a large bungalow marked Executive Offices.

"Wait for me to open your door," Rick instructed,

purposely tucking his collar under his jacket. "When we get out, I want you to adjust my shirt collar. After that, follow my lead."

He walked around the car and opened her door. He took her hand and helped her out, pulling her close. What, she couldn't help but wonder, was the point of this playacting before they even saw Sabrina? Did he think that she was spying on them from a window? Or was it just for rehearsal's sake? Despite her hesitation, Lessa did as she was instructed, carefully adjusting his collar. When she was finished, Rick smiled and put his arm around her, guiding her to the door. His arm weighed against her back as they walked. To be so close to him felt strange, but, surprisingly, not uncomfortable. In fact, there was something sensual about the way he held her, as if he were publicly claiming her as his.

The secretary led them into a large, airy office with overstuffed furniture upholstered in tropical prints. When a statuesque woman stood behind a desk, Lessa stopped in her tracks. Blond, busty and completely made-up, she was the same woman Lessa had seen that night in Rick's apartment. And suddenly the cold, hard truth hit her like a slap on the face. It was she, not Sabrina, who was being duped.

"Rick," Sabrina said. She held out her hands, signaling him to greet her.

What was going on? As Lessa watched Rick walk toward Sabrina, her heart banged against her chest so hard she was certain they both could hear.

Sabrina took his hands and kissed him on both cheeks. Without letting go, she said, "It's been too long."

How could he do this? Lessa thought. *How could he have pretended not to know who Sabrina was?*

Rick stepped back from Sabrina, as if suddenly remembering his date. "Sabrina, this is Alessandra Lawrence," he said.

"Well, well," Sabrina said, giving Lessa a careful once-over. "She's a beautiful girl, Rick."

"You two know each other," Lessa said coldly.

Sabrina smiled. "Rick and I are old friends."

"I've met you before," Lessa said. "At Rick's apartment." Rick glanced at her, startled. "I seem to remember that you two were more than just friends."

"We were lovers," Sabrina said, flashing her a pearly white smile. "Rick? You didn't tell Alessandra about me?" she teased. "I'm insulted."

Rick looked Lessa in the eye and said, "Sabrina and I haven't seen each other in years."

"Has it been that long?" Sabrina said. "It seems like only yesterday." She turned back toward Lessa and said, "We spent Christmas together one year."

Lessa couldn't take her eyes off Rick. Had he set this whole thing up? Was the whole "takeover" staged simply so that he could get his job back? As tempted as she was to confront him right there and then, she couldn't risk it. What if was just an awful coincidence? After all, she knew Rick had engaged in many affairs. Perhaps Sabrina was just another one of his women.

"We've come to make you an offer," Lessa said, glaring at Rick. She wanted to get this over as soon as possible.

"She's all business, isn't she?" Sabrina asked him.

"She's determined."

Why were they talking about her as if she weren't there?

"As Rick will attest," Lessa said, flashing him a smile, "I don't believe in wasting time."

"Something else we have in common," Sabrina said.

Something else? Lessa had nothing in common with the overly made-up, phony woman standing across from her.

Sabrina motioned toward the chairs and took a seat on the couch across from them.

"I don't mean to pry, Rick," Sabrina said, "but I was a bit surprised to get your phone call yesterday. After all, I had heard that you weren't working at Lawrence anymore."

"Reports of my demise were greatly exaggerated," he said.

"Were they?" She focused her black eyes on Lessa. "I had heard that Alessandra fired you."

"A lovers' quarrel gone public," he said, putting his hand on Lessa's bare knee.

"Really?" Sabrina crossed her arms and leaned back in her chair. "So you and Alessandra are…together, shall we say?"

Rick nodded. "For some time now. Of course, we've been hesitant to take our affair public, for obvious reasons."

"And she got mad and fired you. Tsk, tsk, Rick. What did you do to deserve such treatment?"

"It was all a misunderstanding," he said, giving Lessa a squeeze.

Sabrina's lip curled up suspiciously, as if she didn't believe him. "Very vindictive of you, Alessandra. Not to mention stupid. You should've been aware that firing him would make your company vulnerable."

How dare she? "I was acting under—"

Rick gave her knee a light squeeze and she knew he was signaling her to be careful. "I wasn't thinking very clearly at the time," Lessa said, doing her best not to take Sabrina's bait. "And it cost me dearly." *Very dearly,* she felt like adding.

Sabrina said nothing; she merely glanced at Rick.

"She's a very passionate woman," he said with a shrug. "For better or worse."

"And I remember how much you enjoy passion," Sabrina said, giving him a little smile.

Lessa couldn't stop herself from sending Rick a look of her own, an angry one.

"Oh dear, Rick," Sabrina continued. "It looks like she's not very happy with you. I certainly hope I didn't cost you your job again." Sabrina laughed. It was a cold, empty sound, just as haunting as Lessa remembered.

But the laugh was enough to remind her of her mission. Pretending to be Rick's lover was bad enough. She would not play the weak and hurt mistress. "Oh, no," Lessa said. "It's just difficult for me to keep all of Rick's old lovers straight. In fact, when I first heard about your takeover attempt, I assumed it was the move of a bitter ex-girlfriend. You know, retribution for his new romance."

The smiled faded from Sabrina's lips. "She's very spirited, Rick. I can see why she caught your eye. Although she looks a little buttoned-up for you."

Buttoned up? "I'm losing my patience," Lessa said, standing. Rick took her arm and raised his eyebrow, motioning for her to sit. She knew that he was right. She had no choice but to continue.

When she was seated, Rick turned to Sabrina. "The

bottom line is that the situation is not what you thought. I am not leaving Lawrence Enterprises."

"You can't defeat both of us," Lessa added.

"So my purchasing stock was enough to heal a…" Sabrina glanced at Rick. "How did you describe it? A lovers' quarrel? Perhaps you should be thanking me, Rick, for winning back your job."

"Let's face it, Sabrina, If not you, it would've been someone else."

"If I remember correctly, there was someone else," Sabrina snapped. "There were several in fact."

Was she implying that he'd been unfaithful when they'd been seeing each other? Lessa wondered.

"Let's hear your offer," Sabrina said.

"We're willing to buy back your stock at a decent premium," Lessa explained as Rick opened his briefcase and handed Sabrina the contract.

After scanning the document, she put it on her desk. "Why should I agree to this when I could have all the properties?"

Rick leaned forward. "Because you're never going to get all the properties."

"I'm not so sure. You two seem to have a tumultuous relationship, to say the least. One that is not having positive repercussions on the company. Your stock has dropped rather dramatically."

"Actually," Lessa said, "when you look at our revenues in the context of the economy, we had an excellent year. And Rick has some properties due to open that should dramatically increase our value. But then again, you know our property is valuable, otherwise you wouldn't want it so badly."

Sabrina hesitated and glanced down at the contract. "I'll need some time to discuss this with my advisers. Unfortunately, they're out of the office right now, inspecting some properties. Perhaps, if you're not in a rush, you could stay until dinner. They'll be back by then and we can all discuss this further."

Lessa felt her heart stop. As excited as she was to think that perhaps Sabrina would abort the takeover, she couldn't bear the thought of carrying on this charade any longer than necessary.

"We would be happy to," Rick said, glancing at Lessa. The look in his eyes was clear. *Don't blow this.*

"It's settled," Sabrina said. "We have a couple of hours to play before we return to business. I'll have my secretary show you to your room. Why don't you change into your suits and meet me at the boat docks? I know how Rick loves to water-ski."

Water-ski? "Unfortunately," Lessa said quickly, "we didn't bring suits."

"I'll have some sent to your room."

Her heart jumped into her throat. Room? As in one room, not two? "It's not necessary," she said quickly. "We'll just pick some up at the gift shop."

"The gift shop is closed temporarily. Renovations," Sabrina said with a shrug.

"Well then, thank you," Lessa managed to say.

Rick took her arm and they followed the secretary, Christa, outside and down a palm-shrouded walkway. Beyond the walkway was a white sandy beach framed by the Caribbean. Christa stopped at a bungalow just feet away from the crystal-blue water. Their quarters were isolated from the rest, a special little love nest next to the sea.

Christa slid a card through a lock and opened the door. "Enjoy," she said cheerfully, handing Rick the card.

It was an opulent and meticulously appointed suite, with French doors that were open to the sea. A bottle of champagne sat chilled in an ice bucket, while two plush robes lay across a bed.

Lessa shut the doors and turned to face him. Her eyes were cold, her face set in a frown. "I thought you didn't like games."

"If you have a problem, Lessa, I suggest you tell me about it. I don't like dissent in the office."

"You know Sabrina Vickers?"

"I knew her," he said.

"Why didn't you tell me she was your girlfriend?" she asked. The accusations once again filled her head. Was he working with Sabrina? Was this all a joke? Had he arranged this just to get his job back? Was this just a ploy to get her stock?

"She was never a girlfriend."

"If she wasn't your girlfriend, then why did she insinuate that you cheated on her?"

"I don't see how that's any of your business."

"It most certainly is my business. Your girlfriend is threatening to take over my company and—"

"Your company?"

This conversation was going nowhere fast. He should at least be able to admit that he had made a mistake. "You should've told me this before."

"Would it have made any difference? I would think if anything, it would've made you more eager to retain my services. After all, I have firsthand knowledge of how to handle her."

The look in his eyes was of a confident victor. She had been deceived and he was enjoying every moment.

"Look," he said, his tone softening, "my relationship with Sabrina was casual. It lasted for a couple of days in Acapulco and then we got together a couple of times when she was in New York for business. Like I said, I haven't seen or spoken with her in years. But I do know that she is one of the toughest and smartest women I have ever met."

Lessa felt a tingle of…what? Jealousy? Why would she care if he thought that bubble-headed blonde with the beautiful lingerie and sexy laugh was intelligent? "You and I both know that I would not have asked you back if she wasn't threatening a takeover," Lessa said. "Do you expect me to believe that this is some sort of coincidence?"

"You're welcome to believe whatever you want. I would suggest, however, that you at least listen to the truth."

"And the truth is…"

"Exactly as I told her. If she hadn't attempted a takeover, someone else would've. This company is weaker than it's ever been. When a twenty-six-year-old with only two years of experience uses her father's connections to take over a company, the sharks start circling."

"I'm more capable than you give me credit."

"Maybe," he said. "Yet here I am."

"The question is why am *I*? Why didn't you just go see her yourself, considering your past relationship?"

"Whatever Sabrina and I shared has nothing to do with this. I know her well enough to realize that she cares little about our past relationship. She's only interested in making money. You're with me because we need to convince her that we're a united front. The heir to the Lawrence fortune and the man who has given you his fortune are friends. If she suspects our relationship is not sincere, she will never accept a deal. She will simply wait and strike again."

He shook his head and absentmindedly ran his fingers through his hair, as if frustrated. "Look, Lessa, as I told you last night, the only one for you to blame for this mess is yourself. Sabrina never would've attempted this if I were in charge. You should've spent more time doing your homework. If you did, you would've realized that any corporate upheaval makes a company ripe for this sort of thing."

There was a knock on the door. Rick opened it and accepted the package, handing the man a tip in exchange. Rick looked inside the bag, and, with a wicked smile, pulled out the tiniest swimsuit Lessa had ever seen.

She whipped it away from him. "She didn't by chance include a cover-up in there, did she?"

He opened the bag again. It was clear he was enjoying this. "Not unless you want to wear this," he said, pulling out his bathing-suit trunks.

She went in the bathroom and slammed the door. She was fuming as she looked at the bright yellow string bikini. It was the type of suit guaranteed to get attention, one that left little to the imagination. She slipped it on, afraid to look at herself in the mirror. She knew without looking that her underwear covered more turf than the suit. She had always been extremely modest, preferring swimsuits that covered her essentials and then some. She wrapped a towel around her waist and, after a moment's hesitation, opened the door. She hurried past Rick without looking at him. "Let's go," she said, heading outside.

"Wait." He grabbed her arm. "Sabrina might think you don't care," he said, tormenting her with his teasing tone.

She hesitated and he let go of her. He had changed into his bathing suit as well. She was not surprised to see that he had the physique of a natural athlete, finely sculpted and strong.

He gave her body a raking gaze. She pretended not to notice his obvious examination and approval, but she could feel her cheeks grow warm. "Take my hand," he instructed. His hands were large, swallowing hers. He could crush her, but instead he held her as gently as he could. "Take your time," he instructed. "Slowly. Don't forget, I'm your lover, not your enemy."

"It's easy to forget," she said.

His eyes gazed over her once again, slowly drinking her in. She could smell Rick, feel his presence.

"Let's get on with this," she said. She found herself thinking once again of Sabrina. She had done a lot more than just admire Rick's muscles. While Lessa had been worshipping him from afar, Sabrina had been experiencing his skills as a lover. She had no doubt Rick was as skilled at lovemaking as he was everything else.

"I'm curious about one thing," Rick said. "When did you see me with Sabrina?"

"At your apartment," she replied, not intending the words to sound as bitter as they did. "About ten years ago. My dad sent me over to deliver some papers."

"That was a long time ago," he said. "I'm surprised you even remember."

Of course she remembered, she felt like saying. She had been madly, wildly in love with him. But before she could say anything, his hand settled on top of her rear end. She could feel herself grow short of breath as he pulled her to a stop. "Sabrina is behind you," he said. "She's watching us."

He brushed the back of his hand across her face. "I'm going to kiss you, Lessa," he said quietly. "It's going to be a tender, passionate kiss. I want you to take your hands and wrap them around my neck. Can you do that?"

Oh God, oh God...

"Just relax," he said softly. "I'm not going to hurt you."

As he leaned forward, she closed her eyes and puckered up. His lips pressed against hers as his hand slipped around her small waist, pulling her in to him. As her bare flesh pressed against his, she was overwhelmed by his physical strength and power.

Slowly, he stopped. He smiled softly, his eyes caressing her. And for a moment, she forgot it was not real. He loved her and she loved him and that was all that mattered.

But instead of sweet nothings, he said, "You didn't put your arms around my neck." With a nod toward Sabrina, he added, "Next time follow instructions."

Four

"**A**s I told you, Mr. Parker," Lessa said, still shaky from the kiss. "I'm not an actress."

"Well, you better try. Because this is the only way to get back your father's business. So no more tantrums." He swung her back into him.

"Every time you touch me, it makes me dislike you even more."

"Well, if all goes according to plan," he said, pulling her so close she could feel his breath on her cheek, "by the end of the evening you'll hate me." He released her but still held on to her hand. "Shall we?"

The afternoon sun reflected off the blue Caribbean, beating through the palm trees that flanked the path. They made their way to the white sandy beach toward a waving Sabrina. Lessa was surprised to see that Sabrina was wearing a suit even skimpier than hers.

"This way," Sabrina called out cheerfully.

Lessa glanced sideways at Rick. If Sabrina was wearing the bikini to impress him, it didn't appear to work. He was looking intently at Lessa. "Showtime," he told her softly.

"Well," Sabrina said, the smile fading from her face as she saw Lessa, "I see you got the suit. Who knew you had a figure underneath those big, bulky clothes of yours?"

"Lessa's in great shape," Rick said, smiling at her proudly. Lessa couldn't help but wince at the discussion of her physical attributes. She tightened the towel around her waist.

"She's a competitive tennis player," Rick said. "She even played at Wimbledon."

"The Wimbledon Juniors," Lessa corrected him, embarrassed by the exaggeration.

"How impressive," Sabrina said, obviously unimpressed. "But does she water-ski?"

Why did Sabrina insist on talking to Rick as if Lessa weren't there? "No, she doesn't," Lessa said, referring to herself in the third person.

"Oh, that's too bad," Sabrina said, with mock sincerity. "Perhaps you'd like to stay here and settle into a beach chair. We won't be long, will we, Rick?" Once again, she flashed her pearly whites.

"I'm always up for trying something new," Lessa said as enthusiastically as she could.

Rick jumped on the boat and held out his hand. She made herself take his hand and climbed onboard.

The boat took off and Sabrina fell against Rick. "Whoa," she said. Rick steadied her as Sabrina smiled at him gratefully. And that was when it hit Lessa. Sabrina was not only an ex-girlfriend, she was vying to be the current one as well. But did she really like him? Or was she, as Rick maintained, just trying to determine his response? After all, what better way to see if his relationship with Lessa was real?

As if thinking the same thing, Rick moved behind Lessa and slipped his arm around her shoulders. She glanced up at him and he smiled back.

"Does the rest of your office know what you're up to?" Sabrina asked, staring at them intently.

"No," Lessa said.

"Yes," Rick said, at exactly the same time.

He squeezed her shoulders again and said, "They didn't for a long time, but due to the most recent issue—"

"When I fired him," Lessa added cheerfully.

"It's become obvious that something is going on."

"I see." Sabrina said, picking up a bottle of sunscreen. She squirted some in her hand and stretched out one of her long legs, swinging it up and over the side of the boat. In a scene worthy of an X-rated film, she began slowly to smooth the lotion over her leg. It was obvious that Sabrina was doing some performing of her own. When she was done, she looked at Rick and said, "Lotion?"

He turned to Lessa and asked, "Would you mind putting some on my back?"

His back? "No," Lessa said, taking the lotion. She squirted some on her hands and forced herself to touch his bare skin. His skin was smooth and his back was outlined with well-formed muscles. She dug in deep, running her fingers against the muscles that seemed to grow hard with her touch. It was sensual and intimate, not the type of activity one would normally perform with a business associate. But she could not allow herself to feel embarrassed. Sabrina was watching.

"Thanks," he said huskily, as Sabrina signaled the boat's driver to stop. "You've got quite a touch," he added, giving her a mischievous grin.

Sabrina handed Rick a life jacket and said, "Why don't you go first." She helped it on him, making a point of rubbing in some lotion that was on his shoulder. "You missed a spot," she said, smiling evilly at Lessa.

Lessa couldn't help but resent the blatantly flirtatious act. If Rick really were her boyfriend, she would be fuming right now.

"Thanks," he said, then plunged into the water.

"Don't forget your ski," Lessa said, tossing it in. He moved out of the way just in time to avoid being clobbered. "So sorry, darling," she said.

Rick slipped on the ski and gave them the thumbs-up sign. He easily got up on the first try, all of his muscles taut.

Sabrina clapped her hands before focusing her attention back on Lessa. As Lessa watched Rick ski in and out of the wake, Sabrina said, "Rick and I met on a ski boat. It was very romantic. I took a bad tumble and had to be carried off the boat. Naturally Rick volunteered. All the other men, including my date, were sitting on the boat sipping their drinks. Well, that was that."

Lessa nodded. What was she supposed to do? She had the feeling that Sabrina was testing her, but what could she say? "Rick is a very gallant man."

"I take it you two met at work," Sabrina stated.

"I met Rick when he came to work for my father." Lessa could still see Rick standing before her, with his hair slicked back and his deep blue eyes, resplendent in an expensive suit. She remembered the feeling that had surged through her, a primitive need and desire so great she felt as if she might wilt away if he didn't love her in return. "I fell in love with Rick the first moment I saw him. Of course, he didn't know that," she said. And suddenly, she wasn't acting anymore. It was a true story, and recalling it now, after all these years, she could still feel the dull ache of longing for her old crush. "I was only fifteen and I don't think he even knew I existed. But I was so infatuated with him. I used to think of excuses to go to work with my dad just to see Rick. There was a drinking fountain right outside his office. I spent hours at that fountain."

"Love at first sight," Sabrina said sarcastically. "How sweet. So there's a significant age difference."

"Not really. About eleven years. Rick was pretty young when he started. It's one of those age differences that grows smaller and smaller through the years."

They glanced back but Rick was no longer there. Oops. Lessa was so into recalling her past love that she had forgotten to keep an eye on him.

"Turn it around," Sabrina said to the driver, pointing to a dot on the horizon.

They went back to Rick and he climbed back onto the boat. "You looked great out there," Sabrina said.

He nodded toward the towel, as if hinting at Lessa to get it. She jumped up and snatched it away just as Sabrina got up. "Thanks, babe," he said casually.

Babe. He called her *babe.* She had never liked that term of endearment. Macho slang for *baby,* it radiated sex.

He eyed them both and said, "What have you girls been talking about?"

"It was so sweet. Alessandra was telling me how she loved you at first sight. How she used to spend hours at the drinking fountain outside your office, just hoping for a smile from you." And with that, Sabrina touched his cheek. "It seems as if you were just too irresistible." Sabrina took a life preserver and fastened it on.

"Is that true?" he asked Lessa, looking at her quizzically.

"It was a long time ago," she said. "I was a kid."

Neither said anything else as Sabrina jumped into the water and put on her ski. As the boat took off, Rick wrapped his arm around Lessa, holding her tightly against him. They were flesh to flesh. She felt the movement of his breathing, the dampness of his skin. This was a little too close for comfort. She scooted away as she pretended to get a better look at Sabrina. She looked like a true professional gliding across the water with one ski. And then she began to show off, turning around backward and forward, smiling and waving at Rick. "She's good, isn't she?" Lessa remarked.

But Rick wasn't looking at Sabrina. He was looking at Lessa. There was something lazily seductive in his eyes, as though he were thoroughly enjoying the moment.

"I think Sabrina is still interested in you," Lessa said.

"No. We were together a long time ago. Besides, Sabrina's not the type to fall in love."

She raised an eyebrow. Women's intuition said differently.

When Sabrina was done, Rick leaned over the boat and helped her out of the water.

"Would you like to go again, Rick?" she asked as she stood in front of him, stretching every which way to pat herself dry.

Oh no, Lessa told herself, this was not how this was going to work, with her sitting on the sidelines watching Sabrina and Rick show off. "I'd like to give it a try," she announced.

"Good for you," Sabrina said in a patronizing tone. "She's got some spirit, Rick." She nodded toward the water. "Jump in and I'll throw you another ski."

"What's wrong with the one you both used?"

"It's easier if you get up on two skis," Rick said.

Out of the corner of her eye, she saw Sabrina smirk, as if mocking her.

"I'll do one," Lessa said.

"Take another ski," Rick said firmly.

No thanks. They did one, and so would she. "Don't worry, dear," she said, jumping into the water. She waded over toward the ski and attempted to put it on. But the boot was set for Sabrina's tiny size-five feet. Her size nines didn't stand a chance.

She struggled with the latch and glanced up. There was no mistaking the evil gleam in Sabrina's eyes. Then Lessa heard a splash as Rick jumped in the water. She couldn't help but feel relief as he swam over to help.

"It's stuck," she said, handing him the ski. He looked at her and said softly, "What's the deal? Why won't you use two skis?"

Why? Because his girlfriend had only used one. And she was…being silly?

"It seemed more convenient," she lied.

She tried to ignore Rick's disbelieving look as he called out, "Toss in another ski."

Sabrina threw it and it landed in the water beside them, barely missing Lessa's head. "Hey," Rick yelled. "Be careful!"

Rick adjusted the skis to fit her. "Hold on to me," he said. Lessa reluctantly put her arms around his neck to steady herself as he slid the skis on her feet. "You don't have to do this," he said.

"I want to do this," she said adamantly, letting go of him.

"All right," he said finally. "It's a little choppy so stay in the wake."

The wake. She got it. She could do this, she told herself. She had won the NCAAs, won the Wimbledon Juniors. She could certainly handle a little waterskiing. How hard could it be?

Rick climbed back on the boat. What had gotten into her? He knew Sabrina had been trying hard to goad her into action, but Lessa was too smart to let Sabrina get to her.

He was impressed with the way Lessa was handling herself. She was doing a good job of playing the concerned lover. He had been surprised at the sensuous way she had applied the lotion, massaging his shoulders and leaning close enough for him to feel her breasts pressing up against him. She had been effective. So effective that his body had sprung to life—a fact that Sabrina, with her eagle eyes and ability to read men, no doubt noticed.

But hell, who could blame him? After all, Lessa was half-naked in that bikini. Every ounce of her firm and toned body was exposed. It was all he could do to keep from staring at her large, upturned breasts, at her slender, perfect hips.

"She's ready," Sabrina said, telling the driver to go. The boat jolted to a start and Rick watched with dismay as Lessa flew out of the water and onto her head.

"Cut the engine," he yelled and jumped in, prepared to retrieve an unconscious woman from the water.

But she poked her head up. "I almost had it," she yelled out cheerfully.

"That's enough," he said sternly, swimming toward her. "Let's go in."

"I'm not about to quit now," Lessa said, grabbing a ski and slipping it back on.

"Lessa," he began.

"Go back up on the boat," she said, reaching for the other ski. "Please. I can do this."

He glanced back at the boat. Sabrina was leaning over the side, watching them. He could not argue with her here.

He hesitantly handed her the other ski and swam back to the boat. "She's determined," he said, pulling himself out of the water.

But he was about to learn just how tenacious she was. Time after time, Lessa went back down. Yet she showed no indication of being tired nor wishing to call it a day. She was hell-bent to succeed.

As Lessa took yet another tumble, Sabrina sighed and said, "How long will she keep his up?"

"Until she skis." He had no doubt that, if necessary, they would be at this all night.

"So, Rick," Sabrina said, leaning back against the

boat and stretching seductively, "you never did explain why you broke things off."

This was one conversation he had been hoping to avoid. "I thought we had an understanding," he said. "I wasn't ready for any commitment."

"And now you are?"

"I—" He hesitated, glancing in Lessa's direction. Her hair was a tangled mess but she didn't seem to care. She wiped her nose with the back of her arm and once again flashed the thumbs-up sign. He had to admit, there was something endearing in her refusal to give up. "I didn't plan on this happening with Lessa," he said quietly. "It was just one of those things."

He found himself encouraging Lessa silently from the sidelines. Her face set in grim determination, she slowly rose to her feet. Caught up in the moment, he jumped up and applauded. Lessa let out a whoop of joy.

Sabrina motioned to the driver to spin around. Rick knew that this would push Lessa outside of the wake, something which he thought was too dangerous. "No!" he shouted to Sabrina, but it was too late. Lessa sped outside the wake and in a split second, her slight form was lost in a spray of water.

He dove out of the boat, certain that no one could escape a fall like that unscathed. But once again, she surprised him.

"Did you see me?" she asked, bobbing in the water and grinning from ear to ear.

"You're lucky you didn't get hurt," he said gruffly, grabbing the skis.

"Lessa, I'm so sorry," Sabrina said, as they climbed

back onboard. "We were getting too far out, so I turned the boat…."

"You should've told her to drop the rope," Rick said angrily. No matter what Sabrina said, he knew better. It was intentional, and she was damn lucky that Lessa wasn't hurt. As it was, he thought, glancing at the big pink mark on Lessa's leg, she was going to have a hell of a bruise. "Do you have an ice pack?" he asked Sabrina.

"It's not necessary," Lessa said.

But Rick didn't listen. He helped her to sit down before holding the ice pack against her leg. "We've had enough. Let's head back."

Sabrina shrugged innocently and they drove back in silence. Rick's initial joy over Lessa's achievement faded into anger. What had she been trying to prove? It was stubbornness mixed with a sense of competition. She should've known when to throw in the towel, known when to say enough was enough. And as a result, she got hurt.

When they got back to shore, Rick made a point of keeping his arm around Lessa, helping her off the boat and down the dock.

"I'll see you at dinner," Sabrina said with a cheerful wave.

When they were out of earshot, Rick said, "What the hell were you doing back there—trying to kill yourself?"

"What are you talking about? I was waterskiing."

"You know very well what I'm talking about. You were trying to prove something. And your competitive nature almost got you seriously injured."

"I guess I should be touched that you're so concerned."

Why *was* he so annoyed? Maybe because the whole

scenario reminded him of what she had done at work. She had refused to give up, and as a result, she was about to get hurt. "You didn't have to prove anything, Lessa," he told her.

"I know that," she said, before shrugging off his arm. As she did so, her bathing-suit strap fell down over her pale, white shoulder. The wind gently blew the strands of her still-wet hair. Her eyes sparkled and her pale cheeks flushed with anger. He felt a sudden urge to kiss her.

"So how do you think it went with Sabrina?" she asked.

He forced himself to look away. The sight of her bare, slender body was enough to confuse even the most resolute intentions. "Hard to say."

"I think Sabrina is still interested in you."

"I told you that's over."

"Yeah, well, she had to look high and low to find a suit that skimpy."

"That's just how she dresses."

"And the way she kept touching you. Pretending to fall against you and putting on a show with the lotion."

"Jealous?" he teased.

"Me?" she asked. "Hardly. But I think Sabrina is."

But he knew better. Sabrina's flirtation was merely a test to see if he bit. He had no doubt that her line about her advisers reviewing the contract was just an excuse to stall for time. He and Lessa still had a lot of work to do if they were going to convince Sabrina. They needed to prove that their love was tempestuous and passionate. A love capable of desperate breakups and tearful reunions. "At dinner I'm going to ask Sabrina to dance. I want you to act like a jealous lover. I want you to storm out."

"Storm out? In other words, you want me to act like an idiot."

"No. I want you to act like a woman who believes her lover is flirting with another. I want you to act like a woman who cannot bear the thought of the man you love touching another woman."

"The man I love…" Her voice drifted off as the implication sank in. "Not all women behave so immaturely."

"True, but we are selling the whole firing as an act of passion. She needs proof. And she certainly didn't get it on the boat."

"Did it ever occur to you that the firing could've been your fault? Perhaps you quit because you saw me flirting with another man. And you couldn't stand the thought of me touching another."

"Sorry, sweetheart, but Sabrina knows me, remember?" he said, touching her cheek. His eyes hardened and he took her hand. "I'm not the jealous type."

Five

"So I'm not only immature enough to fire you over a love squabble, but I'm also jealous. What exactly do you see in me?"

What Rick saw was a woman with beautiful green eyes and exotic cheekbones. A woman with one of the most seductive bodies he had ever seen. A woman so stubborn and determined, she would suffer bruises and sprains without the slightest complaint until she learned how to water-ski. Instead, he said, "Perhaps you excel in other areas. Perhaps you're skilled—"

"In the bedroom? Is that what you were going to say?" She rolled her eyes and pulled her hand away.

"Actually, no. I was shooting for a good listener or cook, but I'd be more than happy with bedroom skills."

They walked back into the bungalow and shut the door. The air-conditioning was off and the room felt like an oven. She turned on the air conditioner and said, "This is going to be one long evening."

"Do you want to shower first or should I?"

"Go ahead," she said, sitting on top of the air-conditioner vent. "I'm set for a while."

Her long, slender legs were splayed out before her. The other bathing suit strap fell down. His eyes grazed down her neck and onto her bare shoulders. He swallowed and attempted to look in the other direction, then yanked off his shirt.

"You're not going to get undressed right here, are you?" she asked.

"No." In fact, he wasn't thinking about undressing himself, but her. What the hell was going on here? This was a business relationship. She was Alessandra Lawrence, the chairman of the board. The one who had fired him.

So why did he want to rip off her suit and take her right on the bed? Because Alessandra Lawrence just happened to be a beautiful woman. He always suspected as much, of course. But with her conservative suits and reserved manner, he'd never seen her as anything more than a wolf in sheep's clothing. He'd had her pegged as an uptight prude. He had not expected a spirited and feisty athlete. Nor had he ever expected her to look so good in a string bikini.

But there was something else that gave him pause. She had a quality, a way about her. There was a spark there. A connection. But whatever it was, it needed to be ignored. She was off-limits. Forever and always. This whole thing was make-believe. And he needed to keep it that way.

He let the freezing cold water of the shower pound

against him as he shut his eyes, trying not to notice his body's reaction to the woman just outside the door.

What had she gotten herself into? She was alone in a hotel room, ogling Rick Parker. She was—God help her—attracted to him. But how could she help it? They had spent the afternoon playing boyfriend and girl-friend. She had run her fingers over his raw muscles, felt the power of his kiss. And now here she was, only one closed door away from a naked Rick.

But, she attempted to reassure herself, it was normal, completely normal, that she feel some sort of attraction. After all, he was a good-looking man. Very good-looking. And she had a history with him. Like she had told Sabrina, she had suffered a painful crush.

But she couldn't allow herself to get confused. He was a business associate and that was all, one whom she did not even like. So why did a part of her wish that per-haps they were truly lovers? Why did a part of her wish that all their kissing and cuddling could lead to some-thing else?

She would simply block it from her mind. She closed her eyes. *Just breathe,* she told herself. *And again…*

But she couldn't stop thinking about Rick. She re-membered overhearing a conversation about him in the ladies' room a while ago. A woman in a neighboring stall had apparently known someone whom Rick had dated. Not realizing that Lessa was in the bathroom as well, the woman had said to her friend, "She said Rick told her on their first date that he didn't want any commitment."

"So what happened?" the other woman had asked.

"She slept with him anyway," the woman had said.

"Did he call her after that?"

"Nope. She was disappointed, of course. You know how it is. We all want to believe we're 'the one.' But she said it was worth it. She said he's great in bed."

"Great in bed?"

"Between you and me," the woman said, "I made a pass at him right after that."

"And?"

"He said no. He was very nice about it, but he said we work together. You know, he didn't want an office affair."

Great in bed...

Lessa turned up the air conditioner, as if a blast of cold air might cool her off. She had to stop thinking like this. Maybe if she had more of a social life, maybe if she *had* a social life, she wouldn't even notice Rick.

Unfortunately, it had been years since she'd been intimate with a man. And her last date had been months earlier, when her aunt had fixed her up with a friend's grandson. On paper he had sounded great, an engineer and part-time pro at a tennis club in the city. But it had been a disaster, right down to the three gold chains around his neck and the way he'd referred to every woman they'd encountered—the waitress, the hostess, the old lady whose cab he'd tried to steal—as "doll." The icing on the cake had been when he'd told her that for a businesswoman she had a "nice rack." And he should know, he'd added, because he'd "known"—big wink—a lot of businesswomen.

She knew her aunt blamed her long hours for her lack of a social life, but Lessa knew the problem was more complicated than that. After all, what twenty-six-year-old woman these days had only slept with one man?

One sexual affair to her credit and that had ended five years ago. Since then, she hadn't dated anyone longer than a week or two. And it wasn't just her love life that was suffering. Her entire social life was lacking. She had tried to make friends since she had come to New York to work for Lawrence, but it was difficult. Everyone she met was connected with Lawrence. Men were intimidated by her position and women tended to avoid her like the plague. One time she had invited a potential friend out for coffee only to find that the woman had not slept the night before, so worried was she that Lessa's invitation had been a ruse to fire her.

The truth of the matter was that Lessa didn't fit in with people her own age any more than she fit in with her fellow board members. Patience, her aunt had told her. It will all change with time.

But how could it when she spent all of her time at work? There was no way around it: She was lonely. It had gotten so bad that lately she had begun to wonder if perhaps she was destined for a life without love.

"It's freezing in here."

At the sound of Rick's voice, she turned. The sight of him, standing in the doorway with a mere towel around his waist, was enough to take her breath away. "You couldn't get dressed?" she asked, quickly averting her eyes.

"Not without my clothes."

She hurried past him and into the bathroom. He had left the shower running for her. She hurriedly took off her suit and stepped into the warm water. Only then did she realize that her clothes were still in the other room. She had been so flustered when Rick had come out in a towel that she had neglected to get her things. Now she had no choice but to do the same thing she had faulted Rick for—parade through the room in a towel. She finished her shower and grabbed the sole remaining towel, drying off and wrapping it tightly around her. Sabrina's decor might be nice but her towels left a lot to be desired. Thin and small, it barely covered Lessa's backside.

She opened the door and took a deep breath. What was the big deal? Rick had seen her in a bathing suit, and the towel covered more than that did. She glanced at her clothes on the chair and quickly calculated the amount of time she would be half-naked in front of Rick. To walk over and grab them, twenty seconds max. The key was to act as if she weren't embarrassed. To appear cool and in control.

Rick glanced up when the door opened. And there she was, wrapped only in a towel. For a split second he thought that perhaps she had come out to seduce him. But when she didn't look at him, when she walked right past him, he realized what had happened. She, like him, had forgotten her clothes. But if nothing else, he was a gentleman. He pulled a contract out of his briefcase and perused it, trying not to notice the way the towel slid open, revealing her leg. The way her plump white breasts peeked out of the top.

She hurried back inside the bathroom and when she came out again, she was dressed in her suit skirt and sleeveless blouse, holding her jacket in her hand.

She tossed her jacket on the bed and checked her watch. "Should we go?" Without waiting for him to answer, she walked outside.

"Lessa, wait," he said, tossing down the contract and following. "Aren't you forgetting something?"

She shook her head. "I don't think so."

"We're lovers, remember?" he said, sliding his arm around her waist. But the unhappiness in her eyes was almost enough to cool his desire. "It's almost over with," he said, as much to her as to himself. "As soon as she signs the papers we can go back to business as usual."

They walked down a winding path, following the signs to the restaurant. Although the sun had nearly set, it was still hot and muggy. They wove their way around thick patches of bougainvillea and tropical ferns, lit with multicolored spotlights. The restaurant was situated on a hill overlooking the sea. Completely open to the outside, it was lit only by candles, their flames flickering in the warm breeze. Rick gave the hostess their names and they were promptly led to a small, intimate table in the corner.

"I don't see her," Lessa said.

"I don't either," Rick said, taking the seat next to her. "But that doesn't mean she's not watching us."

"What should we do?"

"Let's just talk like two people who are interested in what the other has to say."

She glanced nervously at the door. She looked so uncomfortable he felt almost sorry for her. What had happened to the cool and collected woman from the office? The one who had fired him and then just as quickly negotiated his return?

"Where are you from?" she asked.

"I grew up outside the city. In fact, my parents still live in the same house."

"Do you have any brothers or sisters?"

"I have a sister and a brother."

"Do you see them often?"

"Fairly."

This was painful. She was looking everywhere but at him. "So, Lessa," he said, touching her hand to get her attention, "what are your plans for Christmas?"

"My Gran and I are going to have a quiet dinner. Just the two of us."

"Your grandmother?"

"No. She's my great-aunt. My only family. She fell down a year ago and hurt her hip, so I moved her in with me. She's better now but I like having her around."

She lived with her aunt? The image of Alessandra as a sweet and caring niece did not jive with the cold, self-reliant woman he knew from the office. "That's nice of you to take care of her."

"It's the least I could do. After all, she took me in after my dad died. She'd never had any children and she took the role of surrogate parent very seriously. She was great about the whole tennis thing. Even though she was already older she flew with me all over the world. She attended every match."

"I heard you turned down an opportunity to go pro."

"I don't know about that," she said modestly. "But I knew that if I chose to go any further, it would've taken all my energy and time. I wouldn't have been able to go to school or get my MBA."

"Education is important, but not many people turn down an opportunity to be a professional athlete."

"Ultimately I felt like I had little choice. I made a promise to my father."

"You promised him you'd get your degree?"

"No," she said, her eyes meeting his. "I promised him I'd get his company back. I knew in order to do that, I was going to need all the education and experience I could get."

He sat there for a moment, too stunned to speak. He had always known that she was on some sort of mission to take over the company, but he had never imagined that it was an instruction that had come from Howard Lawrence himself.

"But I still play tennis," she said. "At least, as much as I can. I've even fantasized about investing in a tennis camp one day. Either on my own or through Lawrence…and now we're back on business." She grinned apologetically and shrugged. "I'm not very good at this small talk, am I?" Without giving him a chance to answer, she asked, "What are you doing for Christmas?"

"I'm sure I'll be working," he said. He wanted to question Lessa more about her promise to her father, but now was not the time. Not with Sabrina lurking about. He had to take advantage of Lessa's question to steer the conversation back to neutral ground.

"At the office?"

"No. I usually visit one of the resorts, " he said.

"Not exactly Norman Rockwell."

"Norman Rockwell?"

"The big family sitting around the table while the father carves the turkey. My aunt is always apologizing for my lack of family. She blames herself for not having children. She'd like nothing better than the big family gathering, crammed with kids and noise."

"Well, if noise is what you're looking for, you'd love

my family get-togethers. Deafening." He smiled and said, "My brother and sister aren't too bad, but I have a big extended family. Lots of cousins, nieces and nephews. Family dinners are pretty crazy. "

"Your brother and sister are married?"

"They've both been married and divorced. In fact, my sister is about to get married again."

She took a sip of her wine. "So you're the only one who has never been married?"

"Or divorced, as the case may be. I'm the anomaly. They can't quite figure me out. So every time we all get together the big discussion is usually about who they are going to fix me up with."

"But you hardly need help finding dates."

"Apparently they don't like my choices."

"You've brought a lot of girlfriends home?"

"I've only made that mistake a couple of times." He shook his head. "Disasters. But then again, they all loved Karen." All these years later, it was still difficult to talk about her.

"Karen?"

"I was engaged a long time ago."

Conversation died and the room seemed to go quiet. So much for neutral ground. Why had he mentioned Karen? He never spoke of her. Most people at the office had no idea he'd ever been engaged.

"And what happened? No, let me guess. You stood her up at the altar in front of three hundred guests."

"No." *Let it go,* he warned himself. *Switch the subject.* But for some reason, he couldn't. It was the way she was looking at him, so certain that her impression of him as a cold, uncaring bastard was correct. "She died."

She sat still, stunned.

"I was still in grad school. I was studying, so I asked her to come to my apartment after work. She was half a block away when a drunk driver hit her. I don't think I'll ever forget that moment. To pick up the phone and hear a stranger tell me that she wasn't coming home…that she was never coming home."

"I'm so sorry."

He expected her to glance away, to do what most people did when they found out. To make some off-the-cuff comment and attempt to change the subject, but she didn't. She looked straight at him and said, "I can't imagine anything more awful. You must miss her."

"We were high-school sweethearts. We dated all through college. I thought I had everything planned out. We were going to buy a house, have kids. And in a split second, it was all gone." He ran his fingers through his hair. Why was he telling her this?

"My father suffered the same kind of loss," she said. "My mother got sick and died only a month later. They had been high-school sweethearts, too. He never got over it either."

He had known that Howard's wife had died and he had known that she had been his original partner. But he had never thought about the implications of that partnership.

"You know, when my father died, my Gran said he was still right here," she said, putting her hand over her heart. "And that part of him would never die, it would always be right there. And she was right. I can still feel him."

He could see the pain in her eyes and was struck by an urge to soothe her. "How old were you when your mother died?" he asked.

"I was three. I don't really remember much about her. My dad never really spoke of her but my Gran said she was one of the most determined and feisty people you'd ever want to meet. She said that from the first moment my father met her, he fell in love. My aunt said he was devastated when she died. He shut down. He dated, but he never saw the same woman longer than a month. I think he just couldn't stand any more pain. He couldn't allow anyone in because he was afraid of getting hurt again."

Rick glanced away. Without realizing it, she had just summarized his life. "Or maybe," he said, "he never again met anyone that special."

"Maybe," she said. "I'd like to think my parents shared the kind of love that comes along once in a lifetime."

"I'm sure they did," he said.

Her eyes, misty with emotion, narrowed. "I know what you think about me, Rick. The spoiled woman motivated by greed. I know you think I have no right to this company. But you have no idea how important this business was to my dad. It was more than a job, much more. He and my mother started it together and he felt that this company was *still* an extension of her somehow. That he was fulfilling her dream. Their life together."

"Lessa," he began. But what could he say? She was right. He did think that she was a spoiled girl with a keen sense of entitlement. And although she was turning out to be more complicated than he had thought, he could not—no, he *would not*—allow emotion to cloud his judgment.

But before he could say anything, she spoke. "Sabrina's behind you."

He put his arm around Lessa and slipped his hand under her shirt, caressing her bare shoulder. "Act as though I just said something very sweet," he whispered.

She smiled at him, but it was obvious that his touch made her uncomfortable. Apparently their conversation had done little to change her feelings toward him. If she wasn't careful, Sabrina would be on to them.

He felt a presence behind him and heard Sabrina say, "Well, what do you think of my dining room? It truly is romantic, isn't it?" She walked around the table and took a seat across from him.

"Did you bring the contract?" he asked.

She shook her head. "My adviser is looking it over. He should have it to me momentarily. So you might as well enjoy your dinner," she said, signaling a waiter.

Lessa ordered a steak and a side of rice.

"I'll have the same," Rick said. He appreciated a woman who was willing and able to eat.

"How compatible," Sabrina said. "You even order the same food." But it was obvious from the tone in her voice, she thought them anything but. They were going to have to lay it on thick to convince her.

"So do you two live together?"

"I live with my aunt," Lessa said.

"Your aunt? How sweet. And what does she think of your romance with Rick?"

"She's pleased with…our relationship," Lessa said, hesitating.

"Really? After what Rick did to your father?"

He could feel Lessa stiffen.

"I don't know what you're talking about," she said.

"Rick didn't have anything to do with my father leaving the company."

Unfortunately, it was obvious her defense of him was an act. He could practically see the strain on her face.

"Besides, my aunt wants me to be happy," she said with some effort. "She knows that I didn't plan this. But she respects my decision."

"Isn't that wonderful?" Sabrina said, studying Lessa carefully. Sabrina was suspicious and things were getting worse by the minute. He needed to get Lessa away from her. Just then the band began to play.

"Darling," he said, standing and offering Lessa his hand, "it's our song." He turned back toward Sabrina. "Will you excuse us?"

"Of course," she said with a smug smile.

He led Lessa to the dance floor. He pulled her in close as he whispered in her ear, "I think I need to kiss you again."

If Sabrina wanted a show, she was going to get it. He brushed a gentle kiss across Lessa's porcelain cheek. She turned toward him and their lips touched. A sensuous tremor passed between them as he pulled her tight against him. Momentarily forgetting about his mission, he kissed her long and hard, as if she were a true lover. Suddenly, Lessa broke away. Her breasts heaved as she struggled to breathe. She glanced at Rick and he knew from the look in her eyes that they were in trouble.

"Lessa," he said, leaning forward and touching the back of his hand to her cheek. "Are you all right?"

"I'm sorry," she whispered. Before he could stop her, she turned and hurried toward the door.

Damn her! What was she doing? He went after her,

following her outside the restaurant. He grabbed her arm and spun her around to face him. "Just what in the hell do you think you're doing?"

"I can't do this," she said, shrugging off his arm. The look on her face gave him pause. She didn't look like a woman in control of her feelings and actions. She was shaking and appeared to be on the verge of tears.

He hesitated and, without touching her, nodded toward the beach. "Let's get away from the restaurant." He had no doubt Sabrina was bending over backward to get a peek of the action. "Let me guess," he said as they walked toward the beach. "There's a boyfriend back home and you're feeling guilty."

"No. There's no boyfriend."

He felt a small gleam of relief. But why should he care if she was seeing someone?

"I'm just…unsure of the ground rules."

"The ground rules?" What the hell was she talking about? Did she interpret his touch as true longing?

But if she did, would she be wrong? After all, there was an undercurrent of…something. "Look, Lessa," he said, "this isn't one of your tennis matches. There are no rules or regulations. When Sabrina's around, I touch you, you touch me. That's all."

He saw her wince as if in pain. Was the mere idea of touching him so repulsive to her?

"Just pretend I'm…someone else. Someone you care about. Someone you saw in a movie once, hell, I don't care. Forget about my face and just respond to my actions. That's all."

"I'm trying, but it's difficult."

"Dammit," he said, getting even more frustrated.

"Let me make this clear. I'm not enjoying myself either. But this is business. You almost cost me my company and you better try damn hard to get it back."

She did not speak. She looked at him with all the fear and loathing to which he had become accustomed. But for some reason, it wasn't okay anymore. He felt like a bully.

He should've realized that this was too much to ask of her. After all, she hated him. How could he think that she was capable of pretending otherwise? "I should've known that you couldn't do this." He turned away, heading back toward the restaurant. "Go back to the room and wait for me. I'll handle Sabrina."

Rick's words hit Lessa like a splash of ice water. Couldn't do this? Was she really ready to forfeit simply because she didn't like the way the game was being played? Because that was what their whole fake love affair boiled down to—a strategy. The problem was, she couldn't help but wish it were real. With a kiss and some kind emotional words, Rick slashed through the paper-thin barrier surrounding her heart. The promise of love was enough to make her question even the most fundamental of views. But she had to get over it.

She hurried after Rick and took his hand, stopping him. Then, gazing into his eyes, she stood on her tip-toes and pressed her lips to his. She moved her mouth over his, allowing her instincts to take over. She kissed him long and slow, as if he were the man of her dreams and this was the chance of a lifetime. When she was done, she pulled away and said, "Better?"

He was breathing hard and his eyes smoldered with fire. "I'd say."

She smiled, pleased at his reaction. "I can do this. Let's go."

They walked back into the dining room. Their dinner had arrived but Sabrina was nowhere to be seen. He led her back to the table and gulped down his entire glass of champagne, then poured himself another.

"Careful, dear," she said, leaning forward just enough for him to get a peek at her cleavage. "You know how you get when you drink."

She saw his gaze wander down to her breasts before gulping down some more champagne.

"There's Sabrina," she said. As she watched Sabrina work the crowd, flashing various diners a fake, almost frightening smile, Lessa tried to imagine the woman arm in arm with Rick. "I don't see you with her," she said in between bites.

He glanced at Sabrina and said, "I think she was different then. She wasn't as…hard as she is now."

"Hmm. That's probably what my old boyfriends say about me."

"Oh? There are a lot of them?"

She'd meant it as a joke, but he seemed to take her seriously. "No. Not really."

"And why is that?"

"Because…" Why was she suddenly feeling as if she were in a therapy session? Was he going to pay the kindly uncle and give her dating tips? "I've been busy."

"An excuse. But not bad. I've used it myself."

"But you date. You date a lot. It seems like every time I turn around there's another mention of you with a different woman."

"You've been working with me now for six months. Is that your impression of me?"

No, at least not in the office. She would give him that. But there was a question she was dying to ask. "Are you involved with anyone right now?"

"No."

A surge of relief flooded her veins. But why should she care? She waited for him to finish his meal and then said, "Let's dance."

She took his hand and led him out to the dance floor. She wrapped her arms tightly around his neck. She could not only act like a lover, she could act like a temptress. And she was just getting warmed up. "Aren't you going to hold me?" she said softly.

"What got into you?"

"I don't like to give up a game."

"Ah, I see. Everything changed when I told you to go back to the room. You took it as a dare."

"I took it as intended. A challenge."

"And Alessandra Lawrence does not back away from a challenge."

"I know that you have me pegged as a spoiled rich girl, but that couldn't be further from the truth. I'm very determined and I'm willing to work hard to get what I want."

"I believe that, Lessa." He gazed at her, as if drinking her in. "So who am I tonight?" he asked. "Are you pretending I'm a famous movie star…or a—"

"Andre Agassi." The truth of the matter was that there was no need to pretend he was anyone other than himself. But she could not admit that to him.

"A tennis player, of course. I should've guessed." He

smiled. "You're not what I expected, Lessa. I never thought that I would enjoy spending time with you."

Her heart jumped into her throat. He was enjoying her company? "Is this part of your plan to convince Sabrina?" she joked. "You sweet talk me and I fall madly in love with you?"

"Do you think that would work?" he asked, flashing her his famous grin.

He was teasing and she knew it, yet she couldn't stop herself from answering. "If that's your plan," she said, playing along, "I should warn you it might be more difficult than you think. I've never been in love before."

"That's too bad," he said.

"I'm not so sure," she replied. "I've seen the havoc it wreaked on some of my friends."

"Not all love affairs end badly," he said. "And even those that do...well, sometimes it's still worth it."

His eyes grew distant and she knew he was thinking about the woman he had loved all those years before. She was possessed by a sudden urge to comfort him. "I'm sorry," she said quietly.

He did not speak but cupped her chin tenderly.

She closed her eyes, reveling in the touch. His arm slid around her as he pulled her closer. The act caught her off guard, taking away her breath. He leaned forward to kiss her, and her senses charged to life as a delicious shudder rippled through her body. He softly touched his lips to hers.

"There you are!" Sabrina said, interrupting. "I was wondering if I might be able to steal him away for a moment." Looking at Rick, she said, "You promised me a dance."

To Lessa, it almost looked as if he regretted leaving her. She stepped aside and Rick swept Sabrina into his arms. As Sabrina wrapped her arms around his neck and nestled her cheek against his, Lessa felt jealous. Real, honest-to-goodness jealous.

What was happening here? She wasn't supposed to feel jealous. She wasn't supposed to feel anything at all. It was all an act. He was Rick Parker, her nemesis, the man who'd stolen her father's company. There was no possibility of anything happening between them, ever.

But she couldn't help wishing things might be different. She couldn't help her body from enjoying his kisses and hoping for more.

Sabrina put her arms around Rick's neck. Lessa was once again the girl in the doorway, lusting after a man who did not even know she existed.

If she was going to storm out in a fit of jealousy, now would be the time. With one last glance, she made her way toward the door. Just as she got to it, she felt a hand on her arm. Rick spun her around and, pulling her close, kissed her once again.

Six

It was the velvet kiss Lessa had dreamed of, the one she had longed for all those years ago. She wrapped her arms around Rick's neck, welcoming him. His arm slid around her as he pulled her closer. Her senses charged to life. It was as if time had stopped. Nothing else mattered. She wanted to feel him, all of him.

And then, just as suddenly as it had all started, it stopped. "Let's get out of here," he said, breaking away.

His words suggested an intimacy, a desire to be alone. But she knew better. She could tell by the look in his eyes that something was wrong. "But the contract…"

"She's not signing the contract tonight. It was all a game."

Accepting his hand, Lessa followed him out the door. Once outside, he stepped away from her.

"What did she say?" she asked as he led her down to

the beach. It was a warm tropical night. The sky was littered with stars and a heavy, full moon that reflected off the glittering sea.

"She's put us off until morning." He stopped and let go of her hand. "I think she's playing with us, Lessa. I don't think she bought our story, unless our last-ditch effort convinced her. I don't think she has any intention of signing that contract tomorrow."

"I'm sorry. I'm afraid I wasn't very convincing as the jealous girlfriend."

"You did fine." He smiled at her again. It was genuine and sincere, not like the patronizing grins to which she had grown accustomed.

"What are you suggesting we do?" she asked.

"We can go back to New York and try to come up with another way to fend off this takeover. Or," he said, after hesitating, "we can give it another night."

Another night. A night sharing the same room. She glanced toward the water slowly licking the shore. "I didn't bring a change of clothes, or anything," she said.

"I know how you feel about this, Lessa," he said. "So if you want to go home tonight, I understand. I'll stay and deal with Sabrina alone tomorrow morning."

As she followed him back toward their bungalow. She felt the jealous whisper of uneasiness. She thought back to the way Sabrina had leaned into him, the way she had looked at him. Did he want Lessa to leave so that he could have a secret rendezvous with the enemy? Perhaps he had decided on a different way to convince Sabrina to abort the takeover. "She propositioned you, didn't she?"

"How did you know that?" he replied in a tone that let her know her hunch was correct.

The thought of Sabrina propositioning the man Lessa was supposed to be with was infuriating, to say the least. The thought of him accepting was even more infuriating. "What did you say?" she asked, her voice cold.

"I don't mix business and pleasure, Lessa," he said, stopping in front of their bungalow.

"Not even with an old girlfriend?"

He unlocked their door and pushed it open. When she walked inside, he stepped in front of her. "Not even with an old girlfriend," he said, his voice low and threatening. "Now make up your mind. Are you staying or not?"

She looked at the solitary bed. She could've sworn the room was even smaller than when they'd left it. "I'm staying," she said.

He paused for a moment and then stepped away. He loosened his tie and closed the blinds. It was obvious he was angry with her for suggesting that perhaps he would have a liaison with Sabrina. But how could she not suspect the worst? After all, the image of him dancing with Sabrina was burned in her mind. The way he had held her in his arms. The way he had looked at her.

Lessa walked over to the bed and sat on the edge. "Did you love her?"

"Love her?" he asked, surprised. "No. I told you, we had a brief affair. I don't think it lasted more than a week. That was all." He sat down next to her and said, "You're going to have to trust me on this one, Lessa."

"I'm sorry, Rick. Regardless of what you say, I don't think I can ever trust you. Actions are stronger than words."

"I assume the action in my case is what happened to your father. And that doesn't define me as anything but a businessman. I was given an offer and I took it. I did what I could to help him. I'm the one who put together his severance package. I'm the reason you inherited your stock."

"Do you think I should thank you? Losing this company destroyed him." It had literally broken his heart. He had suffered a fatal heart attack and died less than a month later.

"Lessa," he said softly. "He was a good man who did a great job building this company—but he is the one who took it public and hired the board. And you know as well as I do that whenever you take a company public you lose some control."

"He fought so hard to keep his job. I hardly saw him during that last year."

"I'm sorry, Lessa," Rick said quietly. "It's not all about hard work. Sometimes people are simply outmatched."

Was he talking about her father or her? "I realize that. But if you're referring to me, I conceded, remember? And now we're partners on the same team."

He glanced away. Whatever may have transpired between them, it was obvious he still harbored doubt about her.

"I need to have your support, Rick," she said.

His eyes softened and he smiled slightly. He glanced at her leg. "How is it feeling?" he asked, running his finger around the bruise.

"Great," she said, her response indicating not the pain from her bruise but the exquisite feel of his touch. Their eyes locked and she could feel her heart turn over. Her entire body ached for him. He leaned forward and she closed her eyes, readying for his kiss.

* * *

In the nick of time, Rick stopped. What the hell was he doing?

He needed to get back to business. The night, the wine, the romantic setting…it was all making him lose his head. She was not a lover he had brought on vacation, nor would she ever be. She was the chairman of the board and he couldn't allow himself to forget it.

He grabbed his laptop and sat in the chair, trying not to notice as she settled herself on the bed. She fluffed up the pillows before situating her computer on her lap. If anyone had looked in the window, he would think they were a happily settled domestic couple, albeit one not romantically inclined.

He sorted through the day's mail and messages before scouring the recent stock activity. "Sabrina has been buying more stock," he said.

He picked up his laptop and took it over to the bed to show her. He sat beside her and said, "Look at this."

She scanned the information. "So she has no intention of selling her shares to us?"

"Not necessarily. She might be doing this just because she knows we want it. She figures whatever she has is worth twice as much."

"Maybe we should draft a letter to the stockholders and tell them what's going on. They need to know that now is not the time to sell."

"I agree," Rick said.

Together they began to work. At close to two in the morning, Lessa fell asleep, her head on Rick's shoulder. A copper ringlet had fallen over her forehead. He gazed across her face, slowly lingering on her temptingly curved mouth. He slid his hand under her head and gently set her down on the pillow. She sighed and the corners of her lips turned upwards in a sweet smile as she nestled into the soft down.

Damn, but he wanted her.

He swallowed hard and, utilizing every ounce of willpower he could summon, rolled out of bed. Her rubbing up against him in the middle of the night could trigger a chain of events that he didn't want to think about.

He settled himself into the chair and leaned backward, absentmindedly running his fingers through his hair. Who would've thought he'd want to make love to Alessandra Lawrence? She had been nothing but trouble. He'd found her uptight and rigid, a prim and proper woman with a narrow vision. And, so he thought, they had nothing in common besides their desire to run Lawrence Enterprises.

But beneath that cool exterior was a warm and passionate woman, one with her own struggles and demons. And one who just happened to look damn good in a towel.

He barely slept that night. He tossed and turned until a sliver of light was shining through the rose-colored curtains. As he massaged his stiff neck, Lessa sighed slightly and turned on her back. Her long eyelashes curled over her sleeping eyes, and her hair was splayed out behind her. Her body, long and elegant, rested on top of the covers. Daylight had not helped his willpower. With the light radiating around her, she looked like an angel. At the very least, she was the most beautiful woman he had ever seen.

He needed to get out of there. Fast. He showered and

dressed as quickly as he could. When he walked back in the room, Lessa was sitting on the side of the bed.

"Good morning," she said, stretching like a lazy kitten. Her hair was tousled and her shirt half-unbuttoned. And the fact that she was unaware of her sexiness only added to her allure.

"I'm going to find some coffee," he said, looking away. "How do you take it?"

"Black, please," she said as he shut the door.

He picked up the coffee in the restaurant and took his time getting back to the bungalow. He paused outside the door and saw Sabrina stepping off a boat, dressed all in white. She was a beautiful woman, but she paled in comparison to Lessa. He found it amazing that he had ever been attracted to her. She seemed so superficial and insincere. But he had not been looking for love when they'd gotten together. He had been looking for sex and adventure and had found her significantly lacking in both.

He could not imagine coming home to a woman like that. He wanted a woman more like Lessa, one who was spunky and tough. A woman who could be sensitive and strong at the same time. Sabrina saw him and waved. He nodded in her direction and pushed open the door.

Lessa was standing with her back to him, wearing only a pair of lace panties. She pulled her dress over her head and spun around.

"Don't you knock?" she said, picking up her bra and heading back into the bathroom.

"Look, Lessa, I'm sorry. Sabrina is right outside the door. It never occurred to me that you would be naked in the middle of the room. After all, the blinds aren't even closed."

The bathroom door opened and she reappeared. "It's all right," she said. "No harm done."

He would beg to differ. He had seen her full, ripe breasts, her tiny flat belly and the panties that hung over her slender hips. It was a sight he was not going to forget anytime soon.

He suddenly realized that he hadn't moved. He was still standing in the doorway, holding the coffee in front of him.

"Is this mine?" she asked, taking a cup. He watched her sip the warm liquid. She sighed and closed her eyes. "Mmm. This tastes great," she said, running her tongue around her lips. "Thank you."

What was she trying to do, drive him crazy?

Oblivious to her charm, she smiled and said, "Now I'm ready for another round." She opened the door and waved to Sabrina. Then she turned back toward him and whispered, "We should kiss."

Without hesitation, she stood on her tiptoes and wrapped her arms around his neck. As her lips touched his, he could feel his body respond.

Unaware of the seductive spell she had cast, she pulled away. "Did she see?" she asked cheerfully.

"I'd say so." Sabrina was walking straight toward them. "Good morning, Sabrina," he said as Lessa turned around.

"How did you sleep?" Sabrina asked.

"Did we sleep?" Lessa teased with an obvious wink.

"No," he answered truthfully. "I didn't sleep at all."

Ignoring the fact that Lessa was practically glued to him, Sabrina touched his cheek. "Tsk, tsk. And the mattresses are guaranteed to provide a good night's sleep."

"Oh, we did enjoy the mattress," Lessa said, rubbing her hand against Rick's chest.

"Are you ready to sign?" he asked Sabrina. Any more talk like this and he was going to have to toss Lessa back onto the bed and test out the mattress himself.

Sabrina sighed dramatically. "I'm afraid we're going to have to postpone once again. It seems my research has not been thorough."

"How unfortunate," Lessa said.

"I'm going to need a few more days," Sabrina said with a shrug. "It was nice meeting you, Lessa. I certainly do hope you enjoyed your stay. Rick," she said, pausing to flash him a stiff smile, "I'll be in touch." She spun on her heels and turned away, walking quickly back toward the office.

"You were right. She had no intention of signing that contract," Lessa said when Sabrina was out of earshot. She let go of Rick's arm and stepped away from him. "This whole strategy was a bust. It won't be difficult for her to find out that we're not together. After all, everyone at the office knows how we feel about each other."

"Perhaps we can change that."

"I don't know," she said. "Pretending we're together for a stranger is one thing, but doing this on a day-to-day basis?"

"We'll give them just enough to assume."

"What do you mean?"

"The office Christmas party is in a couple days," he said. "We'll go together. It should be enough to get the rumors going."

After all, everyone knew that he and Lessa had fought tooth and nail over the party. He had never liked

Christmas parties. Too much alcohol and partying had turned an otherwise diligent worker into the murderer who was responsible for Karen's death. But that was not the only reason he disliked office Christmas parties. They were a complete waste of time and money. It was a momentary pleasure at best, an obligatory occasion in an otherwise busy season at worst. But Lessa had insisted. The annual Christmas party had been a Howard Lawrence tradition.

"Right," she said, after a moment's hesitation. "I just hope it'll be enough."

"We'll get this company back one way or another," he said reassuringly. And then, before he could stop himself, he gave her hand an encouraging squeeze even though no one was there to see it.

Seven

Lessa knew from playing doubles that if a partnership was not strong there was little hope of winning the match. And so she had returned from the Bahamas with a fine-tuned strategy. There was only one way to win Rick's respect. She needed to prove she was a worthy partner.

Fortunately, she had found a way. She had studied the financials and had come to the conclusion that in order to increase the value of the stock, they needed to sell off some of their more expensive assets. That money could then be used to expand, to buy and develop other properties.

Like the property she had found in Florida. Located off the Gulf of Mexico, Mara del Ray was a former luxury resort, a diamond in the rough. Lessa had attended a tennis tournament there as a teenager and from the moment she'd heard that it was for sale she knew it would be perfect for Lawrence. But where would she get the money to buy it?

Fortunately, there was one resort in particular that was ripe to sell. Located in Antigua, it was now one of their most profitable. But that was certain to change. There was another major resort opening on the island and the resulting competition was bound to affect its value. Better to sell while they were on top. She had made some inquiries and was close to finding a buyer. When she found one, she hoped to present the whole package to Rick and prove once and for all that she knew what she was doing.

"But do you care what Rick thinks?" her aunt asked when Lessa shared the details of her plan.

Yes, she did. So much that when he had walked in and seen her naked, she had done her best to act as if it weren't a big deal. Even though she was mortified, she was not about to act like the hysterical woman who had run out on him the night before. And so she had swallowed her pride and pretended that showing her half-naked body to Rick Parker was something she did every day.

She told none of that to her great-aunt. All she said was "He's my partner, Gran. We have to get along."

"What exactly happened in the Bahamas?" her aunt asked suspiciously.

"Not much. We had a terrible meeting with Sabrina, and then…" Then they had gone back to the hotel room they'd shared. She'd put on a string bikini. They'd kissed, gone waterskiing, kissed again, gone dancing, kissed yet again and then she'd fallen asleep in his arms. Oh, and then, just in case he hadn't gotten a good enough look at her in the string bikini, she'd shown him what she looked like topless. "That was about it."

How could she give her elderly aunt the whole truth and nothing but the truth? She didn't want to upset her. And Lessa had no doubt Gran would be upset to learn that since returning from the Bahamas, her niece had been unable to forget about those damned kisses. They were enough to make her forget who she was and where she was going. But it was more than just a few kisses. It was the way he made her feel, as if she were the most interesting person in the world. More than interesting. He made her feel beautiful.

Her aunt was looking at her curiously, as if attempting to decipher the secret meaning behind her words. Lessa knew the woman was hot on her tracks and, in order to throw her off, she had to toss her a bone. "I must admit that Rick surprised me. He can be very charming when he wants." It was a gift, actually. He was blessed with the gift of sexual magnetism. She could still remember the way the assistants used to flutter around him at her father's office. The giggles and the seductive glimmer in their eyes when they referred to him.

Time, she thought. She just needed some time to clear her head before seeing him again.

"What do you mean?" her aunt asked.

"He was kind and considerate. He was actually worried about me when I was waterskiing."

"He sounds human. That doesn't make him kind."

"Did you know he was engaged? She died in a car accident. From the way he spoke about her, he still hasn't recovered. I think that's the reason he never married. He's still nursing a broken heart."

"Be careful, Lessa. A man like that, one who's been

so wounded, is not the best choice. It'll take quite a bit to heal his broken heart."

"I'm not going to heal his heart."

"But you would like to."

A heavy silence filled the room. Was her aunt right? Did she want to heal his heart?

It was true that she couldn't forget the feel of his hand on hers, the way she had felt when he had looked into her eyes and whispered her name. But it was ridiculous, the whole thing. A romantic fantasy inspired by a romantic setting. That was all.

"Of course not," Lessa finally responded. "If I feel anything, it's a crush. It's not real."

"I can't say I'm surprised you have a crush on him. It's the first time you've been alone with a man in how long?"

"I've been busy," she said defensively.

"Yes, yes, I know. You've been working. As I've told you before, a company can't take you out to dinner. They can't bring you soup when you're sick. They can't keep you warm on cold winter nights."

"I get it."

"A company can keep you busy, but it can't prevent loneliness. I'd like to think that if I'm not here next Christmas you'll have someone else beside you."

"Don't talk like that. You'll be here. As for my love life, who knows? I must admit, I'm a little more hopeful than I have been."

"Lessa," her aunt said, "a man like Rick may serve as a distraction, but that's all. A relationship with him is a complication you don't need."

"Don't worry, Gran. I'm not interested in having a relationship with Rick Parker."

She had told her aunt a partial truth. She may not want a relationship with him, but one thing was certain. She was dying to kiss him again.

By the time Lessa left work, it was close to seven o'clock. The air was crisp and it felt as if it might snow. She paused to wrap her scarf around her neck as she glanced at the store window display. It was a scene right out of a Christmas fairy tale. Snow was falling as a couple kissed underneath trees lined with mistletoe. Just as she started feeling sentimental about the special holiday approaching, a pellet of freezing rain hit her on the nose. She glanced at the cloud-covered sky. The rain was a reminder that in real life, mistletoe trees did not exist and it didn't always snow on Christmas. And sometimes, as much as she and her aunt might wish otherwise, there was no one to kiss under the mistletoe.

She turned away from the window and hurried to the street corner. From the crowd of people desperately trying to hail a cab, she knew her chances of getting one were slim to none. And raining or not, she had promised her aunt a Christmas tree. She would just have to hoof it to the tree vendor as fast as she could. As the horns blew and the people pushed and shoved, her thoughts once again drifted back to palm trees, warm, quiet nights and the man she had kissed.

She had to snap out of this. It was one thing to please a business partner, quite another to dream about seducing him. Although she had spent the day putting together her Antigua deal, pesky thoughts kept interrupting her noble motives. Like how damn good he looked in swim trunks and the expression on his face when he'd opened the door and seen her half-naked.

In fact, several times that day, she had found herself at the water fountain outside his office, unable to quench her thirst. She was as bad as a teenager with a crush. But she had to forget about what happened in the Bahamas. She was not a kid anymore; she was the chairman of the board and Rick was her partner.

A partner whom she had barely seen since their return. In spite of his desire to cultivate the pretense of a romance, the most contact they had had was an occasional hello in the hallway. There were no meaningful glances, no secret rendezvous, no—

"Lessa?"

She turned around. Rick was behind her, looking every bit the dapper executive. He was wearing a black cashmere coat with a maroon scarf tucked inside. "Hi," she managed to say.

"Here," he said, opening his umbrella. "Stand under this."

"No thanks. Contrary to rumors, I won't melt."

"I insist." He smiled as he stepped closer, sheltering her from the rain. "Which way are you going?"

"Fifty-eighth and First," thinking of the Christmas tree lot.

"My car is parked in a lot near here. I'll drive you." Her heart jumped into her throat at the thought of being alone with him. They walked to the next corner in silence.

As they waited for the light to change, she could feel him looking at her. Suddenly self-conscious, she smoothed her damp hair and dabbed at the mascara she was certain had smeared under her eye. "I must look like a drowned rat," she said.

"You look beautiful," he said softly.

Beautiful. He said *beautiful.*

Suddenly she was aware of him, very aware. His masculine presence seemed to fill the night. She felt a chill run down her spine and wrapped her arms around her damp trench coat. In her rush to get out of the house that morning, she had taken a coat that was better suited to a warm spring day than a blustery winter night.

"Hold this," he said, handing her the umbrella. He shrugged off his overcoat and gave it to her. "Put this on."

"No, that's all right. I'm fine."

"I insist."

"But then you'll be cold."

"Put it on," he said again. After she hesitated, he added, "I think you know that I'm every bit as stubborn as you."

Once again she found herself obeying. She wrapped his coat around her, reveling in its musky scent.

"How have things been going for you at the office? Have you been having an easier time?" he asked as they walked down Fifth Avenue. Little gold lights sparkled on the barren trees, and store windows beckoned with spectacular holiday displays.

"No one's poisoned my coffee but they're not exactly standing in line to shake my hand either. I did overhear some women discussing me in the bathroom however. Seems that word of our overnight in the Bahamas is making the gossip circuit. Quite frankly, I think some of the women in the office are hoping that we *are* having a romance. That maybe our office romance will pave the way for more."

"What do you mean, pave the way?"

"Come on now," she teased. "You've noticed how the women there flock around you."

He shook his head and squinted his eyes. "What are you talking about?"

"Rick, you must know that many women who work with you harbor a secret, and sometimes not-so-secret, crush. They know you have a rule about avoiding office romances. They figure you getting involved with me can only be good. After all, if you broke your rule with me, then maybe you'll break it with them as well." There. She had spelled it out.

"So they're assuming we're going to break up?"

"I think it's safe to say the answer is a big yes. After all, you're not exactly a one-woman man."

"I see," he said with a twinkle in his eye. He was obviously enjoying this conversation. "I'll tell you what. When it comes time to break up, I'll let you do the honors."

"That would be quite a claim to fame. I fire you *and* break up with you. I'll go down in history."

He laughed, a deep and hearty response. She couldn't help but feel proud to have elicited such a reaction. His laughs were few and far between. He hesitated and the look in his eyes softened. "Well then, we'll have to give them something to talk about tomorrow night."

As she looked into his eyes, her heart jumped. Tomorrow night was the Christmas party, an event she had worked hard to produce. Up until now, she had viewed it with anxiety, yet another project for which she would be held accountable. But the thought of attending it with Rick, the thought of having to pretend once again that they were lovers, was enough to elicit a tingle of excitement. She cleared her throat, pretending not to be affected. "That's right," she said.

She glanced beside her, suddenly realizing that they were in front of Saks department store. Every Christmas, Saks decorated their windows with magnificent Christmas displays. This year's were the most amazing yet. Each window contained a mannequin dressed in haute couture, posed in fabulous scenes meant to represent a fantasy.

The window directly in front of them contained a mannequin dressed like a woman from the eighteen-hundreds. She looked elegant and wealthy in her diamond tiara and jewelry. But she sat in a slump in an expensive chair, her beautiful gown flouncing around her gold slippers. In her hand was a letter from her lover stating that he would not be back for Christmas.

"I think she's supposed to represent the woman who seems like she has everything, but she herself feels like she has nothing."

"What does that have to do with Christmas?"

"Well, I think it speaks to the fact that for some people, Christmas can be a very lonely time of year. It's hard to be single during a holiday that emphasizes family."

"You sound like you're speaking from experience," he said.

She had not expected such a personal comment and it caught her off guard. "I guess so. There are times when I wish that I had a husband and kids like some of my friends. Times when I can't shake the feeling that I'm missing out on something."

"I think that's human nature, though, isn't it? To wonder if perhaps the grass isn't greener?"

"You feel that way, too?"

"Sure. Sometimes even I wish that—"

"You had someone to kiss under the mistletoe?" she said before she could stop herself. She winced. "What am I saying? You've got plenty of women to kiss under the mistletoe."

"I know what you mean," he said, hurrying to her defense. "And the answer is yes. Sometimes even I wish that I had someone to kiss under the mistletoe. Someone that I loved."

She appreciated Rick making such a personal admission. He may be a pirate, but it was becoming obvious that he still had a heart.

As they stood there, they were joined by a couple carrying a Christmas tree. Off to their right, a young boy sat on his father's shoulders as he hugged a bag from FAO Schwarz.

"Are you done with your shopping?" she asked Rick as they turned to the corner.

"I haven't started. But usually I just give gift certificates. What about you?"

"My aunt is always complaining about the cold, so I got her a cashmere sweater and scarf."

Lessa stopped. The Rockefeller tree, sparkling with thousands of tiny multicolored lights, stood before them. "Do you mind if I take a closer look?" she asked, nodding toward Rockefeller Center. "I don't usually walk this way."

"I'm in no hurry," he said.

"Are you too cold?" she asked. "I'd be happy to give you back your coat."

"I'm just right," he said, taking her arm as they crossed

the street. It was the protective gesture of a gentleman, but suddenly there was an electrical current in the air. Something had shifted between them. By that subconscious response, they had gone from co-workers sharing a stroll to a man and woman sharing an evening out.

They walked to the edge of the street balcony and looked down on the skaters below. Despite the rain, it was a beautiful scene. The giant Christmas tree, the skaters, the shoppers, all framed against a background of sparkling lights. She inhaled deeply, smelling air redolent with fresh pine and roasted chestnuts. "I love this time of year," she said quietly.

He smiled. "Follow me." He took her hand and led her into the building beside them.

What did he have in mind? He glanced at her and winked as the guard got approval for them to enter. Rick led her to the elevator and pressed the button for the top floor. When the doors opened, he led her down a hall to the stairwell. "Where are we going?" she asked.

"Up," Rick said, climbing the stairs. "A friend of mine owns this building. Every year he has a Christmas party on the roof." He reached the top and opened the door.

She followed him out and stopped. Rockefeller Center, lit up in all its holiday glory, was directly in front of them. "It's beautiful," she said, impressed that he had taken the time to show it to her.

He moved closer, holding the umbrella over her head. Their eyes locked. After a moment's pause, he broke the trance and looked away. "I should get going."

"Me, too," she said. "I promised my Gran that I would bring back a tree tonight."

"By yourself?"

"I always do it by myself."

"I guess I shouldn't be surprised. If any woman is capable of carrying a tree home by herself, it's you. Come on," he said, taking her arm. "Let's go get that tree. There's a place I know on Lexington. It's a short walk from there to your apartment."

"But what about your car—" she said, surprised by his offer.

"I'll come back for it."

"You don't have to help me."

"I insist," he said. "Who knows? Maybe it'll help me capture some Christmas spirit."

"Then you have to take back your coat," she said, staunching his protests.

When they made their way back outside, Lessa stopped. The rain had turned to snow. "Look at this," she exclaimed excitedly as she stretched out her hand to catch a snowflake. "A perfect time to get a tree."

He put away his umbrella and, declining a cab, together they walked through the white-dusted world.

The Christmas-tree place could be seen and heard from a block away. "Here Comes Santa Claus" was playing over a speaker, and blinking, multicolored lights stretched from a lamppost to the greengrocer/tree store. A giant plastic Santa sat on the corner, smoking a pipe and watching over the festivities. Usually, picking out a tree was something Lessa did fairly quickly, as if knocking a chore off her list. But not tonight. Tonight she was more than happy to take her time. The salesman pointed to a fat evergreen and said to Rick, "Why don't you get your sweetheart the best tree we have?"

Lessa began to correct the man, but stopped. What

difference did it make if a stranger thought they were lovers?

Rick just grinned and said, "How about it, sweetheart?"

"If that's what you want, dear," she said, playing along.

Before she could stop him, Rick had bought the Christmas tree. "You didn't have to do that," she said.

"I have a secret motive. I wanted to get first dibs on the front. You take the stump," Rick said, holding on to the prickly part. "And lead the way."

Actually he had the tree more or less by the middle and was hefting the majority of the weight. "But you've got the worst part."

"First dibs, remember? No argument."

She smiled at his gallant act, accepted his kindness and started down the sidewalk.

"You usually do this by yourself?" he asked.

"I usually don't pick the biggest tree on the lot."

He laughed and raised it over his head to avoid hitting some fellow walkers. She knew the tree was heavy but Rick made it seem as light as a feather. Once again, she remembered the muscles she'd seen in his arms and torso. She had no doubt he was capable of carrying the whole tree and more. The shrill ring of a cell phone cut off her thoughts. "Hold on a second," Rick said, putting down the tree. He swung open his phone. "Hello." His voice visibly softened. "Yeah, I'm sorry about that. No, don't leave. Give my apology to your family. I'll be there as soon as I can."

She felt her heart drop. It was a woman, that much was obvious. And whomever she was, she was waiting for him with her family. Why had he told Lessa he wasn't seeing anyone right now? Had he lied to her?

"This is it," she said, nodding toward her brownstone.

She buzzed herself in and together they carried the tree up the flight of stairs to her apartment. The smell of pine filled the hall as her thoughts drifted back to the woman who had called, the one who was waiting for him. Lessa couldn't believe she had actually admitted to Rick that she wished for someone to kiss under the mistletoe. Regardless of what he had said, she doubted he was ever lacking a date under the mistletoe, love or no love.

She unlocked her apartment and led him inside. "Right in the corner," she said. The tree barely made it, skimming the ceiling. "Perfect," she said. "Now it feels like Christmas."

Rick's black cashmere coat was covered with needles. Without thinking, she brushed them off and said, "Thank you."

"I'll see you tomorrow," he said. Then he leaned toward her and for a split second she thought he was going to kiss her. Instead he brushed a piece of wet hair away from her lips.

It was an act of intimacy, a lover's touch. She forced herself to move, determined to mask her inner turmoil with a deceptive calmness. Too tongue-tied to say anything, she opened the door.

He smiled but there was something in his eyes that gave her pause. A sadness. With her heart in her throat, she said, "Have fun tonight."

Rick barely made it to the awards dinner in time.

"Where have you been?" Betty asked as he hurried though the door. "I thought you were going to be here at eight."

"I was…delayed."

"Delayed?" she asked, taking his coat and straightening his tuxedo tie. "I barely saw my family tonight. I missed our weekly dinner out because I was worried I wouldn't make it in time."

She had already told him that when she'd called. "I'm sorry," Rick said. "I ran into Lessa on the way out."

"So now it's 'Lessa,' is it?" Betty teased.

"She was on her way to get a Christmas tree," Rick said, ignoring her comment. "She needed help."

"Let me get this straight," Betty said, taking a step back and raising an eyebrow. "You were late to the New York Business Dinner because you needed to help Alessandra Lawrence get her Christmas tree? I'm shocked. You hate Christmas and everything surrounding it."

"This wasn't about Christmas. It was about helping someone."

"Surprise number two." She grinned. "You know, there's a rumor going around that you're falling for a certain chairwoman. I'm beginning to think there might be some truth to that."

Ever since he had returned from the Bahamas, he had been unable to stop thinking about Lessa. The woman he had gotten to know in the Bahamas was much more complex than the narrow-minded woman he knew from the office. He had seen her only occasionally since their return, but each time, his heart had soared. He had actually found himself looking forward to the office Christmas party simply because it would be an opportunity for him to spend time with her again.

When he didn't reply, Betty continued. "Unless it's

something else. You said you were determined to destroy her. Did you mean emotionally as well?"

Did Betty really think that he would seduce Lessa just to get revenge? "Is that what you think of me?"

"I know all about the fake romance, remember? And no one was around to see you picking out a tree. So what's it all about?"

"Am I up yet?" he said, glancing toward the stage as he checked his watch. He had been asked to announce an award.

"It's guilt, isn't it?" she said, ignoring his question. "She fell for you and now you feel guilty. And you should, too. Everyone knew she had a crush on you when she was young. You were her first love. I'm sure she's confused right now, poor thing."

"Poor thing? Just a week ago you were worried she was going to fire you."

"Well, she didn't. And she didn't even manage to fire you either. I just think she bit off more than she could chew. And now she's fallen in love with the man she thought she hated. She's probably imagining a romantic Christmas with you and her snuggled in front of a fire, and instead—"

"Betty," he said sharply, stopping her. "It's only been a week. She's not confused. She's got a lot of confidence. She's fully aware that this truce between us is only temporary."

"She may be saying that, but her actions proved otherwise, right?" She crossed her arms. "I can tell you right now that a Christmas tree is not going to be enough. If you feel bad about her getting her own tree, I can't imagine how you must feel taking away her company."

"I wish there was some other way to handle this, but there isn't."

Betty hesitated and said, "So you're going through with this?"

He didn't have to ask what she meant. He knew. Could he really destroy Lessa? "There's no choice."

Eight

She had just finished slipping her new red velvet dress over her head when Lessa heard a knock on the door. She glanced nervously at her aunt and said, "He's here and I'm not ready."

"Take your time," her aunt said, cracking her knuckles. "I'm looking forward to meeting this Rick Parker."

Her aunt's gracious words didn't fool Lessa. She knew that her aunt did not trust Rick, nor did she approve of her niece spending time with him...even if it was for the sake of Lawrence Enterprises.

"Be nice," Lessa pleaded. "Please. Remember, he is responsible for the biggest tree you've ever had."

"I just have a few questions for him," she said in her sweetest, little-old-lady voice.

Lessa yanked a pair of stockings out of her dresser. How had she gotten so far behind schedule? She had left work promptly at five, hurrying to the store to buy a new dress for the party. But she had made one simple mistake: She had taken her aunt with her. And when her aunt had asked to stop at Rockefeller Center to see the tree and the skaters, Lessa had been unable to say no. Nor had she been able to say no when her aunt had mentioned that she was getting hungry and had asked if they could stay for tea. Lessa had had the feeling that Gran was half hoping that Lessa would miss her date altogether.

She finished pulling on her panty hose as she heard the elderly woman say, "You must be Rick Parker. I'm Virginia Lawrence. My friends call me Ginny but you can call me Virginia."

Oh dear. "Rick!" Lessa called out. "I'll be right there."

She grabbed a brush and ran it through her hair. Then she thumbed through her makeup drawer, looking for a lipstick.

But Gran was just getting started. "I'm the aunt of your old boss, the man you fired, and the great-aunt of your new boss, the one who fired you."

Lessa grabbed the lipstick and swiped it across her lips. Good enough. "Sorry for keeping you waiting," she said, practically jumping into the foyer.

"No problem," Rick said. "I was glad to have an opportunity to meet your aunt."

Gran smiled sweetly, but she didn't fool Lessa for a minute. Lessa knew she had her talons out and was ready to let it rip. "Don't wait up," Lessa told her.

"You'll see her home tonight," her aunt said to Rick, as if placing a demand.

"Of course," Rick said.

She turned back toward Lessa and said, "Try and have some fun dear," as if she knew there was no possible way Lessa would be able to do that.

"Maybe you could make some cookies or something while I'm gone," Lessa said with a wink. "Something grandmotherly."

"Maybe I could give you a good kick in the—" Lessa shut the door before Gran could finish.

"She's very funny," Rick said.

"I don't know about funny but she's feisty. I'm sorry if she was insulting."

"I can't say I blame her. After all, she thinks I fired her nephew."

"You did fire her nephew."

"Lessa," he said with a hint of exasperation as he led her to his car. She had expected something flashy and she was mildly relieved to see he drove an SUV. As she climbed inside, she couldn't help but wonder how many other of his women had sat in the very seat she was in. He climbed in beside her and shut the door. "We've been over this. I didn't fire your father."

She was not anxious to start this argument again. Not right then, at the start of their fake date.

He sighed and she knew he was not going to let it drop. "I was traveling almost nonstop back in those days. I had no interest in office politics. One day, I got a message stating that your father wanted me to return immediately. When I got back, he told me that he had heard from a reliable source on the board that some members were unhappy with his performance. He said he had even heard they had already picked out a successor. He asked me what

I knew, and I told him. Nothing. No one had spoken to me about getting rid of him or replacing him. That night I got a call from Ward Harding. He said that the board had voted and it was unanimous. They had fired your father."

Lessa glanced out the window at the thought of the pain her father must have felt. Ward Harding had once been one of his closest friends. "Only then did Ward ask if I would be interested in replacing your father."

"And you said yes."

"No. I needed time to think about it. I liked the travel and I had no desire to get swept up into office politics and become a manager. But when I found out what they planned on doing to your father, breaking their contract and giving him only a pittance of what he deserved, I felt I had no choice. Assuming the presidency was the only way I could help him."

She would have liked to believe that Rick was totally selfless and that his assuming the presidency had been a personal sacrifice, but try as she might, it was a hard nut to crack.

"Believe it or not, that's the truth," he said, his blue eyes radiating sincerity.

One thing was clear. She *wanted* to believe him.

"He thought you lied to him. That you were the one who convinced the board to fire him."

"He needed someone to blame. And he preferred me to his oldest and dearest friends."

She thought about the uptight, stuffy board over which she now presided. Ward, Franklin, Constance, John, men and women she'd known since childhood. And she wanted to throttle them.

But it was the night of the Christmas party. She

wasn't about to ruin it by picking a fight with an old, opinionated and ridiculous board member. She had to change the subject. She had to prepare mentally for the task ahead of her. After a few moments of uncomfortable silence, she said, "By the way, I really appreciate what you did last night, helping me with the tree."

"It was my pleasure."

"I hope you got to your date all right. She wasn't too mad at you, was she?" Lessa managed to say as nonchalantly as she could.

"My date?"

"I overheard you on the phone last night—"

"I hardly think a business dinner with Betty counts as a date," he interrupted.

"Betty?" Lessa felt a surge of relief. His secretary was the mystery woman?

"Of course. I always make Betty go to these functions and she always complains. As she is always reminding me, she doesn't need another man to take care of."

"What's the game plan for tonight?" Lessa asked, feeling suddenly refreshed, as if a weight had been lifted from her shoulders.

"Look, Lessa," he said, "I know you're not happy about this ridiculous pretend game. But I really think it will work."

How wrong he was. She was actually beginning to enjoy this game. "I hope so."

"Tonight I'm going to try and make this as easy for you as possible. I don't think we need to fall over each other. I think it's enough that we show up and leave together."

"Good," she said as enthusiastically as possible. How

could she tell him that she had been anxious for another opportunity to kiss him?

They drove the rest of the way in silence, until they pulled into the parking garage and he said, "Wait for me to open the door and help you down."

"I thought you said no open displays of affection."

"I'm not worried about what others might think. I just didn't want you falling out. It's kind of steep."

"I think I can handle it," she said. She thought back to Sabrina's story about how she'd met Rick when he'd carried her off the boat. He was obviously used to the fragile type. "I used to do plyometrics—jumping up and down off a step while holding a medicine ball."

He nodded toward her shoes. "In heels?"

Just to prove her point, she swung her door open and jumped out. "Can't pass up a dare, can you?" he asked, walking around to greet her. He took her arm and together they walked inside the building next door. Lessa couldn't help but notice the shocked looks on her co-workers' faces when they saw Rick's arm casually looped through hers. They endured a strained elevator ride up to the main floor of Lawrence Enterprises. It was crowded with office workers dancing to the live band and enjoying the free-flowing champagne.

"Looks like your party is a success," he said into her ear.

"It's in full swing," she agreed. Standing so close, she could feel the sexual magnetism that made him so self-confident.

"Can I get you something to drink?" he asked, as if he really were her date.

"White wine, please," she replied. He smiled at her and she felt her insides turn to mush.

"What was that all about?" her assistant asked, approaching her after Rick had left. "Did you come here with him?"

"Yes," Lessa said quickly.

Fran looked at her silently, as if waiting for her to continue. Lessa liked her but knew that she couldn't confide in her. There was too much riding on the whole scheme. But she couldn't lie to her either. And so Lessa said nothing on the subject. Instead she glanced around the room and said, "They did a good job with the decorations."

"After you left today," Fran said, "we heard from one of the buyers in Antigua. He's ready to make an offer."

Lessa felt a surge of excitement as she thought about the property in Florida. Her dream was one step closer to reality. "Great. I just need to run it past Rick," she said casually, trying to minimize the importance of his approval.

"I hope he's not furious," Fran said. "Antigua's his baby, his pride and joy."

"It's not a baby, it's a property. And Rick is a businessman. He'll appreciate all my research and my hard work."

Fran shook her head. "The last person who tried to do this without his approval got fired. But then again, they weren't *friends*," she said, emphasizing the word.

Lessa felt a hint of anxiety. She suspected Fran was only joking about him firing her. But he could make things unpleasant. After all, he had before.

She glanced around the room. Where was Rick anyway? Wasn't he supposed to be getting her a glass of wine? "I don't want to talk about business. How does everyone seem to be enjoying the party?" she asked.

Fran shrugged, as if she weren't impressed. "The shrimp is good."

After Fran had left to check out the desserts, Lessa headed toward the inner office staircase. The offices of Lawrence Enterprises took up the top five floors of a downtown building. In her attempt to make this party special, Lessa had spared no expense. Each floor had been decorated and had its own private bar. She walked up the ivy-lined staircase and found Rick outside his office, deep in conversation with the head controller. She was just about to make her way over to them when she recognized one of the senior board members flirting brazenly with a woman young enough to be his grand-daughter. John Roberson was a nasty old man, one who had long been a thorn in her side. She glanced away, hoping to avoid eye contact. But it was too late.

"Look who's here," he said a loud and slurred voice as he made his way toward her. "The woman who sin-gle-handedly took ten points off our stock."

His remark had the intended effect. The crowd was stunned into silence. Lessa choked back her humiliation, aware that, once again, every eye was on her.

John slammed a big, fat finger into her chest and said, "Just because you studied history in school you think you're qualified to run a multimillion-dollar company?"

"Keep your hands off her," Rick said with a growl, stepping in front of Lessa.

"We made a mistake giving her the chairmanship," John said, his face red with anger. "The stock has gone down ever since."

"There were other factors at work."

"How can you defend her?" John asked. He shook his

head, disgusted. "Her father almost ran this company into the ground and apparently that's her intention as well."

And suddenly all the anger Lessa had felt regarding her father's shabby treatment burst to the surface. Her father had considered John Roberson a friend, yet according to Rick, he had betrayed him. "How dare you talk about my father that way," she said, clenching her fists as she took a step toward him. But Rick was too fast.

"Time to go," he said, grabbing John by the lapels and hoisting him away.

As Rick hustled John toward the elevator doors, Lessa glanced around at the crowd that had gathered to watch the fireworks. "Sorry about that, everyone. Go enjoy the party."

As the crowd slowly dispersed, misery set in. After all this work, what people would remember about the Christmas party was not the shrimp or the decorations or the fact that there was a bar on every floor. It was that the chairman of the board had almost punched a fellow board member. She made her way over to the bar and ordered a glass of wine. She had already drunk half of it by the time Rick reappeared.

"Thank you," she said.

He gave her a look that said all was not well. "Could I talk to you privately?" he asked.

She set down her wine and followed him toward a darkened hallway. Suddenly he pulled her into an empty office and shut the door. He turned on the light and faced her, his eyes dark and controlled. "Are you attempting to sell Antigua?"

"Not yet, no," she said calmly. "Although there is an interested buyer."

He took a step toward her. He was towering over her, his mouth set in a frown. "We're not selling Antigua. You've wasted your time."

"I found a property in Florida that has a lot of potential," she said, growing more uncomfortable by the minute. "It makes sense to sell Antigua now, before the other resorts on the island are developed. We could use the money to finance the Florida property. Anyway, I'm still getting my ducks in a row. I wanted to lay it all out for you."

"And what if I disagreed?" he asked. "We've ruined a relationship with whatever buyer you've strung along."

"I haven't strung anyone along. I told them exactly what the circumstances were."

She could see him hesitate.

"Let me show you what I've done. Give me a chance."

Before Rick could respond, the door flew open. The director of marketing entered arm in arm with the director of finance. When they saw Lessa and Rick standing in front of them, their jaws dropped in surprise. They moved away from each other. "We were just, um, looking for…some more napkins," the director of finance said quickly.

"So were we," Lessa said. "None in here." Rick followed her out.

"We can't talk here."

"Tomorrow morning. We'll discuss everything before I contact the buyer."

"Tomorrow morning won't work," Rick said. "I have a meeting that I can't change."

"Please, Rick, give me a chance. Let me prove to you that this will work."

He hesitated, looking at her sternly. She could almost see the inner machinations of his mind. "Then we'll do it now. Get your coat," he said. "I'll meet you downstairs."

Lessa found Fran on the second floor. "I have to go."

"You're going? You can't go! We haven't done the toast."

"You're going to have to take care of it. Rick and I need to discuss Antigua."

"You're *both* leaving?" she asked, her eyes widening.

"Yes, but—" But what? She couldn't very well deny an affair. So instead she shrugged her shoulders. "Thank you for taking care of things."

"Sure," Fran said, obviously stunned that the CEO and the chairman of the board would be leaving so soon and so together. "Have fun."

Fun, she felt like saying, was the last thing she would be having. She had never seen Rick so angry—not even when she'd fired him.

"All right," he said as they walked to the car. "Where to? Your place?"

Her place was not a good idea. She could just imagine trying to work with her aunt sitting at the table with them, making snide comments about Rick. "Your place," she said without hesitation.

Without saying a word, Rick turned the car toward his apartment.

Even though Lessa was the one who'd suggested that they go back to his apartment, Rick couldn't help but feel that this was a bad idea. It might have been okay if she weren't wearing a skintight red velvet dress that left little to the imagination.

But where else could they go? he asked himself defensively. Besides a restaurant, a coffee shop or any of the other million places that were available in New York City.

"How long have you lived here?" Lessa asked as they stepped inside the elevator in Rick's building.

He thought for a moment. "Five years."

Anger. He had to hold on to his anger. How could she presume to sell his property without even conferring with him first?

The doors opened directly into his apartment and they stepped out. He turned on the light. He took her coat, trying hard not to notice the curves beneath her dress. He hung up her coat as she walked over to the window and admired the view. She turned back to face him and asked, "Are you putting up a Christmas tree?"

"No. I never do. As I told you, I'm usually gone for Christmas."

"But you'll be in town this year," she said.

He would not allow himself to indulge in another personal conversation. It was too dangerous with them alone in his apartment. "Let's get to work, shall we?" he asked gruffly, nodding toward the table. She sat down beside him and began to talk.

An hour later, she looked at him and said, "Well? What do you think?"

He sat back, impressed. He had to admit that the proposal was not as farfetched as he'd initially thought. She had done her research. She understood the problem of the competing marketplace in Antigua as well as the potential and future worth of the property in Florida. "I'll take a look at this Florida property," he said after thinking it over. "Set up an appointment."

She smiled, obviously proud of her accomplishment. A lock of her hair fell over one eye and he had to stop himself from pushing it away. She may not have succeeded in convincing him entirely, but one thing was certain. He was not ready for her to go. He suddenly realized he was hungry. He hadn't eaten at the party and was fairly certain she hadn't either. "Are you hungry?"

"A little."

"I have a housekeeper who keeps me stocked with some basics. Or we can order in."

"Let's see what you've got," she said with a smile. He led her into the kitchen and opened the refrigerator door. She bent down and looked inside.

"Anything good?"

"You're right," she said. "Basics." She handed him a package of eggs. She put a block of cheese on top and grabbed a loaf of bread.

"Omelets?" he asked.

"No. I'm going to make a soufflé."

"A soufflé. Can you cook? I thought your aunt cooked for you."

"I've picked up a few tips along the way," she said with a smile.

An hour later, his apartment was filled with the warm, homey smell of fresh-baked biscuits and a fluffy soufflé.

When they sat down at the table, she waited for him to take a bite. "It's great," he said, eliciting a smile from Lessa.

There was something about her smile, something about the tenderness in her eyes that tugged on his heart. He felt a sudden surge of protectiveness, a desire to take her in his arms and protect her from the world.

And suddenly he remembered how he had felt when he'd made Karen smile. He could still see her laughing at the beach, her blond hair flowing in the wind. He had loved her with all the passion and naïveté of youth. But would their love have survived? If Karen had not died that day, would she still be beside him?

It was something he was ashamed to admit that he questioned. But how could he not? He had seen friends marry the woman they claimed to be madly in love with then file for divorce several years later. But, he reminded himself, those were his friends. He knew himself well enough to realize that he would never make the same mistake. When he fell in love again, it would be forever.

"Rick?" she asked and smiled. "Where did you go? You look so deep in thought."

"I'm sorry," he said. *Focus.* She was a business associate. The line was drawn. There would be no reprieve. But he couldn't help but wish otherwise. He remembered the way she had felt in his arms, the way she had looked up into his eyes. He had felt something, a stirring in his soul that he hadn't felt for years. But it was ridiculous. He could not have her. Never. His very career depended on it. "I should get you home," he said. "Your aunt will be worried."

"I'm not a child, Rick. I don't have a curfew."

What was that supposed to mean? "Just leave the dishes here," he said, standing. "The maid will take care of it tomorrow." He grabbed her coat and headed toward the elevator.

"Wait," she said, touching his arm. "Did I say something to upset you?"

How could he explain that he needed to get her out of there before he did something he would regret?

She stood in front of him, looking at him with her big emerald eyes. And then that damned lock of hair fell into her face again. But this time he didn't hesitate. He gently brushed it out of her face. And then she kissed him.

Nine

"I'm sorry," Lessa said quickly, breaking away. What was she doing? What had possessed her to kiss him like that? "I don't know what got into me."

But Rick did not look offended. There was electricity in the air as he gazed at her seductively. "Stay with me tonight," he said finally. He stepped toward her, trailing his hand down the side of her neck. She held her breath, closing her eyes as she enjoyed the delicious sensation. He tilted her head slightly upward, as if to kiss her. She felt her resistance fade away. He kissed her again, rough and hard. It was as if every part of her were on fire. She was powerless to do anything but give herself to him.

He took his time, intimately exploring her mouth. His tongue tickled and probed, claiming ownership. She arched against him, craving more. She ran her fingers up and down his back, feeling the strength of his muscles underneath his starched cotton shirt.

Her brain had long ago stopped working. Lawrence Enterprises seemed like a name from a distant past. All that mattered was what she was feeling right then and there.

She inhaled slightly as his hands slipped under her dress. His fingers made their way up her legs and sides, lightly touching her lacy bra. She arched her back, silently begging for more. Within a second, he had unhooked her bra and, with one hand, he began to finger the soft, plump flesh of her breasts while the other hand lifted her dress over her head. As her dress fell to the floor, he dropped to his knees in front of her, kissing the bare skin of her belly, working slowly, taking his time. He gently pushed her back onto the couch. As she sat against the smooth leather, he moved over her, working his way toward her breasts. He freed her breasts and took her nipple in his mouth, gently sucking and kissing. In one smooth maneuver, he removed her bra and leaned over her. In the light of the moon, she could see him stare at her, his eyes gazing up and down her body as if committing her to memory.

He reached his fingers inside the waistband of her panty hose, carefully taking them off. Still looking into her eyes, he slid his fingers in between her legs and underneath her panties. A ripple of excitement surged through her as she arched her hips. His touch was as light as a feather as he made his way toward her most sensitive point. The pressure slowly increased as he continued with his most intimate massage. She closed her eyes and her body began to surrender. "Let it go," he whispered. "Let it go."

When the release came, he silenced her cries with a kiss and cradled her in his arms, kissing her ear and brushing the hair, damp with perspiration, away from her forehead.

But if he thought that one orgasm was enough, he was wrong. It had done little to quench her desire for him. She was consumed with what it might feel like to have him inside her, to feel his naked body against hers. To have him make love to her.

"Your turn," Lessa said, staring brazenly into his eyes.

She unbuttoned his shirt, kissing his chest as she went. As he shrugged off his shirt, she kissed his neck while running the flats of her hands over his bare chest and down toward his belly. Her fingers slid over the hardness inside his pants, then reached for the zipper. He grabbed her wrist, stopping her.

"Are you sure?" he asked.

She had never been so certain in her life. "I want you to make love to me," she said, looking deep into his eyes.

He paused, as if giving her another chance to change her mind. She gave a tug on his pants and he kicked them off.

Like a Greek god, his finely carved body stretched out beside her. Every muscle seemed taut, as if his whole body were tense with desire. She ran her finger over his lips, working her way down his chin and his chest. As she moved down his belly and toward his hard self, she could see him swallow, fighting for composure. She took him in her hands, wrapping her fingers around him.

"I want you inside me," she said. "Now."

Staring deep into her eyes, he pulled her down beside him and skillfully flipped her underneath him. She opened her legs and he gently put himself inside her. He slowly began to move, thrusting deeper and deeper. She buried her hands in his thick hair as he kissed her, his lips hungry and demanding. It was unlike any sensation she had ever felt. Her body filled with a lush feeling of pleasure as she submitted her heart and soul to a primitive power.

Still pushing himself deep inside her, Rick stopped kissing her, hoisting himself up so that he could look directly into her eyes. It was even more intimate than a kiss. It was as if he could see directly into her soul. She fought off the climax that was threatening, desperate to maintain the luxurious tension between them. As if reading her eyes, Rick smiled slightly, and she could see his muscles tense. It was a dare to see who would lose control first. He gave a final thrust and together they relinquished control, releasing their bodies to pleasure.

When Lessa woke up, it was nearly two in the morning and she was naked on Rick's bed, locked in his embrace. She was filled with a feeling of bliss, a sense that all was right in the world. And then, just as quickly, the bliss did a one-eighty and turned into remorse. What had she done?

She had slept with Rick Parker. And not just once either. Twice.

He moved slightly in his sleep, his hand brushing against her bare breast. And just like that, the bliss was back. She was half tempted to reach under the covers and start everything all over again. But that would be a bad idea. If she didn't get home soon, her aunt would start to worry. Of course, she thought optimistically, she could call her and tell her she was, um, detained.

But that was a really bad idea. Because soon it would be morning and she would be forced to endure the official "morning after," complete with awkward conversation and embarrassing attempts to explain their behavior. Better to leave on a high note.

She slid out from underneath Rick's arm and scooted slowly out of bed. She grabbed her clothes and tiptoed quietly into the other room. She called a cab and dressed as quickly as she could. She arrived home and was thankful to discover her aunt sound asleep. She crawled into bed, her head spinning.

She had spent so much time hating Rick Parker. How could so much change so fast? As much as she was tempted to explain her behavior as an aberration, the truth of the matter was that she had known exactly what she was doing and to whom she was making love. And she hadn't cared one iota. It had been worth every single orgasm.

After a nap and a shower, she headed back toward the office, eager to return to the normalcy of work. It was only six o'clock, yet she felt certain that a long, hard day was just what she needed to snap her back to reality. But as she made her way through the office, occasionally passing a half-empty glass of champagne, she couldn't help but feel a little sad the evening was over. Although she knew she shouldn't, she couldn't help herself from wishing she could go back in time. That she could once again feel the strength of Rick's arms around her and the emotional power of their lovemaking.

She stopped. There, standing in her office, leaning up

against her desk as if waiting for her, was Rick. His normally slicked-back hair was tousled and he was unshaven, wearing jeans and a black turtleneck. He had, she thought, never looked so good.

"Good morning," he said.

"What are you doing here so early?"

He paused for a moment and said, "I came looking for you." He sighed. "I have a meeting and I wanted to talk to you before everyone else arrived."

But she didn't want to hear any I-don't-know-what-got-into-me excuses. That was exactly the reason she had left so early.

"Look, Rick," she said, raising her hand. "Let's not make a big deal about this. It happened. Let's just forget about it."

She thought she saw him hesitate. That was what he was going to say, wasn't it? She felt like kicking herself. Why had she cut him off? Why couldn't she just let the man speak?

"Forget about it? Is that what you want?" he asked.

"Yes," she said as confidently as she could, flashing him her best all-business smile as she sat behind her desk. "I thought I'd try and set up a look-through at Mara del Ray later today," she said, referring to the Florida property she had told him about. "I figure including air time, it would take us about eight hours."

"I don't think so."

"Rick, if you're worried about what happened last night, you don't need to be. It was just one of those things, a one-night stand, so to speak. We got it out of our systems and now we can move on." She tried to sound as casual as she could.

"It's not that," he said.

Well then, what was it? Was he still mad at her about Antigua? "I thought we worked out our difficulties last night. You said you were willing to look at the property and we have to do it today. I don't want to risk losing the buyers for Antigua."

"Look, Lessa. I have…another commitment this afternoon. A personal commitment. I can't make it."

Her heart fell. *Another commitment.* "What's her name?" she asked quietly.

He glanced toward her. "Her name?"

Normally she wasn't a masochist but, in this case, she couldn't seem to help herself.

He shook his head. "I don't have a date," he said. "Believe me, if that was the case, I'd cancel it. I have a family obligation."

She felt a sense of relief wash over her. *His family.*

He smiled and said, "My sister's getting married."

"On a Wednesday?"

"She wanted a Christmas wedding and it was the only time she could get the reception hall she wanted. It's a…well, a last-minute affair." He hesitated a moment and said, "Maybe you should come."

"What?" He wanted to introduce her to his family?

"Makes sense. The wedding's in White Plains at two o'clock. There's an airport in Westchester. After it, we'll leave directly for Florida. We should get there before sundown."

"I'd love to, but—" She hesitated. "Do you think it's a good idea? How's your sister going to feel about you bringing a co-worker to her wedding?"

"She knew she ran a risk having her wedding in the

middle of a work week. She'll just be happy that I'm there."

She saw herself surrounded by his devoted and loving family, all asking the same questions: Who are you and what are you doing with Rick?

"It's business," he said, summing it all up.

He made it sound so simple, as if meeting his family would be the most inconsequential event of the year.

Ten

Ten

Lessa arrived home shortly after lunch. She had given herself less than a half hour to get ready for the wedding and throw some items into a bag on the off-chance they ended up staying over. It was a time squeeze, but she had no choice. Her aunt had a lunch date and Lessa wanted to arrive home after she was gone so that she could postpone the confrontation she knew was coming. After all, she would have to confess her love affair to her aunt. She couldn't keep something that big a secret.

Unfortunately for her, Gran's lunch date had been postponed and she was still there when Lessa got home. As Lessa hurried to get ready, her aunt took a seat on the bed and wasted no time starting her interrogation.

"Well?" Gran asked impatiently. "I want details."

"The party was a bust. I certainly tried, but it doesn't seem to do much good." She pulled her blue dress over her head and said, "Sometimes I think I'm fighting a losing battle. I don't think anyone will ever see me as anything more than Howard Lawrence's daughter."

"You have to prove yourself."

"I haven't done a very good job so far. A board member accused me in front of everyone of destroying the company and I almost took him out. Nothing like punching an old man I could've blown over by whistling."

"Fire him," her aunt said defiantly, crossing her arms.

"I can't go around firing people. That's not going to solve anything. I think it was a mistake to fire Rick."

"I'm sure you do." Her aunt shook her head as she continued, grumbling, "You arrive home all disheveled at two in the morning. I wasn't born yesterday, you know."

"All right, here's what happened," Lessa said resignedly, taking a seat next to her. Whether she liked it or not, her aunt deserved an explanation. "During the party, Rick found out about my proposal to buy Mara del Ray. He was pretty upset so I volunteered to go over it with him."

"At his place?"

"We couldn't come here, you were sleeping. And the party was still going on at the office."

"So you went to his place."

"And…one thing led to another."

"You're not a virgin anymore?" her aunt asked calmly.

"Gran, I'm twenty-six years old. I haven't been a virgin for a long time."

"Tommy Winston?" her aunt said with a grin.

"Tommy Winston? No! I was in seventh grade when I dated him. We didn't even really date." In reality, she'd lost her virginity when she was in college, at the ripe old age of twenty-one, with Kevin Blane. He had been a popular fraternity boy with whom she'd had little emotional attachment. She had endured the whole thing with a let's-get-it-over-with attitude. They had slept together exactly twice.

"So now Rick wants to take you home to meet his family?" Gran asked. "Sounds serious."

"It's not like that. It only makes sense. I want him to see this property before sunset."

"And you couldn't take separate flights and meet him there?"

Gran had a point. "But there's only one corporate jet," Lessa said.

"So? You take the corporate jet and make him fly commercial."

"We need to go over everything first."

"I thought you did that last night."

"We discussed selling Antigua last night."

Her aunt raised her hands as if admitting defeat.

Lessa sighed. "It's no relationship, Gran. I don't think he's capable. And I know I'm not."

"You don't know that at all. You've never been tested. That's the problem. I always thought you were picky, just waiting for the right guy. Not the wrong one."

"I'm sorry, Gran. I know this seems strange. I spent all that time plotting revenge and thinking about how I was going to get rid of him. I hated him."

"There's a fine line between love and hate."

"I never thought this would happen. But I'm going to try and keep it all in perspective. I have to. I could be working with him for a very long time and I can't afford to be jealous or distracted."

"How in the world do you plan on preventing that?"

"I just can't allow it. That's all there is to it."

"I don't want you to take this the wrong way, Lessa, but how do you know that Rick didn't do this just to confuse you?"

"You think he slept with me just to bring me pain?"

"It's a possibility. It's also a possibility that it meant nothing to him."

"I don't think he did it out of spite, Gran. I know how I must sound, but he really isn't a bad person. Underneath it all, I think he's sweet and sensitive."

"I hope you're right, Lessa. I really do."

"I'm a big girl, Gran. I can take care of myself."

"You're going to have to if you insist on playing with pirates."

Normally, he would've been relieved to wake up and discover that his lover from the previous evening was gone. But not this time. It had only made him crave her more.

How had that happened? After all, Lessa was opinionated, stubborn and one of the most frustrating women he had ever encountered. But the truth of the matter was that underneath her bravado was warmth and tenderness. She had made him feel things he'd never thought possible again.

And so, when the opportunity had presented itself, he could not deny his mind or body the pleasure. But he would have to. As much as he was tempted to pursue their relationship, he had to agree with her. They would put the previous evening behind them. This was the only solution. After all, he was on the verge of winning back his company and firing her. As much as he might wish otherwise, Lessa did not belong at Lawrence Enterprises. She was resented and distrusted. The board would never again allow her any independence.

Although she was certain to be furious with him when she discovered that she had lost the company, in the end, he had no doubt she would be happier. She could take the money he paid her for her shares and start her own company. She would move on with her life, as he would with his.

But before then, he was going to introduce her to his entire family.

He must be crazy. After all, only a crazy man would do something so ridiculous. But it only made sense, right? They needed to go over their briefs before the meeting. They could do that on the plane.

Yeah, right.

The truth of the matter was that, like or not, he cared about Lessa. And, although they had promised each other that it was a single night, he was already longing for the moment when he could touch her again, when he could make love to her once more. He was not willing or able to go back to business as usual.

"Hello, Rick," Lessa said as she opened the door to her apartment. She looked beautiful. Her long hair was swept up, away from her face. She was wearing a blue dress that alluded to the beautiful curves underneath. "Come on in," she said, motioning for him to follow.

He glanced around nervously. "Where's your aunt?"

"She's not here. She went out to lunch with some friends."

He entered and shut the door. In the foyer, he looked

at the wall of pictures. They were old family photos featuring Lessa and her father. At the top was a picture of Howard with his arm around a woman who looked very similar to Lessa.

"That was my mother," Lessa said. "That was taken at El Vitro, their first property."

"Your mother was beautiful," he said. "She looks a lot like you."

"Thanks." She pointed out another picture. "There they are with me outside of my father's office. That was the day he incorporated Lawrence Enterprises."

From the pictures, Rick could almost feel his deceased boss giving him the evil eye.

Lessa put on her coat and grabbed an overnight case from beside the door. "Ready."

"Are you planning on staying a while?" he joked, nodding toward her bag.

"No," she said quickly, embarrassed that he might think she was plotting to get him alone. "After our last trip, I wasn't leaving anything to chance. I prefer my own swimsuit, thank you very much."

"I thought that other one looked kind of nice."

"Thanks," she said uncomfortably, ushering him out the door and down the hall.

They didn't speak until they were seated in his car. She asked, "So do you like the guy your sister's marrying?"

"Sure," he said with a shrug.

"You don't seem that happy about it."

Not happy about it? The truth of the matter was that his sister had suffered a nasty divorce that had been finalized only months before she'd met her new fiancé. Rick thought she was a fool to open herself up to more pain, but she was determined to be with her new love. And he gave her credit. "It's her business."

"Not a very romantic thing to say on the way to the wedding."

"Maybe not. But it's practical. She's been married before. You wouldn't know it though. She's going all out for this."

"She hasn't given up on love."

"Or maybe she'd just a glutton for punishment. She should've learned her lesson the first time."

"Does she seem happy?"

"That's how most relationships begin, don't they?" There were exceptions, of course, like his and Lessa's. They had begun as unhappily as most marriages end. What did that say for them?

They rode the rest of the way in silence, talking only when necessary. When they got to the chapel, Rick ushered Lessa past his stunned family, not stopping to introduce her. When he went back into the lobby, his sister said, "*You* brought someone? You actually brought a girlfriend to a family event?"

As a groomsman, Rick was required to work the crowd, seating people on either side of the church. Every now and then, he found himself glancing back toward Lessa. She seemed to be totally relaxed, busying herself by making conversation with the elderly woman next to her.

After the ceremony, Rick barely had time to say hello to Lessa before being whisked into the family photo session.

"I'll meet you at the reception," Lessa said.

An hour later, Rick and the rest of the wedding party

finally made their way across the street to the reception. As the bride and groom made their grand entrance. Rick scanned the room, looking for Lessa, but it soon became clear she wasn't there. He finally found her in the hall, helping an elderly woman out of the ladies room.

"This is Rick," Lessa said, introducing him to the woman.

"Oh, your wife has been so sweet to help me," she said. "I don't know what I would've done without her. My daughter was late and—"

"Here I am, Mom," a woman said, hurrying into the hall. She thanked Lessa profusely as she took hold of her mother's arm and helped her the rest of the way.

"Wife?" Rick asked when they were out of earshot.

"It was a misunderstanding. She knew I came here with you and she just made an assumption. I didn't see any reason to correct her."

"Look," he said, "I just have to stay for a little bit longer—"

"And who is this?"

Rick turned to see his parents were standing behind them.

"This is Lessa Lawrence," he replied.

His mother smiled and held out her hand. "How nice to meet you, Lessa."

"Lawrence," said his father, shaking her hand. "Any relationship to Howard Lawrence?"

"I'm his daughter."

"You're the one," his mother said, then looked at Rick. It was obvious by his mother's confusion that the only thing she had heard about Lessa was that she was a pain in the neck. Lessa smiled sweetly.

Rick felt the need to explain. "Lessa and I have a meeting later on. It makes sense to bring her here."

"I see," his father said. "Well, welcome, Lessa. It's very nice to meet you. You're so much younger and prettier than I imagined. Rick, you didn't do her justice." His father winked. "He told me you were pretty but he didn't say you were a knockout."

Her heart did a little flip as Rick winced. Rick had told them she was pretty?

As his parents walked away, Rick looked at his watch. "I think it's time to go."

"Don't be silly," she said with a smile. "We haven't even eaten yet. Besides, you don't have to entertain me. I'm perfectly fine by myself. Go be with your family."

A woman in a red bridesmaid dress came barreling their way. "Rick? Rick Parker! How have you been? I'm Jane Turner, remember?"

Rick shot the woman a grin that Lessa recognized immediately. Rick had no idea who the woman was.

"Would you dance with me?" she asked.

He glanced at Lessa, looking for help.

"Oh," the woman said, her face dropping. "Is this your date? I'm sorry. I thought your sister said you were coming alone."

"I'm not his date," Lessa said quickly. She turned to Rick. "Go ahead. Take your time. I'm fine."

Giving her a pained look, he walked to the dance floor with Jane Turner. Lessa went to the ladies' room and found Rick's newly married sister in there alone, struggling with her dress.

"Let me help," Lessa offered.

"You're Rick's date," Susan said with a smile. "I'm

so glad he brought you. How long have you two been seeing each other?"

"Actually, we're not really seeing each other. We work together. We have a meeting later today and it made sense to go directly from here." Before his sister could say anything, Lessa added, "I'm so glad I could be here, though. It was a lovely wedding."

"You're not seeing each other?" his sister asked suspiciously.

"Not technically."

His sister laughed. "Technically, huh? I saw the way he was looking at you. He appears quite smitten."

"We've only spent a couple of days together."

"So? I only met my husband three months ago. My mother married my father only six weeks after meeting him. Fast courtships are a family tradition. When Rick was engaged before, he proposed after only…" Her voice trailed off as she looked at Lessa. "You did know he was engaged before, right?"

Lessa nodded.

Susan smiled. "You see? I knew you were special. He must really care for you if he told you about Karen." She sighed and said, "We were all so worried about him after Karen's accident. He just withdrew from everything. Fortunately, he found that job. It was just what he needed. Or at least we thought so at the time. With him traveling to all those exotic locales, we felt certain he'd come home one day with a bride. But he hasn't dated anyone seriously since."

"Really? His reputation is as such a Don Juan."

"Oh, yeah. And he is, don't get me wrong. But I don't think all these casual relationships are what he really wants. He's like a nomad, wandering the earth. He's never around for family birthdays or holidays. He just gives a hundred percent to his job." She squinted her eyes. "Lessa Lawrence… Wait a minute. Aren't you the one who fired him?"

Uh-oh. "Yes. I was…well, not happy with what happened to my father."

"Rick felt bad about your dad. I remember him talking about it. But I don't think he had much to do with it, if that makes you feel any better. He told us that they were going to fire him whether or not he took over."

"I'm not sure of the details," Lessa said. She didn't want to get into this with his sister, that was certain.

"I bet you can find out. A lot of the board members are still there, right?"

They were and Lessa had done her best to check Rick's story. The board members she had spoken to had all told her the same thing. If Rick hadn't been there, they wouldn't have fired her father. "I would like to believe that he didn't have much to do with it," Lessa said. "But the truth of the matter is that he didn't stop it either."

"Did he have the power to stop it?" his sister asked. "From what I remember, they had already made their decision by the time they told him." She took Lessa's hand. "In any case, please don't hold it against him. I know he didn't want to hurt your father, or you, for that matter. He was numb back then, still reeling from Karen's death. Maybe he shouldn't have taken the job, but we all make mistakes, don't we? I've made my share." She leaned forward and said conspiratorially, "I was married before. It didn't work out, though. Have you ever been married?"

"Me?" Lessa laughed. "No."

"What's so funny?"

Why was she laughing? Because she had not even had a serious boyfriend. She couldn't very well go from not dating to getting married. "The concept of me having a serious boyfriend is funny, I guess."

"You and Rick sound like you're perfect for each other."

"I'm not like Rick," she said quickly. "I have the opposite situation. I rarely date."

"But you're dating Rick."

"Am I? I don't think so."

"You're dating. You're here, aren't you? I would bet you that he cares about you more than he's admitted. He never brings anyone to meet us."

"But we have to go to Florida—"

"Mumbo jumbo. He's had other meetings and inconvenient family obligations. He still never brought anyone."

There was a banging on the door. "Susan?"

"That's my husband," she said, her eyes lighting up. "Isn't he cute? Have you met him?"

"Yes. He seems very nice."

"Susan?" they heard again. "What in the world are you doing?"

She smiled and grabbed Lessa's hand. "Come on. Let me introduce you to the rest of the family."

Rick sat at the table, nervously looking around for Lessa. He had a feeling she was in trouble, and his fears were confirmed when he saw her arm in arm with his sister. He watched as Susan took Lessa's hand and proceeded to lead her smack into a group of cousins, introducing them one by one.

Rick's younger brother saw the interaction and laughed. "We're all intrigued by your mystery woman. Why didn't you tell us you were bringing someone?"

"Because I didn't realize it until this morning. And besides, she's not a date. She's a coworker."

"Sure," he said sarcastically. "This is me, Russell, your brother. I don't need the party line. Now, how long have you been seeing her?"

"She's the chairman of the board."

"Kind of young to be chairman of the board."

"My sentiments exactly."

"She's beautiful. And smart. And rich." Russell glanced at Rick again. "And she's not yours?"

"I already answered that question."

"So…you don't mind if I ask her to dance?"

"No," Rick said, his jaw tightening.

Susan came over, pulling Lessa by the hand. "Lessa and I were just getting acquainted."

"I think it's my turn," Russell said. He smiled at Lessa and said, "Would you like to dance?"

"I'd love to," Lessa said, accepting his arm.

As his brother led her to the dance floor and the two began moving to the music, Rick couldn't help but notice the way Lessa was smiling at Russell, as if she were actually enjoying herself. And his brother… Well, hell, he looked like he couldn't be happier. And why wouldn't he be? Rick remembered the way it felt to hold Lessa in his arms, to have her delicate arms wrapped around his neck. The way her breasts had felt against his chest.

Out of the corner of his eye, he saw his sister looking at him suspiciously. "Nice wedding," he said.

"I hope you like it," she replied. "It's my last one."

"I don't know," he teased. "Seems a shame to stop. You're just getting the hang of it. This was so much better than the first one."

"Very funny. But it's your turn next."

He laughed. "I don't think so."

They were quiet for a moment as he continued to watch his brother dance with Lessa. What the hell were they whispering in each other's ears?

"She's a beautiful woman," Susan said.

"What? Oh, yes. Attractive."

"She certainly caught Russell's eye."

"So it appears."

The music changed tempo, slowing down considerably. But instead of leaving the dance floor, Russell pulled Lessa close and rested his cheek against hers.

"Just a coworker, huh?" Susan said, motioning toward Rick's fists.

What was he doing? He relaxed his fists. He had no reason to be jealous. Lessa Lawrence was not his and never would be. "More than just a coworker. She's chairman of Lawrence Enterprises."

"Hmm," Susan said, smiling.

"What's that supposed to mean?"

"It sounds like you've got a Hepburn-Tracy thing going on. An office love affair."

"You're wrong."

"I know you. And I can see the way you're looking at her. You can't stop thinking about her, right? And I assume you've…held hands, so to speak."

"Look," he said. "I can guarantee this relationship is not going to go anyplace. She's arranged to give me half her stock in the company once this takeover threat is aborted. What she doesn't know is that I'll then own more than her."

"So you're going to fire her?" Susan asked. There was no mistaking the horror in her voice.

He paused. That was what he was going to do, right? "Yes."

"Rick," she said, shaking her head, "it's Christmas."

"Look, if there was any other way… But there's not." He had gone over it every which way. The truth of the matter was that he had no choice.

"But you care about her. I can see it in your eyes. Why can't you work together?"

"It's complicated." He didn't want to discuss it anymore.

"This is so typical of you. Dating someone that you think is safe. You only like relationships that come with automatic brakes. Did it ever occur to you to get rid of the brakes? Maybe you could have the ride of your life."

"I think you better lay off the champagne," Rick said.

She rolled her eyes and shook her head, frustrated. After a pause, she asked, "Are you going to Mom and Dad's for Christmas?" Every year his sister attempted to get him to come home.

"I don't think so," Rick said, sitting at the table. "You know how I feel about Christmas."

"It would mean so much to everyone if you were there. I thought that perhaps this year things might be different."

"Nothing's changed," he said, his eyes drifting back

to Lessa. With relief. he noticed that they had stopped dancing and were making their way back to the table. "You know what I say—"

"Christmas is for families and kids. Yes, I know what you say. But you're part of our family. And we would love it if you came."

"Hey, Susan," Russell said as Lessa sat down next to Rick, "Lessa doesn't have any plans for Christmas. I told her that she and her aunt should come to our house."

She was going to his parents' house?

"It might be better if I didn't," Lessa said, meeting Rick's eye. "After all, Rick and I work together...."

"He's never there on Christmas anyway. And the more the merrier. Besides," Russell said gleefully, "if the tennis club is open you promised to hit some balls to me." He looked at Rick and shook his head with disbelief. "You didn't tell me she beat Korupova. I saw that match on ESPN2."

"Good for you," Rick said stiffly to his brother. He turned toward Lessa and said, "I know my mother would love to have you."

"Russell, come with me," Susan said. "I need to show you something."

"What?" Russell asked. "What's so important?"

"Now, Russell."

"My brother's a great kid, isn't he?" Rick asked after Russell and Susan had left.

"Kid? He's a year older than me."

"He seemed to really like you." Rick hesitated and then asked, "So are you going?"

"Going where?"

"Christmas at my parents. He asked you, didn't he?"

"It didn't seem like you wanted me to accept his invitation."

"As they said, I won't be there. I don't care what you do. Outside of the office, that is."

She became quiet. Right away he regretted what he'd said. How could he tell her that he did care? That he didn't want her going near his brother or any other man? That she belonged to him.

She raised her hands. "What do you want from me? To not talk to anyone? That's why you're upset, isn't it?"

"Don't be ridiculous," he said gruffly.

At that moment, a team of waiters began serving, and the table soon filled with fellow guests. As he attempted to enjoy his meal, Rick found himself looking at Lessa. Seemingly relaxed and happy, she regaled the table with stories of her tennis exploits. Several times, she glanced at him and smiled, causing warmth to spread through him.

He poured her champagne and picked up his glass as they toasted the happy couple. He found himself wondering if he would ever walk down this road. It wasn't that he had completely written off the idea of marriage. It was just something distant, out there, that he felt he would address when it hit him.

Lessa, however, was the type of woman who would not stay single for long. Some man, some lucky man, would find her, and when he did, he would never let her go.

What the hell was happening to him? They had shared one night. One damn night. Yet the vision of her was seared into his mind. He couldn't forget the way she had felt in his arms, the smell of her, the feel. He had only one option. He would go to Florida with her as agreed. And then he would stay the hell away.

Eleven

Located on the Gulf of Mexico, Mara del Ray had been built in the 1970s and had immediately become a leading resort, frequented by the rich and famous. But in the 1990s its allure had faded. Although still open for business, the present owner had done little in terms of upkeep and renovation. It was almost dark when Lessa and Rick arrived, but even in the dim light, it was obvious that the buildings were in need of paint and repairs. Some still had visible hurricane damage. But, as Lessa discovered, the property, although over-grown, was still lovely. A white sandy beach ringed with palm trees offered a spectacular view of the Gulf of Mexico.

"You have to use your imagination," she said after the owner had given them a tour.

Rick could see immediately why Lessa was interested. Although the buildings would need to be completely refurbished, the setting was one of the most romantic he had seen. But an Antigua, it was not.

He turned toward the owner. "Could we have a moment alone, please?" After the man stepped back, Rick said, "I don't think this property is going to work."

"Why not?"

"Because it's going to take a lot of money to get this place up to our standards. And where are we going to get the start-up capital?"

"From Antigua."

"I don't want to risk a known quantity on this."

"Perhaps we should take it back to the board and let them decide."

"You should know by now that the people on the board are no friends of yours."

"All right," she said, in an obvious attempt to be fair, "why don't you tell me what your concerns are so I can address them."

"I already did."

"This has nothing to do with Antigua, does it? This has to do with who's in charge."

"I'm all for picking up cheap properties and turning them around. Unfortunately, this property is neither cheap nor is it capable of being turned around."

"We're interested, " Lessa said, signaling the owner back over. "Very interested. But my partner and I have to discuss it further."

"We have two other bids," the owner said. "Not much time for discussion."

"It's hard to see in the dark," Rick said. "For all we know, this place could be falling down around us."

"Stay here tonight as my guests," the owner said. "In the morning you will see that it is every bit as beautiful as it is at night."

"There's an idea," Lessa said cheerfully.

It was an idea, but not a good one. "I can't," Rick said. "I have to get back."

"Please, Rick," she said. "Like you said, how can you make a decision when you can't see what you're buying?"

As he looked into her deep green eyes, he could feel his resolve fade. His phone rang and he flipped it open. It was Betty, calling with good news. Sabrina was ready to sell. He snapped shut his phone and said, "We heard from Sabrina. She wants us to meet with her tomorrow morning."

Lessa's face lit up. "We did it," she exclaimed, spontaneously throwing her arms around him. He held her stiffly, trying hard not to enjoy the feel of her body pressed up against him.

As if suddenly realizing what she was doing, she stepped back. "I'm sorry. I guess I got a little carried away."

"You have reason to be excited," Rick said. "Apparently Sabrina is also interested in this property. I have a feeling that when she heard you and I were coming to look at it together, it convinced her we were romantically involved."

"It's foolish to go all the way back to New York when we have to be in the Bahamas tomorrow morning," Lessa said. "It makes sense to stay here tonight. In the morning we'll give this property another look and then head over to see Sabrina."

Telling himself that he had no choice, he acquiesced.

They followed the owner back into the lobby. "I have the perfect room," the man said, grabbing a key at the front desk. "Facing the ocean. You will get a true feel for the resort."

"That's rooms," she said, correcting him. "We need two rooms."

The man looked at Rick. "But I thought—"

Rick shook his head. "Two rooms." As far apart as possible, he felt like adding.

They followed the owner down the hall and back outside, to a two-story stucco building located just steps from the beach. The owner slid the key into one lock and then another. "Adjoining rooms," he said, opening both doors at the same time.

"That's not necessary," Lessa said.

"Oh," the owner said, disappointed. "But these are the two best rooms."

"They'll be fine," Rick said, walking into his room. "Thank you."

He shut the door and immediately opened the adjoining door that separated the rooms.

"What are you doing?" she asked.

"I don't like you staying in here by yourself. We'll keep the door open."

"Rick," she said, "we agreed that last night was—"

"Believe me, Lessa, I have no intention of repeating anything. But I feel a certain…responsibility to return you to the company in one piece. Now," he said, turning the light on in the other room and setting up his computer. "We have some work to do. We need to track down the board and set up a meeting for when we return." He knew it wouldn't be easy. Most members had left town for the holidays and were spread out across the country at their various vacation homes.

He heard Lessa go into the bathroom. When the door opened, he glanced up and, as she walked past, he caught a glimpse of skin. A lot of skin. "I'll see you later," she called out.

He jumped up so fast he almost knocked his computer off the table. "Where are you going?" he asked, heading into her room.

"I'm going to take a quick swim," she said, wrapping a towel around her waist.

"It's not safe."

She rolled her eyes. "I'll be back soon," she said, shutting her door. He ran his fingers through his hair and rolled his neck. What the hell was happening to him? He sounded like a cross between a doting father and a jealous lover. What he didn't sound like was a businessman who was on a trip with a coworker.

But he didn't like the idea of Lessa walking along a deserted beach at night. He didn't care if they were in paradise, sometimes things happened. Some guy might get the wrong idea. And what about the water? Who knew what dangers lurked in there? More than one swimmer had been lost in a riptide. It was ridiculously stupid to go swimming by oneself.

And just like that, he was out the door after her.

It was nearly ten o'clock and the beach was deserted. It was a clear night and the sky was littered with stars. "Lessa!" He scanned the water, looking for her. Damn. Why had he been so pigheaded? It was he who would be responsible if anything happened to her. "Lessa!" he yelled again.

He saw her in the distance, swimming back toward shore. He felt a surge of relief as he picked her towel off the beach.

She stood up in the water, her long body glistening in the moonlight. He stood on the shore, watching her walk toward him. She looked like a beautiful mermaid come to life.

He had every intention of handing her the towel and heading back to the room. Instead, he gently wrapped the towel around her shoulders. She touched his cheek and then he saw the hunger in her eyes. It was all he needed.

Like a lit match to an oil slick, the passion he had been trying to hold at bay burst forth. With a hint of desperation, he pressed his lips against her, hungrily claiming what he desired. He ran his hands down the front of her swimsuit, feeling her nipples harden with his touch.

Suddenly, she broke away and stepped back. "I thought we agreed this was supposed to be a one-night affair."

"There's a problem with that whole one-night thing."

"Problem?" she said weakly as he kissed her long and slender neck.

"Well, there's a lot of problems with it," he said, and with that, he swept her up into his arms.

As he carried her back to the room, she relaxed against him, resting her head on his chest. He kicked open the door and set her down on the bed.

Her hair was tousled by the wind, her cheeks still flushed from his kisses. She looked beautiful and wild, a woman possessed with an almost ethereal natural beauty. Staring into her eyes, he slowly peeled down her suit so that he could caress her breasts. Her head tilted backward and she closed her eyes as he touched her. Within seconds he had her completely naked, her form illuminated in the soft light. He took a moment, his breath ragged as he took in the sight of her long legs and voluptuous curves.

She gingerly ran her fingers across the starched linen of his shirt. Looking him in the eye, she took on the role of temptress. She ran her hands down his front, a smile touching her lips as she pressed against the hard mound in his pants. She unzipped them and took him out, caressing him with her fingers.

Lessa knelt over him and guided him inside. She moved above him like a woman possessed, determined to seek her own pleasure. He watched her carefully, controlling his own desire until she inhaled sharply and her body trembled with release. Only then did he let himself share in the pleasure.

As Lessa kissed him tenderly, he wrapped her in his arms.

"What have you done to me?" he whispered. "What have you done?"

The next morning, Lessa woke up in a tousled mess of sheets. Unlike before, she felt no urge to sneak away. She was happy right where she was, nestled in Rick's arms.

"Good morning," he said, running his finger across her bottom lip.

"Morning," she said, nestling even deeper into the crook of his arm as she listened to the sounds of the hotel coming to life. A breakfast cart being wheeled past their room, a mother scolding her children. A shower was turned on; an alarm clock was turned off. In fact, she could hear…well, everything.

"These walls certainly aren't soundproof, are they?" she said.

"I'll have to sneak you out of this hotel after last night. I'm surprised no one called security."

She laughed and then fell silent.

"It's too late for regrets," he said.

"I don't have any regrets."

He kissed her on the lips. "I'm glad to hear that."

She leaned over him, glancing at the clock on the table. It was almost time to go. As if reading her mind, he said, "I guess we should get going."

"You first," she said, nodding toward the bathroom. "I just want to lie here for a minute."

He gave her a kiss and then, reluctantly, broke away. As she watched him walk into the bathroom, she couldn't help but wonder how long it would be before she saw a man naked again.

The pit in her stomach, the emptiness that was filling her heart…it was all about sex, right? No. The sex had been amazing, no doubt about it. But the impending dry spell would not cause this kind of pain. It was Rick she would miss.

She was suddenly overcome with sadness. She couldn't help but wish things were different. Wish that perhaps they had met under different circumstances. If they didn't each carry their own complicated baggage, would they have had a chance? She didn't know. The only thing she was certain of was that he was still there and still naked.

She heard the shower going and followed the sound into the bathroom, opening the shower door. His thick hair was slicked back. He looked like he was ready for a black tie affair, minus the tux and undergarments. He smiled his sexy half grin and held out his hand toward her.

She stepped inside. The water beat down as she ran her fingers up and down his naked and wet torso. She could see his shaft grow heavy as he pressed against her. He took the soap and slid it around her back, up and down her legs. He reached between her and fingered her as the warm water beat against them. Only when she thought she couldn't take it anymore did he lift her up and enter her, holding her against the side of the shower with his bare strength.

Afterward, he wrapped the towel around her shoulders and kissed her. "I'm liking this hotel more and more."

A knock sounded on Rick's door. "Mr. Parker? Are you ready for your tour?"

They dressed hurriedly and headed back outside. A steamy heat and the threat of a storm welcomed them. As they were led around the property, she couldn't help but notice the change in Rick. Perhaps it was their lovemaking or perhaps just the knowledge that Sabrina was ready to give them their shares, but Rick was joking, even laughing with the owner as he offered Lessa suggestions on ways they could improve the property.

As she walked by Rick's side, she thought about her parents and how they must have felt viewing their first property. It wasn't the same, of course. Rick, unlike her father, had been doing this for years and was at the top of his game. But this was her first property, the first one that she had discovered and wanted to buy, and she felt an excitement in the air. A big what-if.

And although, in the end, Rick did not agree to purchase the property, he at least agreed to consider it. She knew that whatever decision he made, she would have to trust him. For the first time ever, she saw a light at the end of the tunnel. He was her partner but he was also much more. He was her friend.

Twelve

As Rick watched the world disappear beneath them on the flight to the Bahamas, he thought about the previous evening and something became painfully clear: He could not take this company away from Lessa.

He had gotten too involved and there was no turning back. This was no simple affair. He could not hurt her.

So what should he do?

He had already bought the stock; their contract was signed a week ago. Once Sabrina sold him hers, he would automatically be the new owner of Lawrence Enterprises. He would then officially give Lessa back her stock and, at the board meeting, he would announce his support of her chairmanship. If Lawrence Enterprises was what Lessa wanted, it was exactly what she would get.

Their flight arrived shortly before noon. Sabrina had

sent a car and together they drove to her office, where Sabrina was waiting for them. She leaned over her desk in front of Rick, causing her cleavage practically to fall out of her shirt as she pretended to sort through some papers.

"Well, well, well. It's so nice to see you again."

"I can't tell you how happy we were to receive your phone call," Lessa said.

She raised an eyebrow. "I bet you were."

She motioned toward the chairs, encouraging them to sit. "Can I get you something? Tea? Coffee? Water?"

"We're anxious to sign the contract," Rick said.

"I have it right here," she said, waving it in front of them. "Before I sign it and we make this all official, I wanted to take a moment to congratulate you both on your ridiculous performance. Although I must say, Lessa dear, you were a little stiff. But your trip together to Mara del Ray was a very nice touch."

"I'm sorry?" Lessa asked.

"You, Rick, however, almost had me convinced. There was a look in your eye, one that gave me pause." She laughed. "But you, Lessa…I never quite bought it. Then again, you had a much more difficult job. After all, how could you take up with the man who ousted your father? But I was willing to give you the benefit of the doubt." She shrugged her shoulders. "I'm such a romantic at heart. And of course, everyone knows that for some, love is blind. Also, having tasted the goods myself, I know how, well, persuasive Rick can be." She stood before Rick and caressed his cheek. "And now that you got what you wanted, Rick, and you're through with Alessandra, perhaps you and I can rekindle what we once had."

Rick froze. Sabrina knew. "Sign the contract," he commanded. "Now."

"What's going on?" Lessa asked.

Sabrina looked at Lessa and flashed her an evil smile. "Is it possible she doesn't know what you've done, Rick?"

"I bought some shares, after you fired me," Rick said to Lessa.

"Some shares?" Sabrina said. "How modest."

"Things have changed since then," he said to Sabrina.

"I'm afraid you've been double-crossed, my dear," Sabrina said to Lessa. "But don't feel bad. I have all sorts of people working on this and I just found out myself this morning. Unfortunately it doesn't change much for me. Because once Rick gets your shares, he'll be quite invincible."

Lessa glanced toward Rick, as if looking for some sign of reassurance that Sabrina was making the whole thing up.

"Lessa," he said, "I have several other business ventures. Each one of them bought a significant share of stock during the period of time I was not working for Lawrence."

"Spell it out, Rick, for God's sake," Sabrina said. She turned to Lessa and explained, "Once he gets your stock he'll own the majority. Enough to wield significant control, like making himself chairman and CEO."

Lessa sat silent, her eyes blazing with the pain of betrayal. "You were going to fire me?"

What could he say? Until he'd gotten involved with her, he had hoped to do just that. But everything had changed. "Originally, yes. I felt as if I had no choice. But I've since changed my mind."

He could tell from the look in her eyes that she did not believe him. He wanted to take her in his arms and get her the hell out of there. To prove to her that he was sincere.

"Actually, Lessa," Sabrina interjected, "considering the recent turn of events, I'm hopeful that you and I might work out a deal. You only have to give him the company back if he prevents a takeover, correct? Which is dependent upon me selling you my shares."

And suddenly he saw where Sabrina was going with this. She wanted to take advantage of Lessa's emotions to try and talk her out of her stock.

"We're two women who have been betrayed by Rick," Sabrina continued. "Sisters in pain, so to speak. Sell me your shares. Give *me* the company instead of Rick."

Lessa appeared to hesitate. She couldn't really be considering this, could she? "Lessa," he began, "I didn't want to hurt you."

"He betrayed not only your father, but you," Sabrina said. She grabbed the contract and ran it through her fingers, as if ready to rip it to shreds. She walked over and sat on the edge of her desk, directly in front of Lessa. "I sign this and he gets the company. Sell me your stock instead and I'll give you the same deal you were going to give me."

"That's enough," Rick said angrily to Sabrina. He took Lessa's hand. "I had changed my mind. I wasn't going to go through with it. You have to believe me. When I bought that stock you'd just fired me. I had no other options."

Lessa pulled her hand away and closed her eyes, as if fighting back the pain.

How could he have allowed this to happen? The last thing he wanted was for her to get hurt. "I don't want your stock anymore. We'll renegotiate."

Sabrina's voice snaked in. "Desperate words from a desperate man. You can't possibly believe him, can you, Lessa?"

"You're right, Sabrina," she replied. "I don't want to give this company to him. But I don't have a choice. I can't bear the thought of you breaking it up and selling it off piece by piece." She took the contract out of Sabrina's hands and laid it on the table. She picked up a pen and handed it to her. "Could you sign this, please?"

Sabrina hesitated before finally signing. She begrudgingly handed the contract to Lessa. "You just lost everything," she said. "For what?"

But Lessa didn't answer. She walked over to Rick and handed him the contract. "You worked hard for this." And with that, she walked out of the room and out of his life.

How could she have been so foolish as to believe he really cared about her, to believe he would not betray her? And finding out through Sabrina only added to her humiliation. How could he have done this to her? Tears stung her eyes as she hurried toward the car. Just as she was about to get inside, she felt a hand on her arm.

"I need to talk to you," Rick said, steering her toward a private area by the beach. "This is a misunderstanding."

"A misunderstanding?" She shook her head sadly. "You warned me, didn't you?" It had been a brilliant yet simple plan. A trap that she had walked right into. Did she really think Rick would ever agree to be partners, especially with someone he held in such low esteem? Their affair had been nothing but a distraction for him, an opportunity that she herself had offered. She didn't blame him so much as herself. She had been a fool.

"When I bought that stock we were not involved," he said.

"But after we were involved you didn't tell me, did you?"

"I didn't see any point until I could prove to you otherwise."

"You planned everything, right down to your own firing. You pushed me into firing you just so you could buy stock. And then when I asked you back, you knew that you'd be able to get rid of me."

"And I planned on firing you just as soon as I got my company back. That's all true."

"Revenge," she said softly. She had fired him and he'd planned on doing the same thing to her.

"But that was before I got to know you. Before I began to care about you."

She desperately wanted to believe him. But how could she? It might be another lie. The more she thought about Rick and Sabrina, the more she felt they deserved each other. Sitting there in that office, the two of them had been wily and frightening, firing each other, sleeping with each other, making deals behind each other's backs. It made her sick. Maybe she didn't have the stomach for this business after all. She needed a little time to digest all that had happened to her and consider her next move.

"When people care about each other, they help each other," she said. "They look out for each other."

"I'm giving you back your stock," he said, as if that made everything all right.

"I don't want it back."

"I'll pay you for it. I'll pay a premium. Whatever you want."

She looked into his eyes, desperately searching for some sign of the man she had grown to care about. She wanted to believe him, believe that this had all been a colossal misunderstanding, but how could she?

"You don't get it, do you? It's not about money. It never was."

Thirteen

It was official. She was lost.

Lessa scooted forward in her seat as she drove slowly down the two-lane dirt road in Connecticut, hurrying toward a board meeting in the middle of nowhere. On either side of the road was a landscape more appropriate for Halloween than Christmas: deserted farmlands, their brown, dried-out grasses blowing in the wind. Every now and then she would see a lone abandoned house or barn with the roof caved in. Lessa followed the winding road down a hill and found herself enveloped in fog. She turned on her fog lights and continued, slowly making her way through the thick, cotton clouds. She had agreed to have the meeting at this out-of-the-way location because it was Christmas Eve and many board members were already at their vacation homes throughout New England. This just happened to be the halfway point. But the last thing she felt like doing on Christmas Eve was driving around dirt country roads in search of an ornery board and their deceitful, if charming, president.

At the thought of Rick, her stomach turned over. This would be the first time she had seen him since they had returned from the Bahamas. Despite his repeated phone calls over the past two days, she had not spoken with him. What was the point? He had her shares. Although she had been a fool, he had played by her rules. And she had lost.

And now she had no choice but to resign her position on the board. It was ridiculous to think that she could stay on. After all, she had never fit in with the stuffy and shortsighted people she was surrounded by, the same people who had fired her father. And now that she had lost her stake in the company, why would they keep her on? They would not. It was time to bow out gracefully.

Unfortunately, it was proving easier to walk away from the company she had thought she loved than it was to walk away from Rick. She had barely slept all night, filled with dread at the thought of seeing him again. Instead she had walked the floor, analyzing and reanalyzing the situation. She didn't need Psych 101 to figure out what had happened. It boiled down to one issue: honesty. This whole thing could have been avoided if she had just been honest with herself. After all, did she really think that Rick would agree to be her partner? Did she really think that just because he had made love to her he would fall in love? Rick had remained honest to himself and his business. It was she who was the traitor.

She had underestimated his immense attraction. With one kiss, Rick could make a woman forget who she was and where she was going. It was the way he listened, the way he looked at her when she spoke. He made her feel as if she were the most interesting person in the world.

Time, she thought. She just needed some time to clear her head before seeing him again. She needed some time to think before even mentioning his name. But she didn't have any time. In fact, according to her watch, the board meeting had already started.

She thought of the scene that awaited her. Were the board members eager to give her the evil eye? Would they jump with glee when she informed them she was resigning? Or did they already know? Some, she suspected, had been aware of Rick's plan from the beginning. She was on her way out, Rick was back in power and the stock was already going back up.

She checked her watch once again and pulled out her cell. Still no reception. A psychologist would have a field day with this one. She, who was never late, was going to be late for her own resignation. Was her tardiness intentional? And why wasn't she more upset about leaving Lawrence?

True, her time there had not been happy. She had been fighting an uphill battle, one that had been doomed from the beginning. The only reason she'd had even attempted it was because of her promise to her father. She had never asked herself whether being a part of Lawrence Enterprises again was something she really wanted, because it did not matter. It was an obligation, something she had to do.

But she'd always known her aunt was right; if Lessa had succeeded at Lawrence, she would have paid a steep price. Lawrence Enterprises was a public company and she knew from her father's experience just how taxing and emotionally exhausting it was to run. There would always be someone looking over her shoulder, someone trying to take her place.

Perhaps she should think optimistically. It was very possible that this was a blessing in disguise. She did not want to work for someone else. She wanted her own company run by her own rules. Unfortunately, the whole experience made her wonder whether had she chosen the right business. Was she destined for a career in the resort industry? She had always thought that if she worked hard enough, like she had in tennis, she would succeed. But she had had talent on the tennis court. Was it possible she had no talent for this business?

One thing was obvious—hard work alone was not enough. Perhaps, she thought optimistically, all she needed was a little luck.

As if the forces were listening, her car suddenly began to shimmy. She fought for control of the car, yanking the throbbing steering wheel and pulling over to the side of the road. With a groan of despair, she hurried outside to inspect the damage. So much for luck. The right wheel looked like a deflated inner tube.

Lessa glanced around the desolate area as she tied her scarf more securely around her neck. Although the fog had cleared somewhat, a cold and bitter rain still fell. She headed around the side of the car toward the trunk. Her only hope now was that she would find a spare. And figure out how to use it.

Rick had been looking forward to this meeting. Since their return from the Bahamas, he had struggled to focus at work. He was like a man possessed. Lessa haunted his thoughts and dreams. The board meeting at least would provide another chance to explain himself to her, another opportunity to prove himself. He would succeed, he had no other choice. He did not want their relationship to end, not like this.

What had gotten into him? After all, wasn't the inevitability of the relationship's demise what he'd found so attractive in the first place? Wasn't this his pattern? Hadn't his sister accused him of only getting involved with women who were "safe"? Women who, for obvious reasons, he could never love? He had done this ever since Karen had died.

But this time, something was different.

He had never met a woman like Lessa. She was brilliant, determined and feisty. Not to mention her obvious physical attributes. She was a classic beauty, with eyes that seared right through a man, the kind that haunted his dreams. But she was more than a compilation of superficial qualities. There was a vulnerability that he saw in her, a sweetness that made him want to protect her from the world.

Rick checked his watch again, then glanced around the table. The board was getting agitated. Where the hell was she? His heart filled with dread. What if something was wrong? What if something had happened to her?

No. That was ridiculous. He was certain there was a logical reason for her tardiness. He checked his watch again.

"Let's vote," Ward said. "I think we have a consensus anyway. We don't need her here to fire her, do we?"

"We're not firing her," Rick said quietly.

"You can't be serious," John said. "We're certainly

not going to keep her on the board. Why should we? After all, thanks to you, she's got a minority stake. And we all saw what she did to the company. She almost led us to ruin."

True, Rick had once thought the same thing. The stockholders had made it clear they did not consider Lessa an asset. But they didn't know her. They, like the board, had not given her a chance. "You're all forgetting that I now own a majority. And I say she stays."

The room silenced as everyone looked at him, their faces drawn and pale. "You can't be serious," Ward said.

"I am serious."

"She doesn't even have the courtesy to show up on time."

"Maybe something happened," Betty said quietly, voicing his own fear. The muscles in Rick's neck tensed as the color drained from his face.

Rick pushed back his chair. He couldn't take this any longer. He stood up and began walking toward the door.

"Rick?" Betty asked. "Where are you going?"

"I'm going to find Lessa," he said. And before anyone could protest, he left.

Lessa glanced at the mud surrounding the tire. How was she going to do this without becoming a big mess? In an attempt to protect her suit she took off her pretty wool coat and laid it smack in the middle of the mud. She knelt down, fit the tire iron on a bolt and twisted.

Nothing. The bolt didn't move.

Droplets of rain splashed mud on her clothes as she heaved the iron once again. But her efforts were in vain.

She took off her gloves, as if her bare hands might do better. She tried another bolt and then another. Finally, Lessa put down the tire iron and leaned back against the flat tire still on the car. The freezing rain pelted her face and the cold wind whipped through her drenched clothes. But she didn't mind the rain. In fact, it suited her mood just fine.

The distinct whirring of a car engine filled the air. At the sight of headlights, she jumped up, ready to flag down the motorist.

The car pulled beside her and stopped. Her heart caught in her throat as she recognized the vehicle. Rick? In a sudden stab of vanity, she smoothed her mud-spattered suit. She tucked her hair behind her ears and licked her lips.

The car stopped and Rick jumped out. He stood there looking at her, his brow furrowed in worry, his features dark and handsome. The mere sight of him was enough to make all her angst flood to the surface. And suddenly, whether it was the stress of the morning or simply the stress of seeing him once again, she felt like crying. She bit her lip, trying to gain control of her emotions. She could do this. It was almost over.

"What the hell happened to you?" he asked.

She motioned toward her car. "I got a flat tire."

"Why didn't you call?" he asked, looking at the tire.

"No cell service around here," she said, shivering.

He shook his head, his eyes scanning over her. Once again she was aware of how she looked, the mud-spattered suit, the motley hair. She crossed her arms as he approached. She had imagined this encounter many times in the past few days. Would she slap him and insult him? Or act cool and collected, as if he and the company meant little to her?

"What is it with you and coats?" he asked.

"I used it to kneel on. I didn't want to get dirty."

He took off his coat and attempted to loop it around her shoulders.

"I don't want your coat," she said, stepping away from him. She didn't want to touch him or anything that belonged to him.

She might as well have slapped him. His eyes darkened and narrowed. "Get in the car," he said.

She might not have wanted to touch him or anything that belonged to him, but she was willing to make an exception when it came to his car. She picked her wet and muddy coat off the ground and followed his instructions, stepping into the warm vehicle.

He got inside and slammed the door. When he pulled the car back on the road, he said, "I've been trying to reach you."

Trapped in a car, she was helpless to escape his masculine power and deep, stirring sexuality. She couldn't look at him without seeing the lips that had made her forget her name, the hands that had caressed her so tenderly. She could almost feel herself once again falling under his spell.

"I need your account information," he continued, "so that I can transfer the stock back to you."

"I don't want it."

"Then I need your account information so that I can pay you for it."

Now she was getting it. He was afraid of a lawsuit, afraid that she would make a big stink at the company and drag down his net worth. Well, he needn't have worried. She had told him once that she was not a hysterical woman and she had meant it. She planned on walking away with whatever dignity she had left.

"Look, Lessa, talk to me. We need to communicate if we're to work together."

"We're not going to be working together, Rick. I'm a minority shareholder. There's no way I'm going to keep my position on the board."

"I'm giving you my support, Lessa. No one can do a damn thing about it."

"You mean, whether they like it or not, I'll stay on as chairman?"

"That's right."

"I don't want to work someplace like this, Rick. How would I justify my position? The president's mistress? Former mistress."

"So take back your stock. You'll be the principal stockholder once again."

"I don't want it back. It was a deal, Rick. Fair and square."

"You can't leave Lawrence Enterprises, Lessa. You said yourself that it's meant to be. It was what your father wanted. And the work you did on the Antigua/Florida deal was very good. You took charge of it and brought it all together without my help. I need someone like that."

"I'm resigning, Rick. It's my Christmas present to the board."

He hesitated. "Lessa, I bought Mara del Ray. It can be yours. To remake, do whatever you want."

So he had bought it after all. "You were smart to buy it. It's a good investment. You'll see."

"Lessa, think about this. You've wanted to be at the helm of Lawrence for years. Don't let your anger toward me get in the way of your dreams."

It was tempting, but she couldn't stay. She couldn't bear the idea of working side by side with Rick, knowing that he didn't care about her. That he never would.

"I thought you weren't a quitter," Rick said.

How dare he insinuate that she was giving up, admitting defeat? It was taking every ounce of courage for her to leave the company she had fought so hard for. "I have no choice. I realize now that although this company still uses my father's name, it's not his anymore. And it hasn't been for a very long time. It's your company, Rick. You worked for it. You deserve it."

"Don't do this, Lessa," he said, pulling in front of the building where the meeting was being held. "You can't walk away from something that you love."

"Thought I loved. But I was wrong." As she looked at him, she felt a stab of sadness. She was no longer talking about the company, but him.

"I'm not going to let you do this," he said, parking the car. "I'm not going to let you walk away like this. What will it take?"

"Why do you care, Rick?"

"Because I...I care about you," he said, taking her hands in his.

The words hung in the air. She wanted to believe him so badly. He slid next to her and pressed his lips against her, gently covering her mouth. She could feel herself letting go, her defenses melting away. She wanted to believe him. And she did. But it wasn't enough.

No matter what they did or how hard they tried, they

could never be partners at Lawrence Enterprises. Despite the fact that she had given it her all and had played the match of a lifetime, she had lost, and one thing she knew was how to accept defeat gracefully. There would be only one victor in this match. She pulled away from Rick and stepped out of the car. As she walked toward the inn, she felt as if her heart were breaking.

I will miss you, Rick Parker, she said in her mind. *I will miss you.*

Fourteen

That night, Rick did something he had not done in a long time. He went home. At least thirty people were crammed into his parent's small house and the result was bedlam. A fire was burning in the fireplace, an oversize tree was stuffed in the corner of the living room, torn pieces of wrapping paper were scattered about and presents were piled all over the place. Most of the children had escaped downstairs, but every now and then the door to the basement would fly open and a child would burst into the room, excitedly talking about Santa Claus. But Rick did not partake in any festivities. He stood off by himself, his mind focused on Lessa. Only hours ago, he had watched Lessa give away the company she loved. Up until the final moment, he had been sure that she would come to her senses and change her mind.

"I'm glad you're home," his sister, Susan, said, walking up to him. "I've forgotten how much fun you are." He knew she was teasing but he was in no mood.

She sighed and motioned for their brother, Russell, to join them. "Rick is in trouble."

"I'm not in trouble," he said. "I just don't like watching someone throw their career away."

"What did you expect?" Susan asked, "That she would go back to work as usual? You just swindled her out of her company. She doesn't want anything to do with you."

"So let her hate me. But giving away the company just hurts herself."

"For one," his sister said, "she hurt more than herself. She hurt you." She sighed deeply. "But I doubt that she realizes that. I'm sure she's convinced you care little for her."

"I tried to talk her out of this."

"I'm sure she felt as if she had little choice. She didn't exactly throw anything away. You took it. And by the time you changed your mind, it was too late. I understand completely why she did what she did. How can she go back to Lawrence Enterprises knowing that she will have to see you every day? It's just too hard."

"What happened after the board meeting?" his brother asked.

"She rode back to the city with one of the assistants." Rick had attempted to talk to her, but she had escaped immediately after her resignation. He had sat there, helpless to stop her as she'd walked out of his life.

"I can't believe you threw away a perfectly good opportunity to improve your serve. I bet she would've given you some lessons," Russell teased, swinging a pretend racket. "Oh well, you're back at the helm of your company, and that's what's important, right?"

"I'm going to resign," Rick announced suddenly. His brother and sister grew quiet and exchanged worried glances. He knew it seemed sudden, but he had never felt so clearheaded in his life. The truth of the matter was that the company he'd fought so long and hard for no longer mattered to him. He had paid too high a price.

"Does Lessa know that?" Russell asked.

"I don't think it would make a damn bit of difference. She doesn't want to be with me."

"She was upset," his sister chimed in. "What did you expect?"

"I told her I cared about her. I don't just toss that out there."

"You *care* about her? What's that supposed to mean? I'll tell you what it doesn't mean. It doesn't mean that you love her."

Rick was silent for a moment. "But I do." He felt like a burden had been lifted from his shoulders. Dammit, he loved her. He *loved* her.

"We know that. But she doesn't."

"Look, I know a thing or two about women," Russell said as Susan rolled her eyes. "And one thing I know is words are not enough. Women need proof. You have to *show* her how you feel."

"She lives with her aunt, right?" asked Susan. "Does she know how you feel?"

He shook his head. "I don't think she's too fond of me."

"Well, that was your first mistake. She loves Lessa

and wants the best for her. Plead your case to the aunt and wrangle an invitation to Christmas dinner."

"Just show up?"

"With an invite."

"Susan's right," Russell said. "If you love her, you're going to have to fight for her. She's not one of your typical women who takes one look at you and swoons and falls into your arms. She's got spunk."

His mother walked over and joined them. "I'm so glad you came for Christmas," she said to Rick.

"I'm afraid he has to leave, Mom," Susan said.

"Business?" she asked.

"No," he said, "not this time."

Susan smiled. As Rick left the room, she said, "Don't be disappointed, Mom. He'll be back next year—and he won't be alone."

"I'm sorry, Gran," Lessa said. "I've lost everything."

"You didn't lose Lawrence Enterprises. Your father did. You did everything you could to get it back."

"Well, I lost the stock."

"You sold it for a fair price." Despite Lessa's protests, Rick had given her the same deal they had promised Sabrina. "I didn't think the loss of some stock is responsible for keeping you up all night." Her aunt took a sip of her tea. "Perhaps you should give him a chance. Let him prove himself. It is Christmas after all."

Lessa looked at her aunt, surprised. She had expected Gran to jump up and down for joy when Lessa had told her she was finished with Rick Parker and Lawrence Enterprises. Instead Gran had looked at her as if she had made the biggest mistake of her life. But what did her aunt expect her to do? Fall into Rick's arms after the way he had treated her? And how could she work with him after what had happened between them?

Her aunt sighed. "This is not the way Christmas is supposed to be spent."

"Oh no, Gran. Please don't give me the spiel about family and kids. I can't take it."

"Actually, I was talking about the lack of eggnog."

"I told you, Chapman's was out."

"Oh, Lessa, I just feel so bad for you. Stuck here with an old woman and no eggnog."

"I guarantee you there's no place I'd rather be." That was true, wasn't it? She wouldn't want to be wrapped in Rick's arms. No, sir. Lessa finished off her tea. "It's wonderful that there's snow," she said, eager to change the subject. The rain had turned to snow shortly after dusk. "When's the last time it snowed in New York on Christmas?"

"A white Christmas," her aunt said. "How romantic. Maybe you should invite Rick over."

"Invite him over?" Had her aunt heard a word of what she had said? "Rick is probably off in some exotic locale drinking a piña colada and dancing with a beautiful woman. I'm sure he's forgotten all about me by now."

"I'm not so certain. From what you've told me, I think he was as surprised as you by the whole turn of events."

Lessa closed her eyes as the wave of pain washed over her. She wanted to believe that; she really did. She would like nothing better than to think that Rick was by himself, mourning her loss. But she knew better. And she could not allow herself to feel sad. It did no good. She had made her decision.

"It doesn't have to be like this, Lessa."

"There's no choice, Gran. When people love each other, they treat each other decently. You don't have deceit and lies. Real love doesn't hurt like this."

"You've been reading too many storybooks. Real life doesn't always work that way. I never told you about your uncle and me. We dated for two years, and I was madly in love. I thought we were going to get married. And then he went off to the war."

"And then he came home and married you."

"That's the story we've always told. I didn't mention what really happened because it bothered him too much."

"What are you talking about? He loved you. He thought about you every day he was away."

"When he came home, I found out that he was engaged to someone else."

Lessa couldn't believe what she was hearing. Her uncle? The kindly bespectacled man who had worshipped her aunt?

"Apparently he never got any of my letters, but I didn't know that then. He assumed I didn't care about him, and naturally, when I found out about his engagement, I assumed the same thing about him. It broke my heart. Well, he went off and married that other woman. And you know what? It was the best thing that ever happened to me."

"Uncle Stan was married before? Did Dad know this?"

"Of course. But what difference did it make? The point of the story is that he eventually came back. And you know what? I had changed—for the better. I was so much stronger than I had been. I knew I could make it on my own. And he knew what he wanted all along.

Me. If he hadn't married that other woman, he might've always wondered if he made the right decision. Instead, I was appreciated. Very appreciated. Until the day he died, he would've done anything to make me happy."

"So what are you saying? Do you think Rick will go off and marry someone else? Or do you think I will?"

"I think that Rick learned a valuable lesson here. And I believe him when he said he cared about you." She smiled. "I think I know a thing or two about men."

"I can't think about Rick, Gran. I have to move on with my life. I'm going to look for a little property to buy. I'm going start over, build my own company from scratch. And I'm thinking about going back to tennis. Not as a player, but a teacher. I could combine my knowledge of resorts with my love for tennis. Maybe I could start a camp somewhere."

There was a knock on the door.

"Why, who in the world could that be?" her aunt said, feigning surprise.

"Maybe it's Santa," Lessa said, glancing at her aunt suspiciously. What was she up to?

Lessa got up and opened the door—to Rick Parker. He stood before her, covered in snow.

"Rick," her aunt said, brushing past Lessa to get to him.

"Wh-What are you doing here?" Lessa asked, so surprised she could barely speak.

"Your aunt said she needed eggnog."

"Oh, you found some." Gran said. "You're a dear, Rick. Thank you."

"This isn't funny." Lessa gave her aunt the evil eye.

"Who's joking?" Rick asked. "I had to go to three different stores to find this."

"Come in," her aunt said warmly, taking his coat and the container of eggnog. "I think this'll need some brandy, don't you?" She stopped and turned back toward the doorway. "Would you look at that," she said, motioning above Rick and Lessa where a small piece of greenery had been tied to the light fixture. "Mistletoe." She looked at Lessa and winked.

When she was gone, Rick stared into Lessa's eyes. "I told you once, Lessa. I don't give up."

"Look, Rick, I don't want to be a part of Lawrence Enterprises anymore."

"I'm not asking you to." He reached inside his jacket. "I just stopped by to give you something." He pulled out a manila envelope. "Open it," he said, handing it to her.

She ripped open the envelope. It was the deed to Mara del Ray. "I don't understand...."

"I'm giving it to you. A chance to build your own hotel."

He came over on Christmas Eve to sell her a property? "How much do you want for it?"

"I don't want money," he said, looking at her hungrily.

"What do you want?"

"A partnership."

"What about Lawrence Enterprises?"

"I'm resigning. I want to build a corporation step by step, just like your parents did. I was thinking that a tennis camp might be a good place to start." He put his hands on her waist. "You spoke once about expectations...well, I didn't expect this either. I can't seem to stay away from you. I don't *want* to stay away from you."

They were words she had waited a lifetime to hear,

but it was the heartrending tenderness of his gaze that melted her remaining defenses.

"I know what it's like to be frightened of love, Lessa," he said. "I know what it's like to close off your heart. I've spent years like that. But I also know that true love is damned hard to find. It took me a long time to find you, Lessa. And now that I have, I'm not about to lose you."

As she looked into his eyes, she was filled with the same sense of desire that had haunted her from the first moment she'd seen him. She moved toward him slowly, and then, standing underneath the mistletoe, she tentatively pressed her lips to his.

He kissed her back, gently and tenderly, a lover's kiss. She wrapped her arms around his neck and pulled him toward her, knotting her fingers through his thick, wavy hair. "Thank you for my Christmas present," she said.

"That wasn't your Christmas present." He reached inside his coat pocket and pulled out a small box. "*This* is your Christmas present."

Her heart jumped into her throat as she took it and opened it. Inside, nestled on satin, was an emerald-cut diamond ring.

"I love you, Lessa, and I want to be with you. You make the world a better place."

She was too excited to speak. She just stood there, staring at the ring, not believing her ears.

"Say you'll marry me, Lessa," he whispered. "Give me a reason to like Christmas again."

"Yes, Rick, I'll marry you." She threw her arms around his neck and kissed him with all her might. When she was finished, she said the three words she had wanted to say for a long, long time. "I love you."

* * *

The wedding was held exactly three months later, on the grounds of their first joint venture, a Florida resort that specialized in tennis. It was intended to be a low-key affair, with only close friends and relatives. For Rick, Lessa discovered, that meant two hundred people, who filled Mara del Ray to capacity. And Lessa loved every moment of it. The entire Parker clan had accepted her and her aunt as welcome additions.

Lessa and Rick were married on a clear, sunny day in the hotel garden. Lessa wore a sleeveless white chiffon gown and walked down a stone path toward the most handsome man she had ever seen.

As Rick watched her walk toward him, he had no doubt that Lessa was the woman he had been waiting for all those years. With her by his side, he knew that anything was possible. She, and she alone, was the treasure for which he had combed the world.

Afterward they celebrated on the beach, complete with blazing tiki lights and a steel drum band. The guests feasted on fresh fish that had been caught that day. It was a fitting celebration for a former pirate. Rick took her hand and kissed it, giving her a smile that made her tingle all the way to her toes.

She and Rick stood at the water's edge, discussing their honeymoon plans with Susan, Rick's sister. "What made you decide on the Bahamas?" Susan asked. "After all, you've been to so many romantic places. I thought you'd pick something really exotic."

"Betty suggested it," Lessa said, nodding toward Rick's secretary. Instead of retiring, Betty and her husband had moved to Florida a little bit early and Betty now worked for them part-time. In fact, they had received many inquiries from former employees of Lawrence, asking if they might join the new venture.

"There's a property there we're interested in," Lessa added with a smile. In fact, they were considering buying Sabrina's resort. Sabrina, in fact, was the one'd who suggested it to them. She had decided that being the owner of a large corporation was adversely affecting her love life, and so she had decided to sell her business and embark on a trip around the world with her sailing instructor.

"Rick!" his sister said, swatting him. "It's your honeymoon!"

"It was my idea," Lessa said. "It seemed to make sense." The transition from enemy to beloved had gone as seamlessly as the beginning of their new corporation. Rick and Lessa were both equal shareholders and partners. And although Rick was still the same tough negotiator he had been at Lawrence, as a lover and husband he was unrivaled. There were few grievances. They had melded together in the boardroom as easily as the bedroom. In fact, she was having the time of her life. For once, she had no doubt that she was in the right field, no doubt that this was what she was meant to do.

"Well, that doesn't sound very romantic to me. A working honeymoon."

But Lessa knew different. They were simply taking a tour. There would be plenty of time for…other activities.

"Mom," Susan's youngest son said, tugging on her dress. "Richard's swimming in the pool," he said, referring to his seven-year-old brother.

"It's okay," Lessa said. "There's a lifeguard."

"But he went swimming with his clothes on."

As Susan ran off to attend to her son, Lessa saw her aunt sitting under a palm tree. She was fanning herself as she sipped some frothy pink drink with an umbrella.

"I'll be right back," Lessa said to Rick.

"What are you thinking about?" she asked her aunt as she sat beside her on the sand.

"I'm just thinking about that mistletoe. See? Aren't you glad you didn't throw it out or stick it in the closet?"

"You think this is all due to mistletoe?"

"Well, I certainly got my wish," Gran said. "And so did you."

Lessa caught the eyes of the man she loved, and smiled. "And then some. I can't wait to see what you ask for next year."

Her aunt nodded toward the beach at the children playing. "It might be nice to have some children around."

Lessa just laughed. As it turned out, she had been thinking the exact same thing.

After the wedding, she and Rick retired to the private bungalow they had built for their home. The French doors were open and a warm breeze blew the silk sheers. Lessa stepped outside, followed by Rick.

"Gran asked me to give you this," he said, holding out a small brown paper bag.

Lessa opened the bag and peeked inside. She laughed as she pulled out a sprig of mistletoe. She held it up to the moonlight and said, "My aunt swears that mistletoe is associated with miracles. You simply hold it and make a wish."

"Should we test it out?" he asked.

She put a hand on her belly. "I should warn you that

I have a feeling I know what she's wishing for next Christmas."

"Next Christmas?" he asked, flashing her a devilish smile. "Let's see, April, May, June…" He counted out the remaining months. "Nine months exactly. We better start working on this miracle right away."

And holding the mistletoe over their heads, he gave her a long, passionate kiss.

* * * * *

With This Fling...
by Kelly Hunter

Charlotte Greenstone's convenient, fictional fiancé *inconveniently* resembles sexy stranger Greyson Tyler! Grey agrees to keep Charlotte's secret as long as they enjoy *all* the benefits of a real couple...

Girls' Guide to Flirting with Danger
by Kimberly Lang

When the media discover that marriage counsellor Megan Lowe is the ex-wife of an infamous divorce attorney, Megan has to take the plunge and face her dangerously sexy ex.

Juggling Briefcase & Baby
by Jessica Hart

A weekend working with his ex, Romy, and her baby, Freya, has corporate genius Lex confused. Opposites they may be, but Lex's attraction to happy-go-lucky Romy seems to have grown stronger with the years...

Deserted Island, Dreamy Ex
by Nicola Marsh

Starring in an island-based TV show sounded blissful, until Kristi discovered her Man Friday was her ex, Jared Malone. Of course, she doesn't feel *anything* for him, but can't help hoping he'll like her new bikini...

On sale from 7th January 2011
Don't miss out!

Available at WHSmith, Tesco, ASDA, Eason and all good bookshops

www.millsandboon.co.uk